Weil felt in his pocket for the sets of keys he carried with him for both vehicles. He shuffled round the lorries, checking locks. At the back of Gotz's lorry he paused, then on a whim fitted the key and turned the lock so that he was able to swing the door and peer inside. His eyes ran over the silent ranks of pictures, some in their gilt frames, some naked canvas, all tethered together for safety. There was the Bruegel. And the von Rayski portrait group on which he had worked extensively before the war. Slung precipitously across the top, almost touching the roof of the van, was the large Courbet. He nodded at them as if they were old friends, unchanging and reliable. Yes, they would be safe enough here for the time being. Tomorrow would be time enough for them to reach their refuge underground. He relocked the doors. This was a haven for them all, of course it was. Gotz was probably right about the special status of Dresden. It was to be preserved. He could sleep easily in his bed tonight.

Also by Philip Hook

The Island of the Dead

The
Stonebreakers

Philip Hook

CORONET BOOKS
Hodder and Stoughton

Copyright © 1994 Philip Hook

First published in Great Britain in 1994
by Hodder and Stoughton

First published in paperback in 1995
by Hodder and Stoughton
A division of Hodder Headline PLC

A Coronet paperback

The right of Philip Hook to be identified as the Author of
the Work has been asserted by him in accordance with the
Copyright, Designs and Patents Act 1988.

10 9 8 7 6 5 4 3 2 1

A CIP catalogue record for this title
is available from the British Library

ISBN 0 340 63531 2

Typeset by
Letterpart Limited, Reigate, Surrey.
Printed and bound in Great Britain by
Cox & Wyman Ltd, Reading, Berks

Hodder and Stoughton
A division of Hodder Headline PLC
338 Euston Road
London NW1 3BH

To Angélique

1

'Beware the month Lenaion, ox-flaying days.'

The line had come to him suddenly, at six-thirty that morning. The men had been chipping ice from the windscreens of the lorries, their breath turning to steam in the bitter cold. They had cursed prodigiously as they worked, unleashing grotesque torrents of verbal obscenity. He had paced uneasily about the preparations, angry and impotent, wondering whether he should react, and if so how. He was too old for this sort of thing. Didn't they realise he was seventy-one, for God's sake? He was a scholar, not a porter's foreman; a connoisseur, not a driver's mate. Then he'd thought of the line of poetry, and taken from it an obscure comfort. Where was it from? The *Greek Anthology*, perhaps. Its repetition as the day unfolded had eased his spirit. Their progress over rutted and crowded roadways had been painfully slow, every delay knocking them further behind schedule; but he had clung on to the words, savouring them as some sort of link with civilisation, setting his suffering in a more sympathetic context. The month Lenaion: that was the Ancient Greek February. This was February too. And these too were ox-flaying days. But the Greek poet had lived two thousand years ago and could not conceivably have understood the agony of an ox-flaying day spent juddering across the plain of Saxony incarcerated in the cab of a draughty furniture van, the irregular pounding of its engine never quite loud enough to extinguish the low thud of distant Bolshevik guns. Dr Arnold Weil, Classical graduate of Göttingen University, was cold, peevish and afraid.

It was curious that he should now seek refuge in a line of Greek poetry. He had abandoned his Classical studies many years ago, turning instead to art history. Latterly he had discovered a gift for art restoration. In this capacity he had been working for the Dresden Museum for the past twenty years. It must be half a century since he had read those words in the original Greek; apparently forgotten, they had stuck in an obscure corner of his memory like barnacles welded to some submerged hulk. Now the shock of his present ordeal had dislodged them, suddenly, into circulation again. They spoke of another, vastly preferable world, where cold was no more than a picturesque feature of the pastoral idyll, where culture and reason might find a refuge unthreatened by Soviet artillery.

He sat perched on the passenger seat like a nervous crow. Glancing uneasily across at the driver, he delved deep into the pocket of his dilapidated great-coat for a cigarette packet. He clawed at matches with gloved fingers. Two in succession would not strike and fell broken to the floor. The most basic facilities of life were unreliable these days. There: at last he had done it. Light sprang from his shaking hand, and he inhaled gratefully. God knew with what substance they lengthened the meagre quantity of tobacco in these things: boot-laces, he had heard it suggested, or rat's faeces. One of Dresden's main industries was the manufacture of cigarettes, and some strange rumours had been coming out of the factories recently. But any cigarettes were better than nothing. He was putting them back into his pocket when he remembered the driver. Clumsily he proffered the packet.

'Would you . . . er?' What was the fellow's name?

The man did not speak, but nodded his head curtly without removing his gaze from the road. He was blond, in his thirties, with three days' growth of beard on his chin, and watery, unhealthy eyes. It was hard to tell whether he was actively hostile or merely uncommunicative. Weil hastened to remind himself in mitigation of his companion's surliness that the road demanded concentration, and the preciousness of their load outweighed all other considerations. The way was pitted with pot-holes and patches of black, treacherous ice. You couldn't afford to relax. Now, as Weil fumbled with the packet, the driver shot out a quick and practised hand to extract a cigarette and, placing it between his lips, motioned Weil to light it for him. Two more matches failed, then the third flared. Weil's shaking fist moved the flame towards the inclined head whose eyes never left the road ahead. He lit the tip, just as the fire licked his own fingers. The pain was sharp and shocking. Weil dropped the spent stick and nursed his hand in his coat, determined to hide his distress from his companion lest it might compromise his authority. But he could not quite suppress a lingering sense of horror at the incident; an irrational but deep-seated horror of burning flesh.

He must speak to the driver again; the situation demanded it.

'What time do you think we'll get there, Gotz?' he asked, and was relieved to find that the driver's name had returned to him, drifting back into his consciousness with the same unexpected fluidity as the line of Greek poetry.

Gotz frowned. He slowed, in order to manoeuvre round a group of bedraggled refugees forlornly attempting to right an upturned cart on the edge of the road. He appeared to be considering whether the question was even worth answering.

'Where?' he said finally.

'Schieritz.'

'No chance. Not today. Not at this rate. Be lucky if we

3

even make it back to Dresden.'

'The road could be clearer later.'

'You must be joking.' They slowed almost to a stand-still, reduced to the pace of the slowest straggler in a larger knot of hobbling refugees ahead of them. Gotz sounded his horn sharply, with suppressed violence. 'Get out of it!' Exhausted faces peered up at them with hopeless eyes. Some of these people had been on the road from Breslau for three weeks, denied all transport but the power of their own feet. But as the van charted a none-too-careful course around them, neither Gotz nor his elderly companion registered them. Gotz was concentrating bitterly on the road. The other man was peering back yet once more into the darkness of the hold behind them, checking anxiously on the cargo.

'Is Walther still behind us?'

Gotz glanced perfunctorily in the mirror. 'He's there, Herr Doktor.'

Beware the month Lenaion. Weil wound the scarf once more about his throat and relapsed into silence, drumming nervous fingers on the briefcase resting across his knees. His worries were too great to quantify. These drivers, for one thing – Gotz and Walther. They had been foisted upon him by the authorities without sufficient preparation; they were completely unknown to him; their qualifications for handling pictures were non-existent. That much had been clear earlier in the day at Schloss Milkel, where over a hundred canvases had been loaded aboard with much swearing and maladroitness. In the biting cold of the winter morning, preserving their co-operation had been a delicate business, challenging his moribund powers of diplomacy to their limit. A few frames had been chipped, but there had been – thank God – no discernible damage to the picture surfaces. But the exercise had endeared neither the drivers to Weil nor Weil

4

to the drivers. As the day progressed he sensed this undercurrent, not quite of mutiny, but certainly of obstructiveness. He was dealing with an alien force. He felt the same unbridgeable gap between himself and these men as he had felt when confronted with the porters in the old days at the museum, with the plumber who came to mend the bath in his small apartment in the city, or the garrulous, beery builder who climbed out of his window to repair the guttering on the roof and whistled at girls below. Their ultimate resort was physical; his was intellectual. That was the difference that precluded any sympathy or understanding between them. It was a difference that had special significance in these days lived on the edge of the abyss. For, as this quite intolerable war continued, as conditions daily deteriorated, as suffering, personal and communal, became ever more insistent, as the barbarian approached closer to the gates, so there loomed more threateningly that moment of ultimate resort.

At that moment what use was an art historian-cum-restorer by comparison with a plumber or a driver? Reason would succumb to might; civilisation would be submerged in chaos. Works of art would be employed not to adorn palaces and museums but to build barricades. Anarchy, glimpsed already rumbling not far below the surface, would finally erupt. They had heard those Russian guns not forty miles away as they loaded the pictures at Schloss Milkel. The Bolsheviks were the harbingers of unreason. For the first time, as he listened to their artillery, he had felt real fear of the hordes from the east. He shivered, a lonely old man weighed down by a responsibility too great to bear. On his inadequate frame rested, as it seemed to him, a terrible burden. The pictures with whose rescue he had been charged became emblematic of all German culture. If he failed to preserve them safely, everything was lost. It was not right that he should be subjected to this ordeal. It was too much for him, too much for any man. And yet what choice had he had? At the museum there had been no one else left to go. If he had not acquiesced, this crucial mission would not have taken place.

He took off his little round glasses and gave them a tentative rub with a handkerchief in order to relieve the feelings of mounting panic which bubbled up periodically. Beware the month Lenaion, ox-flaying days. He clenched his teeth and peered out of the window at the unyielding Saxon landscape, still solid with frost but bathed momentarily in a milky light by a pale sun. It was three o'clock: perhaps if they made better time now it would still be possible to reach Schieritz this evening. They had set out from Dresden at an ungodly hour, heading east. They had stopped to pick up pictures first at Kamenz then at Schloss Milkel, suddenly too close for comfort to the Russian lines. Now they were headed back towards Dresden, and beyond, to Schieritz, a further two hours to the west of the city. A further two hours into safety. His instructions were to unload there at two main destinations for underground storage. What blessed relief it would be to deposit the cargo intact at those points, his duty discharged, that moment of last resort kept at bay a little longer. He cursed the crowds of refugees who impeded their way, Silesians heading mindlessly westward in front of the Russian advance. Stupid wretches, with their children and their carts. Hadn't he read that there were perfectly decent trains laid on for these people? That being so, why had they felt it necessary to clog up the roadways? The fecklessness of the masses was a constant source of irritation to him in peacetime; how much more infuriating was it now, when great issues were at stake.

Gotz brought the lorry to a sudden halt. Weil looked up, startled and concerned.

'What's this?'

'See for yourself. Look ahead – hundreds of them.'

An apparently endless column of tanks, armoured cars, and troop transport lorries was approaching them, rumbling ominously east. Motorcycle outriders had motioned them to halt, and one was now knocking at the window.

'Off the road,' he shouted. 'Pull over!'

'What do you mean?' asked Weil, shocked.

'Get off the road. Come on, you heard.'

A sense of outrage overwhelmed all else in Dr Weil. 'But we have priority. We can pass, the road is wide enough. We have to reach Schieritz tonight.'

'Priority? Don't make me laugh, you old fool. Why should a couple of furniture vans have priority?'

'Here, see this.' Weil fumbled in his briefcase, then handed over a sheaf of papers.

The outrider inspected them. He shrugged his shoulders and passed back the documents. 'I'm sorry. I thought you were refugees. How many are you, just the two vans?'

'That's right.' Breathless with the exertion of the interview, Weil peered back anxiously and was reassured by Walther's continued proximity.

The outrider blew a whistle sharply and motioned them on. Solemnly they proceeded past the line of military vehicles, the tanks, the armoured cars, and the troop lorries packed with uniformed men who cast curious glances at the unfettered progress of two incongruous furniture vans.

Unexpectedly Gotz whistled. 'Priority, heh? Those pictures in the back, they're pretty valuable, then?'

'Extremely valuable. Thank God the authorities still have the sense to understand that, at least.'

'How valuable?'

'How valuable? My dear man, you really can't quantify these things. Let's just say they're supremely valuable.

7

They have to be withdrawn from the vicinity of the front line, that's of paramount importance.' Weil paused, suddenly embarrassed that his speech had shown unprecedented animation, and uncertain how the driver would react.

'So that's why this journey has priority,' mused Gotz.

'Exactly.'

'Supremely valuable,' repeated Gotz, as if savouring the phrase. 'Supremely valuable.'

'That's right.'

There was a pause, then Gotz asked: 'What's more valuable to the Fatherland, do you reckon, Herr Doktor, soldiers or pictures?'

Weil thought for a moment. Privately he felt it was preferable to sacrifice an entire division of men rather than imperil a single Rubens; but he was wary of the tone of Gotz's question. 'They're both valuable, of course, to the Fatherland. But soldiers are . . . expendable. Most of these pictures are unique, irreplaceable. You have to understand that.'

Gotz gave a mirthless laugh and shook his head. 'Who are they by, then, these irreplaceable masterpieces?'

'Bruegel, for instance. Lucas Cranach. And about two metres behind you we are carrying a supreme work of French art. One of the greatest pictures ever painted by Gustave Courbet.'

'They all come from the museum?'

'That's right. You're from Dresden yourself, aren't you? You probably saw some of them before the war, when you visited the Gemäldegalerie. Before they were all moved out for safekeeping.'

'The Gemäldegalerie? I never visited any galleries. Why should I visit galleries?' Gotz frowned, and there was silence for a moment. They were still passing crowded troop-carrying lorries, serried ranks of helmets atop sullen, steely faces. 'There they go, poor bloody expendable soldiers.'

Weil shifted uncomfortably in his seat. Gotz went on: 'I suppose you realise what my orders are once this jaunt is over?'

Weil shook his head. He would prefer this conversation not to proceed, but he saw no way of cutting it short.

'I'll tell you what my orders are, Herr Doktor. Just as soon as we've delivered these so-called irreplaceable pictures to wherever we've got to take them, the moment they're under guard and tucked away out of all danger, then I've got to report straight back to the sodding clearing camp. You know what they'll do to me then? They'll shove another helmet on my head, stick another gun in my hand, maybe if I'm lucky they'll find me a warmer coat, they'll attach me to another division, then – how long? – seventy-two hours from now I'll be one of those poor buggers on their way back to the front. Back to fight the Russians again.' He stared implacably at the road ahead. 'You see, Herr Doktor, I'm expendable.'

'That's the war.'

'Once you get to that front line, you know who the lucky ones are, don't you?'

Weil shook his head miserably.

'The lucky ones are the dead ones, the people that get killed outright, because you know what those Russians do to you if they capture you, don't you? They castrate you. No questions asked, they just cut you up and leave you bleeding. And another thing you should know, Herr Doktor: there's no stopping the Bolsheviks. They just keep coming and coming, millions of them. There's no stopping them, they'll get us all in the end. And these bloody precious pictures, most likely they'll get them too.'

Weil pursed his lips in disapproval. Such blatant military defeatism could not be condoned in a man like Gotz, of course, but what was even more upsetting was the image of greedy, philistine eastern hordes surging irresistibly onward. Eastern hordes appropriating the museum's pictures.

'I think you'll find they'll be safe where they're going.'

But would they? The doubt was insidious. Where would it all end? He'd heard something on the wireless about a final push being planned, a magnificent last-minute counter-attack to wreak disarray amongst the enemies of the Reich, enemies who were already quarrelling amongst themselves. But was this likely, when every day brought new floods of refugees from the east – frightened, desperate men and women who had abandoned everything in the headlong flight, irrefutable testimony to the Bolshevik advance? There was a dangerous gap between what the leaders of the Fatherland were telling people and what one could see with one's own eyes. He cursed them all – politicians, generals, those in authority responsible for putting him in this intolerable position. He had not asked to go to war. He was a restorer and art historian, not a soldier. His needs were modest. All he asked was physical warmth in his small apartment, enough light to work by, and the freedom to continue his work with pictures. He knew only one great challenge in life, that of entering into the creative mind of the artist whose work he was attempting to conserve and reconstitute. Up till recently his acutest anxiety had been the weakness of his eyes; some days were better than others in this respect, but if the Russians came what would it all matter? Their arrival would herald a new Dark Age akin to blindness.

Was it possible that this disaster would actually happen? This venture, hastily organised, to chase priceless pictures from one hiding place to another, further west, was bringing the full dimensions of the horror home to him. In the earlier years of the war, as news of fresh triumphs flashed out daily, he had indulged in an unthinking confidence in the people who guarded the destiny of the Fatherland. In Dresden there had been shortages, certainly, but not the deprivation and destruction that had undermined other less fortunate cities in the Reich. Up till last summer life had continued as a passable imitation of peacetime existence. But it was last summer that the cracks had begun to appear: schools shut down indefinitely in order to accommodate military casualties and refugees; theatres and opera closed; restrictions on travel; yet more stringent rationing. The nagging suspicion grew that the process of disintegration had set in ineluctably: the situation was now beyond the control of the authorities. A horrific image played in his imagination: a constant stream of refugees and pictures fleeing, from enemies in the east, from enemies in the west, from enemies in the north and south; Germany, safe, unviolated Germany, contracting in size daily like a puddle shrivelling in the sun, till the entire surviving civilian population and the entire cultural heritage of the Fatherland were concentrated into a tiny island in the middle. And then the enemy's final thrust, bringing destruction, defeat and humiliation. Weil shivered. The ox-flaying days offered no shelter.

The cold grey clouds of the morning had ebbed away just long enough to reveal a sunset now, a recession of infinite melancholy. The sky in the west was suffused with a milky yellow light, pointing up the swathes of cloud strung across the horizon like contours of a distant seashore, an imaginary coastline. Running his gaze across the flat expanse of Saxon landscape below, Weil's eye was caught and held by a series of lakes, perhaps no more than a pattern of flooded fields, in which the sun was momentarily reflected. He experienced that shock of familiarity which came to him periodically in front of exceptional beauty, the recognition of nature's power to imitate art.

Many of his sharpest perceptions of the outside world were conditioned by paint. The landscape which he gazed at from the window of the lorry suddenly moved him because he saw it painted by Caspar David Friedrich. He knew it to be true because it vividly reminded him of a particular picture in the museum's collection, one in front of which he had stood many times before the war. And now in a moment of revelation he recognised it again, spread out before him, refracted through the eye of the painter: the evening light, the reflections in the water, the line of trees at the horizon, the melancholy. Friedrich had lived and worked in Dresden, painting the city and its surrounding countryside. His landscapes were mysterious, timeless, and hauntingly sad. But it was an innocent, romantic sadness, thought Weil, in the same way that the Greek poet's Lenaion evoked an innocent coldness. The past was always innocent, of course. By contrast the sadness Weil felt now was more profound, tinged with the desperation of his times, a misery inconceivable to Friedrich; the cold, mixed with the horror of impending catastrophe, was more chilling than any winter the Greeks had known.

He was an old man with little hope and an unfair weight of responsibility on his shoulders. In the old days, the days before the war, when something had occurred to which he objected, there had been clear and civilised lines of recourse. In the museum, for instance, when he had met incompetence or inefficiency, he had proved himself a master of the sardonic memorandum: he had even rather relished the composition of those crisp little notes, drawing the director's attention to this or that malfunctioning of the system. And very often they had produced the desired effect. He liked to think that his relationship with Dr Posse had been a special one: he had admired the man, and felt a reciprocal appreciation from the director. This was the man who enjoyed the confidence of the Führer himself, had been chosen to head the Sonderauftrag Linz, charged with the task of creating a collection of works of art of supreme quality for the city of the Führer's birth. That had taken Posse away from Dresden for considerable lengths of time, and now he was gone for good. So there was no one in the director's office to receive Weil's sharp little memoranda any more. Written complaint had been superseded by physical action in the new scheme of things. He was a forlorn and solitary figure struggling in silence against intolerable adversity, unable to compete in the conditions threatened by the new barbarism. He drew his coat tighter about him and reached for his cigarettes.

It was all but dark when he distantly discerned a series of tiny lights, some flickering, some dimmed, but stretching in a wide arc across the horizon. For a moment he did not recognise what he saw, then, with a gasp of exultation, he cried out: 'Dresden!'

'About bloody time,' said Gotz.

Even now the blackout was not strictly enforced in the city. The number of genuine air raids suffered during this war could be counted on the fingers of one hand, of course, and only two of them had done any damage to speak of. The first, back in October, had provoked only voyeuristic curiosity, with coach-owners running special excursions to view the blitzed streets in the suburbs of Friedrichstadt and Loblau. The second, last month, had been directed against the oil refinery and the goods marshalling yards. They had been exceptional events, not enough to alter the prevailing opinion that the enemy would not waste bombs on Dresden. Not Dresden. Not the Florence of middle Europe. Not when they had their eyes on it as the successor to Berlin as capital of the conquered Reich.

Now the sight of the lights momentarily charged the

13

spirits of the footsore travellers beside them on the road. There was a marginal quickening of pace amongst the refugees, now that they saw their goal beckoning. The twinkling vision of the city enhanced its promise as a refuge for the weary, a miraculous haven from the conflict. For Weil, however, the approach to the outskirts only increased his anxiety. People flocked and milled along the way in ever larger numbers, impeding the vans. There were more vehicles, too. A feverish impatience seized him again.

'I think we should head on to Schieritz tonight,' he said again. 'It would be better for the pictures.'

Gotz took his gaze from the road. For the first time in the brief acquaintanceship of the two men closeted together in the driver's cab, their eyes met.

'No.' It was said firmly, unequivocally.

Weil looked away. 'I mean, it's not so late. The road will be clearer the other side of the city,' he muttered.

'We are tired. We must pass the night in Dresden.'

'We have a very precious load. I do not like to expose it unnecessarily.'

'What is there to worry about, Herr Doktor? The pictures will be safe locked in the lorries. And I do not think the Russians will come tonight. Another night, maybe, but only at the very end.'

'What do you mean?'

'You will always be safe in Dresden. It is the safest city in the Reich. It's true, you may rely on it: I heard it from a man who knows, a man with special contacts in the government.'

Weil was intrigued despite his preoccupations. The theory wasn't new, but it remained seductive. 'You cannot be sure . . .'

'Oh yes, you can be sure. That's just it. Why do you think we in Dresden have had so few air raids, when other cities – Hamburg, Berlin, for instance – have been attacked every night? It's because our enemies propose to destroy Berlin, and when our Reich is conquered the new capital will be here, in Dresden. It's been agreed.'

'Agreed?'

'Agreed amongst our enemies,' declared Gotz authoritatively.

Weil considered the matter. 'But the pictures must reach Schieritz as quickly as possible. I have orders.'

'Screw your orders.' Something snapped, frighteningly. It did not take much pressure for reason to give way to anarchy. Weil sat on in the silence of dread, uncertain how to react. They continued their unswerving route towards the centre of the city, driven forward by Gotz's superior will power. Nonetheless, when Gotz spoke again he did so more gently: 'You should have pity, Herr Doktor. Do you know what it is like for Walther and me, in our situation? This is our last chance. After this journey we go immediately to join new units, then straight back to the front, where we will die. Oh yes, we have no illusions. You, who stay behind in Dresden, you will live to see the city as the new capital of Germany once our enemies have control. But by that time Walther and I will be dead. So you must understand that we will not be denied our last night in Dresden. It is our last night to live, and tonight we will live.'

'I think I have no choice.'

'I think you have no choice.'

Defeated, the old man gave in. The fight was gone from him. He gazed unhappily from his window at the streets packed with thronging pedestrians, moving briskly in the cold, pummelling themselves to keep warm. The city was swollen with soldiers in transit to the front, fugitive Silesians, Pomeranians and East Prussians moving in the opposite direction, Berliners and Rhinelanders from the west, evacuees of all descriptions. It seemed the buildings could not contain them, so they spilled on to the streets, a mass of uncomfortable humanity. And yet, extraordinarily, when he looked closer he saw that here and there people were actually enjoying themselves, they were laughing and shouting, there were children dressed in carnival costume. Down another street he caught a glimpse of the brightly coloured lights of a circus. Perhaps this city was some sort of haven after all.

'Look, it's Mardi Gras,' continued Gotz. 'Carnival night. A time to enjoy yourself.'

The convoy of which Weil was the nominal commander rolled slowly towards the River Elbe. They passed over the Augustus Bridge and turned left on to the embankment, beneath the Bruhl'sche Terrasse. There, in the heart of the old city, they drew to a halt. Walther pulled up behind them. Three weary figures lowered themselves to the ground, swinging their arms to reactivate circulations. Weil's whole body ached with cold and exhaustion. Beware these days, beware the month Lenaion. But at least he was back on familiar ground, surrounded by landmarks that he had known for the past thirty years: he peered up at the Frauenkirche and the Hofbau, monuments of continuing civilisation which loomed impervious to the flux of humanity below.

Gotz and Walther drew aside and entered into muffled conversation. They cursed and laughed. Weil found it hard to avoid the conclusion that their refusal to continue further tonight was long prearranged, and that they were congratulating each other on an objective attained.

Walther looked disturbingly like a rat. He was a smaller, darker, older man than Gotz. He grinned at Weil, revealing sharp little teeth.

'So, we start again tomorrow, Herr Doktor. It is a wise decision you have made, I think.' He gesticulated towards the lorries, laughing stupidly. 'These treasures will be safe here, you can rely on that.'

'I very much hope so,' said Weil severely. 'And I insist that we start early tomorrow. We meet here, seven o'clock.'

'*Ja, ja*, seven o'clock, it is agreed.'

'Are the lorries secure?'

'*Ja, ja*. Sure they are secure.' Gotz and Walther were already edging away into the crowds. Walther called back: 'And Herr Doktor . . .'

'Yes?'

'It's carnival, Mardi Gras. Enjoy yourself tonight. But don't do anything we wouldn't do.' Guffawing, they disappeared into the evening, stepping over an elderly couple of Silesian peasants who had installed themselves with all their worldly goods on the pavement nearby and had apparently sunk into a dreamless sleep, oblivious even to the cold.

Weil felt in his pocket for the sets of keys he carried with him for both vehicles. He shuffled round the lorries, checking locks. At the back of Gotz's lorry he paused, then on a whim fitted the key and turned the lock so that he was able to swing the door and peer inside. His eyes ran over the silent ranks of pictures, some in their gilt frames, some naked canvas, all tethered together for safety. There was the Bruegel. And the von Rayski portrait group on which he had worked extensively before the war. Slung precipitously across the top, almost touching the roof of the van, was the large Courbet. He nodded at them as if they were old friends, unchanging and reliable. Yes, they would be safe enough here for the time being. Tomorrow would be time enough for them to reach their refuge underground. He relocked the doors. This was a haven for them all, of course it was. Gotz was probably right about the special status of Dresden. It was to be preserved. He could sleep easily in his bed tonight. His apartment beckoned him. There would be no heating again, but that was nothing new, and he could sleep in his great-coat as he had done often that winter. He imagined the familiar smell of turpentine which would greet him from the small room that he used as a studio. It was reassuring. But God in heaven, he was tired. And at seven o'clock they must be off again. Beware the month Lena-ion, ox-flaying days. He picked his way past the two sleeping peasants, swathed in derelict coats and blankets, and shivered. The idea occurred to him suddenly that they were not sleeping but dead. He hurried on without looking back.

Gotz separated from Walther two streets later. Walther pressed him to come to a place he knew where they could drink and play cards, but Gotz felt disinclined to indulge his companion's passion for gambling. He had other plans. They had crystallised on the slow, infinitely tedious drive across the Saxon plain that afternoon. He remembered her from his last leave in Dresden, the one before Christmas. He had been on the way to rejoin his unit when he had met her at the Central Railway Station. It had been a short encounter in the refreshment hall. They had fallen into conversation at the bar and she had told him where he could find her, if he so wished, the next time he was in town. She worked in a tea-room; her shift ended at six. She was a widow – her husband had been killed on the eastern front last year. OK, she was no longer in her prime, but Gotz had cast a judicious eye over her and decided that the blondness of her hair was not unattractive and that her figure was still serviceable. More important, she wanted it, he could tell. A few preliminaries might be necessary, a little encouragement; to his annoyance there had not been time to put the issue to the test at their first

18

meeting as he had had to catch the train. But the more he
thought about it the more confident he felt that she would
prove ultimately compliant. And compliance was an
attribute to be prized above all others when you were
choosing a companion for your last night of freedom. He
hadn't forced that miserable old sod Dr Weil to abandon
the idea of driving all the way to Schieritz that night in
order to spend the evening playing cards. Of course, she
might no longer be employed at the place she'd told him,
many things might have happened in the last two months,
but he'd decided to try her first.

He saw her almost as soon as he got through the door.
She recognised him and smiled. 'You again? I thought
you'd come in sooner or later.'

He approached her. She was piling plates and cups on
to a tray. 'Free tonight?'

'Give me ten minutes.'

They drank beer in a bar, then, as she said she wanted
to go to a circus, they went there, to the Sarassani circus in
the Neustadt. She said she loved circuses, and she laughed
uproariously at most of the acts, too loudly at times. Gotz
didn't laugh much himself, because his mind was on other
things. The place was packed, so he pushed closer to her,
rubbing his leg against her thigh. She didn't move away.
In the darkness he managed to put his hand on her knee,
and under the cover of her coat work it further up the
inside of her leg. She let him reach high enough to make
him impatient to leave.

'Let's get out. There are only three more acts to come.'

'Oh, let's stay a little longer.'

'No. Come on, we're getting out before the rush.'

He pushed her out into the street. It was 9.30. Still the
crowds jostled on the pavements. He drew her into a shop
doorway and kissed her heavily on the lips.

'Take me somewhere,' she breathed.

He put his arm round her and guided her, back towards the Augustus Bridge which led to the old city. They crossed the silent Elbe, in the shadow of the Hofkirche, with the dome of the Frauenkirche looming in the distance. Then they turned left on to the embankment beneath the Bruhl'sche Terrasse.

'Where are we going?'

'You'll see.'

He felt in his pocket. The key was still there. It was a simple matter to open the driver's cabin door and hoist her in.

He kissed her again. Soon he felt her woollen stockings, and the ample flesh above them.

'No!' She broke away breathless, her lipstick smudged. 'Not here. Not now. It's too public, anyone could see us.'

He cursed and looked around. There were still pedestrians passing. The Silesian peasants slept on against the wall. Too many people in this bloody town. Too many people with nowhere to go, nothing better to do than tramp the streets.

'Very well,' he said. 'We'll drive a little while, find a better place.'

It was 9.41. He switched on the engine, and at that precise moment a new sound arose, the shrill and plaintive moan of the air-raid siren, echoing suddenly and clearly across the length and breadth of the city, from Klotsche in the north to Rachnitz in the south.

'Shit.' He glanced across at her.

She leered back at him. 'They're always false alarms, you don't need to worry.'

He released the brake and pulled out into the road. What he had in mind would not take very long.

2

'How are we doing for time, Dakins?'

Captain Victor Meer leant forward from the back seat of the jeep to ask the question. The sun was irritatingly hot for September, and his uniform felt heavy against his skin. He was sweating and uncomfortable.

'Should be at Augstein in about ten minutes, sir.'

'On schedule, then.' The Americanism was distasteful to him, but he found himself using it nonetheless. He didn't quite know why. The Army made you do strange, uncharacteristic things, speak and think in ways wholly alien to your normal civilian persona. Perhaps he said it to impress Dakins. But as far as he could judge Dakins was impervious to anything except an order. His driver was an emotionless machine. To anyone in authority he presented a bland and dispiriting front of expressionless compliance. It bordered on the insolent. God knows what the man really thought. He probably didn't think at all, reflected Victor. And that was the clue to getting by, of course. It was the way you survived. You had to cultivate an unquestioning mindlessness. You had to become obsessed with meaningless detail. You must stifle all curiosity. Individual flair must be suppressed and submerged in the lumpen mass. The longer he served in it, the more contempt he felt for the Army. Military life was an affront both intellectual and aesthetic.

God, this heat. He ran a finger inside his collar and felt the wetness of his perspiration. They rattled along the dusty country road, and once more Victor looked up and about him at the ravishing Carinthian countryside under the clear blue late-summer sky. But the beauty gave him no pleasure. He had often imagined coming to Austria. Through the long years of war he had yearned for the great European museums which were barred to him. It had been an intolerable penance for his generation to pay, to be locked out of Italy for six years, to be excluded from France, to be kept ignorant of the major German collections. And Vienna, too. He was twenty-eight, and he'd never been to Vienna, never seen the treasure houses of the Albertina and the Kunsthistorisches Museum. Now, irony of ironies, the war was just over and he'd been posted to Austria. He was an Intelligence officer in the British Army of Occupation. He'd been here the best part of eight weeks, and had not got near Vienna. Nor was he likely to, as far as he could see. He was fretfully confined to duties here in the British Zone. He was starved of all that made life bearable: good food, good company, good conversation, good pictures.

Intelligence. When he'd first arrived here he'd wondered what on earth the tasks he was being required to perform had to do with that faculty. He'd spent most of his waking hours in checking lists, like some sort of automaton: lists of vehicles, lists of equipment, lists of towns, even lists of lists. He had felt suicidal with frustration and boredom. What the hell was he doing here? Oh yes, he knew the official answer, the Army's answer, well enough. Colonel Keith, his commanding officer, had made it clear from the first briefing. They were here to de-Nazify the local population. But initially he'd scarcely encountered the local population. He'd seemed to be living in a vacuum at Brigade HQ, checking these bloody lists, surrounded by brother officers who were so profoundly unsympathetic that he could scarcely support being in the same room, let alone conversation with them. Then – thank God – his work had become sporadically more absorbing. That was when the lists he'd been allocated had started comprising people rather than things. Lists of known Nazi Party members, lists of known non-Party members, lists of people denounced as Party members, lists of people who had done the denouncing. And then, because he spoke fluent German, he had started actually meeting some of these people, fleshing out the bare names on the lists with details of their physical appearance, their characters, the evidence they had to give. A month ago he had conducted his first interrogation. Many more had followed. The experience had been something of an insight into the duplicity of the human mind, particularly the duplicity of the human mind when cornered or under pressure. He had been intrigued by the varieties of deception he had encountered: there was intentional dissembling, of course, out and out lying, people denying their Nazi pasts when it was a simple matter to check up on their careers in the Party records; and there were subtler forms of it, men and women coming forward with plausible stories about the transgressions of others, allegations that might be true or might equally be motivated by local neighbourhood feuds and jealousies; and entwined in all this was frequently a strand of self-deception, a belief held fervently that something was true simply because it was pre-eminently desirable that it should be true. Separating all these deceptions was a challenge that he had come almost to relish. Certainly it represented the only remotely intellectual stimulus in his present existence.

The succession of country roads along which Dakins was guiding him were for the most part deserted. These were roads where the only other motorised traffic was likely to be military, for fuel was a luxury denied to the native agricultural population. Occasionally they passed an Austrian farmhand driving a horse and cart laden with hay. Even in this year of upheaval the harvest must still come in, and those who worked the land had no alternative but to get on relentlessly with the task, reaping now under British occupation the crops that had been sown in spring under another form of political domination. Yet even here appearances could be deceptive. They had picked up one man last month from a gang of harvest labourers: he had looked as agricultural as the hoe he wielded, as though he had never known any other life but this simple regime of subservience to the seasons, impervious to the viciousness and violence that had disfigured Europe these past six years. But he had proved an impostor, a fugitive who had tagged on to the community only weeks before, an SS officer with a record of appalling crimes in concentration camps, crimes he had still been committing when the crops he was now reaping had been sown.

Victor had sat opposite this man, spoken to him at length, asked him questions, and concluded that he had never before encountered such naked evil. There were no personal qualities to him that in any way engaged his sympathy or his pity, no mitigating factors to temper the horror. Certainly no contrition. What had Victor felt, faced with this monster? A curiosity, certainly. And a sudden realisation that while man had within him the spiritual power to rise far above the beasts of the field, an obscenely warped intelligence could give him the capability by that same margin to sink below them. It had been a salutary experience. He didn't think he'd ever forget it. Certainly not the last exchange: as the man had been led out, under guard, from the interrogation room, he had looked back suddenly over his shoulder and spat out at Victor two vitriolic words: *'Verdammter Jude!'* Verdammter

Jude. Jewish scum. He had felt slightly sick. He'd never thought of himself as looking particularly Jewish. But the man had instinctively recognised him.

The landscape grew hillier as they approached Augstein, and along the terraced escarpments it was possible to make out straggling groups of peasants picking the last of the ripened vines. The new vintage was already available in the *heurigens*. Casks of the local wine had been delivered to the mess last week. It was deceptively easy to drink, but it gave you a head like a donkey the next day. Beside him on the back seat lay three bottles of something rather more rarefied, a 1929 Hock that had been requisitioned for the mess in large quantities from a local hotel. He was bearing these as a peace-offering, a good-will gesture to the man he was on his way to meet. It was a liaison mission. He was approaching the extremity of the British Zone. By the time they reached Augstein in a few minutes they would hit the border with the Soviet Sector, and there, at 15.30 hours, he had an appointment with his Soviet opposite number. Their brief was to discuss 'matters of joint concern'. Of course in practice this meant nothing very momentous. Policy was handled higher up: Victor and his Soviet colleague addressed themselves merely to joint problems of operation, to the cross-boundary pursuit of suspects, to logistical questions arising out of the need for the exchange of essential supplies. Nothing profoundly significant was ever decided at these meetings, but they were regarded – by Colonel Keith at least – as a useful point of contact. 'We need to know what the Soviets are up to, Meer,' Keith had told him briskly. 'Keep your eyes and ears open.'

Victor had to confess that to date he had brought very little back in the way of hard information about Soviet activity as a result of his liaison role. But today at least would bring a development of mild interest: a new Soviet liaison officer was due to make his appearance this afternoon. No longer would the humourless, heavily jowelled features of Captain Sirov glower across at him, challenging his adequate but far from perfect command of spoken Russian. Sirov had been re-posted, and, as they drove into the small town of Augstein that September afternoon, Victor wondered vaguely what the new man would be like: Captain Boris Venetsianov.

They met in a tavern. It was a new venue, suggested by the Soviets. Dakins deposited him at the door and prepared for one of those infinitely tedious periods of waiting which men like him seemed to accept unblinkingly. Victor walked inside. The interior was old and unexpectedly beautiful: the mellow woodwork was carved lovingly but unpretentiously; here were tables and benches worn by sheer usage, moulded into gentle undulations by centuries of being sat on and eaten at. The smell of the place was distinctive, compounded of wine, wax and flowers, the flowers cascading out of the boxes at the open windows. On entering he felt a welcome coolness after the stinging heat of the sun outside. He placed his briefcase, bulging with superfluous military paperwork, on the table. Next to it he stood the three bottles of Hock. Then he strolled over to look at the view across the valley from the window, and lit a cigarette. A little later he heard the door opening behind him.

'Captain Meer?' said a deep Russian voice.

It was the first time he heard it, that voice which was to haunt him for the rest of his life.

He turned round to meet his new opposite number. He had expected another Sirov: the man he saw before him could not have been more different. He was much younger than his predecessor, like Victor still in his twenties. He was blond, tall, clean-shaven, with memorable blue eyes. Victor was instantly attracted to him. There was something about the way he stood there, the way his limbs related to each other, his whole physical presence, that stimulated Victor. He wanted to be near this man. He instinctively relished his company. It was absurd, really. Absurd, and exciting. But instinct also told him not to show any of this. Experience had taught him caution. You didn't expose yourself to people, you didn't allow them that advantage over you. So he replied gruffly: 'Captain Venetsianov?'

They shook hands formally. Then Victor presented him with the three bottles of Hock. Immediately Boris produced six of powerful Russian vodka in return, and when Victor protested that his offering looked meagre by comparison he laughed loudly. It was the laugh of a man who enjoyed life. 'No, no, Captain Meer. In our country vodka is like water. What are six bottles of water by comparison with these three magnificent bottles of wine?'

They finished their business within an hour or so. There was not much to deal with this week. Boris was as intractable over areas of disagreement as his predecessor, but he managed to convey his intransigence with infinitely more charm. Victor then suggested that they should open one of the vodka bottles and that Boris should join him in a drink. He surprised himself by the invitation. Such a thing would have been unthinkable with Sirov. But now it seemed the most natural course conceivable to seek to prolong time spent in Boris's company.

'Venetsianov,' Victor said after they had toasted each other. 'Are you by any chance a descendant of that excellent Russian painter of the early nineteenth century?'

'Alexei Venetsianov?' Boris asked, alert and intrigued. Then, unexpectedly, he shook his head in mock distaste. 'That, Captain Meer, would be most unsound.'

'Unsound?'

'But of course.' He grinned at Victor roguishly. 'We are

now taught that Venetsianov's excessively charming pictures of the Russian peasantry show him to have been a prisoner of the bourgeois values of his time. I have heard respected Soviet authorities declaring that in his paintings the truth of nature does not achieve the truth of social reality. Therefore, while I think he may be a distant ancestor of mine, I do not make too much of such an embarrassing connection.'

Victor was enchanted. Boris was the first Russian he had met who was prepared to poke a little gentle fun at the system. It was thrillingly illicit to hear him talk like this. That he was prepared to do so to Victor seemed a personal compliment, formed an immediate bond between them. 'But you have seen his work?' Victor persisted.

'Certainly, in Leningrad and Moscow. I have spent many hours in the public galleries before the war. But it is rare to find an Englishman who knows his pictures.'

'Only from photographs,' Victor admitted. 'Perhaps one day I will see them in the flesh.'

'Then you shall come to see my collection in Moscow also,' Boris declared, pouring out more vodka. 'To your visit!'

'To my visit, thank you.' Victor raised his glass again to this extraordinary man, and added, 'I didn't know there were such things as private collections in the Soviet Union.'

'But of course there are. If you are prepared to look about you, there are many beautiful things to find in the Soviet Union. And I have been lucky in this war, too.'

'Lucky?'

'During the Red Army advance it has been possible to make some exceptional acquisitions.'

'Really? Where?'

'After the fighting finished, there was what you British

like to call "mopping up". I was in many places: in Prague, in Dresden, in Leipzig . . .'

'And you found pictures in those places? Pictures you could buy?'

Boris smiled enigmatically. 'Pictures I could acquire. One or two superb items, real discoveries.'

'What were they?'

'Ah. That is my secret.' He shook his head. 'No, to find that out, you must come to Moscow. Then perhaps I will show you, one day.'

'One day,' repeated Victor, staring into his vodka.

'And you, Captain Meer,' continued Boris, 'I think you too love pictures? Am I right?'

He was right. Victor had always loved pictures. Even as a twelve-year-old he was already spending much of his free time in solitary visits to the National Gallery, escaping the atmosphere of moneyed philistinism prevailing in his parents' house in St John's Wood. To the chagrin of his father, a successful banker in the City, Victor had shown no aptitude for cricket. What did he get up to in those museums all day? There was something morbid about it, something unhealthy, when you could be out in the open air enjoying yourself. But Victor was not to be shaken from his passion. He had gone up to Oxford to read history. He had got a first. He had been toying with the idea of an academic career, but his real wish had been to work with pictures professionally. And then the war had come, changing everything, forcing him to join up and abandon his immediate ambitions. He told Boris Venetsianov a little of his life before the war, and his ultimate hopes. It seemed easy to talk to him in this sweetly scented room, with a third glass of vodka in his hand. Remarkably easy.

Boris looked at him very intently.

'I think you and I have much in common,' he said with

great seriousness. 'We shall be friends.'

'I hope so.'

'I call you Victor, yes?'

'Please do.'

'And I am Boris.'

'Boris.' The explicit formalisation of such intimacies would normally have embarrassed him, but now he felt no such unease.

'So what do you think, Victor? Do you like being here in Austria? Do you like these Austrians we have to deal with?'

'One or two of them, perhaps. I don't really know.'

'I tell you I have no respect for them.' Boris frowned with contempt.

'In what way?'

'For me they have no dignity. Therefore I have no sympathy for them. They are duplicitous, not to be trusted. They laugh, they sing, they enjoy themselves. But they welcomed the Germans in 1938, and now they welcome us as liberators. They want to have it both ways, they are unreliable, insubstantial, like the froth on the beer. They want to be everyone's friends, but beneath the surface they have only one loyalty, to themselves. They were the ones who decided to unify their country with the German Reich. Now, when they see the way the wind is blowing, they are claiming the status of an unwillingly occupied territory. They are cheats.' He thumped the table with his fist. Victor was intrigued by his anger. There was something exciting about his passionate response to life.

'You know,' Boris went on, 'I preferred the Germans. In Leipzig, in Dresden, their cities were shattered, but they still kept some pride. They still stood up to you. They were not for ever trying to win you with meaningless laughter.'

'I wonder,' said Victor. 'Do you think the Austrians have always been like that?'

He shrugged. 'Probably they have always been a frivolous people.'

'Now come on, Boris. What about Klimt and Schiele? What about Freud? What about Mahler? These were not frivolous intelligences. I don't believe these men were always laughing meaninglessly.'

'But that is something else!' Boris exclaimed vehemently. 'That is the other strand in the Austrian spirit, complementary to the laughter but the reverse of it. How can it be expressed? A dangerous morbidity. A dark and self-indulgent introversion.'

'You have a very low opinion of the inhabitants of this country.'

'No one is past redemption, but now they must find it through socialism. It is the only way.'

'We shall see what happens in the elections, then,' Victor said. This first national poll was only a few weeks away, at the end of November. The country was being offered a much-vaunted opportunity for self-determination. 'That will be the Austrians' chance to embrace socialism.'

'Yes,' said Boris thoughtfully. 'This is the moment when they must seize their opportunity.'

Victor glanced up, half expecting a glint of irony in the Russian's eye, a flavour of that irresistible self-mockery which he had already shown him. But for once there was none. Boris was serious now. He looked closed up, suddenly impenetrable. So Victor said nothing more on the subject. He sensed that if they were to be friends, they must discuss politics on Boris's terms or not at all. Instead he asked:

'And what of Austrian art? Do you despise that too?'

Boris shook his head emphatically. 'But of course not.

There have been excellent pictures painted in this country in the past, I do not deny it.'

'Such as?'

Boris looked up at him with sudden excitement. 'Victor, you know something? You ask me what Austrian painting I admire? I tell you: I could show you an Austrian picture in a house not thirty kilometres from here which, if you saw it, you would not forget. I could bring you there, and I guarantee it would take your breath away.'

'What is this picture?'

Boris looked at his watch, enthusiastic again. 'Perhaps it is too late now, there is no time for it to be arranged. But next week, Victor, yes, next week we shall do it. After our meeting you shall be my guest for dinner. You come to the Soviet Sector, we eat, we drink, and I show you something you won't forget. It will be a pleasure to show it to someone who will appreciate it.'

'You're very kind, I shall look forward to it. But won't you tell me what it is that I'm going to see?'

'No,' Boris said, delighted at Victor's curiosity. 'You must wait, and come and see it yourself. And then you shall tell me if it was worth waiting for. Is it agreed?'

'Definitely agreed.'

They shook hands and parted. Even as they said goodbye Victor found himself looking forward to next week's meeting with an unprecedented intensity. This man was unlike anyone he'd ever met before. This man was beautiful, with his blue eyes and his big, bear-like body. This man loved pictures, made him laugh, and lived life with a captivating gusto. And in the end, a very faint voice in the depths of his soul was warning him, this man would be dangerous.

On the morning of Victor's second meeting with Boris, he attended a briefing given by Colonel Keith. There were ten or twelve men gathered in the room at Brigade HQ, ten or twelve of his brother officers, laughing and smoking together. Victor sat a little apart, pretending to study a sheaf of typewritten notes. He contemplated his fellows sourly. He had little in common with them. They were a second-rate bunch of schoolmasters, junior civil servants and provincial university lecturers. Socialists to a man, of course. Not that Victor himself was a particularly political animal, but he had felt mildly affronted by the mood of pious self-congratulation that had prevailed when news had come through of Mr Attlee's summer election triumph. What depressed him most was that these men clearly considered themselves the coming generation. They were smug, earnest, and anti-élitist. They were mediocrities, who would rather listen to a radio than contemplate a Raphael. If they were indeed the future of his country, then Victor wanted no part of it.

Keith strode in and everyone stood up, scraping chairs on the wooden floor. 'Sit down, chaps,' said Keith briskly. 'Smoke if you want to,' he added redundantly. He was a tall man who made a point of holding his shoulders unnaturally straight, as if he kept a coat-hanger in his tunic even when wearing it. He had a greying moustache, and spoke with carefully controlled vowels, as if in his larynx he had installed the elocutionary equivalent of the coat-hanger. Victor looked up at him, and wondered if any of his colleagues objected quite as strongly as he did to being addressed by Keith as a "chap". He thought probably not.

'I'll come straight to the point,' began Keith. 'You're all in the course of your various duties in regular contact with Soviets. I'm here to give you some revised guidelines for dealing with them.' There was something about him that reminded Victor of his housemaster. The same futile lectures. The same futile injunctions to take actions for which there was no rational justification. The same inclination to impose rules dictated by the lowest common denominators of behaviour and intelligence. Perhaps it was just that the Army was essentially no more than a rather depressing extension of school life.

'Now don't misunderstand me,' Keith continued, 'the Reds are still officially our allies. No change there. But part of our job in Intelligence is to see one jump ahead. Plan for the future. There are changes in the air, and Stalin and his boys have got to be watched, watched very carefully. I've told many of you before, but I'll tell you again, because it's advice that's worth repeating: don't make the mistake of treating your average Russian as a European. If you do, chances are you'll come to grief. Don't necessarily expect from him the normal civilised European response in any given situation. No, Russians are Asians, and have to be treated accordingly. Bear that in mind, and you won't go far wrong.

'Right, you're all bright chaps, and you're no doubt aware of the way the wind's blowing. National elections coming up, end of November. Free and fair opportunity for the Austrians to choose their own government. Except we know damned well that the Soviets are pushing their own candidates like merry hell, trying to manipulate the outcome. They want to stage-manage the return of a communist regime here. That would give them the authority gradually to edge out their co-allies from any sort of influence in this country. We'd all be standing in a very different relation to them then, very different indeed. We know it. They know it. And if they know it, you can bet they're taking their own precautionary steps with regard to us. That means that all contact with them has got to be extremely guarded from now on. Don't give anything unnecessary away. Think carefully what you really need to tell them. And don't get too friendly with them.' He paused, then gave the sort of breathless little laugh which with Keith generally preceded an attempt at a joke. 'Not that that's likely. Personally I've never met a Russian who I wasn't perfectly happy to keep my distance from.'

Everyone laughed. Victor was obliquely reminded of his housemaster again. Of his housemaster lecturing him on the dangers of friendships with boys from other houses. What absurd and panicky restrictions the authorities in closed communities dreamed up for their members. Restrictions designed for idiots. They had absolutely no relevance for Victor, of course. As Dakins drove him to Augstein that afternoon, he relished the prospect of seeing Boris Venetsianov again. It was ridiculous to impute a political dimension to his friendship with Boris, to fear some sort of security liability. There couldn't be. There couldn't be, because he knew in his heart that he and Boris had something crucial in common: they both valued pictures more highly than ideologies.

Two hours later Victor was with Boris. They were penetrating the forbidden territory of the Soviet Sector, driven by Boris's driver now. They wound through hilly country, past villages that had hitherto been only names on the map; villages that nonetheless looked from the outside remarkably similar to those in the British Zone – sleepy, agricultural communities under alien control, populated by peasants who were alternately surly and mystified at what was happening to them. For Victor, being on the other side of the line was intriguing but strangely unsettling. Ever since the conclusion of their routine business at the inn in Augstein, his excitement at being with Boris had been tempered by an anxiety that expressed itself in questions.

'What about Dakins?'

'Tell him to wait for you here. We shall use my driver, it is simpler.'

'What time shall I tell him to expect me?'

'We shall make a night of it, huh? Let him be ready any time from midnight. I shall drop you back here.'

'Where are we going?'

'To Murnsee. It is forty-five minutes' drive, not more.'

'Who are we going to see there?'

'Ah, Victor, do not worry yourself with these questions. No one will kidnap you.' He turned towards Victor and touched his arm, his mesmerisingly beautiful eyes filled with amusement. 'We are going to see Kalb.'

'Kalb? Who is he?'

'Kalb is a man whose acquaintance I have made in the past two weeks. He is an artist.'

'Why are we going to see him?'

'You want the official story?'

Victor nodded.

'Officially you and I are going to see him because he has significant evidence to offer in the Hauptmann case, evidence of such importance that I felt my British opposite number should hear it at first hand. It will be an excellent example of Anglo-Soviet Intelligence liaison.' Boris laughed merrily, produced a hip-flask and swigged heavily from it, then passed it to Victor. It was vodka. Victor derived a guilty physical pleasure from not wiping the rim before he drank, savouring the secret taste of Boris's saliva in his own mouth. His sense of bravado returned to him.

'And unofficially why are we going to see him?'

'Because he has interesting pictures on his walls.'

'Is he a good artist?'

'Victor, he's the worst bloody artist you ever saw.'

They both laughed hugely at this, Boris presumably because he knew what the joke was, and Victor because his courage had returned. He was relishing his night out, he was happy in the company of this extraordinary man, and he was enjoying his merriment.

The terrain about them had grown more rugged, even mountainous. Suddenly, as they passed into a new valley, there lay spread out before them the picture-postcard lake of Murnsee. They negotiated the circuitous road which snaked down into the small town that bore the lake's name. A lingering sunset had been visible higher up, but now the shadows of the hills had fallen across them and they were in twilight. There was a café at the water's edge, lit by lanterns and fairy lights. It was late in the season, of course, but it was strange and a little eerie to see it deserted. For a moment Victor imagined how it would have been only twelve months ago: full tables, many Nazi uniforms, a lot of beer being drunk. And singing, probably, the sort of singing that brought sentimental tears to the singers' eyes. The sort of singing that made your flesh creep. The sort of singers whose smiles masked hatred. "*Verdammter Jude.*"

Only a year ago. And ten years ago, who would have been sitting here then? A more international clientele, certainly. Americans, British, French; hikers, backpackers, and more leisurely tourists, rhapsodising over the Alpine scenery. Perhaps even the eighteen-year-old Victor Meer, had things worked out differently, on his way to Vienna. But these people too were gone for ever, swept away; they were the generation whose innocence was lost. It would never be the same, not for them, not for Murnsee. As dusk spread over the town, Victor sensed the atmosphere of almost tangible melancholy that inhabits holiday resorts bereft of holidaymakers. But there was also something more chilling here. All was quiet. But it was as if the town were not so much asleep as resolutely clenching its eyes closed in anticipation of some awful retribution.

They drove through the centre past the church, and about half a mile the other side of the village turned into the gate of a comfortable-looking villa whose garden sloped down to the water's edge. Now the engine was switched off, they could hear the lapping of the lake.

'Come and meet Kalb,' said Boris, jumping down from the jeep.

They walked up towards the front door. In the gathering darkness Victor was aware of flowers and trees, gently rustling in the breeze. The garden felt peaceful, with a faint smell of autumn. A place to sit and think. A place to escape. He was safe out here, he could breathe. But this house? Suddenly, irrationally, Victor didn't want to go in. It oppressed him, filled him with an overwhelming foreboding. No, more than that, a horror. A conviction that he shouldn't see inside, that if he did it would set in motion some indefinable evil. But the next thing he knew Boris was beating with a suppressed violence on the door, and there was no way of avoiding what must come.

The man who answered the knock swayed indecisively in the doorway for a moment, peering out at them. He looked ill. He had thinning grey hair, a cadaverous face, and his forehead and upper lip were beaded in sweat. He said nothing, no greeting, no protest, but with a gesture of resignation he shuffled aside to let them pass into the house.

'Kalb, I have brought Captain Meer with me. He is British, and a great connoisseur. He has come a long way to see your pictures. This is a big honour for you.'

The man nodded. He was rubbing his hands together distractedly. It was only now that Victor realised he was almost paralysed with fear.

Boris led the way into a salon. It was a musty, unpleasant room, overwhelmed by heavy late-nineteenth-century furniture. Victor shivered, and looked about him at the pictures hanging on the wall. There was a series of insipid Austrian lake landscapes. In one or two compositions nude women were bathing in the foreground, frolicking vacuously at the water's edge. They simpered as they bathed, as if aware of the spectator's voyeuristic gaze.

'Oh, don't look at those,' said Boris. 'They're all Kalb's own work. They're rubbish.'

It was true that they were not good. Victor felt obscurely embarrassed looking at them in the presence of the artist. His eye lingered on the monogram with which each was signed, a pretentious entwinement of the initials KK executed with a flourish in one corner. It was that self-confident flourish that was pathetically incongruous with the abject figure who stood head bowed beside his creations, rubbing his hands furiously as if the motion were the only thing that would stave off disaster.

'Come on, Kalb. Get us a drink. Then we'll come through and have a look at a real picture.'

Kalb shuffled off into a back room. Victor looked enquiringly at Boris, who shrugged, and said in a lowered voice: 'He's a filthy Nazi, of course. He knows it, we know it, although if you give him any encouragement he'll come out with all sorts of stories justifying himself, all of them lies. He was in Vienna, he did some terrible things. The evidence is all there against him. Now he's fled here, to his country retreat, and hopes to put us off the scent. But I know everything about him. And he knows I know. I'm just biding my time with Herr Kalb, waiting my moment.' Boris smiled to himself, then went on: 'As for his pictures – well, you can see for yourself what sort of an artist he is. He's not worth this much.' And he spat disdainfully.

'But you didn't bring me here just to show me these?'

'Most certainly not. In a little moment I have a surprise for you. Really, a surprise.'

Victor laughed, but he felt uneasy. Kalb was like a rat caught in a trap. There was something desolate about any doomed creature, even a rat.

Kalb came back into the room with a bottle of wine and two glasses which he carried shakily on a tray. Boris took the bottle, inspected it, then poured out drinks for both of them. There was no question of Kalb joining them.

'This had better be good,' said Boris, holding up his glass for a moment before drinking. 'Captain Meer is a great connoisseur of wine as well as of pictures. It would not be well for you if Captain Meer was disappointed.'

Victor drank, awkwardly, sensing Kalb's frightened eyes upon him. He had to say something. 'Not bad,' he muttered.

Boris nodded, then smiled. 'You are lucky, Kalb. Captain Meer is a difficult man to please.'

There was a pause, then Boris added: 'So. Shall we go through to the next room now? Kalb will show us his study.'

The shuffling figure moved forward, pushing open the double doors that led off the main salon. Victor and Boris followed.

Then Victor saw it, hanging there, above the fireplace. A single picture, on its own. It was of such quality that it dominated everything else. The eye was drawn irresistibly to it. Coming face to face with it so quickly after Kalb's own pictures was a journey of such swiftness from the ridiculous to the sublime that he felt momentarily disoriented, in a state of shock. He registered first that it was a landscape, a landscape executed in a distinctively jewelled style which was familiar because he had seen it employed in figure subjects by a famous hand. He thought suddenly, My God, if Klimt ever painted a landscape, that's what it would look like; and then it dawned on him, almost simultaneously, that that's exactly what it was. It was by Klimt. It could not be by anyone else. He caught sight of the signature, and the whole thing fell into place. He was transfixed by it. He felt elated, light-headed. And the reaction was suddenly familiar: he realised he was feeling about this picture the same emotions he had felt not long ago in another context. The same emotions he had felt when he first saw Boris himself. This picture was so breathtakingly impressive that he no more wanted to be separated from it now than he had wanted to leave Boris Venetsianov after their first meeting.

Some minutes later, he couldn't be sure quite how long, he heard Boris addressing him gently. 'Have you seen enough? It's time to go now, I think.'

He was slightly dazed. Obediently he followed Boris out, glancing back once for a last look at the Klimt. Kalb held the door open for them. As Victor passed silently by him, Kalb suddenly opened his mouth as if for the first time that evening he was going to speak. For a brief moment he looked at Victor with anxious, pleading eyes. But no sound came.

Victor hesitated. Then he hurried out to join Boris in the jeep. No one said goodbye. The driver started the engine and they were away.

'He's vermin, that man. Scum,' said Boris a little later. 'But what about that picture? Was I right to take you to see it?'

'You were right. It was utterly exceptional.'

'You are pleased you came?'

Victor was touched by his persistence, the realisation that his own approbation meant something to Boris. 'Very pleased, Boris. I congratulate you on finding it. It was far, far better than anything I could have imagined.'

As they followed the winding road away from Murnsee,

Victor asked Boris: 'How did a man like Kalb get hold of such a picture?'

'I think he bought it for nothing from some Jew trying to get out of Vienna in 1938 or '39. But you know something, Victor? I doubt if Kalb really knew what he was doing when he bought that Klimt. No one who could paint the dreadful landscapes that Kalb produces would be able to acquire a picture like that except by the sheerest chance. It is a travesty, no, to see such an object in the possession of such a bastard?'

'A travesty, yes,' agreed Victor.

'Now we go to celebrate?'

'Now we go to celebrate.'

He'd had quite a lot to drink, and felt suddenly a sense of profoundest well-being. It was delightful to be driven through Austria in the company of Boris Venetsianov. It was miraculous to have seen such a beautiful picture as that ravishing Klimt. Contemplating each of them gave him nothing but pleasure. In fact, after several more drinks from Boris's vodka bottle, the two entities began to blend into one, an inseparable mixture of alcoholic desire. The physical and the aesthetic. Boris and the Klimt. He couldn't tell them apart any more.

And it was easy to forget the anxious, pleading eyes of the man standing wordlessly in the doorway.

He woke suddenly, with a start. He hadn't so much been asleep as in a reverie, rocked by the motion of the jeep. He hadn't been dreaming for long, not more than twenty minutes or so, but he was aware that it was cooler now, cold even. He drew his coat closer about him.

'We are nearly there,' said Boris. He was excited, and his eyes were bright with anticipation.

'Where are we going?'

'To the place where we shall celebrate. I think you would like a good time, no?'

'Why not?' But Victor felt suddenly weary and uncertain of what Boris was proposing.

They drew up at a brightly lit tavern. At first sight it looked like any large country inn in this part of Austria. But it was unusually noisy. Victor heard raucous men's voices singing and shouting inside, and snatches of music playing. He shivered involuntarily. There was something strange, something alien about the place. Still, it was not until Boris led the way inside that Victor realised what it was. These were not the local inhabitants merry-making. The men were almost exclusively in military uniform, in uniform that was not immediately familiar. Then he understood: these were Soviet officers at play. The Austrians that were here looked different, too. They were mostly women. Painted, compliant Austrian women provided for the amusement of the occupying force.

Boris and he sat down at one of the few unoccupied tables. The atmosphere was foetid with sweat. Victor looked about him. The Russians were very drunk, pawing at the girls and shouting at the waiters. The women had glazed eyes and mechanical laughs. Victor found that the only way he could assimilate the scene was by relating it to those bawdy-house interiors of which he had seen so many painted by lecherous Dutch artists of the seventeenth century. These figures were gross, he decided, unpleasant to look upon. He imagined Boris would not want to stay here long. It was all a mistake. He leant towards him and said: 'It's like something out of Jan Steen.'

Boris laughed. 'You think so?' he said, but his mind was not engaged on the conversation. He was looking around the room for something. Or someone. They were brought more vodka, and a plate of borsch, which Victor started to eat but could not finish. He was just pushing his plate aside when the girl joined them.

'Boris,' she said coquettishly, 'where have you been?

It's too long since I saw you.'

She was pretty, in a coarse sort of way, highly coloured and plump with a sickening voluptuousness. Boris greeted her and drew up a chair for her. She sat down close to him, possessively, leaning forward so that her breasts bulged out of the encasement of her dirndl.

'This is Clara,' said Boris, putting an arm round her and squeezing her flesh. 'You like her?'

Victor shrugged. She reminded him of a cow. A prize cow, absurdly prettified with a bell about her neck and ribbons decorating her head.

Clara giggled, motioned Boris aside and whispered in his ear. He nodded, laughing himself.

'Clara says she has a friend who would like to meet you.'

'Does she?'

'She's as pretty as Clara. And she likes Englishmen.'

Clara agreed, leering eagerly at Victor. The evening was suddenly turning into a nightmare. He could think of nothing he would like to do less than meet this girl's friend, a duplicate mass of cheap-scented bovine flesh. No. No. No.

'Look, it's been a long day. Perhaps I should be getting back.'

'Oh, come on, Victor. What is this?'

'No, I've stayed long enough.'

'Don't you like these girls? They're clean, I promise you. They're reserved for officers.'

Victor shrugged again. The place was becoming intolerable. It was hot, oppressive, raucous, and alien. He wanted to get out.

'No, I don't think you do like them, do you,' said Boris softly. Then he added, almost under his breath, 'What do you like, I wonder?'

'I'm tired,' said Victor, rising stiffly from his seat. He

was conscious of appearing ridiculous, but he didn't care now so long as he got out.

'Come with me,' said Boris, getting up too. 'I'll get Gregor to drive you back to Augstein.'

Victor would have liked to have waved away his offer of assistance, to make an angry assertion of his independence, but reason told him that there was no other way of getting home. Boris put an amicable arm about him and guided him to the door. Over his shoulder he told Clara to wait, he would be back in a minute. He settled Victor in the back of the jeep and gave Gregor instructions.

Then he looked intently into Victor's eyes for a moment. 'I am sorry that this evening was not quite to your taste. Really I am sorry.' The words came out awkwardly. Victor sensed that he was genuinely upset to have displeased him, and despite everything he was touched.

'It doesn't matter. I'm tired, it's better that I go home.'

'You see,' Boris explained, smiling apologetically, 'it is a simple matter of physical gratification. The body has its needs.' He paused; then, patting the bonnet in a valedictory gesture, he added: 'I won't be staying longer than I have to.'

Where did he take her? Victor wondered as he was driven silently back to Augstein. Was there an upstairs room that could be rented by the quarter-hour? Or did they just go out into the trees behind the tavern and do it in the open air? Was it an act of casual congress in the night, dirndl bunched up above her straining thighs, underclothes wrenched aside? Victor's gorge rose, and he thought he was going to vomit; but the moment passed. He was sweating, but he was all right as long as he did not think about her actually touching Boris. Didn't think about her clutching his flesh. Didn't imagine her brushing his lips with hers.

Victor reached Augstein and rejoined the patient Dakins. As they drove the last leg of the return trip to Brigade HQ he finally mastered his nausea. He mastered it by concentrating on the one untainted feature of the evening. By reliving his rapture in standing in front of it. By recreating in his mind's eye its every jewelled branch and exquisite blossom. By remembering the Klimt.

The day that everything fell apart was the first Monday in December 1945.

It was also the first really cold day of the winter. The distant mountains had a thick covering of snow, and as Victor walked across the courtyard of the old monastery that served as Brigade HQ he noticed that there were patches of ice on the paving stones. It was hard to believe that the sweltering afternoon when he had driven through fields of harvesters to his first meeting with Boris was barely ten weeks ago.

Neither Boris nor he had talked again about the night of the encounter with Clara. Victor sensed that both of them found the incident too tender to probe, that in their separate ways each of them had exposed himself too revealingly to the other, and by tacit consent they left it alone. But their official weekly meetings continued. And Victor discovered that, despite the mortification of that night in the Soviet officers' tavern, he still relished Boris as much as ever, that he looked forward to seeing him with the same intensity. On the one hand it was the attraction of opposites. The Russian's exuberance, the gusto with which he attacked life, contrasted with Victor's own natural introspection, his innate suspicion of people. And on the other, Boris's enthusiasms – for pictures, for music – exactly mirrored Victor's own. On top of that Boris's reciprocal pleasure in his company was a constant source of surprised delight to Victor. Boris was the only real friend Victor had made since his posting to Austria. Looking back as far as he could remember, to Oxford, to school, Victor realised that he was the closest friend he had ever made in a life of guarded remoteness from his peers. It was a bloody existence out here in Austria, with winter coming on. Without Boris Venetsianov it would have been intolerable.

Keith called a briefing that Monday morning. People sat about in their great-coats, cursing the cold. The monastery heating system was erratic, and the stove in the corner of the room had failed again. But Keith looked pleased with himself. He began a résumé of the Austrian political situation. The national elections had just been held and it was becoming clear that through the ballot-box the Austrians had rejected a communist future. He announced the result with satisfaction, as if he himself had not only foreseen the outcome, but had even subtly orchestrated it.

'This vote represents cause for considerable relief,' he declared. 'The Austrians aren't stupid, of course. The Reds overestimated the likelihood of people voting for a political system proposed to them by an occupying force whom they regard as oppressors. When you've raped and pillaged to the degree that the Soviets have here, you can't expect the local population to want to vote for the candidates you've made it clear you're supporting. The important thing is, this country isn't lost to Western influence. It has clearly indicated which way its preferences lie. What will be interesting will be to see how our Soviet friends react now. Someone's bungled, misread the situation. Heads may roll. And it's important that all of you keep your wits about you in dealing with them. Make a note of any changes you detect in their line. Report back. Thank you very much, chaps.'

That afternoon, as Dakins drove him along bitterly cold

roads to Augstein, Victor said: 'What do you make of them, Dakins? The Soviets, I mean?'

'Couldn't say, sir.'

'But you've met a few, haven't you? You've talked to them, surely? Other drivers, for instance?'

'Not much at all, sir.' He stared woodenly at the road ahead.

Victor suddenly wanted a reaction, any sort of positive human reaction from the man. 'There are probably some decent chaps amongst them,' he suggested encouragingly.

'Wouldn't know, sir,' said Dakins.

He met Boris as usual at Augstein at 3.30. From the first moment, Boris was preoccupied. Victor reported dutifully to him on the various niggling and ultimately insignificant issues that were their professional concerns. A former mayor of a nearby town had disappeared under a sudden cloud of accusation about his conduct during the war. It was rumoured locally that he had fled to relations who lived in a village in the Soviet Sector. Would the Soviet authorities make the appropriate enquiries? There had been a complaint from a British platoon commander about an unannounced Red Army incursion over the border in pursuit of a suspect. Could the British be assured that this was an isolated incident, not to be repeated? And for what exactly had the suspect been wanted? Boris said he could give no such undertaking, nor could he supply any further details until he had checked the matter with the relevant authorities. Then he shrugged, smiled ruefully, and leaned across and patted Victor's shoulder.

'Enough, Victor, huh? All these matters can wait, they are not important. What about another dinner tonight?'

'Tonight? I don't know . . .'

'Please, Victor. You would do me a big honour. No visits to the tavern tonight, I promise you. We can have food served to us in my quarters, I can arrange it. And more important, I have urgent things to tell you. There is some bad news and also some good news.'

'What is this news?' Victor asked, alarmed.

'Come to dinner and I will explain.'

Not long after, Victor was in Boris's jeep again, being driven by Boris's driver. Being driven deep into the Soviet sector. A succession of sentries examined papers, saluted, waved them through. And then they were there, drawing up in the yard of the imperial hunting lodge commandeered by the Red Army for its officers. Boris led the way down broad passages hung with the sporting trophies of a distant age. Here were the antlers of animals once shot by the guests of Franz-Joseph, antlers now used carelessly as coat-hooks by the soldiers of another, alien, empire. Boris drew Victor into a room that was apparently his own private quarters and settled him in a chair.

'Vodka?'

'Thank you.' Victor lit a cigarette and settled back. Boris wheeled out a large and antiquated gramophone which he cranked wordlessly into life. He played a cracked but beautiful recording of Prokofiev. Both men sat in silence for a while, smoking as they listened. Once Boris leaned forward to prod the coal burning in the grate. Victor studied him, marvelling at the strength of his shoulders, the grace of his head and neck, the inordinate length of his eyelashes. It was then, for the first time, that he allowed himself to think the unthinkable.

Could it be that he was in love with Boris? With a sudden shock of confused revelation, he realised that he was. He realised what it all meant. He was in love with this man. In love with a Russian.

For a while, Victor didn't dare speak. Then he said, in an unnaturally gruff voice: 'So, what is all this? What's this bad news you've got to tell me?'

Boris got up from the fireside, rubbing his hands in the small of his back and stretching.

'I'm returning to Moscow,' he said simply.

For a moment Victor didn't understand him. 'But you'll be coming back here?'

'No, I regret not. There will be other plans, other duties for me there.'

The words reverberated in Victor's head. He could think of nothing to say. He was numb with disappointment. He was losing Boris. He was losing everything that made his life in Austria worth living. As the emptiness of this new reality sank in, bitterness followed.

'This is something to do with those bloody Austrian elections, isn't it?' he demanded. 'This is happening because they didn't go as expected.'

Boris looked at him. 'Why do you say that?'

'Bloody politics. Bloody, bloody politics.' Victor felt tears of frustration welling in his eyes. 'Why can't people understand that there are more important things in life than politics?'

'What things are more important?' asked Boris softly.

'Things like pictures. Like music. Like friendship. I know it. You know it. You do know it, don't you, Boris?' What he was saying had become crucially important to him suddenly. He turned on the Russian with a sort of violence. 'In the end, pictures are more important than political ideology. They are, aren't they? Tell me you believe it.'

Boris shrugged and looked away.

'Please, Boris.'

He still said nothing, kicking with his boot at a piece of coal that had fallen from the fire.

'Boris.'

Then he spoke, slowly, still staring into the flickering flames. 'All right. But this is said only between us. I would not say it to anyone else. Yes, pictures are more important.'

There. It was out. Even in his unhappiness, Victor felt an enormous sense of relief, of justification.

'What will you do in Moscow?' he asked.

'Some special duties, I cannot say more. I am sorry. In army life, there is no choice.'

'So this was our last Monday meeting.'

'Our last one at Augstein.' Boris turned and looked at him. 'But you know, Victor, I have the feeling we will meet again.'

'What, when I come to Moscow?' he said, bitter again. 'I'm about as likely to visit you there as I am to fly to Mars.'

'Don't be so sure, my friend. If you don't come to the Soviet Union, perhaps one day my work will bring me to your country. Or we will meet somewhere else. I do not intend that we shall lose touch.' He shook his head with a defiant assurance. 'And you. Tell me what will be your plans now?'

'My own plans? If I had the choice, I'd get out now. But that's not possible in this bloody army. I'll probably be in this wretched country for at least another twelve months. I won't get leave till Easter. Perhaps they'll finally let me go home next autumn.' He paused, then added in a rush: 'Dear God, Boris, I'll miss you.'

Victor had never before made such a confession of personal attachment. Perhaps Boris sensed it. He put a hand on Victor's shoulder.

'It won't be so bad.'

'It'll be bloody awful. I'm sick of Austria. I mean, what the hell are we doing here anyway? What's the point of it all? This meaningless de-Nazification process, sorting out their local feuds for them, that's all it is. British Zones, Soviet Sectors: what good does it do? I reckon we should just hand the whole enterprise over to you lot and let you get on with it. You seem to have much more stomach for it.' Victor gazed miserably into his vodka glass.

'Is this the official British position, Captain Meer?' Boris could ask these mock-serious questions with an enchanting wide-eyed irony. Victor laughed despite himself.

'I will have to check with the appropriate authorities,' he said, imitating one of Boris's own favourite stonewalling responses.

Boris arranged for dinner to be served to them in his room. It was an unexpectedly good meal. As it drew to a close, he leant across to Victor and asked: 'So you would like to leave the Army?'

'Very much. I'm sick of it.'

'Then you will work with pictures?'

'I intend to, yes.'

'You will be excellent. One of the top men, I know it. Perhaps in future years I may consult you?'

'About your collection?'

'About my collection. Maybe in the future I will find new pictures for it and need advice. Then I will come to the great man in London. But I think perhaps I will never have chances again like I have had in the past months. Here, and in Germany. I have been very lucky.'

'Won't you tell me what you've found?'

'Ah, Victor. These things are sensitive, it is too soon to speak of them. But one day. One day, I promise you.'

Victor nodded. Boris wasn't going to tell him more, even now. And it was late, time for him to make his departure, say sad farewells. As he got up, a little unsteadily, Boris said to him:

'I cannot let you go yet.'

'Why not?'

'You have not heard the good news.'

Victor paused. The bad news and its implications had

cast such a shadow over the evening that he had forgotten the second part of Boris's promise. 'Tell me,' he said.

'It is something which I hope will please you. I have a gift for you, a token of our friendship.'

'Boris, this is very kind.' What was Victor expecting? A book or a photograph; perhaps one of his battered Prokofiev gramophone records.

'No, no. It is a pleasure for me to give you something. Perhaps you have not realised that our time together has been dear to my heart?' He paused, and Victor thought he was going to say more. But then instead he ducked back into a large cupboard and emerged with an object that was flat and oblong, an object hidden under a blanket.

'Oh my God!' Victor said; even before Boris revealed it he knew with a sick horror and guilty excitement what it was.

Seconds later he was looking at the picture of the orchard. The blossom. The ravishing jewelled colours. The Klimt.

'There, it's yours. My gift to you. Take it.'

Victor was transfixed. 'But . . . but it belongs to Kalb.'

'Kalb? No, it does not belong to Kalb. That vermin never deserved to own it.'

'But it was hanging in his house.'

'Well, it's not hanging there now.'

'How did you get it?'

'The details are not important.'

'How, Boris?'

He shrugged.

'Boris, you have to tell me. I've got to know.'

'Kalb was executed last week. I confiscated some of his property.'

'But . . . but you couldn't do that.'

'Why not? I have the power to do what I think best in these matters.'

'On what grounds did you confiscate it?'

'I confiscated the picture because it was doing no good on the wall of a dead man. Why leave a picture like that in an empty house?' His tone softened: 'And then there was an even more compelling reason.'

'What was that?'

'I thought you wanted it. I wanted you to have it.'

Perhaps Victor should have refused it. Perhaps he should have turned on his heel and walked out of the room. Perhaps he should have insulted Boris, destroyed their friendship, destroyed everything for both of them. But he couldn't do it, not then, not just at the moment of their separation. If he was leaving Boris, then he had to leave him happy. He couldn't bear his parting memory of the man to be a sad one. And the way to leave him happy was to accept his present.

And there was a second, equally irresistible reason for not refusing it. He wanted that picture. He craved it. He found it breathtakingly beautiful, and the thought of owning it was so miraculous that in itself it was compensation for a year's misery in Austria, made his Army service worthwhile, even without the added dimension of its connection with Boris. So he took it. He clutched it under the blanket and carried it with him to the jeep. And before leaving he embraced Boris in the Russian style, felt his warm body against his own. I love you, Boris, he said under his breath as he held him. And later as he drove back in the jeep he could think only of what Boris had done for him, the extent of the sacrifice he had made. Boris could have kept the Klimt for himself. It would have been an adornment to any collection, and Boris was eagerly building his own. But he had resisted the temptation. He had preferred to get it for Victor, to give it as a token of his friendship. How could Victor have refused it? When he measured the feeling behind the gift, tears came to his eyes and he sobbed quietly in the back seat behind the impassive Dakins.

He had to keep thinking about Boris. If he hadn't, his mind would have strayed, strayed in directions that had to be prevented at all costs. To a frightened man with beads of sweat wobbling on his upper lip. To a frightened man who couldn't stop rubbing his hands together in paroxysms of anguish. To a frightened man who now lay dead with a Soviet bullet in his back.

Over the years that followed, Victor found many ways of blotting out the memory of that man. A man called Kalb. A war criminal. A war criminal whose only war crime might just conceivably have been that he was lucky – or unlucky – enough to find himself the owner of a very desirable landscape by Gustav Klimt.

3

Oswald Ginn visited Dresden in 1985.

In those days you had to fly to West Berlin to get there if you were coming from London. It was raining when he landed at Tegel that April afternoon, raining very hard indeed. He watched the sheets of water cascading against the aircraft windows as they drew to a halt and prepared to disembark. The skies were dark, almost apocalyptic. He shivered. Berlin. For a moment he felt the weight of history on this place: you were always threatened by the past here. And by the present. Today it was the microcosm of the modern world, where east abutted west in concentrated confrontation. You couldn't come to Berlin without feeling insecure.

There were only a handful of people waiting in the arrivals hall. He guessed at once which was the man detailed to meet him: Dr Gunther Dresch of the East German Cultural Affairs Department looked exactly as he had anticipated. He wore a shapeless grey raincoat, a small hat, and steel-rimmed spectacles. He was frowning, as if he was concentrating very hard on something. Perhaps he was concentrating on not looking at the line of naked women decorating the magazine covers displayed at the kiosk six feet from where he was standing. Or perhaps as a good communist he was merely expressing his distaste for the decadent Western lifestyle which any trip through the Wall forced him to confront. There was something faintly ridiculous about him; but there was also something strange and unfamiliar, something to beware of. Oswald approached him with a sudden diffidence.

'Dr Dresch? I am Oswald Ginn.'

'*Ja? Ah zo.* Mr Ginn.' Dresch's face cranked itself into a smile of greeting, then sprang back as if on a coil into its habitual set of diligent suspicion. 'I was concerned. Your plane is twenty-five minutes late.'

'Oh, well,' said Oswald jocularly, 'you know British Airways.'

Dresch looked at him mystified. 'No, I do not.'

There was a pause. Oswald felt he was going to dislike Dr Dresch. He tried again: 'Anyway, it's a great pleasure to be here.'

'It is a great honour to welcome the representative of so distinguished a museum, Mr Ginn. I hope you will find your visit enjoyable and productive.'

'I am sure I shall.'

'Please follow me. There is a car.'

Dresch strode on ahead and Oswald followed, wondering if the man was real. 'It is your first visit to the DDR?' Dresch asked him over his shoulder as he pushed through the doors.

'It will be, yes. But I have been to Berlin before. I saw the Liebermann exhibition here some years ago.' Dresch was marching remorselessly on, so Oswald added encouragingly, 'A wonderful show, you probably remember it well.'

He stopped and turned to Oswald. 'This exhibition was in the West, I think?'

'In West Berlin, yes . . .'

'I thought so.' Dresch spoke firmly and resumed his stride. The point had been made.

Oswald followed him into the open air, where the rain pelted down relentlessly. He was appalled but intrigued. It wasn't every day that the museum sent him on official business across the Iron Curtain. This trip was a break in the routine, and a bloody welcome one. Back in London he felt stifled. The demands of his job increasingly irked rather than stimulated him. He was forty, for God's sake; in his prime. He was a senior curator. But he was surrounded by bureaucrats and time-servers, frustrated by his colleagues' jealousies and pettiness. So this journey to East Germany was important, offering a little unexpected excitement and putting a bit of distance between him and his problems. It was a step into the unknown, an adventure. Glamorous in a way, too. Even Daphne had paused for a moment last night to get him to repeat where he was going, shown a flicker of interest in his movements. Unusual for his wife, that.

Dresch reached a large blue saloon. It wasn't a make of car that Oswald recognised. Dresch held the rear door open, motioning him to duck in from the rain. Then Dresch took the front seat next to the driver, and gave an abrupt command to move off. Oswald pondered this arrangement. Up front with the driver, Dresch was emphasising proletarian solidarity, avoiding the effete capitalist image of fat cats in the back being chauffeured about by a solitary underling. The car wheezed into action, coughing black smoke from its exhaust. Disconcertingly, one windscreen wiper moved more slowly than the other. It was raining harder than ever.

'So, Mr Ginn,' said Dresch in an unexpectedly smug tone, 'you see that it is not only in the West that you build big automobiles.'

'No, indeed.'

'No doubt you observe there is considerable room for the legs where you sit at present?'

'Very spacious, yes.'

'I have to tell you something: you would have less room in a Mercedes. It has been compared.'

'That's extraordinary.'

'I assure you it is true. There have been tests.'

They proceeded through the neon streets of West Berlin, edging uneasily past strip-clubs, luxury hotels, department stores and hoardings advertising American jeans and Coca-Cola. They travelled for the most part in silence, although in order to emphasise his point about relative sizes Dresch for a while took to issuing a little whistling noise of disparagement every time they passed a Mercedes.

A little later Oswald looked down a side-street and saw, thrown straight across it, a twenty-foot concrete barrier. Glancing upwards, he glimpsed the cone of a control tower behind. For a moment he mistook it for a prison; then, with a sick shock, he recognised what it was. The Wall. That wall. It was totally arbitrary, the way this barrier terminated the street in mid flow, cutting off a block of flats which fell away into oblivion beyond the line. Randomness always frightened him. He had a recurring nightmare, of the moment when the tenuous hold that reason and good order exert over human proceedings snaps and everything is washed away in a flux of illogical and utterly chance occurrence. This was the beginning of that dream – surreal, disturbing, unmanageable.

Dresch said: 'Shortly we shall pass through into the DDR. You have of course the requisite papers?'

'I do, absolutely.' Oswald checked in his passport for his new visa.

'And fifteen Deutschmarks will also be necessary.'

'Oh. Right. What is that for exactly?'

'An unavoidable clerical charge for processing your entry.'

'Probably what Charon called it.'

'Excuse me. Charon?'

'Didn't he demand a coin for ferrying passengers across

the frontier of the Styx?' The Styx was an arbitrary barrier too, of course.

'I do not know the area you speak of,' said Dresch severely. Oswald could see he thought the Styx was like the Bronx, some undesirable urban wasteland thrown up by American capitalism. He left it at that.

They had to leave the car in order to negotiate the western border control at Checkpoint Charlie. Finally they were motioned through by gum-chewing American marines in spotlessly white leggings. Oswald observed them curiously. They seemed unmoved by their proximity to the hostile east, as unconcerned as if they were on sentry duty at some barracks in Omaha. Christ, these men were the very front line of civilisation. Didn't they realise that? All they did was stand about chewing gum. Oswald watched them receding as he and Dresch were driven the hundred metres to the eastern control building. Looking back, he felt a sudden surge of panic. In travelling those hundred metres he had put himself as far beyond the protection of those marines as he would have been in Moscow. He was through the curtain. And he was on his own.

Being back on the soil of the Democratic Republic seemed to relax Dresch a few degrees. He turned round in his seat and announced that if there was no objection, they would drive straight on to Dresden. The journey would take no more than three hours, and they would arrive in time for dinner. Fortunately, he could not resist adding, the car was a powerful one. He even gave one of his brief, mechanical smiles. Oswald agreed politely, and kept his eyes on the view from the window.

East Berlin in the rain. Dear God, it was depressing. The contrast with the streets he had just left was extraordinary: no neon lights, no commercial advertising, no colour. Granite grey buildings, looming wet and menacing. How could the West be so near and yet so far? There were fewer cars, fewer pedestrians, fewer umbrellas. The people: what were they like? Oswald peered closely at those he could see hurrying past on the pavements, sheltering in doorways. Were they a different race? Did communists wear different clothes, do their hair oddly, walk in a distinctive way? They were dressed more drably than in the West, that was noticeable. There were more uniforms to be seen, too. People looked tenser, more serious; or was that just the rain? The women seemed less attractive; or perhaps they were just less tarted up than in the West. Still, there was something dispiriting about the atmosphere. You sensed it was unyielding and inflexible. You sensed an undercurrent of regimentation. People weren't laughing much. Their individuality was shackled, their self-expression muted. He yearned for some evidence of an independent spirit, just one small sign, one spark of colour in the grey uniformity. He wanted to see graffiti on the walls, something.

The car left Berlin and headed south through fields and rural villages. Oswald's depression lifted. Perhaps things weren't so bad after all. He felt suddenly invigorated by his trip, emboldened by it. He was doing something new at last. London was stultifying, and it was good to be away, to find himself in an unfamiliar environment, with a challenge to meet. Back in the museum people talked and thought, then thought and talked; but they never got around to doing anything. They were paralysed, clogged up in a sort of cerebral morass. But here, in a speeding car threading its way through East Germany, he could fancy himself in the unfamiliar role of the man of action. He liked it. Maybe visiting Dresden to discuss with the local cultural authorities a loan exhibition of German Romantic painting wasn't exactly a perilous assignment. But it was a change. And there was a hint of menace implicit in any passage to the East which set the adrenalin running. His life needed adventure. The truth was he'd been too long in his job. In London it was hard to find anything worth taking seriously any more. His colleagues' absurd enthusiasms for their own pitifully parochial projects – rehanging the North Wing, repositioning the bookstall, issues that ten years ago might have galvanised him too – now seemed futile in the extreme, exercises in the irrelevant.

'How do you see the role of the museum in today's world, Oswald?' he had been asked by Denzil Burke, the dreadful new director of publicity, only last month. Burke had actually gone to the length of organising an internal seminar on the subject.

'I see it as a centre of excellence,' Oswald said shortly. He was an unwilling participant in this nonsensical jamboree.

'Could you define excellence for us in this context?'

Oswald detested him with his pink spectacles and his ridiculous little bow-tie. 'Excellence means the best,' he said. 'A focus for the best pictures, and a focus for the best in art-historical scholarship.'

'That's all very well, of course. But what about our duty to the public?'

'Sod the public.'

Denzil had laughed with a great display of broad-mindedness, as if to show that he could humour eccentrics with the best of them. 'I see a slightly different emphasis needed here,' he had continued smugly. 'Can I put it like this? We need to promote this museum as a machine for heightening visual awareness.'

A machine for heightening visual awareness. God, what crap. Meaningless PR gobbledegook. Why did they all put up with it? But Oswald was aware that his capacity to be gripped by any new enterprise was waning. It was hard to find anything worth taking seriously any more, and as a cover he lived his life in a cloud of cynicism, constantly on the verge of self-parody. He followed the progress of a droplet of water across the outside of the car window, watching how the speed of the car drove it in an ineluctable course laterally across the glass. He had a will, didn't he, and the strength to assert it? He was more than that droplet of rain. He felt a sense of hope. But he must act. His life needed a new direction.

He had been at the museum for fifteen years now, ever since leaving the Courtauld. Middle age was creeping up, drawing its tentacles insidiously about him; unless he made a move soon he would be ensnared for the rest of his working life. He had seen it happen to others. The longer he left it, the less capable his flesh would become of taking the action that his spirit willed. The greyness that he'd seen in East Berlin depressed him, but it was no more than a reflection of the greyness of his own existence. He must get out, break free, assert himself before it was too late. Take a paint can and spray a bit of graffiti himself. Otherwise all that lay ahead would be bitter and rancorous old age. And as if this were not compulsion enough, there was the further factor of money. A gallery curator's salary was pitifully inadequate, and not merely by comparison with those Oxford contemporaries like Geoffrey Cornforth whose ambition had driven them into senior positions in merchant banks. It was iniquitous how much a man like Cornforth made, of course; but even normal people, like dentists, publishers and solicitors, seemed appreciably better off than he was. Nor could he even enjoy the decent pleasures of out-and-out penury, because he was ignominiously cushioned by Daphne's private income. Daphne's bloody money. The boys' education (Jasper and Gordon were at boarding-school), the original capital to buy the house in Hammersmith, even the financing of the car – she had provided it all. He resented her for every penny of it. She seemed to think it gave her the right to patronise him, to treat him as an irrelevant adjunct to her life. It was emasculating him. He yearned to make enough to free himself, and that emancipation would not come working in a museum. The problem was taking the first step, breaking out of the inertia that the security of her private income prolonged.

Oswald considered the back of Dr Gunther Dresch's head in the seat in front of him. Dresch held himself erect and attentive. What was he thinking as he scoured the view ahead through the windscreen? How old was he? Early fifties, perhaps. What secrets lay hidden in the private life of this apparently inscrutable figure? Was he married? Did he have a lover? Was his salary adequate? What ambition drove him on? Did he nurture a secret passion for ten-pin bowling? What books did he read?

'Do you live in Berlin yourself, Dr Dresch?' Oswald asked.

Dresch bobbed round in his seat. '*Ja*, I live in Berlin.'

'Is it a pleasant place to live?'

'I am sorry?' The question perplexed him.

'Do you enjoy it? I mean, do you have many friends in the neighbourhood, how are the theatres, the restaurants, that kind of thing?'

'The cultural amenities are outstanding.' Dresch spoke slowly but firmly. The matter was closed.

Oswald fell silent. He observed a line of tanks drawn up on the roadside as their car laboured by. He looked closer and saw they were Russian. Soviet soldiers were standing around them, smoking and exchanging swigs from a flask. It was chillier now, and still raining. He shivered. He was after all a visitor to enemy territory.

Later he tried conversation again. 'I suppose you know Dresden well?' he asked.

'Dresden?' Dresch paused. 'Yes, it is my native city.'

'Ah, that's good. So this is something of a homecoming for you?'

'A homecoming, yes. That is correct.'

'Do you still have some family there?'

Dresch turned again and looked at him. 'No, Herr Ginn, I regret I do not. My parents, they were both killed in the firestorm of 1945.'

'Oh. I am sorry.'

'It was many years ago now. But we can never forget.'

'Of course not.' Oswald felt awkward, wanting to change the subject.

'The destruction was total,' Dresch continued. 'In the inner city, the Altstadt, there was scarcely one structure left standing. You will see for yourself the works of rebuilding and restoration that have been carried out. I believe the full extent of the damage has never been widely publicised in the West?'

'I really don't know. I mean, I think most people are aware . . .'

'Herr Ginn, take yourself as an example. You are an intelligent, well-informed man. Do you yourself know what was the loss of life sustained in one night's air raid on Dresden in February 1945?'

Oswald shifted uncomfortably in his seat, appalled at the directness of the interrogation. 'I'm afraid I'm really not sure. Not precisely.'

'According to reliable estimates, there were dead some one hundred and thirty thousand persons.'

'That's dreadful.'

'One hundred and thirty thousand. More dead than in the bombing of Hiroshima.'

Oswald shook his head, acutely embarrassed, and at the same time angry. It was not right that he should be subjected to this history lesson. At best it was an error of taste.

'It was an undefended city, Herr Ginn, of no military significance. And in the course of one night it was destroyed from the air, saturated with incendiaries.'

What did Dresch want him to say, for God's sake? Was he meant to apologise? There was a perversity in Dresch's persistence. He was getting a retributory satisfaction out of retailing these statistics. What was Oswald meant to feel? Chastened? Or threatened?

'No, it is right that we do not permit these things to be forgotten,' continued Dresch. 'The state has directed that every year on the night of 13 February this tragedy is commemorated. At 10.10 we keep silence for a period. This was the time at which the first bombs fell on the undefended city.'

Suddenly, despite himself, Oswald glimpsed the horror of what had happened that evening in Dresden forty years ago. He saw the scale of the thing, imagined the unimaginable. More than a hundred thousand people dying within a few hours of each other in a very small area, compressed together in basements and flimsy shelters, burned, asphyxiated. More than a hundred thousand people with nowhere to run to, bombed mercilessly from the unprotected skies. The fires raging out of control, the utter destruction. And then the hundred thousand corpses. Flame-charred corpses. How do you cope, physically, with a hundred thousand dead bodies? How do you dispose of them? Each one once a living human being; each one once the child of parents. For a moment he understood the depth of the city's bereavement. For a moment the enormity was overwhelming.

Then, unexpectedly, Dresch brightened. 'You will, however, see for yourself that the task of rebuilding the city has been achieved triumphantly. It has been a supreme joint effort between the workers of the DDR and their Soviet comrades, a monument to socialist endeavour.'

Oswald paused, shaking away the images he had conjured up for himself. 'And the public collections of works of art, they were largely saved?' he asked.

'Only by heroic Soviet actions,' Dresch assured him.

'Weren't most things being held safely at sites well away from the city throughout the war?'

'That was so at the outbreak of hostilities. Museum personnel were obliged to crate and evacuate hundreds of thousands of objects from the museum's holding. They were sent for storage in distant castles and in some cases under the ground. However, in 1945, as the liberating Red Army approached, an atmosphere of chaos prevailed. Many of these objects were moving on senselessly ordered flight-paths. Orders had been given that everything stored east of the Elbe had to be moved to western depots.'

'You mean works of art were lost track of?'

'It was inevitable. And very major pictures were destroyed for ever under tragic circumstances.'

'How many?'

'To be precise, one hundred and ninety-seven. All burned on the night of 13 February in the firestorm.'

'So they were actually in the city?'

'There were forty-two hanging in the Residenz. These were too big to move. But then there happened also the most tragic coincidence. A transport containing one hundred and fifty-five paintings was en route through Dresden that night. On any other night of the war their passage would have been a safe one. But as it turned out supreme canvases by – amongst others – Bruegel, Cranach and Courbet were lost through the action of the RAF. Thousands of tons of incendiary bombs were deposited on a small area of the city creating fires of enormous heat. Nothing and no one survived.'

'Terrible,' Oswald agreed. His unease was returning. The numbers reverberated through his head. One hundred and thirty thousand people; one hundred and ninety-seven pictures. How much did the pictures matter by comparison with such appalling loss of life? Sod the public, he had told Denzil Burke. It had been in a completely different context, of course. But bugger that bastard Burke for making him say it.

Dresch was continuing his relentless catalogue of communist achievement: 'Immediately after the surrender of the Third Reich, the Red Army entered Dresden. Almost at once a Soviet Special Command of art historians, museum experts, restorers and artists began the rescue of art treasures.' He paused. He seemed genuinely moved by what he was describing. He looked Oswald in the eye and went on with feeling: 'You know, Herr Ginn, we in the DDR owe an enormous debt to those selfless men and women, those Soviet comrades of ours. They became the heroic saviours and guardians of our cultural heritage. We never forget that without their prompt and unstinting efforts many magnificent paintings and art objects would have been lost. Lost for ever.'

Once again Oswald was uncertain how to reply. This was a different Dresch. Dresch the humourless cog in the Party machine, Dresch the unsmiling executive of the collective will of the state, these things Oswald had come to terms with. But Dresch the man of emotion was a new and disturbing phenomenon. There was something indecent about him in this guise, something that made Oswald want to turn away from the spectacle.

'I suppose there was the problem of looting?' he ventured. 'In the chaos at the end of the war, I mean?'

'Looting?' Dresch was incredulous.

'Spoils of victory and all that. I suppose conquering armies consider themselves entitled to a bit of plunder. It must be hard to stop, anyway.'

'You misunderstand, Mr Ginn. I have heard it said that this regrettable practice occurred with the American soldiers in the Western zones at the conclusion of the war.

That may be so, I do not know. But the Soviet Army was superbly disciplined; they came as liberators not oppressors. There were no instances of looting of treasures in this sector. Oh no, quite the reverse.'

'How fortunate.' Oswald concealed his irritation.

'We in the DDR were fortunate, indeed. You see, all art works were rushed for intensive care to Moscow, Leningrad and Kiev where necessary repairs and restoration could be carried out in the required thorough manner. Enormous pains were taken. And this nation has of course shown its gratitude since.'

'Yes?'

'For instance the Patriotic Order of Merit of the DDR was awarded to several outstandingly deserving members of the Soviet rescue team.'

'And how long did it go on, all this repair and restoration?'

'It was in 1955 that one thousand two hundred and forty saved paintings were returned to Dresden.'

'Ten years,' said Oswald. The East Germans must have begun to despair of their ever coming back, all those pictures spirited away to the Soviet Union. It was surprising that they did return, in a way, considering how many other assets the Russians stripped from the country in the immediate post-war years; but they must have been allowed home as a little reward for a subject state that had so immaculately toed the line.

'*Ja*, ten years. It is hard to believe, no? So much work in so short a time. And tomorrow you will see the results for yourself.'

'I look forward to that greatly,' said Oswald.

The car ground on through the rain, thudding regularly over the joins in the concrete sections that made up the surface of the road. In renewed silence he contemplated the gradual erosion of the number of

kilometres separating them from Dresden. Three hours
in a car with Dr Gunther Dresch had certainly been an
experience. It was hard to imagine a man of more
indomitable pig-headedness. In Dresch he had come up
against something more disconcerting than the extrem-
ism of the zealot: it was something calmer, deeper and
more intractable, this utter absorption in a creed, this
complete conviction of belief which reacted to question-
ing of doctrine not with violence but with incredulity.
Perhaps after all the sooner Oswald saw these pictures
then got back to the West the better. He felt uneasy: he
sensed that in Dresch he was encountering a microcosm
of something huge, horrendous and monolithic. It was
not just that his political tenets were apparently dupli-
cated in literally millions of his rigidly totalitarian
countrymen; there was another way in which Dresch
was but one in horrifically many. This was as a native of
Dresden with a legacy of bereavement. The parents he
had lost burned alive in the city forty years ago were
themselves but two out of a hundred and thirty thousand charred corpses. And while Oswald might legiti-
mately mock him for the naivety of his politics, he
resented the fact that at the same time Dresch's terrible
wartime inheritance involuntarily aroused both his pity
and his guilt.

'Ah. Here is Dr Benz now.'
   At Dresch's words, Oswald looked up from the menu
he was studying. Some of the dishes described in the
antiquated typescript had been summarily crossed out
with ballpoint pen. He was very hungry indeed after his
journey, and he was worried that he would find nothing
edible left to order. The hotel restaurant was a depressing
place. It was a large, characterless room lit by bare fluorescent tubing. The only decoration on the cream-coloured

walls was a shelf of cactus plants. The doorways were hung with bead curtains, and the floor laid with an unpleasant patterned linoleum. He could still hear the rain lashing the window behind him. God, he needed a drink. In these surroundings he was going to have to make conversation with Dresch for another hour or two. Except that they were not, apparently, to dine alone. On checking in at the hotel an hour earlier, Dresch had informed him that they were to be joined by Dresch's Dresden colleague for the evening. Now that this colleague was announced, Oswald glanced across to the far doorway, expecting to see another man in a colourless raincoat, probably wearing steel-rimmed spectacles and frowning.

Strangely, the only person who had entered the room was a slim blonde woman in her early thirties, her hair cut stylishly and pleasingly short. She swayed towards them between the tables with an elegance and poise that were oddly out of place here, shaking out a scarf which she had apparently been wearing to protect her head from the rain. She was dressed in a brown jacket over a yellow polo-neck and a skirt tight enough to emphasise the excellence of her figure.

'I am so sorry I am late,' she said as she approached them. 'The traffic is bad at the moment.'

Dresch greeted her with brisk formality, then turned to Oswald.

'Herr Ginn. This is my colleague, Dr Saskia Benz.'

Taken aback by the gender and attractiveness of Dr Benz, Oswald was even less prepared for the smile she directed at him. It was a warm, open, uncalculating smile, a smile of unfeigned pleasure in his acquaintance. Normally inclined to hold a woman's beauty against her, to treat good looks with suspicion, Oswald was reassured.

'How do you do,' he said, and stood for a moment smiling foolishly back at her.

'I hope your journey was not tiring?'

'Not at all,' he lied.

She smiled at him again as she settled in her chair. 'No, I think I will keep my coat on. It is horrible weather we give you for your visit in Germany.'

After the rigours of conversation with Dresch, Oswald found the excitement of talking to her intense. 'I'm afraid it was raining just as hard when I left London this morning,' he said.

'Was it raining in London?' She sounded intrigued and surprised.

'Even in the capitalist West, I'm afraid the sun doesn't always shine.'

She laughed delightedly. Even Dr Dresch allowed himself one of his mechanical smiles. Oswald was made to feel that he had said something brilliantly witty, and basked in the pleasure of having amused her. God, she was attractive, with a dark, faintly Slavic set to her eyes, and high cheekbones. She seemed simultaneously exotic and approachable, innocent and yet seductive. What was it Bernard Tumbrill had told him the other day? Bernard told him a lot of things, of course, most of them fantasy; Bernard, leering lasciviously over his drink; Bernard, drawing lecherously on his cigarette. You didn't necessarily believe everything Bernard told you, though some of his theories sounded plausible simply because you would have liked them to be true. And Bernard, moderate painter and top-class alcoholic, was good at playing the role of the well-travelled roué whose experience had taught him a thing or two. Now his words came back to Oswald: women from behind the Iron Curtain are sexually fascinated by Western men, he'd said. And then there had followed the Budapest lift story. His fellow passenger had been a voracious Hungarian lady who had practically torn the clothes off him and effected a seduction between the first floor and the sixth. It had been a very slow lift, Bernard admitted that much. It was one of the great set-pieces of Bernard's repertoire, this story, constantly embellished and renewed with ever more imaginative detail. But you never knew. Something like it might just once have happened.

Dear God, imagine being in a lift with Dr Saskia Benz.

Now she said wistfully, 'I should like to visit London one day.'

'You must,' Oswald encouraged her, adding diplomatically, 'but I suppose you don't get much opportunity for travel in your work?'

'Not so much now, but in my previous job, yes. Often in the Ministry of Foreign Trade I was sent as delegate.'

'Where did you go to?'

'Yugoslavia, Bulgaria, Rumania, Italy . . .' With a child-like enthusiasm she enumerated the countries. 'Italy, mmm, yes. Italy was my favourite. I was in Milano.'

'You liked Milan?'

'Mmm . . . wonderful restaurants, wonderful clothes.'

Dr Dresch coughed. You could see he disapproved of the direction the conversation was taking. Oswald turned to him and said: 'And do you travel outside the country at all?'

'It is not frequently a requirement of my work.'

'Dr Dresch has many important responsibilities in Berlin,' explained Dr Benz. To Oswald's amazement, as she spoke she winked at him. It was a private, conspiratorial wink establishing an intimacy between them to the exclusion of her colleague.

'I'm sure he does. But let's hope this exhibition gets off the ground, then you will both have a good reason for coming to London.'

She nodded. 'We must work hard together to achieve this.' To emphasise the point she reached out and touched

Oswald lightly on the arm. It was an unthought, spontaneous gesture, but it sent a sharp thrill through him.

Two other tables in the linoleumed expanse of the restaurant were occupied. At one sat three army officers, locked in grave discussion. At another a party of Swedish businessmen debated their day's negotiations in the lilting, slightly foolish rhythms of their native tongue. One waitress served everyone – an ill-tempered, hirsute mountain of a woman who emerged periodically through the beaded doorway of the kitchen like some ogress from her lair. Oswald looked at her surreptitiously as she loomed over them taking their order. The muscular grip with which she held her pencil threatened to snap it in her hand.

'To drink?' she asked sharply.

Dresch ordered mineral water. There was a pause, and for a moment Saskia looked embarrassed. Then she turned decisively to Oswald and said, 'You will have some wine with me, won't you, Herr Ginn?'

'I certainly will,' Oswald agreed with relief. He grinned back at her, to reassure her that he was on her side, to tell her that two were stronger than one and together they had nothing to fear from Dresch. Even so, he saw her glance quickly across to her colleague a moment or two later, just to check she hadn't pushed her luck too far.

The waitress brought the wine and filled their glasses. Oswald half expected her to bite the head from the bottle rather than bother with a corkscrew.

'My God,' he exclaimed when she'd gone, 'is that woman possibly a member of your Olympic shot-put squad?'

Saskia giggled. Dresch replied almost at once, 'No, this could not be so. You may not realise, perhaps, Herr Ginn, the high level of athletic achievement we have in the DDR. For those who show promise the State provides

Schools of Excellence from an early age. Those pupils who make exceptional progress are then enrolled in the armed forces. Therefore it is unlikely to find a competitor of Olympic standard engaged in hotel work.'

'Dr Dresch,' said Saskia gently, 'I think that Mr Ginn is teasing us.'

'What is that?'

'It was a joke, I think.' She glanced swiftly at Oswald.

'Oh, *ja*. A joke.' Dresch lost interest immediately.

Oswald leant across to refill Saskia's glass. Dresch's steadfast refusal to accept any drink beyond his mineral water only emphasised his isolation. Gradually Oswald lost both the inclination and the obligation to include him in the conversation; talking to the enchanting Dr Benz occupied all his own attention. The way she seemed to find everything he said fascinating was more intoxicating than the wine. He talked with growing animation and excitement; she listened entranced. She wanted to know about the London art world, about major exhibitions, about auctions where works of art changed hands for enormous sums of money. She asked Oswald if he collected pictures himself. She giggled at his accounts of other people's incompetence at the museum, marvelled at his description of his own discovery of a Delacroix two years before. Dresch drummed impatient fingers on the tablecloth.

Finally Dresch announced his intention to go to bed. It was ten minutes past ten. As they all got up, Oswald noticed that the dining-room was now empty of other customers. He shook Dresch's stiffly proffered hand.

'You will liaise with Dr Benz tomorrow morning. She has been detailed to make arrangements for the inspection of individual items from the museum's collection. She will inform you of the schedule. I will meet you again later in the morning.'

'Goodnight, Dr Dresch.'

For a moment Oswald thought that Saskia was going to leave too. The possibility filled him with such an empty despair that when he spoke again he found he was pleading with her.

'Won't you have one more drink with me? So that we can make arrangements for tomorrow?'

She looked at him, surprised, then smiled. 'You are very persuasive man,' she said, sitting down again.

Daphne had been asleep when he got up that morning. He had dressed in the bathroom, knotting in the mirror the same tie that he was now loosening. It suddenly seemed almost incredible that it had remained in place through so many disparate events of the day, that the same knot should have held its position around the neck of a man who was perhaps no longer the same person as when he had put it on. He had not bothered to say goodbye to his slumbering wife. She wouldn't have thanked him if he had. The taxi had been late, and he had waited anxiously for it in the front doorway, finally resolving to go back in and telephone again at the very moment it appeared round the corner. There had been Heathrow, morning newspapers and foul airline coffee; a bumpy few minutes as they had descended through the rainclouds; then landing at Tegel. Daphne had probably still not left the house, perhaps not even left her bed. And he had been removed to a different world by an unreal passage from west to east; across West Berlin, through Checkpoint Charlie, then the drive south to Dresden, finally the lousy hotel. So many unsettling new impressions: the greyness of the architecture, the shoddiness of the facilities, the rigidity of people's minds; somewhere a lingering horror, a distant suggestion of something burning. And now suddenly, at the end of it all, this unexpected and delicious intimacy. He didn't know what it all meant. He knew only that he must prolong it.

Schnapps. That was what was needed. Was it possible to obtain such a thing now, here, at this hour? The Olympic shot-putter, disgusted that they had not gone off to bed like Dresch and the other guests, frowned at his request, but he persisted. If Saskia could order him wine in the face of Dresch's disapproval, then he would prevail over this dragon to get Saskia schnapps. And then suddenly there was the waitress, stomping gracelessly towards them with a half-full bottle of the stuff and two glasses in her hand. She dumped the things on their table and left them to it, ostentatiously switching off the lights in the unoccupied quarters of the room.

'Thank God she's gone,' Oswald exclaimed, filling their glasses. There was a thrilling complicity in their solitude. Things were moving very fast, and he couldn't quite tell where they were going to end. It was the sort of situation in which you didn't dare hope, you just kept pushing along.

Saskia giggled, then said: 'It is a shock for you, no? It is different, our life here compared to the West?'

'In some ways, yes.'

'But you know, not everything is bad here. The system, it has merits as well. Society is well organised, people are cared for; unlike in the West everybody has jobs . . .'

Oswald took his glass and raised it to her. 'To the system,' he said.

She looked uncertainly at him, then laughed and drank herself. 'Now I too must make a toast. To the exhibition.'

'The exhibition?'

'The exhibition of German Romantic painters that you will make in London.'

'Oh, of course. The exhibition. I'll drink to that too.' He paused. He was curious about her. He wanted her to tell him everything about herself, so he asked, 'Are you a specialist in German nineteenth-century painting yourself?'

'I regret no. I love very much the period, and especially admire some examples in the museum here, but I am not trained as art historian. Not expert like you.'

She looked at him with a shy admiration. She admires me, he thought, this lovely woman thinks I've achieved something with my life, and he was happy. But he confessed, 'I'm not an expert in German nineteenth-century painting, I'm afraid. Seeing the museum's collection tomorrow will be something of an education for me. I look forward to it.'

'I look forward to showing it to you.' She smiled at him again, that big, wide-eyed, entrancing smile, and then looked down. She had inordinately long eyelashes. 'I think . . . yes, it has been a special day for me, this. I think I will have a cigarette.' She produced a packet. 'Can I offer you one also?'

'Why not?' said Oswald.

You want to know something, Oswald? It was Bernard Tumbrill talking again, accosting him blearily one evening a year or two ago, his paint-stained fingernails wrapped around a whisky and soda. You want to know what's one of the most exciting sights in the world? It's when a woman you're after reaches for a cigarette. When you see that, you know you're halfway there, because when she lights up it tells you two things about her. One, she's a sensualist. And two, she gives in to temptation.

Oswald reflected on this theory as he watched the graceful fingers of Saskia Benz insert the cigarette between unbearably tremulous lips, then flick flame to its tip with an experienced hand. His pulse quickened.

'So you are specialist in what, if not in German painting?' she was asking him.

'French painting, primarily.'

'You know we have some French paintings in the

museum here. I would be happy to show them to you also.'

'That would be wonderful.'

'There is nothing outstanding, I am afraid.' She paused to draw deeply on her cigarette. 'The best was I suppose the Courbet.'

'You mean the one destroyed in the war?'

'Yes, it was called "The Stonebreakers". I have seen photographs of it, it was a masterpiece.'

He nodded. 'I know the picture. Dr Dresch was reminding me earlier today of the way it came to be lost. It's the most tragic story. I mean, that this picture should have been on the transport passing through the city on . . . on that one night, when so much else was saved.'

'It was truly the most tragic coincidence.'

'You know, coincidences frighten me.'

'What do you mean, they frighten you?' Saskia was solicitous, as if he had said he was feeling unwell.

He frowned, and tried to explain. 'I suppose it's the randomness of coincidences that I can't cope with. What does it mean, that the one night that picture passed through Dresden was also the one night in the war when the city sustained an utterly crushing bombing raid? It means nothing. It's utterly random.'

'You want it to mean something?' She spoke softly.

'Yes . . . No. Sorry, I'm not expressing myself very well – it must be the schnapps. Perhaps all I'm saying is I can't bear to think that sheer chance is the ultimate regulator of our lives.'

'Come,' she said, 'chance is not always something to fear. For example, if you had come two days earlier to Dresden, we would not be having this conversation.'

'No? Why not?'

'My colleague, Dr Raisbach, would have liaised with you. But now Dr Raisbach is unwell, so I am the replacement. It is chance that we meet.'

'And is Dr Raisbach as beautiful as you?'

She giggled. 'Dr Raisbach is a man.'

'Maybe I shouldn't be frightened of chance, then.'

'Maybe you shouldn't.' She drew deeply on her cigarette, serious again.

'Tell me about your work here,' he said. 'If you're not an art historian, what are you?'

'Ah, Mr Ginn, you will find me very dull. I am an economist. But in the Cultural Ministry, where we are dealing with many artists, sometimes an economist is useful.'

'I think the Cultural Ministry is extremely lucky to have you.'

'You flatter me.'

'Not at all; I bet you are a very brilliant economist.'

She flushed, pleased, but unsure what to say, so he continued: 'And you live here in Dresden?'

'We have an apartment in the Neustadt.'

The personal pronoun lay there before him, ticking like a suspect package. He must tackle it immediately, if possible render it harmless. 'We? That is you and . . .'

'My husband and me.' She paused, perhaps suddenly sensing the detonation. 'But he . . . he is diplomat, posted in Moscow. We do not . . . I mean we are apart often. I have not seen him for nine months.'

'You miss him?'

'We are mostly separate.' Oswald filled her glass again. 'Ah, Mr Ginn, you are a man easy to talk to, you know. You are dangerous, I think.'

'No, you are dangerous because you are easy to listen to.'

'And you, Mr Ginn . . .'

'Oswald, please call me Oswald.'

'All right. And you, Oswald, tell me about you. Your

81

life is happy in the museum? All these beautiful pictures you work with?'

'Pictures, pictures. I sometimes wonder if there's not more to life than pictures. There's certainly more to pictures than museums.' He hadn't meant to sound so bitter, but his disenchantment was unmistakable.

She nodded. 'You know, when I first saw you this evening, I thought you were a man with a – how can I say? – with a dissatisfaction. You intrigued me for that.'

'A dissatisfaction?' He laughed. 'Oh dear. Is it so obvious? I must be very depressing company.'

'No, no,' she assured him, 'you are very good company. Please excuse me, I am being rude. I do not mean to be.'

'You're not rude at all. And I suppose you could be right, I am dissatisfied.'

'Is it your work which dissatisfies you?' She leant forward, concerned, her whole attention engaged.

'Amongst other things, yes. I . . . I suppose I have become stale. I need a new challenge.'

'Could you find a new challenge? Do you know one?'

Did he know one? He did, of course. There had been that conversation with Leonard Sparmann over lunch a couple of months ago. A proposition had been made to him. 'Give it some thought, Oswald,' he had been told. 'We need someone of your experience at Fortescue's. Promise me one thing, that you'll call me first if you're thinking of a change of direction.' His immediate reaction had been: What, me, become a dealer? It's unthinkable, I'm a museum man, I'm a scholar. I'm not made for all that financial chicanery. But then he'd thought about it a bit, remembered people who had achieved a successful transition into the commercial world and how much money they'd made. And finally he'd postponed the question. It involved upheaval and inconvenience, and he'd told himself that perhaps he wasn't quite ready. But how ready do you have to be, for God's sake? Today he had imagined himself a man of action. He should prove it. Prove himself worthy of the concern of Saskia Benz. He should call Sparmann again, take the jump. Now, to please her, he said: 'Yes, I'm considering something.'

'You must do it. It is dreadful for someone like you to be frustrated. You must change. Can you?' She spoke excitedly, as if the question were as vitally important to her as it was to him.

'We'll see.'

'I have an instinct about such things. An intuition.'

He shook his head in wonder. 'I think you are amazing, Saskia.'

'Me? Why am I amazing?'

'I never thought I would meet an East German woman as beautiful as you, as stylishly dressed, let alone one who admitted to being susceptible to anything so unorthodox as her intuition.' There, he had said it. Perhaps he had gone too far.

But she laughed delightedly. 'You expect me to – how you say it – put the shot?'

'No, Saskia, not you.' He stretched out his hand and touched hers. She withdrew it, but not immediately.

'And you are married also?' she asked, looking at her cigarette packet.

Daphne. They had been married for seventeen years. He had first met her at the Courtauld. How could he explain that they had been different people then? Perhaps the two young students had been in love. They seemed distant and unreal, unconnected to the person he had become. Or perhaps they hadn't ever been in love, not even then. They had got on well, accommodated each other, found they missed one another when they were apart. And that had seemed a good enough basis for marriage, buttressed by the security of his first museum job. It was what people did, after all. You went out with girls, and at a certain period in your life you married them. The one you happened to be going out with at the time. That's how it seemed, anyway. How could he have foreseen that they would become different people, he and Daphne, that their relationship would grow increasingly bitter? He thought of her now; he saw her before him, suddenly very vividly. He resented her. He resented her for the money with which she cushioned his life. He resented her for the boredom with which his company often seemed to fill her. He resented her for the way she flirted indiscriminately with other men at parties. He resented her for making him feel resentful. How was he to express all this to Saskia?

'Like you, separated,' he lied.

'She was beautiful, your wife?'

Was Daphne beautiful? The other day he'd caught a glimpse of a long-disregarded photograph of a bride coming out of a church. For a moment he'd drawn a blank. Who's that? he'd found himself wondering; she's not bad looking. And a split second later he'd recognised it was Daphne. On their wedding day, all those years ago. And now? He had heard other people say she was attractive. Were they just being polite? He felt incapable of judging. His critical faculty was paralysed by familiarity, so that the question seemed meaningless.

'Why do you ask?' he said.

'It was a man in Italy I met – you know I visited Milan in my former job – who said to me, those who deal with works of art must always have beautiful wives. Otherwise they should not be dealing with art, they can have no feeling for it.'

He shrugged. 'I am not sure that theory is true.'

What she said made him angry, not so much because of his own inability to decide whether or not his wife was beautiful, but because of the nameless Italian who had clearly been flirting with Dr Benz. She was worth more than the attentions of some second-rate *flâneur*, striving to insinuate himself into intimacy with her. Oswald reached for the bottle and found it empty. He looked across at her. Her head was bowed. She was still toying with her empty cigarette packet, tearing it into little strips. He marvelled at her wrists, emerging from the sleeves of her jersey: they were full, fleshly and graceful. From those wrists he suddenly imagined very clearly the way her limbs would be, how it would feel to hold her against him. He leant towards her and stroked her hair.

She raised her head abruptly.

'I've stayed too long,' she said. 'You must forgive me for keeping you up. Maybe I'm a little bit drunk, you know? But I've enjoyed talking with you so much. I enjoy always to meet new people, people from other backgrounds. It is my weakness.'

'Well, I don't usually enjoy meeting new people,' he replied bitterly. 'But you're utterly exceptional.'

She stood, gathering her lighter into her bag with ominous purposefulness. Oswald got up, and for a moment his head swam. He followed her out of the restaurant into the darkened foyer of the hotel. There was no one about except a somnolent concierge. Everything was strangely silent; it seemed that the rest of the city was asleep. For a moment the two of them also seemed suspended, pausing opposite each other, uncertain how to proceed. This was Dresden. On the other side of the Wall.

'Don't go.' He spoke in a whisper.

'We meet again tomorrow,' she said, knotting the belt of her raincoat. 'Nine thirty at the museum.'

'Please, Saskia.'

'No, it is better I leave. Better for us both.'

He reached out and held her by both arms, facing her.

He held her, Saskia Benz, the official of the East German Cultural Affairs Ministry, a woman he'd known for less than four hours. There, in Dresden, in 1985, in the foyer of that desolate hotel.

'So you shafted her, then?' Bernard Tumbrill, his white hair dishevelled, his eyes bloodshot, his tie hanging from an unbuttoned collar, could not conceal the excitement in his tone.

'You could say so.' As Oswald spoke he hated himself, but it is difficult not to tell people what they want to hear, especially if the story involves sexual conquest. Here he was, back three days in London after his trip to Dresden. Here he was at the private view of some contemporary painter in an opulent Mayfair gallery where drink flowed freely and the waitresses came round with plates of neatly cut squares of smoked salmon, each one topped with a mound of caviar. Here he was back in the West with the East still fresh in his mind; still shaken, still disoriented by it all. Still aching for that bleak hotel restaurant with its stark fluorescent lighting. He had been pleased when he came across Bernard. Together they had retreated into a secluded corner near the cloakrooms, where he'd told Bernard about Dresden. He told Bernard partly because he thought Bernard would appreciate it, and partly because he found it a relief to talk about it, because he felt if he didn't talk about it to someone he would go mad. Of course, he'd made selective reports already: with his colleagues at the museum he had discussed the pictures available for the putative exhibition; to Daphne he had given only a description of the foul food and the poor hotel before she lost interest; but to no one as yet had he mentioned the existence of Dr Saskia Benz. And now he found he couldn't go on any longer without speaking of her. So he'd told Bernard. Only it hadn't come out quite the way he had intended.

Bernard Tumbrill. Bernard was an uninspired painter, a fitful dabbler in the art trade, a voracious womaniser. But his true genius lay in travelling. He was permeated with an irresistible wanderlust, and disappeared for lengthy tracts of time just roaming from country to country, painting a bit here, buying the odd work of art there, and drinking prodigious quantities of Scotch everywhere. From Thailand to Hungary, from Norway to Peru, he crossed and recrossed the globe; just as you had forgotten his existence altogether, he would resurface, press you to a drink after work in a favourite watering hole, and regale you with improbable tales of his travels. He could be immensely diverting. Oswald had known him for years, had initially been attracted to him as many art historians are to practising artists, out of admiration for someone at the cutting edge of the creative process. Closer familiarity with his work had cured Oswald of that delusion, but he was still a little in awe of Bernard as a manifestation of untrammelled waywardness. Perhaps he envied him the easy bohemianism that enabled him to drift fecklessly round the world leading a life of naked self-indulgence. Bernard's glorious sense of irresponsibility was in stark contrast to Oswald's own shackled existence. Was that the reason why he'd spoken as he did of Saskia? Had it been a chance, just for once, to compete, to match Bernard's relentless catalogue of seduction with one of his own? Bernard's response was enthusiastic.

'Good for you!' he exclaimed encouragingly, spilling his large whisky and soda as he spoke and sucking the liquid from his fingers. 'I bet she rutted like there was no tomorrow.'

Oswald laughed uneasily. Now he had spoken about Saskia he wished he hadn't. It had come out wrong, and

Bernard probing for details about her sexual performance was grotesque, a travesty. He had already said much more than he intended. He just wished he could stop thinking about her. Dear God, that shadowy hotel lobby. Her standing there doing up the belt on her raincoat. Don't go, he had said. We meet again tomorrow, she had declared. Nine thirty at the museum. Please, Saskia. No, it is better I leave. Better for us both. Then he had put out his hands to hold her. Then.

'Christ almighty,' Bernard was continuing, 'those Eastern European women, they're bloody incredible. Did I ever tell you about that Hungarian translator I had in a lift in Budapest?'

'You did.'

'Oh. Well. There you are, then.' He paused, thwarted. 'A spot of healthy adultery never did anyone any harm.'

Oswald looked back across the room. His eye caught Daphne, far away, talking intently to a blond young man in a pin-striped suit. Suddenly she laughed loudly; he heard her clearly, across the raging sea of other voices, heard her laughing with that inane braying that he found so exasperating. If only.

'I suppose it's travel,' he theorised feebly. 'Being away from home. Sort of opens up possibilities.'

'Broadens the mind,' agreed Bernard. 'Personally I've always found hotels an extraordinary aphrodisiac.'

'I tried to ring her, actually,' Oswald ventured again.

'Who?'

'This woman. The one in Dresden I was telling you about.'

'Oh, her.' Bernard drained his glass and looked about him for a waitress. 'Always a mistake if you ask me.'

'What is?'

'Trying to make contact after a one-night stand. So what did she say?'

88

'I had this number for her in some branch of the Cultural Affairs Department. It took me hours to get through. Then when I did a strange thing happened.'

'What was that?'

'They denied all knowledge of her. Said there was no one in the Department of that name.'

'That's how it is in countries like East Germany. Someone steps out of line and they're done for, given the chop. Believe me, it's always happening. She's been sacked for getting too friendly with a Westerner, that's probably it. Been reassigned to postal collections in suburban Leipzig most likely. Look, I know how these places work. I've spent a lot of time behind the Iron Curtain. Leave it alone, old son. Be grateful for what you got.'

'You're probably right.' He stared miserably out of the gallery window. Please, Saskia, he had said. No, it is better I go. Better for us both. He had reached out to touch her.

'You know what your trouble is, Oswald,' Bernard went on, 'you need a change. Professionally, I mean. Look, you've been pissed off for years. Why don't you get out of the museum? God almighty, if you've got it in you to knock off this German bint, then you've certainly got it in you to walk out of that dump. Seduction often leads to action, in my experience. It sort of galvanises you, sets the energies flowing. You screwed her, now screw the museum. You know you want to.'

'It's strange you should mention it. I'm having lunch with Leonard Sparmann next week.' He couldn't resist mentioning it, although they had agreed it should all be kept very discreet.

'What, Leonard Sparmann? That wanker at Fortescue's?'

'Fortescue's, yes.'

'Going to become a dealer, eh?' mused Bernard. 'Well,

here's to loadsa money. I think you should go for it.'

'I'm only going to talk, nothing's decided.' This was true. But his resolve to take positive action was hardening. After Dresden; after Saskia. He had to justify himself, give his life back some meaning. To please her.

The waitress finally responded to Bernard's signalling.

'Thanks, love,' he said. 'Make it a stiff one.' She giggled, and he turned back to Oswald. 'You know, it occurs to me: once you're set up with Fortescue's, let's get together. I could put a bit of good business your way now and then. I'm not joking, I've got contacts.'

'Contacts?'

'Yeah, contacts. Sometimes I get offered pictures on my travels, bloody good ones once or twice. It's amazing what can turn up in the out-of-the-way places I get my nose into. The trouble is, I don't generally have the cash available to take advantage. But if you had Fortescue's financial muscle behind you, we could put together a deal occasionally, you and I. I tell you what, as soon as you're on the pay-roll, ring me up. We'll make some money together.'

'You're on,' Oswald laughed.

'Right. Here's the girl with my glass. We can drink to that.'

Later, Oswald let Daphne into the car on the passenger's side, but she insisted on driving home.

'You're probably pissed,' she said.

'I'm not pissed.'

'Anyway, I'd rather be safe than sorry.'

'Look, I am not drunk. You've probably had more than I have.'

'Don't be ridiculous, of course I haven't. Stop trying to make me out as some sort of alcoholic just to justify your own excesses.'

'My own excesses? That's good, coming from you, when you made such a spectacle of yourself this evening with that tailor's dummy in a pin-striped suit. You were all over him.'

'What the hell are you saying?'

'That you were making a spectacle of yourself. Shouting and laughing loudly. People were looking at you.'

'Don't talk crap, Oswald. Now I know you are drunk.'

'Oh, for God's sake.' Too late he tried to be reasonable. 'It really doesn't matter.'

But she was spoiling for a fight now. 'I'm sorry, it does matter. Drink turns you so unpleasant these days, so morose. Where were you all evening? Skulking in a corner with that disreputable artist fellow.'

'Bernard Tumbrill. He's an old friend of mine.'

'He looks like a tramp.'

'I happen to like him.'

'I give up with you. Where's your ambition? You come to a party like the one tonight where there are a lot of influential people about, people who could be useful to your future career, and what do you do? You don't talk to them, you don't sparkle. You just hide in a corner. You've got to snatch your opportunities in this life if you want to get on.'

Snatch your opportunities. He was back in the foyer of the Dresden hotel. It was past midnight.

'Don't go,' he said.

'We meet again tomorrow,' she said, knotting the belt of her raincoat. 'Nine thirty at the museum.'

'Please, Saskia.'

'No, it is better I leave. Better for us both. Thank you, Oswald.'

For a moment she stood there. He put out his hands to her, holding her by the upper arms, just above the elbows. He could feel her flesh beneath her clothes. They faced each other. Then, very quickly, she leant forward and kissed him on the cheek. He smelt her scent, and the warmth of her skin. And then she broke away. She slipped swiftly out of the door. She just went. One second she was there, brushing his cheek with her lips; the next he was alone with the concierge. When he pulled himself together and stumbled outside, there was no sign of her. It had stopped raining. He walked a few paces in one direction, picking his way between the puddles, then doubled back in the other. Somewhere, not far off, he heard a car starting up and accelerating away. He stood in the street, forlorn and drunk. But there was nothing to wait for. There was nothing to do but go to bed.

The next morning his hangover was thick-textured, like a fog. He lay for a while, looking at his horrible room with its ugly ceiling light and beige, characterless walls. His head ached, his eyes stung, and his mouth tasted foul. All that gave him the strength to drag himself out of bed was the thought of seeing her again. There had been nothing last night after she had gone, nothing except a terrible sense of waste, of a priceless chance lost. Why had she gone? Why hadn't he persuaded her to stay? Why hadn't he forced her to? Shit, he'd been so inept. He'd let her slip through his fingers. He'd frightened her away. He'd forgotten the way to treat women, he'd been married too long. They'd both known in their heart of hearts that it would have been better for her to stay; he should have given her the security, the confidence to yield to her instincts. Where had she gone, after all? Only back to the solitude of her empty flat, the flat where her husband didn't live. Perhaps she had made herself a cup of tea, smoked one last cigarette before going to bed. She must have been thinking of him as she turned out the light. Wondering. It was all such a bloody waste.

Oswald walked to the museum through the old town. In

the distance factories belched smoke. An unhealthy yellow mist hung over the Elbe, the visual equivalent of his hangover. He detoured along the Bruhl'sche Terrasse. This embankment had been one of the great views of Europe, painted by a succession of distinguished artists through the eighteenth and nineteenth centuries: Bellotto, Friedrich, and the Norwegian J. C. Dahl, all pilgrims to a city whose beauty had once been on a par with Florence or Rome. Once. Before that night of horrific destruction. Sad vestiges of that former beauty remained. You glimpsed it in the old buildings which had been restored by the new regime. But they were interspersed with depressingly ugly modern constructions: Baroque elegance was brutalised by contemporary concrete. He paused in front of a ruined church – the Frauenkirche. It was deliberately left a shattered shell as a reminder of the war. He caught his breath. The jagged masonry and the sundered walls suddenly brought the terrible images back to him with unexpected vividness. These were the very streets of the firestorm. This was where people had died, and died in their tens of thousands. Burned by flames that roared down streets and ripped up tree-trunks. Suffocated then shrivelled in basements turned ovens. Forty years ago the squares hereabouts had been piled so high with charred bodies that it had been impossible to count them, far less identify them. In the end they had had to douse them with petrol and cremate them in stacks. Dresch's parents had probably been put to the flame not far from here. Ironic that you ended up cremating people who'd been killed by incendiaries. But there had been no other way to dispose of so many corpses. Such a weight of death cannot simply be lifted from a place, no matter how much restoration and rebuilding you undertake. Its immanence was still palpable.

When Oswald reached the entrance to the museum, he saw her before she saw him. She was wearing the same white raincoat, but with a different scarf. 'Saskia!' he called.

'Mr Ginn.' She looked up, marvellously fresh. But she spoke nervously.

'God, it's good to see you.'

'I hope that you have slept well.'

'Very well. I can't tell you how much I enjoyed our dinner last night.'

She frowned. 'We must make a start, Mr Ginn. I have a list of twenty-one paintings for us to inspect. This could be a . . . a nucleus for your exhibition, perhaps.'

Her manner was altogether colder and more distant than last night. Why? It hurt him to hear her talking to him as if he were no more than another official. He wanted to shake her, tell her not to be so stupid. He wanted her to acknowledge that only a few hours earlier they had been very close, that that closeness had meant something. He'd stroked her hair, for God's sake, held her hand. Perhaps she was regretting the intimacy of their conversation. Or perhaps she was protecting herself, denying it because he was due that evening to catch a plane back to the West and she knew she would never see him again. How could he get it across to her that it didn't have to be like that, not if she'd give him some sign.

'Can't we talk somewhere?' he said.

'We must go to look at the pictures. There is not so much time. Soon we will be joined by the senior member of the museum staff.'

They began their tour through mournful, deserted rooms. Oswald's headache returned more powerfully. In a desultory fashion he took some notes. He would have to have something to show on his return to London, some justification for his trip.

'Look,' she said suddenly, 'here is a very special picture. My favourite work. Very important for your exhibition.'

They stood in front of a broad Saxon landscape at sunset.

'Ah, Caspar David Friedrich,' he said. 'Yes, it's beautiful.' It was. He stared at it for some moments, unable to find appropriate words with which to go on.

'I think this is a sad picture,' she said at last.

'A sad picture?'

'It makes me sad to look at it. It is the atmosphere, the mood.'

'Yes, it's melancholy.'

'It reminds me of a discussion that I had once with some friends. We were arguing about which of the art forms had the most power to make you cry, to bring you to tears. One friend said, perhaps because he was a musician himself, that music was the art with the most capability to do this. Then perhaps drama, the theatre and the cinema. Books also, we have all read poetry and novels which move us. The other people all agreed that the art with the weakest power to make you cry is painting. But I . . . I am not so sure they are right.'

She was staring straight ahead, into the breathtaking panorama of distant clouds strung across the yellowing sky, reflected in the pattern of waterways below. A sailing boat bobbed in the shadows, the only sign of human life; it was dusk, the time of evening when the traveller quickens his pace for home. Oswald was aware suddenly that Saskia was deeply moved, not far from tears herself. And in his despair he felt impotent to help her, incapable of reaching out to her. An unbridgeable gulf had opened up between them. The gulf between men and women who are married to other partners. The gulf between East and West. The gulf between communist and capitalist. The gulf between Friedrich and Constable, between the Elbe and the

Thames. And the gulf between the fire-raisers and those who have been put to the flames.

Abruptly, doors at the far end of the gallery swung open, and they both turned to see two figures clattering in and striding officiously towards them. Oswald recognised Dr Dresch with another man.

'Good morning, Herr Ginn, good morning, Dr Benz,' said Dresch. He presented his companion, a curator of the museum. 'You are making good progress, I hope?'

'Good progress,' Oswald said. He sensed that the final chance had gone. He would not be alone with Dr Saskia Benz again on this visit to Dresden. He had been right, of course. In this life you must snatch your opportunities, as his wife had just told him.

Daphne turned the car into their street.

'So what are you going to do about it?' she was saying.

'Do about what?'

'Making something more of your life, what you're always complaining about.'

'I'm looking around. I'm going to leave the museum.'

What had Saskia said, leaning earnestly towards him in the harsh fluorescent light of the restaurant? 'You must do it. It is dreadful for someone like you to be frustrated. You must change. Can you? I have an instinct about such things. An intuition.'

Daphne drew the car to a halt and switched off the engine.

'You won't leave that museum,' she said. 'You mark my words, in five years' time you'll still be there, still complaining.'

4

Daphne was wrong. Five years later Oswald was a director of Fortescue Ltd, art dealers, of Bond Street.

He had left the museum. He left it with surprisingly little regret. Seduction leads to action, Bernard had told him. Well, not quite. But without that trip to Dresden, who knows? It had certainly tipped the balance. So he'd had lunch with Leonard Sparmann. They'd talked terms, set a schedule. Then he'd walked calmly into the museum director's office and announced his resignation, as from 31 August. Just like that. A weight had lifted from his shoulders. He felt renewed, recharged. He'd even managed a polite word or two with Denzil Burke, once he knew he wouldn't have to gaze into those absurd pink spectacles for very much longer.

And then he was out. He'd asserted himself, made the break. Daphne was proved wrong about him. In a strange way he sensed she'd never forgiven him for it.

It was hot that September morning as Oswald walked briskly up Bond Street towards Fortescue's familiar doorway. He had just begun his sixth year in the trade. He was established. Was he happy? He was happier, certainly, than he had been. He was richer, too, although not rich. He was more ambitious now, more worldly; and probably more confident. And yet he had to admit that there were still ways in which he felt walled in, chained down. No, not just by Daphne. There was the gathering suspicion that in moving from the museum to Fortescue's he had merely exchanged one set of incompetent colleagues for another. Christ, Leonard and Magnus. They were the co-chairmen at Fortescue's, his closest working associates. Their shortcomings were a constant source of frustration.

Take Magnus, for instance. First impressions were deceptive. When you looked at Magnus you saw a flamboyantly dressed, apparently confident middle-aged art dealer. He must know his stuff, you thought. Colourful bow-tie, striped Jermyn Street shirt: you didn't dress like that, sport such peacock feathers, unless you had something to offer. No one would have the gall to. No, there must be some substance there, underneath the show. But the truth was different. What you found when you got closer was not so much panache as panic. Magnus was catastrophically indecisive. He couldn't reach a verdict about anything. He was deeply insecure about his own judgment, never wanted it put to the test. When you saw him squirming, frantic, desperate, finally cornered into what he hated most, the confrontation of an issue, you almost felt sorry for him. At least you would have done if Magnus hadn't also had a measure of superficial charm which persuaded people who didn't know him very well to overestimate his capabilities so infuriatingly. 'Remarkably intelligent,' they declared after a first meeting. 'Great flair, Magnus Prior.' Magnus had neither flair nor intelligence, he really didn't. But what he had developed was a sort of sly cunning which he deployed to extricate himself from responsibility whenever possible. That same cunning came in useful with women, too. Women seemed to like him; strangely, he had a lot of success with them. It was that obscure and rather contemptible streak in the feminine psyche which found weakness attractive, no doubt. Oswald could see no other explanation.

Then there was Leonard. He was a different proposition altogether. He dressed in essentially sombre colours:

his shirts were grey or brown, sometimes even black. Occasionally he wore a floral tie, but this would look out of place, like bunting on a rock-face. Unlike Magnus, who luxuriated in a mane of wavy blond locks worn self-indulgently long, Leonard's hair was sparse and close-cropped. He didn't smile often, but when he did you saw so much gold in his teeth that it suggested not so much dentistry as investment strategy. He was devious and obstinate, and would use every means at his disposal to get his own way. Indecisiveness was not his problem: it was just that the decisions he reached with such authority were very often wrong. Then the hand-wringing on Magnus's part would follow. Magnus was excellent at pointing out people's mistakes after the event. 'If only you'd gone one more bid on that Ingres drawing. Then we could have sold it to Cleveland instead of Agnew's doing it.' 'I always felt those Magnasco sketches would be difficult to shift. They've been in stock for five years now.' Or 'I see a Lepine fetched quarter of a million at Sotheby's yesterday. I'm afraid we sold ours much too cheaply last week.'

Magnus and Leonard were second-generation dealers. Their fathers had been partners, having bought Fortescue's for a song just after the war and built it up again, if not to the position of eminence it had enjoyed in the nineteenth century, then at least into a flourishing concern. The Sparmanns had come over from Germany in the 1930s and settled in Golders Green (although Leonard now lived in Hampstead). The Priors were rather more blue-blooded. Magnus had inherited a flat in Chelsea and a large house in Wiltshire. Prior senior had provided the social contacts while Sparmann senior injected the business acumen. Their sons attempted a similar division of labour, without ever attaining quite the same level of success. Their inadequacies had become increasingly clear to Oswald over the years. In fact he had had his doubts as early as the first week, when Jack, the gnarled old porter who had done the framing and odd jobs in the basement ever since the heady days of the old regime in the 1940s, had drawn him aside confidentially and offered the opinion that Mr Leonard and Mr Magnus were 'a couple of tossers'. It was wrong of Jack to talk like that, of course, but you could understand his disenchantment. OK, just occasionally Leonard managed to bully some poor sucker into buying or selling something reasonably advantageously to the company; and it had not been entirely unknown for some friend of Magnus's to descend on the gallery after a good lunch and make a purchase. But, Christ almighty, they were a difficult pair to work with.

'Morning, Olga,' said Oswald, pausing just inside the entrance to the gallery. 'Hot again, isn't it?'

The woman who sat at the reception desk glanced up and grunted. She was a singularly sour-looking spinster in her late fifties, her greying hair gathered in a bun above gaunt and ascetic features. She came of indeterminate Middle European origins, and she had worked at Fortescue's for twenty-five years. It was rumoured that the reason for her recruitment in those far-off days had been that she had enjoyed a fling with the young Leonard Sparmann, but now it was hard to believe that she had ever enjoyed anything, let alone a 'fling'. She was surly and seldom laughed. Jack the porter, himself prone to black moods of ill-natured pessimism, found her oppressive, and once offered the suggestion that she ought to ask for her money back. When asked where from he had wheezed maliciously, 'The charm school.'

'They're waiting for you,' she said.

'Who?'

'Leonard and Magnus. In Leonard's office.'

'Christ. The meeting. I forgot. Just ring through and tell

them I'm on my way, would you? I must collect some papers from my desk.'

She grunted again, unwillingly, but as he began to climb the stairs he noticed she had lifted the receiver.

'Am I doing the right thing?' he'd asked Bernard five years ago over a drink.

'What? Leaving the museum?' Bernard had contemplated him with rheumy eyes. 'You're doing what I'd do in your shoes.'

'But will I make a dealer?' It was the question that had been bothering him most. After all, others had tried and failed to make the crossing from the academic to the commercial world. 'I mean, I've got confidence in my eye, my connoisseurship. I suppose my knowledge is pretty extensive. But will I make a dealer?'

'It all depends,' Bernard announced. 'You've got to have drive.'

'Drive? What sort of drive?'

'The most successful dealers I've come across have been driven by one thing and one thing only. They want to make money.'

'You think that's the only qualification I'll need?'

'Look, Oswald, old son. If you want to make money badly enough, you'll be a good dealer.'

Bernard had been right, he reflected. It was all about money. Everything was about money. He found he did want to make it, wanted it passionately. He'd very soon found himself taking almost unthinking risks in pursuit of a deal. His art historical training came in useful, of course, but he quickly learned not to let an academic approach lure him up commercially unproductive cul-de-sacs. Was there a profit in the picture? That was all that counted. The urge to make money even taught him the rudiments of salesmanship, the basic techniques of persuasion.

He began to understand a little more of the relationship

between money and art, the way you set out to determine the value of a picture. Certainly quality affected price, but it was not a straightforward correspondence. There were other tangential factors which complicated calculations, factors such as rarity, nationality, subject-matter, condition, and historical significance. Then there was the ultimately unquantifiable element, the wild card that defied analysis, the element of fantasy. Fantasy. Pictures could fire the imagination of a buyer. That you couldn't measure. All you could do was play on it, play on it for all you were worth.

He'd made a good start. Within a month of taking up employment at Fortescue's, he succeeded in persuading an American museum curator to buy a Delacroix from stock. Leonard and Magnus were impressed. Then something even more curious had happened. Another dealer – Harry "Shagger" Parks – brought in a Japanese client who wanted a Corot. Oswald dug up from the basement racks a landscape whose existence Magnus had forgotten. Parks said his client would offer £250,000 for it, which after commission to Parks would leave Fortescue's with £225,000. The offer was accepted. But there was a confusion. Oswald intercepted a call from the Japanese client's bank, a call intended only for the ears of Parks. From this it transpired that Shagger was in fact being paid £425,000 for the picture. As a result, it was possible to negotiate a considerably higher share of the available profit. Again, Leonard and Magnus were delighted. But what most struck Oswald was Parks's reaction. There was no shame or contrition, no apology. Only white-faced anger at the bank's slip-up. It was an interesting introduction to the ways of the market-place.

In this business, Oswald reflected, you never quite knew what to expect next. He reached the top of the first flight of stairs and remembered the first time Bernard had turned up at Fortescue's. It had been – what? – in his second year there. The first he had known about it had been Olga calling up frostily on the telephone from her reception desk.

'There is a gentleman down here who says he knows you. His name is Tumbrill.' She paused, meaningfully. 'You had better come, I think.'

Bernard had made no concessions to Bond Street in his preparation for the visit. His clothes were ill-kempt, and he hadn't shaved for a couple of days. Oswald fetched him up to his office and gave him a Scotch. It always surprised him how pleased he was to see Bernard when they hadn't met for a while.

'So where have you been this time?'

Bernard clutched his drink and frowned. 'Here and there. On my travels, you know.'

'And what do you think of all this? Fortescue's, I mean?'

'Not bad.' He paused. 'But, Christ, what a tight-arsed old bitch that receptionist of yours is. Anybody given her one recently? That might loosen her up. Not that I'm volunteering.'

Then he produced a battered photograph from his pocket. 'What d'you make of that, old cock?'

Oswald inspected it with interest. 'Looks like Greuze. Rather a good one, too. Where did you get this?'

'It's a picture we can buy. From one of my contacts. I just got back from Austria and I brought it straight round to you.'

'Where's the picture itself?'

'It's with a man I've known for some time in Vienna, name of Grunwald. Mysterious fellow. Bit of a wheeler-dealer, with excellent contacts in the East. Does a lot of business with Moscow, I believe. One of the lucky buggers who's managed to wangle some sort of unofficial approval from the Soviets, if you know what I mean.'

'Does this come out of Russia?'

'It wouldn't surprise me in the least. But with Grunwald it's better not to ask too many questions. You either take the merchandise he's offering or you leave it. But his prices aren't exorbitant.'

In the end Fortescue's bought it, and then made quite a lot of money when they sold it on to an American collector. Bernard was happy because he got his commission, and Oswald was happy because Leonard and Magnus had been impressed by the way he'd managed to unearth this unexpected treasure. Art dealing is all about buying interesting new material privately, after all, finding things that are fresh to the market, things that nobody else has seen. The Greuze had been perfect.

'Where did you find it?' Magnus had asked, intrigued.

Oswald had been able to shrug mysteriously. 'I've got my sources,' he had replied.

And what had happened to Bernard then? He'd disappeared for several months, to South America as far as Oswald could recall. Soon after that he developed a tiresome ecological obsession, and the next time Bernard presented himself on the doorstep of Fortescue's it was with a poster advertising some Green cause which he wanted Oswald to display prominently in the window. He'd been upset when Oswald had refused. Unreasonably so. But that was Bernard for you, unpredictable and erratic. He'd made no contact for some time now. Maybe one day he'd turn up with another Greuze, you never knew. Oswald rather wished he would. He could do with another opportunity to assert himself. Damn this bloody meeting. He'd forgotten about it. It was always reassuring to go to Leonard's meetings with something up your sleeve, some little surprise to spring, something like another Greuze, for instance.

He ducked into his own office on the first-floor landing for a moment, to dump his briefcase and collect a file. And there was Eugene. Eugene sitting at the substantial partner's desk. Eugene at work in front of the banked shelves of bound copies of the *Burlington Magazine* flanked by a comprehensive collection of the major auction catalogues. Eugene sitting at Oswald's own desk. Yes, this was the room Oswald had liked so much when he'd first seen it, five and a half years ago. Leonard had opened the door and waved an airy hand. 'This will be your office,' he'd declared. A few weeks later Oswald had slid down in the well-upholstered chair behind the desk for the first time and relished everything: the books, the panelling, the drinks cupboard, the pleasingly oblique view of the bustle and style of Bond Street through the window. I can be happy here, he'd thought, I've made the right decision. This is freedom. He'd felt an easing of the walls that hemmed him in. And now here was Eugene, usurping his place, thumbing through a large reference book and surrounded by a welter of transparencies.

He looked up and said casually, 'Ah, Oswald. I thought you weren't coming in today. Would you like me to move?'

Oswald contemplated him for a moment. Eugene Crabbe had been part two of the Sparmann-Prior plan to beef up the firm. Or at least he was Leonard's appointment, with the agonised acquiescence of Magnus. He was nakedly ambitious and, in certain narrow channels, dangerously intelligent. He looked about fifteen, but came with an impressive post-graduate degree from the Courtauld. He was also well connected. A string of dowager duchesses had a weakness for him; and he was not above offering discreetly flirtatious encouragement to homosexual museum directors fascinated by his boyish looks, if they were of sufficient eminence to be useful to him in the future. He was a pompous, opinionated little prick. Worst of all, from the moment of his arrival two years ago, he had been foisted upon Oswald, detailed to share his office.

'Couldn't he go in with Gloria?' Oswald had pleaded with Magnus. Surely it was more suitable for him to sit with the secretary.

'Oh, Christ! Look, Oswald, this is a real bugger, I know, but . . .'

'There just isn't room in my office. It's not big enough for a second person.'

'I know, I know. But it's very difficult to change the plan now. There are so many factors to be taken into account.'

'Why doesn't he go in with you? Your office is bigger than mine.'

'Oh, no, I think not.' It was one of the few firm decisions Oswald could ever remember Magnus taking.

Leonard had settled the issue once and for all.

'He can't go in with Gloria. The secretary's office would be inappropriate as such. And it would be inconvenient logistically speaking for him to be on the second floor with us. No, he must have a table in your room, Oswald, it will be better that way.' He had paused, and then added in a conciliatory tone: 'So that he may learn from you. He is a bright boy, but he can benefit from your enormous knowledge, as such.'

Oswald shook his head now. 'Just move over by the time I'm back, would you?' he asked with icy politeness. 'I'll be in with Leonard and Magnus for half an hour or so.'

'Of course.'

'What are those transparencies, by the way?'

'Interesting, aren't they? Take a look at this one. I found it staying with Lady Lindisfarne this weekend. It's not been attributed up till now, but surely it's by the same hand as this drawing at Chatsworth, which doubtless you know?'

Lady Lindisfarne. Chatsworth. The whole thing was a joke. Here was Oswald, trying to make the business a bit of money, to go out and find a few pictures to sell and a few clients to sell them to; and here was this youth ballsing on about Chatsworth and his weekends with Lady Lindisfarne. Oswald waved the transparency aside. He was suddenly too angry to speak, still less to offer a critical judgment.

Moments later, he entered Leonard's office. Leonard was sitting writing purposefully at his desk while Magnus stood a shade uneasily behind him, examining a catalogue taken from the shelves, no doubt at random. They were waiting for him, that was clear enough; and they were both doing their best to conceal the fact that neither of them had anything worthwhile to do to fill in the time till his arrival.

'Good morning, Leonard, good morning, Magnus. Look, sorry I'm a bit late. Dreadful traffic in Hammersmith.'

Leonard waved a hand impatiently to signify that he wasn't interested in travel reports. Despite the fact that he had lived his entire life in north London, the impression Leonard made was still strangely foreign. It was partly the architecture of his face, partly his style of dress, and partly the way he spoke, the construction of his sentences and the unusual inflections he still gave to certain words. Now he said:

'We wanted to have a chat, Oswald, because we have things happening at last.' He looked at Oswald with a glint of triumph in his eye, while Magnus nodded in judicious agreement.

'Oh? That sounds exciting.'

'Yes. Business opportunities on several fronts. We must

work out a strategy, as such.'

Magnus giggled nervously at the implication that a decision might have to be taken.

Oswald decided to show willing. He eased himself into a chair and said, 'Excellent.'

'I saw Salzman last week,' announced Leonard.

'Ah. Did you?' Oswald's mind was infuriatingly blank.

'He's in a buying mood.'

'Salzman. Yes. Just refresh my memory about him.'

Leonard drew in his breath in frustration. Oswald's request detracted from his perception of the momentousness of the opportunity at hand. 'You know, Conrad Salzman. You have met him, Oswald, you must surely remember the man. He is very rich indeed, and lives in Switzerland. He bought that Ingres from us two years ago. Now he tells me he's on the look-out for something truly exceptional.'

'Like everyone else.'

'That may be so, Oswald. But the difference with Salzman is that he can afford to pay exceptional prices as well. And furthermore he is not too particular about where the picture has come from provided it is important enough. He is not, for instance, always demanding export documents in triplicate and other boring details. He says he is looking for something a little bit special, an unearthed treasure. You know, something that other people don't know about, as such.'

'Ah. You're thinking of the Murillo.'

'Oh, do look at this,' interrupted Magnus, delving feverishly into his catalogue. 'Isn't this Stourhead?'

Leonard ignored him. 'Well, the Murillo is a possibility, don't you think?'

'I suppose so,' Oswald conceded.

'What is the export position, as such?'

'It's a trifle obscure,' Oswald told him. 'The Duke says

108

that it was exported out of Spain perfectly legally on his yacht from Ibiza in 1982, but the papers have gone missing. He says he can get copies from a friend in the ministry.'

'Yes, I see,' said Leonard, frowning. 'What do you think, Magnus? We don't want to get too embroiled, do we?'

Magnus shook his head and pursed his lips.

'It could be dangerous,' Oswald agreed. 'There could be all sorts of unwelcome repercussions. We all know the sort of thing – Spanish Customs getting involved, complaints to governments, investigations that leave us holding the baby . . .'

'But then again,' mused Leonard, 'we could stand to make a lot of money on this deal. I mean really a substantial amount. You can't reject it out of hand.'

Magnus shook his head again. 'No,' he said. 'You can't reject it out of hand.'

Oswald thought how much he disliked Magnus, standing there with such self-importance and contributing nothing to proceedings. 'OK,' he said, 'it can't do any harm to shoot Salzman off a transparency, anyway.'

Leonard supported him. 'You are correct, I think, Oswald. We can gauge his reaction. If he's keen then we'll proceed cautiously.'

For a moment Oswald reflected on the two characters involved in this putative deal, the two principals between whom Fortescue's were aiming to wedge themselves as middle-men. The Duke of Santa Ponsa and Conrad Salzman. He felt no great sympathy for either. He'd spent the past few months, off and on, negotiating with the Duke over the sale of his Murillo. He'd mistrusted him since their first meeting when the Duke, a balding chain-smoker with shifty eyes, had proposed lunch at the Ritz ('My treat, old man') and discovered at the end of the meal that he had forgotten to bring his wallet with him. In recompense he had pressed into Oswald's hand 'a small token', a Cartier key-ring which had turned out to be fake. On their next encounter the Duke had arrived at Fortescue's accompanied by a lady who, although described as his personal assistant, was nonetheless palpably a tart picked up locally in Shepherd Market. Olga had been outraged, but Jack the porter had declared admiringly that the Duke clearly 'knew how to give it some stick'.

Salzman, on the other hand, was an altogether different phenomenon. It was extraordinary, really, that people like Salzman should actually exist. Oswald remembered him clearly now: Leonard had introduced him a year or so ago. He was a small, compact, neat man in his fifties, dapper but anonymous. But when he looked at you it was with the unyielding, almost inhuman stare of the man who is too used to making money. To say that he was rich was an inadequate deployment of language. He represented a confluence of fortunes, a magnet to wealth. From his father he had inherited a highly successful Swiss engineering concern; from his mother, through a happy concatenation of deaths, he had become sole heir to a large German motor-manufacturing business; and by his late uncle in South Africa he had been left a gold mine. What was that old Dutch proverb? Oswald thought bitterly. The devil always shits on the biggest heap. The result of all this was that Salzman, an ardent collector with almost limitless resources, had had his palate jaded by the ordinary 'major' picture. He craved the extraordinary, the unique. Also, buying in the full glare of the public auction no longer attracted him. He hated people knowing exactly what he had paid for this Monet or that Nolde, down to the last penny of buyer's premium. He was therefore prepared to part with an exceptional amount of money in order to ensure that the truly exceptional picture that he was acquiring should remain secret, discreet from the prying eyes and gossiping tongues of the rest of the art market. The money was irrelevant if the object was right. For Salzman millions of pounds spent under these conditions were a drop in the ocean. He didn't feel it. His priorities were different, not just from the bulk of humanity, but even from the ordinarily rich.

'And is there anything else we can tempt him with?' Leonard was asking. He turned to Magnus, who frowned and looked away. Magnus was about as likely to come up with something fresh to interest Salzman as he was to conquer Everest.

'What about you, Oswald? Got anything up your sleeve?'

'I'll work on it. Make some discreet enquiries in certain quarters.'

'Can you be more specific?'

Leonard's tone annoyed him. He refused to be interrogated. 'Rather delicate, I'm afraid. Old museum contacts of mine. Heritage questions, you know.' He laughed, apologetically. 'You'll have to leave it with me for the moment.'

Leonard backed off. 'Well, let's all persevere on this. It's in all our interests to come up with something.'

There was a pause while Leonard made a note on a piece of paper. Then he said: 'We must move on, anyway. There is a second interesting development to consider.'

'What's that?'

'This.' Unexpectedly Leonard placed an index finger on the corner of each eye and pulled, distorting his face horribly in the process. Magnus stepped back in surprise.

'What are you doing?'

'Come on, come on,' cajoled Leonard.

'Are you in pain, Leonard?'

'Oh, for heaven's sake. Look at me; surely you can guess.'

Oswald and Magnus both stared blankly at him. 'Sorry, Leonard, you've got me,' said Oswald.

Leonard removed his fingers from his eyes with a sigh of deep frustration. 'You know, Land of the Rising Sun? Our Nipponese friends? Understand now?' Periodically he made these self-conscious and doomed attempts to disprove the generally held view that he was lacking a sense of humour.

'Ah.'

'There's a new syndicate visiting this country at the moment, and they want to buy. They've been put in touch with us by a banking contact. They need our advice, as such.'

New Japanese clients with money in their pockets were something to get excited about. The speculators were gone now – the investors with limitless cash to launder who had turned to the art market to help them. Only the serious collectors remained. To be put in touch with a new group of potential buyers was a tantalising prospect.

'How can we help them?' asked Oswald.

'They want to meet for lunch to tell us more,' said Leonard. 'Unfortunately the only day they can manage is tomorrow, when Magnus and I will be unavoidably away. We thought you and Eugene could entertain them together.'

Oswald agreed, without enthusiasm.

'There we are, then,' concluded Leonard. 'Let's get cracking on all this because there is money to be made.'

They stood up. Magnus, seeing that proceedings were coming to an end, returned his catalogue to the shelf and smiled. 'A good meeting, Leonard,' he said sagely.

Later that night Oswald emerged from the bathroom in

his pyjama trousers. Daphne lay reading a magazine in bed. She glanced up briefly as he came into the room and said, 'You're overweight.'

That was it. Nothing more. She meant to wound rather than inform, you could tell from her tone of voice. Not that Oswald was fat, of course; but if he had gained a few pounds from the Fortescue's expense account, then that was an occupational hazard, almost a badge of engagement in the front line of the art market. Still, she was speaking from a position of strength herself, in that whatever her other shortcomings she had preserved her own figure pretty well. Oswald stood looking at her for a moment. She lay there, angular, aggressive, flicking through the pages. It had been a bloody awful evening. They'd been to a barbecue. A bloody barbecue, with bloody awful fellow-guests in someone else's bloody awful garden. He felt an irresistible urge to bring the simmering tension of the evening to the boil.

'You know what I feel about barbecues, my dearest?' he said. 'Ultimately you really can't be seen giving one. They're irredeemably non-U.'

'What rubbish.'

'I tell you barbecues are non-U.'

'Since when have you been the arbiter of these things? Anyway, how can they be non-U when the Royal Family have them?'

The Royal Family have them, indeed. He had finally realised something about Daphne: she was a snob. His marriage to her had been a protracted period of gradual reappraisal of all the positive judgments he had made about her in the early stages of their relationship. Originally he had been attracted by what he identified in her as a fierce independence of spirit, a refreshing iconoclasm which prompted her to libertarian, even left-wing views. But this iconoclasm had hardened into nothing more than a massive contrariness, a pleasure in raising other people's hackles for the sake of it; while her last vestige of political revolt now expressed itself merely in an occasional preference for organic food.

'Magnus was in good form tonight, wasn't he?' she continued. Magnus. She would bring him up. Oswald's heart had sunk on arriving and finding Magnus amongst the guests.

'Moderately, I suppose.' Actually Magnus's behaviour had annoyed him intensely. The bastard had turned up, without his wife, and proceeded to maraud the party for attractive women like some overheated peacock in a pink jacket and turquoise shirt open at the neck. Oswald had caught a glimpse of him, coiled against a tree at the bottom of the garden, being charming to someone else's wife. A snatch of conversation drifted up to him in which Magnus held forth about a Delacroix he had sold recently for a quarter of a million. The only Delacroix that Fortescue's had disposed of in the past twelve months had been handled by Oswald.

'He's got a lot of charm. I bet he's a good salesman,' Daphne continued.

'That's where you're wrong. He's useless.'

'I can imagine him being tremendously persuasive.'

'That just shows what a bad judge you are.'

'He makes you feel inadequate, doesn't he?'

'What's that supposed to mean?'

'Nothing, darling. But you may as well be realistic about yourself, just for once. You always abuse people like Magnus because they make you feel inferior, you feel you can't compete with them.'

'Can't compete with Magnus? You must be joking. He's a total bloody disaster.'

'There you go again.'

'What do you mean "again"?'

'I mean you're always abusing people who show a little dynamism. You're frightened of them. What about Geoffrey Cornforth? You remember Geoffrey Cornforth, now, surely? He was the one we had to stop seeing because you were so jealous of him. The one you were so rude to without any reason. It was embarrassing.'

'Has it not occurred to you that I dislike Geoffrey Cornforth simply because he's a third-rate shit? I'm delighted we no longer see him.'

'Plenty of other people didn't find him third-rate. He was enormously popular, I seem to recall. And excellent company.'

'So that's it. I suppose you fancied him too, did you?'

'Don't be ridiculous. God, I think you're drunk again.'

'I'm not drunk.'

'Anyway, I'm going to sleep now.' She laid down her magazine and rearranged her pillows with the elaborate precision that always infuriated him. Then she added: 'By the way, the Volvo's broken down.'

'What, you've driven it into something again?'

'You know perfectly well that last time was not my fault.' She reached to put out the light. 'No, the clutch has gone.'

'Oh, shit,' he said as he got into bed.

He sensed that wall again, that hemmed-in feeling. Conversation with Daphne often brought it on – a barrier of frustration, anger, and futility. Not that they talked much, never really talked at all. Their conversations were rarely more than skirmishes, a ritual probing of each other's weaknesses with a view to laying them bare and thereby scoring points, the give and take of a relationship diseased with resentment. In the past he had borne her deep bitterness for cushioning him, emasculating him almost with her private income. Now she in turn resented his new-found financial independence; far from applauding the steps he had taken to better himself, the steps she had been advocating so strongly when he was languishing at the museum, she seemed threatened by his progress, unable to cope with it, disposed to withdraw her ambition on his behalf. So now he resented her resentment. Since the boys had been away at school they had lost their children as significant common ground. And anyway he now found prolonged contact with them depressing, their surly teenage fecklessness an additional irritant. He felt guilty at the way the end of the holidays lifted his spirits. What way was there through this wall? How could he break it down?

Occasionally, in the street, he thought he saw Saskia. It happened less often now, but there were still times when he would quicken his step, his heart beating with irrational excitement, only to find that the woman whose short blonde hair or slender figure had struck a momentary chord was no more than some suburban filing clerk or shop-girl, an alien travesty of the original beautiful proto-type. He tried not to think of her too often. She was lost to him, a long-gone fragment of history. Perhaps the tide of change that had flowed across her country had swept her into a new prosperity. Or perhaps it had swept her away for ever. There was no means of knowing.

The next morning Leonard rang him at 7.45 from his car telephone. Oswald reached for the receiver, hearing Daphne swearing sleepily and turning away with the bedclothes pulled up over her ears.

'I'm approaching Heathrow now,' Leonard told him. 'Just thought I'd give you a ring to discuss lunch today. With the Japanese it's important to strike the right note, as such.'

'Of course.'

'What I think you should do from the word go is establish trust. Try and make them feel they'll be safe with Fortescue's advising them. Build their confidence in us. I wish I could be there myself, but this trip to Zurich could not be cancelled. Look, I'm just going into the tunnel now so I'll ring off. Anyway, you know what to do: establish trust.'

This was typical of Leonard: a command whose essential nebulousness was cloaked by the precision and authority of its delivery. How did you win the trust of Orientals? In the art trade there was never any shortage of people with theories about how to handle them. 'For God's sake don't talk about cliffs,' one person had told Oswald. 'The Japanese are frightened of them.' 'Stand up straight,' another man had said. 'The Japanese revere tall men. They think they're nearer to God.' 'Don't try and sell them pictures with crows in them', 'Never let them lose face', 'Always let them beat your price down', 'Never allow them to haggle'; it had become a symbol of your status as a dealer to claim sufficient familiarity with Japanese clients to be able to offer advice about doing business with them; and the very variety and incoherence of this advice testified to the irremediable inscrutability of the Oriental mind.

A few hours later Oswald and Eugene Crabbe sat in a very expensive Jermyn Street restaurant awaiting the arrival of their guests. Oswald looked across at Eugene. He was squinting short-sightedly at the menu in much the same way as he sometimes squinted myopically at drawings by Perino del Vaga. Elderly titled ladies and other gullible clients occasionally mistook this short-sightedness for connoisseurship. Oswald put it down to an oddly misplaced vanity, which prevented Eugene from investing in a pair of spectacles. When it came down to it, Oswald had little confidence in Eugene's capacity for winning the trust of Orientals. Oswald would have to do most of the talking.

He glanced across at the neighbouring tables. In pairs, in groups, sharply suited men were talking together, laughing, cajoling, negotiating. Business was being done. Strings were being pulled. Influence was being exerted. It was a microcosm of a certain monied section of the British establishment. And then he saw Shagger Parks. He looked away quickly, but Shagger had seen him too, noted him. Whatever he and Eugene did would not go unobserved now. Bloody Parks. He was the last person they needed here, spying on them. There was something repulsive about him, and yet something compelling. Both physically and metaphorically, Shagger was a wide boy. His reputation as one of the most successful picture dealers in the West End was largely founded on his genius as a salesman. Unscrupulous and aggressive, Shagger was a monument to vulgarity. OK, he wore expensive shirts and Savile Row suits. But they couldn't disguise his ruddy, perspiring complexion, shifty eyes and greasy hair. Looking at him you got an impression of loucheness. And yet his sales pitch was unbeatable. How did he do it? It was one of the mysteries of life how he succeeded in compelling the most hard-boiled businessmen into the sort of extravagant and ill-judged purchases they wouldn't have touched with a bargepole in their own sphere of activity.

Oswald was just thinking how he needed Parks's company today like he needed a hole in the head when the Japanese themselves arrived. There were three of them, all wearing identical raincoats.

An elaborate ritual ensued, involving bows of greeting and the formal exchange of business cards. It quickly became clear that Mr Takomara and Mr Nikohito had scarcely a word of English between them, so conversation had to be channelled through the third member of the

party, Mr Yomara. Mr Yomara was the banking contact
of Leonard's through whom the clients were being introduced to Fortescue's; however, despite having lived for
fifteen years in Hendon, despite having risen to a position
of high rank in an English merchant bank, he too was only
spasmodically intelligible. He spoke in very fast and
breathless bursts, apparently through a mouthful of small
pebbles. It was not going to be easy.

Everyone drank a gin and tonic; everyone ordered
identically, lobster cocktails followed by Dover sole;
everyone seemed pleased when Oswald got the waiter to
bring two bottles of Sancerre. The business of winning
their trust could begin.

Unexpectedly Eugene chose this moment to make his
first contribution to the conversation. He took a sip from
his wine glass, then turned to Mr Nikohito and addressed
him in his most languid and mannered drawl:

'Do you know Lady Dulverton?'

From behind thick spectacles Mr Nikohito peered at
him perplexed and let out a series of unintelligible sounds
which Eugene disregarded.

'You've probably seen Bowick anyway. I've always felt
it was the supreme example of Jacobean country house
architecture. I've been fortunate enough to stay there on
several occasions and each time I return I'm impressed
anew by the magnificent staircase. Of course, it's Grinling
Gibbons.'

'Glinring. . . ?' ventured Mr Nikohito gamely.

'I also happened to notice on my last visit some
fascinating *retardataire* patterning to the western eleva-
tion. In the brickwork, you know.'

'Blickwork?'

'I recommend you have a look next time you're there.
My only reservation about the interior is the Gallery. I
mean those tapestries are in my judgment deplorable.

119

Regrettably Pre-Raphaelite.'

Mr Nikohito roused himself for the supreme effort.

'Leglettabry . . . Ple-Laphaerite?'

This had gone on long enough. Oswald interrupted: 'Mr Yomara, won't you tell us now what Fortescue's can do for Mr Nikohito and Mr Takomara?'

Mr Yomara nodded wisely and accepted a second glass of wine. 'Mr Nikohito and Mr Takomara have own personal museum in Osaka . . . You must understand, Mr Ginn, they take great pleasure in their collection. It is their hobby.'

'Excellent,' said Oswald.

'And Mr Ginn, you should understand that Mr Takomara and Mr Nikohito are of course serious collectors, not speculators who have done harm to the Japanese art market. Perhaps you have read of these scandals? For Mr Takomara and Mr Nikohito they are deeply distressing.'

'Of course. What do they collect exactly?'

'Many magnificent Western paintings: Monet, Sisley, Renoir, Utrirro . . . but they want more paintings, paintings by top French artists. They look for Corot, Courbet . . . when you find major works, they pay big plices.' There followed prolonged exchanges in Japanese with Messrs Nikohito and Takomara. Then Mr Yomara continued:

'I am authorised to tell you that Mr Nikohito and Mr Takomara feel now is good time to buy in art market. They have made available fund of thirty million dollars for financing art purchases.'

'Thirty million dollars?'

'That is this year's allocation, yes.'

'You mean there could be more next year?'

'Most certainly.'

It was too good to be true, the sort of proposition most Western dealers only dream about. Here were serious Japanese collectors whose enthusiasm for picture-buying was undimmed by the setbacks the market had suffered in their own country, clients who were prepared to offer huge sums if the right things became available. Maybe they were right, too. There were opportunities now which perhaps hadn't been there a year or two earlier. Oswald asked tentatively: 'Is there anything they're particularly looking for at the moment?'

'They pay big plices for works in books.'

'Works in books?'

'Illustrated in reference books. That is important. They like to see their pictures reproduced in major publications. Also certificates from recognised expert on artist. In their museum, Mr Takomara and Mr Nikohito like to frame certificates next to pictures. Sometimes even leave pictures in the safe and just exhibit certificates.'

'I see. Well, I'm sure we can help with those.'

'You have works for sale which are photographed in main works of reference?'

'I'm sure we can find some.'

'They do not like pictures recently sold in auction. These are too well known to everyone. Please only offer fresh material.'

'We'll bear that in mind.'

There was a further interlude of muttering in Japanese before Mr Yomara said: 'Also they like big pictures. They have big Monet "Waterlilies".'

'I understand.'

'They want important pictures. Pictures from museum. There is one thing which would make Mr Nikohito and Mr Takomara very happy, that would be to buy pictures from Western museum.'

'Oh, right,' said Oswald jocularly. 'I'll ring up my friends from the National Gallery and see what they've got for sale this week.'

'You do that, please.'

'No, really. It was a joke.'

'You ring up your friends.'

'Of course, I was speaking in jest. I really couldn't . . .'

'Please? I do not understand; you cannot help Japanese clients?'

'No, no – I mean . . . I will do what I can.'

The bill for lunch was enormous, something in the region of seven hundred pounds. To Oswald's relief, Mr Takomara seized it immediately it was placed on the table and covered it with an exotic-looking purple and gold credit card.

Outside on the pavement Oswald tried to cement the foundations of trust which he hoped his efforts had laid. 'I will be in touch with you personally the moment I have something suitably exceptional to offer you,' he assured his guests. Eugene had slunk away already, claiming he had an appointment. Now Mr Nikohito and Mr Takomara disappeared into a very long limousine. Only Mr Yomara was left.

'So, Mr Ginn,' he was saying, 'I bid farewell.'

'Goodbye, Mr Yomara, a great pleasure to meet you.'

'Before I go, I wish one piece of advice.'

'But certainly. What is that?'

'Your colleague – he is also specialist in Impressionist pictures, like you?'

'What, Mr Crabbe? Well, he is my junior. It's probably better to deal with me.'

'No, no, not Mr Crabbe.' Mr Yomara delved into his pocket for a business card and peered at it carefully. 'Mr Parks.'

'Mr Parks?'

'Yes, Mr Harry Parks. He was kind enough to address me in the toiret of restaurant. He said he worked with you, and for us to contact him at any time.'

'Oh, my God.'

Parks was dangerous. Christ, you had to be careful. But as Oswald walked back to Fortescue's, he reflected that perhaps it had not been such a bad lunchtime's work. He marvelled once again at the magnificent imprecision of the art market, that glorious blurring of the edges which rendered the value of works of art unquantifiable by the methods employed with stocks and shares, property, or other commodities. It was the vital element of fantasy again, the fantasy that attended all art market transactions, allowing the same object to be bought for five thousand pounds one day and sold for twenty-five thousand the next. Who could say what a picture was really worth? Only the buyer, and the beauty of it was that buyers came in such a wide variety of tastes, prejudices, moods, and liquidities.

The most thrilling thought of all was that he now found himself in direct contact with two of the most substantial purchasing forces currently in play, Conrad Salzman and Messrs Takomara and Nikohito. Discretion was essential, of course; but if he could only come up with the sort of fresh, privately owned pictures these buyers required, and present them in suitably authoritative art historical packaging, then he really was on the brink of achieving something momentous. On the horizon was the sort of deal which would make so much money that everyone would have to sit up and take notice: Leonard, Magnus, Eugene; Harry Parks; even Geoffrey Cornforth; even Daphne.

So when shortly afterwards something extraordinary happened, and an opportunity of quite unparalleled potential opened up for him, it was like the answer to a prayer. He went for it. He went for it with the single-minded obsession of a much-disappointed man who recognises that this time what he's been offered is unique and determines just for once to make the most of his luck. The three weeks that followed were the most tantalising, compulsive, and ultimately devastating of his life.

The letter arrived next day.

It was from Bernard Tumbrill. Olga handed it to him as he came through the door, and Oswald recognised the handwriting immediately. It was in a large brown envelope on which Bernard had forgotten to stick any stamps. That was probably why it had taken ten days to reach him from London W14.

So Bernard was back in London. He'd been travelling, of course, but where and for how long Oswald could not be sure. They had not spoken for some time, not since the coolness that had developed after he refused to stick up the wretched Green poster in the gallery window. But now Bernard was writing to him, for which he was grateful. He hoped it signalled a rapprochement between them.

Olga called after him: 'By the way, if you were thinking of using the private viewing-room this morning, don't.'

'No?'

'Eugene is having Lady Lindisfarne in there.'

Lady Lindisfarne was seventy-four. 'That should be highly pleasurable for both of them,' said Oswald, and hurried on, eager to take advantage of Eugene's absence from his office.

The first thing he looked at was the photograph. He drew it from the envelope – a glossy black and white print of a painting, a painting that was immediately familiar to him, a painting whose very familiarity triggered a rush of memories. It caught him with his guard down, so the first was of Saskia. Of Saskia. He tried not to think of her too much these days, but here she was, propelled vividly into his consciousness by this painting; Saskia, in the restaurant, animated, intelligent, concerned, as he told her that

124

coincidences frightened him. Why had he said that? He had said it because they had been talking about the picture he was looking at now, the picture of which Bernard Tumbrill had sent him this photograph. The picture that had been on that convoy through the city the one night the bombs had fallen on Dresden. 'The Stonebreakers.'

He knew them well, those two men in the painting. In the past he'd had to find out everything he could about them, in preparation for a paper on the French Realists. Now he saw them again, the facts came back to him. One was called Gagey, the older one of the two. He had spent his entire working life as a road-mender in the neighbourhood of Ornans in eastern France. In the middle of the nineteenth century you didn't retire, although Gagey had passed today's retirement age. You worked till you dropped. There was nothing idyllic about the reality of rural life then, strive though some Salon painters might to present an image of a sanitised, happy peasantry for the edification and reassurance of an urban bourgeoisie. People like Gagey were grindingly poor, and merry only on the infrequent occasions when they could afford to get drunk. He had with him a much younger assistant, hardly more than a boy. They were both breaking stones on the edge of the road. It was October, but it was still hot.

Then an extraordinary thing happened. A carriage appeared in the distance, clattering towards them; but instead of passing them by, it stopped. The carriage was not grand, not an aristocrat's vehicle, but it clearly belonged to a family of reasonable professional status. Its occupant would not normally be the type to acknowledge the existence of humble road-menders, still less to stop and address them. But this is what happened. An excitable, somewhat wild-looking young man accosted them. He had a proposition for them, he said. Would they come to his house in Ornans the next day? He had work for them, for which he was prepared to reward them more generously than the pittance they received for road-mending, and there would be good meals thrown in. What sort of work was it? No, he didn't expect them to break their backs. He just wanted them to stand there. To pose. To model. He was going to paint them.

The impetuous young man was Gustave Courbet. What was he like then, in October 1849? He was young, wild, a bit Bohemian; and he was newly arrived back home in provincial Ornans from glamorous Paris after a year in which he had begun to make it. That summer, for instance, he had just had seven pictures, no less, accepted for the Salon exhibition, and one of those – 'After Dinner at Ornans' – had achieved the honour of being purchased by the State. That meant something. People were talking about him: he was a hothead, a rebel, and his pictures caught the eye. For one thing they were enormous. 'After Dinner at Ornans' showed an interior with almost life-sized figures seated around a table, one playing the violin while the others listened pensively with pipes and wine. This sort of genre subject was not unusual, of course, but it was rare on this scale. The artist was monumental-ising everyday life. There was something challenging about the picture, the way it asserted that ordinary, contemporary men and women were just as fit for this treatment as the heroes of antiquity. And there was something challenging about the rough and ready way the artist handled paint, with a directness and assurance that created an almost disquieting impression of imme-diacy. You only have to look at the normal fare of the Salon, the sort of pictures Courbet's work would have hung next to, to understand the shock he caused: soapy, slightly lascivious nudes, stiff Davidian scenes from the antique, the merry, rosy-cheeked peasantry dancing in the meadows. Their connection with reality was tenuous at best. Courbet's work – and by extension Courbet himself – cried out for attention.

So in October Courbet came back to Ornans from Paris something of a local hero. He was fêted by his friends in the town, and they drank the night away in celebration of the hero's return. He was a famous artist. What he wanted to do now was paint more large pictures, and for this he needed a spacious studio. His mother had recently inherited two houses in Ornans, and Courbet's eye was immediately attracted by one of these, which contained a large two-storey room formerly used as a laundry. This was converted into his atelier. A big window was cut in the north side, and Courbet painted the walls greenish yellow and dark red, the window embrasures white, and the ceiling and upper parts of the walls sky blue. He was creating a world within a world, and to add a touch of fantasy he painted swallows on this blue background skimming across the heavens.

The space was there, the materials were ready. He needed a subject. His intention was to paint a landscape, and that morning he had set out in the family carriage to drive to the Château of Saint-Denis near Masières where he was going to make some studies. As he drove along the road he saw the two men on the wayside and stopped the carriage to look at them. As he wrote afterwards, they were 'breaking stones on the road, the most complete personifications of poverty. An idea for a picture came to me at once. I made an appointment with them at my studio for the next day.'

What did they think, these two road-menders, when this strange figure propositioned them? They presumably weighed up the advantages: money in their pockets, and a good meal. But what did they think of the artist? Perhaps Gagey's attitude mirrored Jack the porter's to Leonard and Magnus: he dismissed him as a tosser, but a tosser who to his face had to be humoured because he provided the meal-ticket. Or perhaps the two of them went with some curiosity to that studio, like locals might today be roped in as extras in a day's filming. Except that these two extras were to be the unwitting stars of the show, immortalised in paint far beyond their time, symbols of the exploitation of labour, landmarks in the history of art. Until, that is, the hour of that tragic coincidence in Dresden nearly a century later. 'Coincidences frighten me,' Oswald had said, thinking of the picture's destruction. The randomness of chance, that was what had upset him. That it meant everything, and nothing. And then she had reassured him. 'Chance is not always something to fear,' she had said, thinking of their meeting.

The next day Courbet posed his models carefully. 'On one side is an old man of seventy,' the artist recorded, 'bent over his task, sledgehammer poised in the air, his skin tanned by the sun, his head shaded by a straw hat; his trousers of coarse material all patched; inside the cracked sabots, torn socks which had once been blue show his bare heels. On the other side is a young man with a dusty head and swarthy complexion; his back and arms show through the holes in his filthy tattered shirt; one leather brace holds up the remnants of his trousers, and his leather boots, covered in mud, gape dismally in several places. The old man is kneeling, the young one stands behind him holding a tray of crushed rock. Alas! In labour such as this, one's life begins that way, it ends the same way.'

Oswald had always been intrigued by this picture. There was something monolithic about the figures. They were forms in attitudes of toil, stonebreakers who had themselves been cast in stone; neither of their faces being visible, you were conscious of no overt attempt to elicit sentimental response from the spectator. And yet there was something in their very postures that commanded sympathy. Why? Perhaps it was only him; perhaps their stonebreaking seemed poignant because it mirrored his own arduous and ill-rewarded efforts in the context of Fortescue's now and the museum before; perhaps he was a stonebreaker too.

Not that he accepted what Prudhon made of this painting. Prudhon turned it into something that it wasn't: what he wrote about it never entirely rang true. Prudhon reconstituted it as a political statement. In 1864 – fifteen years after it was painted, mind you – he called Courbet the first true socialist painter, and 'The Stonebreakers' the first socialist painting. 'Others before Courbet have attempted socialist painting and have not succeeded,' he declared. 'That is because the desire is not enough: one must be an artist. "The Stonebreakers" is a satire on our industrial civilisation, which constantly invents wonderful machines to perform all kinds of labour and yet is unable to liberate man from the most backbreaking toil.' Prudhon could never see anything in a picture except a moralistic, socialist tract. When he tried to visualise Prudhon, he thought suddenly of Dresch: Dresch frowning, single-minded, grey; Dresch, whose view of life would always be ultimately limiting. Anyway, Prudhon's influence certainly ensnared Courbet; under it Courbet convinced himself that his motivation in painting 'The Stonebreakers' was undiluted social protest. But this was with hindsight; when Courbet stopped his carriage at the roadside there was a purely pictorial element in this motivation, Oswald had no doubt. Courbet was primarily seduced by the visual qualities of the scene the stonebreakers constituted. He was always a creature of instinct, not intellect, a sensualist first and a philanthropist second.

He laid down the photograph. The image, redolent with

remembered ideas and associations, had temporarily absorbed him. Almost as an afterthought, he picked up Bernard's accompanying letter. Then it hit him.

Dear Oswald,

In haste – just back, knackered, from extensive travels abroad and trying to sort myself out. This is the one letter I must write before I turn in because it concerns a bloody sensational discovery. So I'm shooting the enclosed off to you at once. I've been offered it by an old friend who's surpassed himself this time, don't you think?

You'll recognise what it is, of course, so I don't need to tell you much more except that because of its size it will be a bit of a problem to get out. But it will be worth it, because as far as I can see the sellers have little idea of its true value. That's the way we like it, isn't it, old cock?

Give me a tinkle as soon as you get this because we must act fast. Your turn to buy me lunch, I think.

Yours ever,
Bernard

He stared at the letter, incredulous, trying to get its fantastic implications straight in his mind. Bernard Tumbrill, Bernard Tumbrill of all people, had been offered for sale Courbet's 'Stonebreakers'. One of the most important lost pictures of the nineteenth century, assumed destroyed, had defied its apparent fate and resurfaced. And Bernard was now offering it to him at what might well be a knock-down price. What would it be worth on the open market? It was difficult to put an accurate figure on it, but surely more than ten million pounds. And its value art-historically could be expressed more simply: its rediscovery would create one of the major sensations of the second half of the twentieth century. Events such as this occurred once in a lifetime, if at all. A picture like that reappearing was extraordinary enough. But being one of the first people it had been offered to – well, that was an opportunity of such stupendous good fortune that it took the breath away, left you winded.

He had to stand up and walk about. He had to draw back from the enormity of the piece of information that had just come into his possession. He looked out of his window at the crowds surging avariciously up Bond Street, oblivious to his secret. He thought of Leonard and Magnus, striving ineffectually in their offices upstairs; of Olga scowling at the Kafka novel she read at her desk when there was no one in the gallery; of Jack cursing as he reframed a watercolour in the basement; of Eugene closeted with Lady Lindisfarne in the private viewing-room; all of their activities were paltry, pitifully irrelevant by comparison with the momentous news he had just received.

Right. Let's have a look at this thing again. Approach it logically. Was he absolutely sure that the picture now being offered to him by Bernard was genuine? He took up the photograph and peered at it minutely, searching for any suspicious indications. He could find none. There was no doubt that the painting reproduced there was by Courbet. It had all the authority and power of the master at his peak. This was unquestionably not a copy. It was the picture that for most of its life had hung in the Dresden Gallery, admired by countless pre-war visitors. It was the picture that had been ferried for safekeeping to some Schloss east of the city early on in the war. And it was the picture that had been carried in a convoy of furniture vans through Dresden on Shrove Tuesday 1945.

So the question was, how? How had this masterpiece fallen into Bernard's hands? How had Bernard been able to come up with it when all the records concluded that it had perished on the night of 13 February 1945? Dresch, Saskia and a thousand other people with better access to the facts than Oswald were convinced of its destruction in the firestorm. But what was the evidence that had convinced them? What were the facts? Where did the facts end and the conjecture begin? The facts were that the picture was last recorded on the evening of 13 February 1945 in an area that later that night was razed to the ground by Allied bombing. Oswald himself had walked along the Bruhl'sche Terrasse and understood the scale and the intensity of the holocaust. But what had actually happened that night? In the end you could never be sure, not of the details. Not of the precise fate of individuals. Nor of individual things. There were many private deaths and secret horrors for ever hidden to history. A merciful oblivion, perhaps. But what else was hidden by that chaos? Not just on that terrible night, but in the aftermath too? There had been a breakdown of order, of official control. In the last two months of the war, events in Germany in general and Dresden in particular were by no means totally documented. Many things must have happened that eluded the official records. The destruction of 'The Stonebreakers', therefore, had been an assumption, not a fact. Its ultimate fate was unrecorded. No one had ever actually identified the ashes of the picture. No one had inspected the blistered strands of canvas, or poked at the charred remains of the wooden stretcher. Somehow 'The Stonebreakers' had survived. Its history since February 1945 remained to be prised out of the shadows, of course; but either Bernard or his source would shed some light on that question, no doubt.

Oswald knew he must move quickly now. He checked his address book for Bernard's number, reached for the telephone, and began to dial.

At that moment there was a knock on his door. He replaced the receiver hastily. Magnus loped in. He wore a yellow bow-tie against a shirt of virulent green. His eye was caught by the landscape that Oswald had recently brought up from the stock room to hang on the wall. Typically Magnus allowed this to distract him from whatever it was he had come in to discuss.

'What a pretty view. Is it Corot?'

'Valenciennes, actually.'

'Oh, right.' He nodded, peering at it again a little feverishly as if hidden in its luminous recessions was the clue to a question that had been bothering him.

'What can I do for you, Magnus?' Oswald found it impossible not to sound impatient.

'What? Oh, right.' He coughed, and ran a hand through his hair. 'No, Leonard was wondering – we both were, actually – how you got on with the Japanese yesterday.'

'The Japanese?'

'You had lunch with them.'

'Ah, those Japanese.' Oswald chose his words with care. 'Well, it was reasonably encouraging. They want to buy important French nineteenth-century pictures, particularly the Impressionists. They've got quite a lot of money to spend.'

'A lot? How much?'

'Really quite a lot.' He didn't want to worry Magnus. And it suddenly seemed wiser to keep the true extent of their spending-power to himself for the time being. 'A million or two, anyway.'

'Excellent.'

'It's promising, isn't it?'

'Of course, we were both sorry we couldn't have been there for lunch ourselves to . . . lend a hand.'

'We got by,' Oswald assured him.

There was a pause. 'So,' mused Magnus, scrutinising the Valenciennes, 'the pressure's on.'

'How do you mean?'

'It's not just Salzman now. It's the Japanese as well.

133

The pressure's on us to come up with some pretty exceptional pictures.'

Oswald's eyes carried to the photograph of the Courbet lying exposed on his blotter. Discreetly he turned it face downwards. 'Have you come up with anything?' he asked Magnus.

'Me?' Magnus looked surprised, and a little uncomfortable. 'Well, I suppose I could be on to something. There might be . . . there might be a Salvator Rosa in the offing. I'm not sure at this stage.'

Oh yes? thought Oswald. That'll be the day, when Magnus comes up with a worthwhile picture. But he hadn't got time to taunt him, not now. He wanted him out of his office as soon as possible so he could get on the telephone to Bernard. On to the track of the Courbet. He had the feeling that every second was vital.

'Fun, wasn't it?' Magnus was saying.

'What was?'

'That party the other evening. The barbecue.'

For Christ's sake, get out. 'Yes, I enjoyed it,' lied Oswald.

'I like barbecues.' Magnus paused again, standing irresolutely in the doorway. Then he added: 'Daphne was looking well.'

'Daphne?'

'Lovely woman, your wife. You're a lucky man, you know.'

Oswald grunted.

'Yes. Well,' finished Magnus. Finally he was on his way.

Alone again, Oswald snatched up the telephone and dialled Bernard's number. It began to ring. Answer, damn you, answer. The line rang interminably. He cursed Bernard's fecklessness, his disorganisation. How could he put something as important as this photograph in the post and then forget to stamp it? Precious time had been lost.

Bloody Bernard. He was getting increasingly erratic, of course. There had been that business with the Green posters. But Christ, if he came up with the Courbet now Oswald vowed personally to plaster the entire street window with the things. Why, oh why, didn't the old bastard answer? Come on, come on. There was a click the other end. At last.

A taut female voice said: 'Yes, what is it?'

'Could I speak to Bernard Tumbrill, please?'

There was no reply for some time. Suddenly he heard sobbing.

'Hallo? Hallo?'

A scuffling noise followed, then a male voice said: 'Who's that speaking?'

'Oswald Ginn. Who are you?'

'Higgs. Funeral directors. Mrs Tumbrill has to proceed to the cortège now.'

'Funeral directors? Whose funeral, for God's sake?'

'Mr Bernard Tumbrill. Passed on three days ago.'

'Bernard? Dead? But he can't be, he just wrote to me.'

'It is most unfortunate, sir.'

'But he can't be dead,' Oswald repeated. 'What happened to him?'

'I believe the deceased was the victim of liver failure.'

'But this is terrible . . . I need to speak to him . . .'

'I'm afraid, sir, that I must cut you short there.' The voice was smooth but authoritative. 'We have to move on. Don't distress yourself, Mrs Tumbrill. First car outside, waiting for you, that's it . . . goodbye, sir.'

The line clicked again and then he heard only the dialling tone. Slowly he put the telephone back in place. He sat at his desk, sick with shock.

It took time to sink in that he'd lost a friend. What registered immediately was that he no longer had access to the Courbet.

5

The villa in the hills behind Cannes was positioned discreetly. From the road all you could see through the trees were two or three green-shuttered windows set in a white wall and branches of bougainvillaea trailing across a doorway. In the seclusion of the garden behind, Orlando Verney unwound himself on to a sun-chair and removed his dark glasses. He had one of those faces that under other circumstances might not have been striking at all – a neutral face, containing nothing remarkably out of place and nothing indisputably breathtaking; however, because he lavished so much attention upon it, it was transformed. You saw beauty there because you perceived the intention of achieving beauty. Its evident accoutrements implied its existence. His sleek dark hair was always excellently cut, longish, and curling in exactly the right places. Even when the wind blew through it as he drove Victor's open-topped Rolls-Royce, it seemed to fall miraculously back into place the moment the car stopped to negotiate traffic lights in Cannes. His skin was tanned throughout the year to a constant and carefully calculated tone, never too deep, but to a refreshingly refined shade which suggested teasing flirtations with the sun rather than the commitment of a passionate affair. Were there hints of wrinkles at the corners of his eyes? Nothing to worry about yet. Still, at thirty-something, the situation needed watching. Watching carefully.

He reached down languidly to brush away a pine needle

from his toe. He was good at doing things languidly: pouring drinks, arranging deck-chairs, helping ladies out of fur coats. Only rarely did his elegance shed its languor, and become a wiry, spring-coiled thing, and on those occasions money was invariably at stake. If an introductory commission was in the offing, the parties concerned would be politely but rigorously pestered until it was forthcoming. If Orlando was meeting a bill for lunch or dinner (and he tried not to let this happen too often), he scoured the figures on the account minutely, querying a stray £1.25 here, withering about an unexplained fifteen francs there. People half expected him to be stupid; indeed, would have felt more secure if he were. But he wasn't. You found you underestimated Orlando at your peril.

It was 10.30 on this September morning and it was hot. The sky was cloudless, and before much longer Victor's immaculately kept pool would beckon. Meanwhile he might justifiably remove the tee-shirt he was still wearing. It was the one he'd been given in Los Angeles that time by Ed Morg, the film producer. They had been all the rage that summer in sophisticated circles, those tee-shirts emblazoned with the single word 'Starfucker'. They legitimised by jest their wearers' serious commitment to being seen about with the most glamorous names. Everyone had worn them and laughed. Orlando had taken an amused but world-weary glance at Ed's gift and wondered about changing the final R into a D.

The small, podgy, bronzed shape that was Victor Meer padded out barefoot from the house carrying a bottle of champagne and a jug of orange juice on a tray with two glasses.

'Good. I'm glad you've removed that vulgar vest,' he said.

'Not your style, is it, old thing?'

'I'm happy to say it isn't.' Victor pursed his lips in a familiar expression of disapproval. His own Aertex shirt, worn over a venerable but well-cut pair of khaki shorts, was discreet and freshly laundered. He placed the tray on the table beneath the parasol, and stood for a moment contemplating it thoughtfully. There was something on his mind, Orlando could tell. Finally Victor said: 'Orange juice or Buck's Fizz?'

How old was Victor? He must be in his seventies now, and for that age he was not badly preserved. Paunchy and short of stature, it was true, so that at times he appeared almost spherical; but you could see that as a young man he'd had looks, even without delving into his photo album. He was a sweet old thing, really, though he could be absurdly difficult. But Orlando was as a rule prepared to put up with a certain amount of difficulty in a person if they had reached Victor's level of eminence in their chosen field, and particularly if they were generous hosts.

'Just give me a glass of champagne, will you?'

Victor frowned as he poured out a generous measure, then gave himself some orange juice with a sprinkling of champagne. He sat looking into the middle distance and sipped distractedly. Orlando decided not to give him the satisfaction of asking him what was on his mind. He had the feeling that Victor was on the verge of being tiresome. Instead he decided to broach a concern of his own.

'I've been thinking about that Klimt of yours.'

'Have you?' Victor looked pained.

'I've been giving it rather a lot of thought, in fact. Have you ever considered what it's actually worth?'

'I know it's the most valuable picture in my collection.'

Orlando nodded. 'Exactly. But are you happy with all that money tied up in one object? Doesn't it worry you, the insurance and the security implications?'

'Now and then.'

'I mean, after all, you're always telling me how the best collections must constantly evolve. Collectors should never stop selling and buying. One's tastes change, don't they?'

'What are you saying?' asked Victor, frowning.

'I'll tell you what I'm saying, darling. I'm saying that if you're thinking of selling that picture, now might not be a bad time to do it. You see, I know someone who's looking for a Klimt landscape, someone who wants one very badly.'

'I don't know, it's difficult.' Victor's voice was querulous. 'I might part with it some time, I suppose. But it's such a wrench, such an upheaval disposing of a picture like that; and it was one of my earliest acquisitions. Perhaps I'm a little sentimental about it.'

'That's not like you.'

'I can be very sentimental about certain things. And occasionally, just occasionally, about people.' A cloying look of longing was being cast in Orlando's direction. He decided to ignore it and asked:

'Where did you buy it? I forget if you ever told me.'

'Where did I buy it? I got it on the Continent . . . I think it may have been in Munich, from a dealer. In the early fifties, if I remember rightly.'

'You probably didn't pay much for it? Not in those days.'

'Not in those days, no. One didn't pay much for pictures then.'

'What a mysterious old queen you are. That was in your Secret Service time, I suppose?'

'Whatever makes you say that?' Victor spoke quite sharply.

'Just a little joke, old thing.'

Victor laughed sourly. 'Just because I served a few unspeakably boring years in Intelligence in the war, that doesn't make me James Bond, you know.'

'No, darling. Of course it doesn't.'

'It was simply that there were a great many good pictures to buy then if you knew where to look.'

Orlando removed his dark glasses and unleashed on Victor a heavenly smile with plenty of eye contact. 'Look, think about it. I know I could get an exceptionally good price for that Klimt of yours. It could all be done very discreetly, with absolutely no upheaval for you. Why don't you leave it in my hands?'

Orlando needed money. He always needed money, but at this moment the need was acute. If he was asked what he did in life, he generally said vaguely that he was an art dealer; but his trading activities were haphazard, and for long tracts of time negligible. The necessity of making money was a tiresome one, the most irksome aspect of his existence. His best deals came by chance, in the course of his wide-ranging social life. 'Orlando, darling,' the bored wife of some industrial tycoon might say to him at dinner, 'we need a picture for our dining-room. Something English, traditional-looking; you're so clever, you know the sort of thing. A hunting scene, or dogs, something like that.' Then Orlando would suggest lunch on Tuesday, when he would promise to show her a couple of things she might like. By that time he would have nipped around his friends in the galleries and selected a few likely-looking items. Agreement would be reached beforehand on prices to be quoted to his client, which would include a generous commission from the gallery for himself. If all went well the after-lunch tour, conducted in an atmosphere of mildly alcoholic flirtation, would end in a purchase. But this sort of ploy was not worked often enough. His mother made him an allowance whose amplitude he had been known to exaggerate when it suited him to assert his membership of the *jeunesse dorée*; but in truth it was meagre, and, while he received considerable amounts of free-wheeling hospitality from a large number of sources, he was nonetheless constantly overdrawn. Continuous labour was not his forte: the effort of prolonged application did not suit his temperament. In the most charming manner possible, he was lazy. A fat commission on the sale of Victor's Klimt would wipe out that overdraft and see him through most of the winter.

Victor frowned again and shook his head. 'You know I really don't think I'm quite ready to part with that picture.'

'It's up to you, of course,' sighed Orlando. He replaced his dark glasses and reverted his gaze to the cypresses at the end of the garden. Dithering old queen.

There was a period of disconsolate silence. Victor sipped his drink through pursed lips, then said: 'You know, it's quite absurd your leaving today. You're not still planning to, are you?'

Orlando had not been sure, but now he replied: 'Oh, for God's sake, Victor, let's not start all that again. I've told you, I've accepted an invitation, and I'm due there this evening.'

'You could telephone her, say you've been delayed a day or two. We've had such a good time these past ten days.'

'I'm not going to be bullied.'

'I'm not bullying, just asking.'

'It's a simple matter of good manners. I've accepted her invitation.'

'How could you want to spend time with that poisonous old cow?'

'Look, darling, Vera's a very distinguished singer and I'm not going to sit here and listen to her being abused like this.'

'Very distinguished singer! She's a clapped-out old

whore. What conceivable attraction she has I cannot imagine. Apart from anything else she's so irredeemably vulgar. She may play the grand lady now, but it's all utterly bogus. Where does she hail from? Some unmentionable place like Sidcup.'

'You're very well-informed.'

'Alphonsina left one of her dreadful magazines in the kitchen. There was an article about her, with some quite ghastly photographs. I've never seen such a face-lifted female.'

'Not very polite about our neighbours, are we?'

'Hardly a neighbour. I thank Providence that there's a distance of at least forty kilometres between this house and hers. I am therefore spared contact with her.'

'God, Victor, don't flatter yourself. I'm sure she doesn't even know who you are.'

Victor scowled petulantly, picked up his glass and padded back into the house.

Orlando lay back again, mildly annoyed. Victor really ought to give him that Klimt to sell; there was no reason for him to adopt such an obstructive attitude. Orlando's decision to decamp to Vera's was a punitive measure, one which once threatened must be carried through in order to sustain his credibility. Did he want to go? It was true that Vera was vulgar, but she was splendidly so, and she had style, that was undeniable too. She had begun her career as an opera singer, and had made the transition to the West End stage, and then to America and films, with considerable commercial success. More to the point, she adored Orlando. Last year she had given him dinner in Paris and they had been snapped by a passing photographer. The photograph had figured in many gossip columns amid speculation that Vera Maskell's new lover was youthful art dealer Orlando Verney, twenty-nine. It was certainly true also that Vera was a little past her prime, being closer in age to Victor than to Orlando. But that sort of consideration had never worried him. His was a simple and on the whole unmalicious philosophy: he was prepared to do anything with anyone provided it was in civilised surroundings and involved no physical pain.

He would probably have a more lively time of it at Vera's. The past ten days with Victor had been relaxing, but only occasionally stimulating. Victor was working at the moment, closeted most mornings in his study writing a book. In the afternoons he rested. In the evening they might drive down to Cannes for dinner. This was the time when Victor could be good company, when his conversation stretched, challenged and amused. His reminiscences were pre-eminently worth hearing. Although the comparison would have annoyed him intensely, his career was like Vera's in that it had been distinguished by a major transition from one successful field into another. Today he was widely acclaimed as one of the Grand Old Men of the English literary scene, having progressed from being an art historian of considerable stature in the immediate post-war years to his present position as one of the most respected and successful serious novelists of his generation. In the process he had claimed the acquaintanceship – and frequently the friendship – of an impressive array of literary, political and social personalities: Nicolsons and Maughams, Mitfords, Coopers and Waughs flitted intimately through his reminiscences. Leafing through Victor's library, Orlando found volumes inscribed to his host by authors as diverse as Kenneth Clark, Graham Greene, Jean-Paul Sartre, and Joe Orton. Victor's anecdotes were rich source material for Orlando, to be appropriated and casually regurgitated on occasions when their repetition could add lustre to his own star.

Orlando had not been to university. He had left school a year early under a tiny bit of a *nuage*. But despite his lack of formal education he was articulate and nimble-witted, having early on learned the importance of cultivating the mind as well as the body. He had a retentive memory, and considerable skill in summoning from his burgeoning store the appropriate (albeit second-hand) remark, joke or anecdote for the occasion. In this respect the company of men like Victor had been an enormously productive investment. But then so in its different way was time spent in Vera's milieu. Chez Vera there was an awful lot of gossip. Not so much of a literary nature, it was true, but nonetheless diverting. In the circles in which Orlando moved it could sometimes be as useful to know Hollywood's amatorial secrets as Bloomsbury's. Orlando fingered the imaginary D on his tee-shirt a little meditatively.

But perhaps the most enduring legacy of Victor and his circle was Orlando's assurance in handling the art world, his own chosen field of operation. He had learned what to say and when, how to tailor his conversation to the company he was keeping in order to convince them of his expertise. He now had a whole repertoire, to which he was constantly adding, of gambits designed to impress his listeners with the range and depth of his art-historical knowledge and critical insight. In idle moments he was fond of rehearsing his various set-pieces. As he reached for his drink and lay back in the comfort of his chair, he now ran through one or two at random.

There was northern Mannerism. Currently this one had considerable potential, being a fashionable subject amongst serious-minded young museum directors. In this connection it was important to remember how to pronounce Uytewael, or at least not to pause before attempting it. Then there was Caillebotte. Here was an artist whom it often paid to praise: those jaded by the clichéd names of Impressionism, or those whose cheque-books were not quite large enough to compete for the artists of the movement's élite, responded to his appeal. You could point out that he was a figure on the fringe who had been unjustly neglected, on his day as good as Degas, and – my God! – what about that wonderful picture of umbrellas in a Parisian street, or, even better, the one of workmen planing floorboards in an apartment? This could be milked from several angles: cowboy builders in late-twentieth-century London could be contrasted with the nobility of these heroic French artisans; or elderly gays could be titillated by having their attention drawn to the muscular bodies of the labourers in the light shafting in through the window.

Sargent was definitely out. One must deplore his facility, and quote, inaccurately if necessary, the contemporary critic who claimed that in the portraits one couldn't recognise the sitter for the likeness. A thoughtful rider could, however, be added: 'I find Sargent acceptable only in those moments when he becomes Jamesian.' Orlando was not afraid of the big names, nor to tread on ground fought over by the heavyweights of art history. At London dinner tables he could be heard eulogising Venetian painting of the early sixteenth century. Ultimately, he would maintain, the distinction between Giorgione and early Titian is immaterial: the main thing is that the pictures were painted. And then there was the almost sensual delight of rolling one's tongue round the Italian word *Giorgionismo*.

He had assured a wide-eyed audience in New York that it was impossible to understand French eighteenth-century painting until you had read the Goncourts; on another occasion he had urged the claims of Italian Divisionism to pre-date French Neo-Impressionism, and on yet another, in a blasé tone, had suggested the possibility that Impressionism itself as manifested in Paris in 1874 was presenting nothing radically different from that which had already been achieved independently in Budapest. Only once, at the end of an alcoholic evening in Sydney, Australia, had he inadvertently mixed up the two theses, but fortunately the rest of the guests (including two directors of State museums) had been too mesmerised or too far gone to notice.

On the whole he thought it unlikely that any of these gambits would need to be brought into play at Vera's. He was not sure what Vera's taste in pictures was, but he would be surprised if it were in any way sophisticated. Conversation would probably not tend in these directions. Still, you never knew whom you might meet anywhere. It was his motto always to travel prepared.

Lunch was served on the verandah at 1.30 as usual. By the time of its appearance, Orlando had reached a provisional decision about his plans for the immediate future. In the late morning he had discreetly withdrawn to his room, showered and packed. He emerged looking immaculate in his white summer suit and light blue shirt, wearing his prodigiously expensive sun-glasses. Victor was already seated and watched in silence as his guest sank gracefully into his chair and inspected his Rolex. Alphonsina waddled out of the kitchen and placed in front of him a bowl of vichyssoise. Through the bougainvillaea one could see the heat shimmering in the garden.

'Thank you, Alphonsina,' said Orlando brightly. The cook, who adored him, giggled happily and withdrew. For a period no one spoke, Victor having apparently withdrawn into a mood of morose introspection. Then Orlando wiped his lips with a napkin and enquired: 'Good morning's work?'

'Not entirely.'

'You must be getting towards the end now, surely?'

'The closer one gets to the end, the more difficult it all becomes.'

'In what way?'

'I've been planning these memoirs for – what? – the past ten years. One way and another I've had quite a number of experiences in my life that are worth writing about.'

'Your memoirs will be the hottest literary property of the decade,' encouraged Orlando. 'People will kill to get their hands on them.'

'When one gets to my age, one's autobiographical urge becomes confessional, expiatory even. I want to tell the truth about people and events with which I was involved, not obfuscate to save feelings, least of all my own. So this book of mine is bound to be controversial. Others may be upset.'

'Darling, I can't wait.'

'That's just it. I fear everyone may have to. I'm coming around to the feeling that the publication of this book may have to be postponed till after my death.'

'God, Victor, what are you afraid of? Libel actions? Prosecution under the Official Secrets Act? Or perhaps you committed an unnatural act with a member of the Royal Family?'

Victor refused to be drawn. He sat glumly sipping his soup with mincing little slurping noises. Suddenly Orlando felt impatient with him. It was all rather tiresome, this pettish show of anguished grandeur. There were more immediate issues to be addressed.

'I've been thinking this morning,' he announced. 'What we should really do is get that Klimt of yours photographed, have half a dozen transparencies made. Then we'd be ready.'

'Ready?' Victor toyed suspiciously with his napkin ring.

'Ready for when you decide to sell it. You can't dilly-dally indefinitely. And I can't tell you how easily I could arrange a really profitable and discreet sale. The money would be in your account without your having to lift a finger.'

'It's not as if I need the money,' said Victor testily.

'Everyone needs money.'

'I really don't think I do at this moment. No, I've got other problems.'

Other problems. What was he talking about? No, Victor was being really quite exceptionally selfish over the issue. Why couldn't he see that his own financial sufficiency was irrelevant, that dwelling on his other problems was sheer self-indulgence? No, the crucial point was Orlando's own need of money. Victor's intransigence over the sale of the Klimt could do nobody any good. Surely, thought Orlando, he must realise that if he yields on the question of its disposal, I will probably give in and postpone my departure to Vera. Probably. Orlando didn't like to be too closely ensnared by such bargains lest his freedom should be shackled unacceptably. But Victor should at least proceed on this hypothesis: it was his only chance.

'So you're not going to sell?'

'I can't make any decision at the moment.'

Orlando looked at his watch again. 'Ah, well,' he sighed. 'There's a train at three I thought I might take. Will you run me down to the station?'

'I'm really much too busy.'

'I know – why don't I drive myself over in the Mini, that wouldn't disturb you. I could get it back to you next week.'

'No, that wouldn't be convenient.' Victor looked angry and miserable at the same time. 'The Mini is needed here.'

'Really?' Orlando raised an incredulous eyebrow.

'If you're determined to go, I'll ring for a taxi.'

So Orlando departed in a white Mercedes from Cannes-Cab. Farewells were muted. Victor waved briefly from the terrace then turned back towards his study before the car was through the gate. He was a mean old man, decided Orlando as the taxi wound a circuitous route down the hill to the station. But it was the right moment to leave anyway. Wherever Orlando stayed, he reached a saturation point beyond which the company palled. Then it was time to move on, before damage was done.

At the station Orlando got out briefly, concluded that the platforms, the carriages and the passengers all looked impossibly tacky, and got back into the car again. The taxi drove him all the way to Vera's at a cost of just under seventy pounds.

Victor, on the other hand, spent the afternoon at his desk. He was not happy. He wrote a little and thought a lot. For a time he thought about Vera Maskell, and wondered if he'd ever hated anyone he'd never met with quite such a powerful and irrational hatred. Then his mind drifted further back into the past. He'd been spending a lot of time in the past this summer. That was partly because of the memoirs, of course. But there was another reason, too, something far more disturbing. The letter. That bloody letter. It had arrived out of the blue six weeks ago, and thrown his life into turmoil. Oh, God, why couldn't he be left in peace now? Surely he'd earned it, after all this time. But no, even now he was to be haunted, haunted by a man he'd met one autumn nearly fifty years ago and seen only two or three times since. A man called Xenophon.

'Mrs Tumbrill? I don't think we ever met. My name's Oswald Ginn.'

She looked at him with confused and hostile eyes. 'Are you the one that telephoned?'

'I did. This morning.'

She was a large, ungainly woman, with long greying hair held up haphazardly in a bun. She was in her late fifties and had perhaps once been a beauty, but no longer. Her skin still retained a suggestion of its original clarity but there was a puffiness now, a puffiness that spoke of too many past defeats. She had let go. A scent of stale garlic lingered about her. She said, 'You'd better come in.'

Oswald paused for a moment on the threshold of the dilapidated mansion flat in West Kensington to which he had traced Bernard's widow. It was the first time he had seen the place: Bernard was the sort of man who didn't invite you home. Looking back, Oswald realised that their relationship had been conducted in a succession of art galleries and more or less disreputable bars. He'd never thought about Bernard's domestic life. Perhaps he had subconsciously assumed Bernard didn't have one, being such an inveterate traveller. He'd never speculated about Mrs Tumbrill, either. Bernard had rarely mentioned her. Of course, he wouldn't have much, would he? Bernard had been a womaniser and no doubt constantly unfaithful to her. Perhaps she'd come to terms with that. But maybe the saddest thing for her to bear would have been that in the end he was happiest out drinking with the boys. His seductions were mere raw material for the real business of recounting them luridly to his drinking companions. What consolation did that leave for his wife? Probably just the dirty washing.

Now Oswald followed her along a murky passage. The walls were hung with posters advertising environmental issues, some in German. Probably amongst these was the one that Bernard had wanted him to hang in Fortescue's window. God, how long ago that seemed now. How long ago everything seemed now, everything that had happened before Oswald had got the letter with the photograph of the Courbet.

She led the way into a large studio-like reception room where because of the high south-facing window the light was much better. It was a mess: sofas and chairs piled high with books, table-tops littered with tubes of paint and abandoned brushes, a desk stacked with paperwork held down by two unemptied ashtrays. It smelt, of turpentine and old cigarettes, as well as the garlic. In the middle of the threadbare carpet was an array of junk, heaped together: bottles, a dead potted plant, a single slipper, a water-damaged roll of wallpaper, various coat-hangers. She followed Oswald's gaze and laughed bitterly:

'Could be by Kurt Schwitters, couldn't it?'

'Could it?' Oswald was lost.

'Didn't he specialise in this sort of crap? You know, Dadaism? Sticking a whole lot of random household objects together and calling it a collage?'

'Yes, I see what you mean.' He laughed politely. 'Maybe you're right.'

'I'll tell you something,' she said with sudden vehemence, 'I wish it bloody was by bloody Schwitters. Then I'd sell the bloody lot and make some money. That's all art's good for, really, isn't it? Money?'

She stared aggressively at him. 'Not always,' he said.

'Oh, come off it. Look, as far as I'm concerned there's only two types of art: Rubbish; and expensive Rubbish.' She picked up one of the half-empty tubes of paint then threw it down. 'It's a pity Bernie only ever managed to get involved with the first sort.'

'I wouldn't say that.'

'Oh, wouldn't you?' She was truculent. But he sensed that part of her wanted to hear him refute what she said, to reassure her. About Bernard, at least.

'No, I wouldn't, actually. I admired Bernard as a

painter. Maybe he never got the recognition he deserved, but he did some excellent things.'

'Before he hit the bottle.' She was right, of course.

'He'll be much missed,' Oswald persisted. 'He had a feeling for painting, he could tell good from bad. That's rare.'

'How d'you mean?' She sank into a chair, and added, 'Clear yourself a seat, by the way.'

Oswald pushed away some books and sat down. 'Thank you. No, I mean he had a discerning eye for quality. He recognised some good pictures, discovered them.'

'What, old pictures, you mean?' Was there a quickening interest?

'Just in general. He had taste.' Steady now. No need to tell her too much. She didn't need to know about the Greuze. And certainly not about the other thing.

'How long had you known him?' she asked.

'Oh, many years. I first met him in the early seventies.'

'I don't remember him mentioning you.' She was suspicious again, aggressive.

'Well, I suppose that could have been because just recently I hadn't seen so much of him.'

'Join the club.'

'He travelled a lot, didn't he?'

'Christ, he travelled. God knows what he got up to. I hadn't seen him for six months before he got back this last time. He seemed to need it, somehow, the being off on his own.' She paused, then added, 'Inconsiderate bugger.' But her tone wasn't entirely without affection.

Oswald was wondering how to approach the question he'd come to ask her. Nothing was easy in bereaved households. 'It's a dreadful ordeal for you, I'm so sorry,' he said.

'I mean, look at the mess he left behind him. It'll take me weeks to clear this lot.'

'I'm so sorry. But this is the moment when everything must seem at its worst . . .'

She turned on him, angry again. 'Oh, spare me all that shit about time being a great healer. If I hear that load of old crap once more, I'll scream. What have you come to see me about, anyway? I suppose he owed you money, did he?'

'No, please, Mrs Tumbrill, nothing like that. No, I really wouldn't have bothered you at all, but there's one thing I urgently need to know, about his most recent travels. Where had he been on this last trip, the one he'd just got back from when he . . . you know?'

She frowned, and shook her head. 'God, don't ask me. I lost track.'

'Didn't he write to you, or ring up from anywhere?'

'Him? You must be joking. Never bothered. He could have been invited to stay in the White House and I'd only have found out about it in the newspapers.'

'But you must have some idea where he was. Didn't he talk about it at all when he got back?'

Mrs Tumbrill stood up, then walked to the window. 'I suppose he would have done, in the end. But the Monday evening he got back he was so shattered, he just pushed off to bed, hardly said a word. The next day he was taken ill, and the day after that they rushed him into hospital. Of course, he'd known about that liver of his, that it was dangerous to carry on the way he had been. But he didn't take any notice. We knew it was always on the cards, but when it all happened so quickly, it was a terrible, terrible shock. He died on Saturday evening. I don't think he even realised I was with him.'

Oswald felt sorry for her then, standing there staring out of the window. But he prayed she wouldn't cry, not now, not before he'd finished. 'So there's really no clue about where he'd just been?' he prompted gently.

154

'Oh, there are clues, I suppose.' She turned and faced Oswald again, and he was relieved to see her more composed. 'If you asked me to guess, I'd say he must have been in Germany and probably Austria, because he liked Austria. You see, he brought back a selection of new leaflets from the German Greens. Here they are, I found them in his suitcase.' She picked up some papers from a chair and offered them to him. 'Take a look at these, they're worth reading. And before that, where was he? Could have been in Spain, or was it South America? Somewhere like that. But I can't be sure, it was all so confusing.'

Oswald nodded, trying to hide the little thrill of excitement he felt. 'Germany and Austria, that would figure.'

'What would figure? Why do you need to know all this?' But she sounded perturbed rather than intrigued.

Oswald said, as calmly as he could: 'Bernard wrote to me just before he died, about a business matter. I'm trying to unravel it now. If I could find out where he had just been travelling, it would be an enormous help.'

She shrugged. 'Well, he spent a lot of time in Vienna, as I say. In fact, he once deigned to take me with him. Big of him, wasn't it? He seemed to have a lot of friends there, and to be honest I didn't much like the look of them. Anyway, he spent most of his time drinking with them.'

Vienna, Vienna. Some sort of pattern was emerging, a coherence. Could Vienna mean Grunwald? The more he thought about it, the more plausible it seemed. Why not, after all? If Bernard had just been in Austria, then there was every likelihood that he had been in contact with Grunwald again. What had he said in the letter? That he had been offered the picture by 'an old friend', one who had 'surpassed himself this time'. That would make sense: the Courbet was an incomparably more significant find than the Greuze.

'When you were in Vienna with Bernard, did you meet a man called Grunwald?'

She gave the question some thought. 'I might have done. I do remember one time, we were in a taxi with one of his mates, a slimy little shit. I didn't trust him at all. To make conversation, I asked this bloke what he did, and both he and Bernard laughed, and the bloke said, "You could call me a bit of a Harry Lime." I asked him what he meant and he said that he made his living finding people things they couldn't always get through legal channels. So I said, "Oh, you're an art dealer, are you?" They both thought that was quite funny, I seem to recall. And, yes, that guy might have had a name like Grunwald, but I can't be sure.'

'And Bernard could have been in touch with this Grunwald on his last visit.'

'Could have been, I suppose. I just don't know.'

Oswald drummed his fingers on the arm of his chair. He was very near to something here, he felt certain. He must press Mrs Tumbrill just a little bit more, prise out of her everything relevant to Bernard's recent movements, but at the same time he must walk a tightrope, calming on the one hand her grief for her dead husband and on the other her suspicion about his own motives in all this.

'Was there anything else in his luggage to suggest where he might have just been? Any other evidence?'

She gestured towards the desk, the desk on top of which lay the stacks of unsorted papers and unemptied ashtrays.

'I put everything that came out of his suitcase on there,' she said.

'May I have a look?' He got up from his seat.

'Help yourself.'

He moved the ashtrays carefully, setting them down on the floor. There was a pile of unpaid bills which he also set to one side, together with some more literature from the

German Green Party. Then, almost immediately, he came across an Austrian fifty-schilling note, crumpled in such a way that it must have been discarded from a trouser pocket not long ago. The evidence was mounting up. Underneath the banknote was an empty packet of Spanish cigarettes: inconclusive. Then came five carbon-copied sheets of closely typed script which he picked up curiously. They comprised an article entitled 'The Barbizon School: The First Greens' by Bernard Tumbrill, due for publication, according to an attached note, in next month's edition of a journal called *European Environment*. Cranky old Bernard. Presumably he'd been revising it on his travels. It was rather poignant to think of it appearing posthumously, but Oswald did not feel tempted to read it now, and he laid the typescript gently back on the desk.

There was nothing else.

He coughed apologetically and said: 'Thank you so much for seeing me, Mrs Tumbrill. I'll leave you to get on. You've been most helpful.'

'You're off, then?'

'Yes, I'll see myself out, don't worry.' He hesitated, suddenly awkward. 'And if there's anything you need, anything I can help you with, just let me know.'

'That's kind of you. Well, there is one little thing.'

'Yes?'

'If you're going past a postbox, you might drop this in.'

Relieved, he said, 'Of course.'

He left with a re-used brown envelope in his hand. Its flap was stuck down with Elastoplast which was already coming adrift. He made a half-hearted attempt to reseal it. As he stepped out of the slightly foetid atmosphere of the flat into the relatively fresh air of the communal staircase, he glanced back. He could see Mrs Tumbrill at the end of the passage, framed in the doorway, staring after him. She lifted a hand and gave a forlorn wave, hardly more than a quick spasm of movement. He waved back a little foolishly.

As he cantered down the steps he felt a surge of regret for Bernard. It was sad, seeing all Bernard's things abandoned like that, visiting his home for the first time under such circumstances, meeting his defeated wife. The wife he'd preferred not to talk about. The wife he'd let down so often. The wife who grieved for him. Yes, it would have been better not to have come, kinder to Bernard's memory. Bernard had been his friend and at times his confidant. Now Bernard had gone, and left him with the last great question of their friendship unanswered. Where was the Courbet he had uncovered?

Oswald was on his own from now on. But he had one lead. And that lead pointed in the direction of Vienna and Grunwald. Grunwald had to be involved in this; Grunwald, with his old association with Bernard, and his long-established ties with Eastern Europe in general and the Soviet Union in particular. What if the picture was coming out of Moscow? What if it was one more trophy which Grunwald had skilfully negotiated out on to the Western market?

Oswald's thoughts raced back to Dresden again. There was Saskia, at the table in the restaurant. They were talking about coincidences, about the night on which the lorry carrying 'The Stonebreakers' had stopped in the city. Somehow this one picture had survived. Out of that night of destruction it had been salvaged, God knows how. But it was possible, just possible. What might have happened to it then? He recalled Dresch's ecstatic account of the Red Army's team of experts setting about the task of saving Dresden's treasures, the treasures they had found strewn about in various hiding places when they marched into the city in May 1945. Recent revelations had shed more light on what had actually happened in this process. Thousands of objects had been carted away. And ten years later over a thousand restored works of art had been returned to the city, true enough. But there had been instances of plunder; even the Russians were admitting it now. It was known that property confiscated from Germany at the end of the war existed in both public and private collections in the old USSR. So, supposing some heroic Soviet liberator had come across the Courbet secreted somewhere in the Dresden vicinity in May 1945? Since it was believed destroyed on the night of 13 February, there would have been no one else out looking for it, nothing to stop an enterprising Russian individual discreetly taking possession of it. It could have returned to Moscow as part of his personal booty and remained there ever since. Now it had been winkled out. Perhaps the original plunderer had died; perhaps some local entrepreneur, encouraged by the new mood of capitalist enterprise, had decided to release the picture on to the Western market and approached the only channel he knew. That channel would have been Grunwald; Grunwald could then have turned to Bernard Tumbrill; enter, finally, Oswald Ginn, alerted by Bernard's tantalisingly inconclusive letter. So now it was up to Oswald to trace the links back in the chain, to track this picture down and repossess it.

To do this, he felt absolutely certain about one thing: that he must continue to keep the picture's existence quiet, protect it from the interference of others. The thought of Leonard and Magnus becoming involved was intolerable, let alone that precocious little twit Eugene Crabbe. Their combined shortcomings – Leonard's obstinacy, Magnus's cowardice, Eugene's arrogance – would only damage the enterprise. The more people who knew about it, the more risky it became. It was much better left in one safe pair of hands. His own.

From the moment he had first received Bernard's letter, he had felt a growing sense of mission. There was the picture itself, of course. The image of Gagey and his young colleague working on the dusty road outside Ornans had always moved him. But there was something else in all this now, something that went very deep inside him. There was Dresden. Dresden, the picture's last known resting place. Dresden, whose harrowing past had simultaneously stirred both his imagination and his guilt. Dresden, where he had once held Saskia for a second or two, felt her shoulders in his grasp, smelt her scent. Dresden, where she had finally eluded him. Could it be that he was driven to pursuing 'The Stonebreakers' as some sort of oblique act of homage to her memory?

Yes, but that wasn't all, was it? The more he thought about it, the clearer it became that by finding 'The Stonebreakers' he might also make a very large sum of money. Conrad Salzman. There was the perfect buyer ready and waiting for it: discreet, unscrupulous, incalculably rich, and in the market for something utterly exceptional. He wouldn't need much persuading to pay a huge price for 'The Stonebreakers'. It was just the sort of world-class picture that he was looking to acquire with no publicity. Alternatively, there was the Japanese syndicate. Whichever way you looked at it, this was a picture that would be a must for their collection. Not only was it of the first rank as a French nineteenth-century painting; it was also something widely illustrated in the definitive art-historical literature; and, even better, it was a picture that boasted a proud Western museum provenance. You couldn't conceive of a more alluring combination. The truth of the matter was that once Oswald had laid hands on it he could practically name his own price. He would have millions of pounds in his power. There would be the opportunity to make a very large amount of money indeed. For Fortescue's. Or for himself.

Returning to the gallery that afternoon, he met Magnus on the stairs. 'Is Eugene about?' he asked him.

'No,' said Magnus. 'He's hospital-visiting.'

'Oh? Anyone we know?'

'Yes.' Magnus spoke with an air of suppressed excitement. 'It's Lady Lindisfarne. She had a minor heart attack.'

'I don't know why Eugene doesn't just set up a nursing home for distressed elderly titled folk and be done with it.'

Magnus shook his head. 'No, seriously, I think it's in all our interests for Eugene to preserve his intimacy in that direction.' He lowered his voice meaningfully. 'There's the Corot, you know.'

'The Corot?'

'A wonderful early one. Been in the family for years. It's on the cards she might sell. Leonard thinks – we both do – that it could be just the thing to offer Salzman. Or our Japanese friends.'

It was pathetic, really, the way they were all flapping around Lady Lindisfarne in the hope that she might yield up some second-rate Corot. For a moment Oswald was tempted to reveal the existence of the Courbet, just to put them all in their places. But he restrained himself. 'Maybe Eugene should be encouraged discreetly to tamper with the life-support system,' he suggested. 'The best client's usually a dead one.'

He greeted Gloria the secretary cheerfully.

'Oswald,' she called after him as he went into his office, 'there's a message for you.'

'From who?'

'The Duke of Santa Ponsa rang.'

'Oh, God. The bloody Murillo, I suppose?'

'No, he wondered if you'd be interested in joining some

sort of club which he's starting here in London. He said there's an initial membership fee of fifteen hundred pounds, but he can get you ten per cent off. The only thing is, he needs the money by the end of the week.'

'Christ almighty.'

'What shall I tell him?'

'Tell him to get stuffed.' He sat down at his desk, then called through again: 'Gloria?'

'Yes, Oswald?'

'Could you dig out some filing for me and bring it through here? I want everything we've got on a man called Grunwald. A man called Grunwald, in Vienna.'

'Herr Grunwald?'

'Who is speaking?' The voice at the other end of the telephone was nasal and suspicious.

'My name is Oswald Ginn. I'm calling from Fortescue's in London. I'd like to speak to Herr Grunwald, please.'

'This is Grunwald.' The admission was cautious, almost reluctant.

'Oh, good. Herr Grunwald, we have never actually met, but you might remember me; I am a friend of Bernard Tumbrill.'

'Ah.' There was a pause. 'Of Bernard.'

'Yes. Actually, you and I have done business before, through Bernard. It was three years ago. Herr Grunwald, I am ringing to ask you: have you seen Bernard recently?'

'It is not so long ago that we were in contact.' He spoke slowly, choosing his words with care. 'Why do you ask me this?'

'Because Bernard is dead. He died suddenly, last week. So I am not able to get in touch with you through him. That's why I've come through to you direct.'

'Bernard is dead? I am sorry.' He said it coldly, distantly.

162

'Yes, it was a shock. Very sad. I was an old friend of his.' Oswald paused. Now. Now he must get to business, broach the matter. 'But the reason why I wanted to speak to you is that I believe you have recently offered Bernard an extremely important French nineteenth-century picture.' There was silence at the other end, unnerving silence. Oswald added encouragingly: 'Is that so, Herr Grunwald?'

'I do not know what you are talking about.' It was not a measured denial. There was a violence in the way he said the words. A violence; or a panic.

Oswald thought quickly. The man was stonewalling, hiding something. What he needed was reassurance, reassurance that Oswald was genuine, that he was serious, that he knew what was going on. So he took a risk and pretended to more knowledge than he had. There was no alternative, no other way forward. 'Look,' he said, 'you don't need to worry. I'm on your side, I want to do business with you. I know about this: it's a picture coming out of Russia, isn't it? Something pretty exceptional; Bernard sent me the photograph before he died, so I've seen it.'

'What picture do you mean?' asked Grunwald quietly.

'The one you offered Bernard.' Oswald took a deep breath. 'The Courbet. "The Stonebreakers", for Christ's sake.'

'Where do you get these stories?' His tone was changed. There was surprise now. And fear.

'Please. I am a serious buyer. I want to pursue this. I'd be grateful if you wouldn't offer it elsewhere until I have the chance to see it. Will you reserve it for me?'

'This is not possible. I do not . . .'

'Please, Herr Grunwald.'

'These are not matters to be discussed on the telephone.' He was angrier again.

163

'When can we discuss them?' Once more there was silence. 'I'll come to Vienna. When can we meet? Herr Grunwald?'

And then the line was dead. Grunwald had rung off.

What was going on? Why this evasion? For it was evasion rather than denial of the existence of the picture. That much was clear. Oswald went back in his mind over the conversation they'd just had. Grunwald was hiding something. But why?

And then of course he realised, and cursed himself for his naivety. Grunwald with his background would never commit himself on the telephone. A man who had been dealing with the Eastern Bloc for many years, operating with one foot either side of the Iron Curtain, had reason not to trust the security of the public communication system. It had been foolish to press him, he saw that now. He hoped he hadn't completely undermined ground for future co-operation between them. Damn. What should he do next?

He telephoned Grunwald again, to tell him that he would come to see him in Vienna and to fix an appointment. But there was no connection. He must have tried eight or ten times. Then, in desperation, he called the international operator.

'I'm sorry, sir,' she reported back finally, 'the number you gave me is out of order. A fault. No, I can't tell you when it will be clear again. Why not? Because I'm not the Austrian telephone repair service, OK?'

He stared unhappily out of the window. They were digging up the street below his office. He watched a very fat workman drilling, bending over so that a gap between his tee-shirt and jeans was exposed. The tops of massive buttocks spilled out, vibrating gently. On an oil drum nearby sat his mate, reading a newspaper and drinking tea. Modern times. In the complaints book open to members of the public visiting the Paris Exposition Universelle of 1855 he'd once found the following anonymous outburst: 'Monsieur Courbet is kindly requested to give his Stonebreakers clean shirts and to wash their feet.' What would that spectator have made of these two Gageys of the 1990s? Would even Courbet himself have bothered to stop and paint them? He doubted it. Give Oswald the originals any day. And he was going to find them; my God, he was going to find them. His instinct told him more strongly than ever before that they were out there, out there somewhere.

That was Friday. Saturday and Sunday he spent frustratedly at home. Those nights he slept badly. He thought constantly about the picture, the same indeterminate theories about its recent history and present whereabouts circling his brain time and again, knotting it up till he felt like screaming. Where did reality end and the dreams begin? Once he woke, certain that he'd found it, that it was standing in the next room, that he had only to walk through the door and there it would be, pristine and intact; and another time he emerged sweating from sleep convinced that the whole thing was a dream, including Bernard's letter, that there was no 'Stonebreakers' anywhere to be rediscovered. And one more time he woke with an even stranger illusion, that he could smell smoke, and burning, and hear people screaming in very confined spaces, and that not far away bombs were falling, masonry was collapsing, and wood was splintering. And canvas was rending.

Even Daphne noticed that something was wrong. On Sunday morning she asked him what was on his mind.

'Problems,' he said vaguely. 'At work.'

She looked at him curiously. 'Such as?'

He had it in mind to confide in her then. He felt a

sudden urge to tell someone, to talk about the extraordinary thing that had happened to him, the unparalleled opportunity that had opened up; he wanted sympathy for the problems he was contending with – Bernard's untimely death, the difficulties with Grunwald, the need to keep everything secret; and he wanted encouragement as he started on this enterprise, this quest to find a picture that could change his life. And hers, too. She was his wife, for God's sake.

'I've been put on to something pretty exciting.'

She walked to the refrigerator and poured herself some orange juice. She stood there, her tall, thin body swathed in a dressing-gown. 'How's that come about?' she asked.

'Through a contact. Well, you know him. Or knew him, I should say: Bernard Tumbrill.'

'Bernard Tumbrill? That drunk? I don't know what you see in him.'

'I don't see anything in him now. He's dead.'

'Dead?'

'Yes, dead. He died last week, of liver failure.'

'I'm sorry to hear that. But I can't say I'm surprised.' She drained her glass and set it down on the table. 'So he put you on to something, did he?'

'Something quite extraordinary, actually.'

'Well, all I can say is, be careful. Check it out before you do anything rash.'

'What do you mean?'

'Frankly, if Bernard Tumbrill produced something, I wouldn't touch it. As I say, I'm sorry he's dead, but he struck me as a deeply unreliable man.'

'Oh, for Christ's sake.' He couldn't stay in the same room as her after that. She was prejudiced against Bernard, he'd always known it. Maybe Bernard had been occasionally unreliable, but that didn't mean the man couldn't be right about something important like this. Not when you knew the facts. But there was more to it than that. Oswald sensed his wife's attitude was also conditioned by something further: a sort of jealousy of himself, a begrudging of any opportunity for him to succeed. There was no point in trying to explain any more to her about what he was planning. She'd made it clear she wasn't interested.

Later she went out, and stayed out till the early evening. He couldn't remember where she'd said she was going. Perhaps she hadn't actually told him. Anyway, by the time she got back he'd made up his mind.

'By the way,' he said, 'I'm going abroad tomorrow.'

'Oh? Where?'

'Austria. On business.'

'So you won't be here tomorrow night?'

'No, I won't.'

'It looks like I'll be going to the Alstons on my own, then.'

It was the way she said it that annoyed him. It was as if going to the Alstons was something with which to taunt him. 'What's going on at the Alstons?' he asked.

'Oh, a dinner.'

It leapt out before he could restrain it: 'I suppose that arsehole Geoffrey Cornforth will be there?'

'Amongst others.'

'I wouldn't sit down at the same table as him.'

'Lucky you're not coming, then, isn't it?'

'Bloody lucky,' he said bitterly.

But at least he'd made the decision and he felt better for it. So what if Grunwald's telephone number was still unobtainable? He would fly to Vienna and go to find the man. Confront him personally. That was clearly the only way to do business with him, face to face. And the sooner he got there the better, because for all he knew there might be competition by now. How many other people were aware of this picture's existence? But he felt a new determination. 'The Stonebreakers' had become so important to him that losing it was a possibility he was not prepared to consider. Tracking it down was to be his private victory. Over Leonard and Magnus; over Daphne; over the academic art world. It was to be the final act in his emancipation from the museum, the ultimate justification of the change he had made in his life: the triumph of commercial action over passive scholarship.

Orlando Verney sat on Vera's bed and considered his reflection in the dressing-table mirror. He liked what he saw: the white silk pyjamas looked good against his brown skin. He ran a hand through his hair a couple of times and was pleased with the effect. In the bathroom next door he could hear Vera turning on taps and splashing essence into the water. He got up and wandered out on to the balcony with the magnificent view over the Mediterranean, the balcony set over the mimosa-clad terrace that led down to the pool. The sun was already hot, and the stone under his feet was pleasantly warm. It was another beautiful early autumn day, the sixth in a row since he'd been here of cloudless blue skies and refreshing breezes. It was utterly idyllic. And he was pissed off.

Vera's villa was very different from Victor's; you felt it immediately you walked in. It was almost on the seashore, so you heard a constant background accompaniment of breaking waves. The rooms were bigger and airier. The expensive decorators whom Vera had employed had gone for a look of pervasive white opulence. In the drawing-room below there was even a white grand piano, on top of which stood a display of framed photographs, all inscribed effusively to his hostess. But the biggest difference from Victor's villa lay in the absence of books. He could practically memorise Vera's library in its entirety. There were hardback editions of novels by James Clavell, Morris West, Taylor Caldwell, Scott Fitzgerald, James Michener and Jackie Collins; the autobiographies of Mohammed Ali, David Niven and Richard Nixon; and a series of lavishly illustrated larger books covering a variety of subjects, from *The English Country House* to *Impressionism*, from *The Golden Age of the Hollywood Musical* to *The World of Marcel Proust*.

'Orlando, Orlando,' Vera had murmured to him at dinner that first day, 'you're looking so beautiful. I've been thinking about you a lot. What have you been doing with your life since I last saw you?'

'Ah, Vera, that would be telling.'

'Are you making it really big in the art world, darling?'

'Enormous,' laughed Orlando, thinking bitterly of that wretched Klimt and Victor's pig-headedness.

'You'll stay here with me for a week or two, won't you, darling?' whispered Vera.

The pleading tone was depressingly reminiscent of Victor, but Orlando had decided to be a good guest. Any undertaking he gave now could always be gently reneged upon later. It was his policy wherever possible to tell people what they wanted to hear. Why not? He had taken Vera's hand under the table. 'I'll stay a week at least. And it's so good to see you, looking so marvellous. In all these months away from you I'd forgotten quite how lovely you were.'

This had been an exaggeration. Vera looked older than he remembered. Orlando, who had a sharp eye for feminine couture, deeply regretted the excessive exposure of her upper arms. The bronzed skin was slack and unappealing, betraying her age much more eloquently than the little tucks round her eyes concealed it. Her blonde hair was, of course, well groomed and her magnificent cheekbones, always the hallmark of her looks, still gave structure to her face. But she was slipping. Longer sleeves, dear.

'I've given you the blue room. Next to mine.'

Orlando had squeezed her hand. 'Vera, you're so naughty.'

'And have you been faithful to me all these weeks?'

'What's fidelity?' He'd trotted it out easily. 'I'm never faithful, it's terribly small-minded to be faithful. But to you, my darling, I'm utterly loyal and always shall be. And that's far, far more important.'

He had been vaguely aware that the sentiments he was expressing were second-hand; where had he picked them up? Perhaps from Victor; perhaps from one of Victor's friends. It didn't matter. Vera had been on the whole appeased. And almost immediately Orlando had been drawn into conversation by the fellow-guest on his right, a hard-nosed American bitch whose husband was a film producer, a woman who wanted only to discuss the iniquitous price of everything, from London hotels to Los Angeles funeral parlours.

Later that first evening, when Vera's other guests had gone to bed, he had reassured her by knocking quietly on her door. She had been waiting for him in a dressing-gown. The sound of the sea breaking on the shore wafted through the open window. There was no light except from the moon. It had been almost romantic. But even then he had been under no illusions about Vera, any more than he was about Victor. He had crept into Vera's boudoir in much the same spirit in which he allowed Victor occasionally to creep into his own bedroom and slide between his covers. The embraces that followed were part of the bargain of hospitality. Whose were preferable? Victor's or Vera's? It was hard to say. He felt like an up-market garage mechanic. Prepared to service any car, of any make. Provided it was expensive.

Now Vera was calling him from the bathroom: 'It looks like another beautiful one, darling.' Annoyed, he ambled back into the bedroom. He didn't reply. The heartiness of her elliptical allusion to the morning irritated him intensely. She herself came through the doorway from the bathroom, wrapped in a towel. Thank God she'd got some make-up on by this stage. She certainly needed it. Half an hour earlier he had been woken by her distinctly garlicky breath in his ear. 'Orlando, hold me,' she had breathed. Steeling himself, he had complied, turning over in bed to embrace her. She had suddenly seemed old, and worse, as she writhed against him, a little bit ridiculous. He had resented her antics as simultaneously both an intrusion into his sleep and an aesthetic aberration. What right had this ageing female to disturb him, to inflict herself on him at will, to force him into close physical contact with her decaying body with its sagging skin. It was bad manners. It was profoundly inconsiderate. She was becoming too demanding altogether. She must be made to realise that Orlando's resources of tenderness were not limitless.

'What are you doing?' she said playfully. 'Admiring yourself again?' Orlando's eyes had strayed back to the mirror, it was true, but her tone angered him.

'At least it doesn't take three hours every morning to make myself presentable.'

'What's that supposed to mean?'

'Nothing. It's just that . . .' He had started the sentence without knowing how he was going to finish it. Instantly he relived the sensation of her capsized breasts pressed against him, her stiff-jointed legs locked around him, her talon-like fingers clawing at his back; he recalled the irksome necessity of rousing something stiff enough to stuff inside her, the simulated motions of passion, the

171

faked ejaculation, her moaned expressions of pleasure, and suddenly he felt vicious, as though he wanted to break something for the sake of smashing it, and went on: ' . . . it's just that I prefer people to grow old gracefully.'

'Look, I'm only fifty-two, for Christ's sake.'

'I'd say that was a conservative estimate.'

She sat down, sniffing. 'Why are you being so horrid to me?'

He had hurt her, as he intended. But it wasn't anything she couldn't take. In the end she was tough, he knew that. It was as well that he should emphasise the limit of their mutual illusions. He watched her contemplating tears, then deciding against, perhaps remembering the mascara she had just applied in the bathroom. In the end they were both realists. Now he said:

'Vera, dear. You know I adore you.' He stood up and walked back out on to the balcony. He felt caged, imprisoned here. Enough was enough. After all, it had been almost a week.

A little later the telephone rang and Vera answered it.

'Hallo. Yes, he's here. Who wants him? Right, I'll give him to you.'

Orlando looked questioningly at her as he reached for the receiver.

'It's a Victor Meer,' she whispered, shrugging her shoulders to signify that she did not recognise the name.

'Victor, how are you?'

'Fine, thank you. And all the better for hearing your voice. Are you enjoying yourself?' The tinge of bitterness could not entirely be eradicated from the question, although the old thing was obviously trying to be reasonable.

'Wonderful.'

'I've missed you, you know.'

'Have you?' said Orlando.

'Yes, very much. I do hope you've been behaving.'

'Like the perfect guest I am, I've slept only with my hostess.'

'For God's sake, Orlando!' said Vera and Victor simultaneously, each unheard by the other. Victor went on resolutely: 'I don't want to hear about it, it's not interesting to me. Look, I was calling to see if you would care to come back soon, stay here another night or two. The thing is, something's come up, a picture which may be to your advantage. A commercial proposition, if you like.'

'The Klimt?' Orlando's interest quickened.

'If you come over I'll tell you about it. But I have to talk to you in person.'

'Well, I'll see. I can't promise.'

'Try and make it this afternoon; it's a matter of urgency. You won't regret it. I'll send a cab for you.'

'I'll think about it.'

'Please, Orlando.'

'We'll talk later, Victor. Goodbye.'

'Who's that?' asked Vera a little peevishly.

'Victor Meer.'

'I know that's his name, but who is he?'

It was shameful, reflected Orlando, that she should be asking such a question. Surely anyone with any cultural pretension at all, anyone who displayed on their bookshelf *The World of Marcel Proust* as some sort of badge of literary awareness, should know the name of Victor Meer. Perhaps after all she was nothing more than a jumped-up singer. Come to think of it, he had never actually seen her reading a book in all the time he had spent with her. Suddenly Vera's ignorance was oppressive. Her house was oppressive. Her guests were oppressive. Yes, it was time to move on. It wasn't good for him to stay too long in one place. And if Victor really did have a proposition for him, perhaps involving the Klimt, then he'd better get back.

The commission on a deal like that would be considerable.

'Victor Meer is a writer. A good writer. That's probably why you haven't heard of him. He's asked me over to stay with him for a few days, and this afternoon I'm going to have to be off.'

She was silent for a while, but reached for a cigarette.

Finally she said simply: 'I suppose he's a fag.'

'I've never really thought about it,' said Orlando, and went down to breakfast.

Oswald never went to Vienna.

He had fully intended to, there was no doubt about that, because the first thing he did when he got into the gallery on Monday morning was call Fortescue's travel agency for a booking on the late-afternoon flight. When the telephone rang again he was expecting it to be the agency confirming his seat. But it wasn't.

'Oswald?' said a precise male voice the other end.

'Yes?'

'I hope you remember me. It's Derek Gilbert here.'

Derek Gilbert. The name meant something, but for a moment he was at a loss to place it. Then it came back to him. My God, Derek Gilbert. He'd lived on the same staircase as the man for two years at Cambridge, seen him practically every day. A clever bastard, Derek. Smug and self-satisfied, he recalled, but undeniably clever. In such a situation it is hard to repress the clichés. 'Of course I remember you. It's been a long time,' Oswald heard himself say.

'Nearly twenty years. I believe the last time we met you were about to get married.'

'That must have been it. And you were about to be posted abroad. Where was it, somewhere like Jakarta?'

'Manila, actually.' That was Derek Gilbert, still as infuriatingly pedantic as he'd been as an undergraduate.

What had he been doing out east? The Foreign Office, of course. Gilbert had become a diplomat. Probably a bloody good one: he'd had all the qualifications. Smug, discreet, intelligent. Buttoned-up.

'Well, it's good to hear you again,' said Oswald encouragingly.

'You must forgive me for ringing you out of the blue like this.' Oswald heard a little clearing of the throat, suddenly a familiar mannerism across the years, a device to gain time for calculation and concise marshalling of thought. 'The point is, something's come up, and I need advice. Specialist advice. So I thought of you.'

'Delighted to help if I can.'

'It's something really rather intriguing that I've come across fortuitously. Something potentially very exciting. A discovery, I think one could say.'

'What is that?'

'It's difficult to talk about it on the telephone. There's a certain amount of documentation I'd like you to see. I don't want to waste your time, but I think you'd find it interesting.'

'What's this all about?'

'I'd like to get your opinion. Could you come over?'

The request was abrupt. For a moment Oswald was too nonplussed to glimpse its underlying steel. 'I don't know whether I can today,' he said cautiously. 'I've got to catch a plane this afternoon.'

'Look, I'm not far away. Just in Bury Street, ten minutes' walk from you.'

Oswald paused. No doubt all that Derek had to show him was some hopeless Rubens copy retrieved from an elderly aunt's attic. But he couldn't on the spur of the moment think of any cogent reason for refusing. And perhaps there was also an element of curiosity. At the very least there would be an oblique pleasure in dashing the hopes of a man whose air of intellectual superiority, Oswald now recalled, had been a frequent irritant at university. 'OK, I'll come at twelve. But I must be away by one, this trip's important.'

The relief was perceptible. Derek gave him the address. 'I'm so grateful,' he said. 'It's something that's been nagging at me for days. I'm sure it won't take you long to put me out of my misery.'

Derek Gilbert answered the door almost as soon as Oswald pressed the bell. His features were immediately familiar. He stood there for a moment, the same slim, neat figure, with the same expression of quizzical self-satisfaction. His hairline had receded slightly, but he had changed very little. Except for one thing. The way he dressed, the way he held himself had altered subtly. He wore an expensive shirt and tie, and flamboyant braces. Not that he was loud or vulgar or anything like that. It was more that the incipient preciousness perceptible in Cambridge had amplified. Was he gay? thought Oswald suddenly. He hadn't been at Cambridge, not noticeably anyway. Whatever he did now, it was doubtless very discreet. 'Nice,' said Oswald meaninglessly as he followed him through the small hall into the sitting-room. It wasn't nice at all, in fact. It was furnished like a dowdy second-class hotel. There was not the slightest evidence of character stamped on this interior. Reproduction Redouté flower prints hung listlessly on the cream-coloured walls. A pair of depressing ochre sofas flanked the empty fireplace. It was a faceless, forgettable flat. It was almost as if it was intended, this facelessness. As if it had been created with the specific aim of not attracting attention.

'It's just a service apartment,' explained Derek. 'I've taken it temporarily, while . . . while one or two things are sorted out.' He was moving about restlessly, with an air of suppressed excitement. 'Look, sit down,' he encouraged. 'I'm sorry if my summons was a trifle peremptory, but . . . well, I think you'll find it worthwhile.'

'I'm sure I will. I'm most intrigued.'

'Scotch?'

'With water, thank you. No ice.'

He measured it meticulously and set it at Oswald's side, fetching a cloth to wipe away a drop of water spilled inadvertently on the table. Neat old Derek. Prissy old Derek. Half dandy, half schoolmaster. But there was also a nervousness, a pent-up anticipation about him as he himself now sat down opposite with a glass in his hand.

'You see, I felt I had to get hold of you. You're the only person I know in the art world. I felt I had to consult somebody who was expert in these matters. Somebody I could speak to informally. Somebody who would know how to follow it up.' He cleared his throat and sipped his own drink. 'Because there may be something quite significant to follow up here. A clue.'

'A clue to what?'

'A clue to the rediscovery of something staggeringly important.' He looked Oswald straight in the eyes, suddenly defiant. 'That's how it seems to me, anyway.'

'What is this thing? A picture?'

'A picture, yes.' He paused, uneasy. 'But I don't want to say anything more about that just yet. What I want you to do is read this and see if you reach the same rather startling conclusion as I did.' He reached across and picked up a wad of photocopied pages of typescript. Of antiquated typescript, tightly meshed across the paper. He patted it possessively, as if still uncertain about handing it over.

Oswald was curious now. 'What is all that, Derek?'

He gave a little self-deprecating laugh. 'Look, forgive my asking, but may I rely on your discretion in all this?

You see, I'm going to show you some classified documents. I've made copies of them, which, strictly speaking, I shouldn't have done.'

Oswald nodded. 'Certainly you may rely on my discretion.'

'I shall destroy them as soon as you've read them.'

'I understand.'

'I have to protect myself.'

'Of course you do.'

'Right, I'll give you the background.' But he paused again, long enough for Oswald to wonder what was worrying the man. He watched as Derek took another mouthful of whisky and swallowed hard. Was it the security risk? Was he merely frightened of making a fool of himself? Or was there something else, something more obscure?

He went on at last: 'Recently, in connection with quite another matter, I've had occasion to consult a variety of wartime files. Intelligence files, I suppose you'd call them. Well, in these files are the records of one or two interrogations conducted by the Allies at the end of the war, in the summer and autumn of 1945. They are interrogations that formed part of the evidence against suspected war criminals. Nothing sensational, you understand. Mostly they were cases that were never followed up because they weren't considered serious enough at the time. So this stuff has mouldered away for years, gathering dust in some store-room of low-grade security material. But on going through it again, I found something of quite extraordinary interest. Something which no one seems to have picked up.

'It's only a detail, really. It comes from the file on a man called Major Heinrich Wenglein, an SS officer who escaped from Germany a little while before the end of hostilities. No steps were ever taken against him, for one reason or another. But the significant thing is the record of a statement made by a young woman called Gerda Helgemann. That's what I've got here, and I want to show it to you. I want you to read it whole, now, and tell me what you think.'

Oswald took the papers that Derek handed to him. He put down his own drink and began to read, there on the depressing ochre sofa in Derek Gilbert's faceless service apartment in Bury Street, St James's.

6

My name is Gerda Helgemann. Yes. I am currently living at a refugee centre south of Vienna. I have been there for five weeks. I was taken there at the beginning of June from another centre for displaced persons in the west of Austria. I think it was near Innsbruck. I want it to be understood clearly that I have made contact with you of my own free will and am giving you this statement voluntarily. I have nothing to gain from it personally. No, the information I shall give you is intended to help you catch a man who is evil, a man who should be brought to justice for the crimes he has committed in the war which has just ended, a man whom I knew well up till three months ago.

I am twenty-two years old. I was born in Lockwitz, five miles south-east of Dresden, on 20 March 1923. I don't remember my father, and my mother died before the war, when I was thirteen. I had two older brothers also, who were both in the Army. They were killed on the eastern front late last year. It was December; they died within three days of each other, you know, but in separate actions because they were in different divisions. Strange, wasn't it, almost a coincidence? Only three days apart. They were older than me, a lot older, and I suppose I was not close to them. We got telegrams, you know, at my aunt's house. I lived with various relations after my mother died, but the last year I was with my aunt, in the southern Dresden suburbs. God knows where she is now, the mean old cow. She ran away. The beginning of that week, perhaps it was the Sunday, she just went. She was scared of the Russians coming. I didn't mind her being scared, we were all scared of the Russians if we thought about it, but she was so bloody hypocritical about it, pretending it was her

181

duty to head off to Augsburg like that to look after a sick friend. She left me behind, alone in the house, didn't she? Oh yes, she claimed she was coming back in a week or so, but who knows whether she would have. Anyway, I stayed, I was happy to, because of Heinrich.

I first met him in November last year. His name was Major Heinrich Wenglein. I was sitting in this café in the old town with a girlfriend. I tell you one thing, we had no shortage of followers. Katya and I, we used to turn a lot of heads; but we were choosy about who we went out with, very choosy. Then this officer came over to our table, very tall and blond and thick-set, and he asked us, cool as you like, if he could join us. He was an arrogant so and so, and I could see Katya liked him. There was this feeling of power about him, you could tell he was used to getting his way. Well, of course, when an SS officer requests your company you have to have a pretty good reason for saying no. He was a self-confident bastard; but I think he was a self-confident bastard before he got into the uniform, it wasn't just the uniform speaking. So he sat down with us and bought us drinks. Anyway, I knew Katya liked him because she slipped off almost immediately to put some more make-up on in the toilet. That was her big mistake. As soon as she'd gone Heinrich leant across to me and said, 'Let's get rid of your friend. Come for a drive with me.' Well, what girl wouldn't have been flattered? I went; we just slipped out before Katya got back. He made me laugh, and he was a good-looking man, no doubt about that.

Yes, all right, we became lovers. I was coming to that, I would have told you anyway, you didn't have to ask. No, I certainly didn't let him the first time. As I say, he was good-looking, he was exciting to be with, and he was a very high-ranking officer. And he liked me, he liked me very much. Every time I said no to him it seemed to hurt him; this look of sadness came into his eyes. In a way I felt proud of having the power to hurt such a powerful man; proud, and a bit alarmed, I suppose. Still, he wanted me so much I gave into him in the end. Quite often he used to pick me up at my aunt's house and take me for dinner or drives in the country. Sometimes he just sent his driver to pick me up and take me to his quarters. We became close. By February, well, we were very close. He told me he loved me. He said he hadn't intended it to happen, he hadn't expected to want to see me more than two or three times. He'd worked his way through a fair number of girls before me. But he found he couldn't get me out of his head. I was different because I was a bit difficult, I stood up to him more than the others. What did I feel? Well, I thought I loved him too, then.

I'll tell you the sort of thing he used to do. You see, I was in the Dresden R.A.D.w.J., that's the Female Reich Labour Service. No, I didn't volunteer, you had to be, there was no choice about it. You had duties, everyone did, you couldn't get out of them. There was a real old hag in charge of my section, Irma Kreuz was her name, and she had a down on me, because she was an ugly old cow herself. Well, one evening, just as I was leaving home for fire-watching duty, Heinrich turned up unexpectedly in his car. I said I was on the way to my shift, and he told me to skip it, to come back with him for the night. *Ja*, that's all very well, I said, but what about the R.A.D.w.J. authorities? I'll write you a letter, he said, don't worry about that, it'll say I commandeered you for special SS work. I don't mind telling you I was shit-scared the next day when bloody Irma started screaming at me. What the hell did I mean by not turning up last night? People were shot for that sort of thing in wartime. If she had anything to do with it, I'd be made an example of. I gave her the letter, and when she read it she just shut up, not a squeak out of her. No one said anything more about it. It was wonderful, really. You see, he had that sort of power and he enjoyed using it.

Yes, he did talk about marriage once or twice. But we were going to wait and see what happened, perhaps till after the war. Heinrich was very optimistic about the future at that stage; nothing would shake his confidence even though we all knew things weren't going well. He told me not to believe all the gloomy stories I heard, he said the important thing was that the Führer was still in charge and the Führer was a man of Destiny, unlike his enemies, so he was bound to triumph in the end. There was a secret plan, he told me; our enemies were arguing amongst themselves, and it was only a matter of time before the alliance against us disintegrated. We would never be defeated. The worst that could happen would be some sort of negotiated peace, which would give us the opportunity to regroup for a final victory later. All that was important for the time being was to hold back the Russians. Once things fell into place, we were going to get married. It wouldn't be long. Do you know, I think that's what would have happened if the war had worked out like he said it was going to. But then came that night, Shrove Tuesday it was, Mardi Gras. It changed everything.

My aunt had gone, as I say; caught the train to Augsburg. I was left alone in the house. The Shrove Tuesday, of course, was a carnival, and we were looking to have some fun. I don't remember that much about the early part of the evening. A lot of people were drunk. And there were crowds of people in the centre of town, swarming everywhere, mostly drunken peasants from Silesia, falling about and lying in the pavements. Bloody refugees. Heinrich and I had a drink in a café, and there was a lot of music and singing. I had my R.A.D.w.J. duties that night. At ten o'clock I was due to report at the Central Railway Station to help receive more refugees. God almighty, didn't we have enough bloody refugees already? But still more poured in, and they all had to be dealt with. Not that there was really any shelter for them, no question of a roof over their heads or anything like that; but they had to be directed to different areas of the town, otherwise the streets would have become impassable. I remember Heinrich looked at me in a special way and said, 'So your aunt's away tonight?' I said yes. 'So your house is free?' Yes. 'We shall spend the night there, then.' It was something we had not done before, and the idea appealed to me. That would teach my aunt to leave me alone, I thought. We would sleep in her bed, just to show her. But what about my R.A.D.w.J. duty? Forget it, he said. That's an order. Exactly like that, he put it. I suppose those words saved my life, because we all know what would have happened if I'd been caught at the Central Station later that evening, don't we? Very few people survived there.

We left the café about 9.30 and Heinrich drove us back to my aunt's house in the southern suburbs. While we were still in the car the first air-raid warning sounded. To tell you the truth, we paid very little attention to those bloody sirens. I remember someone saying that out of 170 alarms we'd had in

Dresden since the war began, only two had led to enemy air raids. And even then not much damage had been done. So those sirens meant almost nothing to us. But quite soon after, we knew this one was going to be different, very different. We had just entered the house and gone upstairs when we heard two or three very loud explosions. 'Scared?' said Heinrich, laughing at me because I flinched when they came. Then a whole lot more followed in quick succession, with amazingly bright flashes of light. Even Heinrich didn't think it was a joke any more. He got up and drew the curtains back; so many buildings seemed to be burning it was like daylight out there. He said, 'My God!' in a voice I'd never heard before, and we both went down to the cellar. We just stayed there. We were both sweating, it was strange; even there the heat seemed intense.

Soon after midnight Heinrich went up to have a look again. He came back to tell me that the whole Altstadt was burning. It seemed the bombing had been concentrated on a fairly small area. Where we were, two kilometres or so from the centre, only a few stray bombs had fallen on our street. Everything else had dropped on the old part of town. It was like the end of the world, he said, not just buildings burning but great sheets of flame engulfing everything in the way, annihilating it. I'd never seen Heinrich shocked before; he looked twisted, kind of unnatural. There was nothing we could do except stay down in the cellar. Then an hour later the second raid came. We couldn't believe it. We heard the drone of a lot more aircraft, followed by more of those terrible explosions. I mean, for God's sake, you can only burn something once; everything was already on fire. But it seemed they wanted to burn us twenty times over, just to make sure. It was mad, more and more bombs, all incendiaries. We stayed huddled in the cellar, waiting to be hit any moment. *Ja*, we spent the night together, but it wasn't the way we'd intended.

In the morning – I suppose it was about eight o'clock – we both went upstairs and had a look outside. We opened the door and stepped into the street. The bombing had stopped, but the centre of the city to the north was just a mass of yellowy-brown smoke. You could smell it everywhere, a sickly, smouldering smell of burning. It made you want to retch. I remember one or two houses in our street were also on fire, but no one was doing anything about it. There were no fire engines left, I suppose. Everyone was in a sort of shock. Shock takes different people in different ways, and with Heinrich he became very nervous and energetic, then every so often he would just stop and say 'God almighty!' Anyway, we came out of the house, felt the heat, and stood for a moment. In the road, about fifty metres from where we were, a lorry was burning. There wasn't much left of it, but it must have been a big van, the sort they use to carry furniture around. I said, look at that, and Heinrich said it must have caught a stray incendiary bomb, a pretty direct hit. If there had been a driver there was no trace of him now in the mangled cab. All that was left was a sort of twisted tracery of bent iron where the cab would have been. But then I looked back, and about a hundred metres behind, just lying there in the road, were two pictures, large ones. Yes, pictures, you know: oil paintings. They must have fallen from the van, been thrown free on impact, I suppose, and avoided the flames. They looked odd there, out of place in the middle of the road. Heinrich went over to them and I followed. One was very badly ripped, the other less so. Heinrich said we should carry them into the house. They weren't that heavy; they hadn't got their frames on them of course. You see he was always mad about art, loved pictures. He told me once he dreamed of having a great collection himself one day. You could tell he felt really strongly about it. Well, we picked them up and we'd just got the second one to the door when it all happened. It was shocking; I mean it really shocked me, this. Well, we were in a state of shock already, of course. We felt we were practically seeing the end of the world; maybe we'd arrived in hell itself, that was what it looked like with that huge inferno just a few streets away, and other fires still burning in our street. But even so what happened now took my breath away.

Suddenly this other man came up. I don't know where he sprang from; perhaps he lived nearby. But we were so engrossed with the picture, we hadn't noticed him approaching. He said to Heinrich, 'What the hell are you doing with that? It's not yours.' His words were slurred, as if he was drunk, but perhaps it was only the shock. Heinrich wheeled round instantly. He had a terrible look in his eyes. He shouted at the man: 'Get out of here!' The man didn't move. He noticed Heinrich's uniform. Normally that should have shut him up, but I think he just saw it as a symbol of the authority which had let him down. He opened his mouth and began a long whining moan about how his house was on fire and where had the emergency services been? He was a bit hysterical. Then I saw Heinrich draw his pistol. He repeated once more in an oddly calm voice: 'Get out.' It was much quieter the second time. Still the man dawdled, whimpering about something. And then Heinrich shot him, just like that. He crumpled up in the gutter. He was dead, you knew at once. Heinrich just put his pistol back in its holster, turned around and pushed me back inside the door with the picture. I was shaking. It was the first time I saw a man killed.

When we got in Heinrich seemed to forget about the whole incident immediately, or at least put it behind him. In a way the shooting seemed to have settled him down, he was no longer on edge the way he had been. He looked at the two canvases with great care, he was totally absorbed by them. It was clear that one of the pictures was damaged pretty much beyond repair. The paint surface was blistered and large areas of the canvas were in shreds. What was it? Some sort of portrait, I think. But it was extraordinary that the second picture was almost unscathed, particularly odd because it was the bigger one of the two. The canvas had come away from its wooden support, but Heinrich took it into the living-room and laid it out. I guess it must have been about one and a half metres high by about two metres wide, something like that. It was beautiful, sort of haunting. Looking at it calmed me down a bit too. It showed two men working on a road. They were peasants, in the costume of another time. Looking back it was odd that I felt so absorbed by that picture, that I was able to stare into it forgetting that the city nearby was in flames, that just outside the front door lay a dead man, and right next to me stood his killer. But it was impressive, it had a sort of power. It took you out of yourself. I can't remember exactly what I said, but I said something; I think I wanted to test my voice because I hadn't spoken since the shooting. I said something like, 'That's good enough for a museum.' He said nothing, but I could tell he was impressed with it too. Very carefully, he started examining the one bit of serious damage the picture had suffered, which was a long rip, pretty much down the centre, separating the one figure from the other. Suddenly he said, 'Yes, that's how it must be!' and very intently he continued the tear to the bottom so that he was left with two pieces of canvas roughly the same size. Then, with some newspaper, he rolled together the two fragments, so that what he had was a portable, tightly packed tube about a metre in length. He taped it up, lifted it, and found it was easy to carry. Then he looked me full in the eyes, and grinned for the first time for a long time. 'My insurance policy,' he said. I didn't immediately understand what he meant, but I was relieved to see him smile.

Heinrich's car was still parked in the road outside. It had a lot of shrapnel in its side and its windscreen had been smashed, I suppose from the direct hit on the lorry carrying the pictures. But Heinrich climbed into it, clearing a way through the broken glass. It was incredible, but the car started up first time. Heinrich told me to wait where I was and he'd be back in an hour or two. He was going to find out what was going on. He told me not to let anyone into the house, and to guard the picture safely.

It was nearly eleven when he got back. I was glad to see him again. But once more he was changed. He looked sick. He said the city was utterly destroyed, that the place was in chaos, that literally tens of thousands had been burned alive. I don't know why, I thought of Katya suddenly. As we'd left the café last night I'd seen her with some soldiers. She'd looked well set for the night, as if she wouldn't have been going home for some time. So she must be dead. He said that you couldn't imagine the destruction, it was hell on earth. The scale of it was dreadful, there was no order yet, no organised rescue work. There would be no counting the bodies, still less identifying them. Apparently there had been some sort of firestorm, a sort of irresistible wind sucking people into the flames. And there were all those bloody refugees, of course, just swilling around the centre of town with nowhere to sleep except the streets. They certainly wouldn't have got into the shelters. They must have died in their thousands. Heinrich

said the strange sickly burning odour we could smell everywhere when we opened the door was something different: it
was human flesh. Bodies were smouldering in every street, on
every pavement. Some had burned at such heat they were
shrivelled, to no more than eighteen inches long. He'd seen a
mother and baby welded together. What he'd just been
through had overwhelmed him. He didn't know how to cope
with it, and that was a new experience for him. He kept taking
swigs of brandy from a hip-flask to steady himself. Well, I
thought about it all for a moment, then it all seemed obvious
to me what was going on, and I said, 'This means the Russians
are coming, doesn't it?' I mean I knew they were only – what?
– seventy miles away. Now they'd bombed the city in preparation for moving in and taking it. They'd be there any moment.
Don't forget, we knew what to expect from the Russians when
they came, we'd all heard the stories. Of course, they raped all
the women, and you could count yourself lucky if that was all
that happened to you; but any German males they took
prisoner they castrated. All that was just round the corner.
We'd seen our city destroyed, burned to the ground. Now they
were coming for the survivors. Normality had gone. Laws
meant nothing. All you could smell was burning flesh.

I said, what now? He said he had come back to collect the
picture from me. Then I said to him – I don't know why, it just
came to me suddenly – 'You're running away, aren't you?' For
a moment he looked at me as if he'd seen a ghost. I suppose he
was horrified that I'd guessed. For a second I thought, 'Oh my
God, he's going to shoot me too.' So I screamed at him: 'Take
me with you! You've got to! Look, we both know it's the end
of everything here, it's probably the end of Germany. If we
get out now, we can escape all this.' He came towards me. I
thought, this is it, he's going to kill me. I just stood my
ground. He came right up to me, and grabbed me. Then he
kissed me, very hard, on the lips.

We set out almost at once in his car. He told me to take a
few warm things in a suitcase. He hadn't got much luggage
himself – just this long canvas bag in which he fitted the
rolled-up picture that we'd rescued from the road. What else
did he have in there? Just a few clothes, I think, and maybe a
couple of other rolled canvases, smaller ones. As I say, he

loved pictures, and I think he once told me that he'd come by one or two other quite valuable things in the course of the war: did he say in Poland? But I'm not sure about that. Anyway, we got going pretty quickly. I didn't look at the dead man still slumped in the gutter as we drove away. The city outskirts were silent. Occasionally you saw the odd civilian stumbling about, shaking their heads in a bemused sort of way. I honestly think the whole population was in shock. And I'll tell you something else. Even when we'd gone forty or fifty kilometres you could still look back and see a pall of smoke rising up out of where Dresden must have been.

'What you have to realise, *liebchen*,' he said to me as he drove, 'is that no one will look for us. As far as the authorities are concerned, if they find we have disappeared they will assume that we are just two unidentified bodies in the ashes. No one will trace us. How many died in Dresden last night? I don't know, but it must have been one hundred thousand, perhaps one hundred and fifty thousand. And they won't identify five thousand of them.' As we headed further away from the horrors, it was extraordinary to see people behaving normally again. We met some traffic, saw a tractor working in the fields. In one village I saw a postman delivering letters. I couldn't believe it. I felt more and more that we were lucky to be alive, and even luckier to be heading south in a fast car, away from it all. The Russians couldn't advance as fast as this car would go. For a while I was almost happy.

Heinrich relaxed a little too. He told me something of his plans. He had friends and relations in Argentina, even some family business interests. Also he had contacts in Zurich. All we had to do was get into Switzerland, he said, and he had papers prepared for that. Once we were in Zurich he'd fix a flight for us to Lisbon. From there we could get a boat to South America without any problem. He spoke of the whole scheme with increasing confidence and optimism. To me it all sounded wonderful, an escape from the most hellish experience I'd ever known to a peaceful and prosperous new life in a continent which was beyond the retribution of our enemies. That was how he put it, and it sounded good. I remember he reached out and took a cigar from the glove compartment of the car. He asked me to light it, which I did. But when I felt the flame on the match in my hand I suddenly felt sick and remembered the smell of burning flesh. But I didn't say anything about it to Heinrich; he seemed to have forgotten it all, put it behind him.

He was strong, Heinrich, you know; he must have driven fairly solidly for the best part of two days. He didn't seem to need rest. We did stop the first night in a wood, not far from Nuremberg, and had a few hours' sleep. But we were away again before first light. I suppose we must have been halted at road checks four or five times, but Heinrich's papers and his uniform carried us through with very little trouble. Very little trouble except once: near Munich we came up against a very jumpy and aggressive guard; you know, at that stage of the war I think a lot of them were drunk, it was the only way for them to get through. Anyway, he said we had no right to enter a new zone. Heinrich shouted at him, screamed. My heart almost stopped as I saw Heinrich's hand move towards the gun in his holster. Thank God, the guard backed down, and Heinrich didn't use the gun. That would have been it if he had. But normally Heinrich's personality was enough to smooth over the difficulties. That and the SS uniform.

It was strange; although I slept a little in the car as he drove, I hadn't had that much more rest than he had, but I felt wide awake, alert, excited by the thought that we were escaping together. I saw an end to our troubles not far away, and I was exhilarated by it all. We skirted Munich, then drove on south-west to Friedrichshaven. We must have reached there about – what? – eleven at night on the Thursday, at the end of our second day's travelling. So it was in the small hours that we drove along the edge of Bodensee. Heinrich suddenly pointed to some lights in the distance, across the lake, little twinkling gleams playing in the water. 'There you are,' he said, 'that's Switzerland.' They couldn't have been more than ten kilometres away; for a moment I couldn't believe they were that close, that our freedom was so near.

I remember it was near a place called Birnau that Heinrich pulled in off the road and hid the car in some bushes. I could hear water lapping not far away. 'What are we going to do?' I asked. 'We're going into Switzerland.' 'How?' 'By boat, my *liebchen*.' 'And what about papers? I have none.' He patted his breast pocket and said, 'That has been taken care of.' I should have realised then that this was unlikely. Maybe he could have had his own false papers prepared, that was no problem, but he couldn't have had anything to cover me as my coming with him was a decision taken on the spur of the moment, an afterthought. But I was under his power. He had brought me this far, and I had submitted to his will. I thought I was also submitting to his protection, didn't I? Subconsciously I suppose I expected him to take care of everything now, I didn't have to worry. All through the journey, and particularly now it seemed to be reaching its climax, I had felt a little light-headed.

He took my small suitcase out of the boot of the car, together with his own long bag. He found his parcel of civilian clothes and changed into them, then he tied up his uniform in the same parcel and weighted it with stones. The clothes he put on were anonymous, a jacket and tie and overcoat. I remember noticing that the coat had a maker's name sewn in: it was a Zurich tailor. His planning had been amazingly thorough. Then he told me to follow him and led the way down by a hidden path to the water's edge. 'How do you know the way?' I asked him. He told me he had an uncle with a summer-house very near by. He had often spent his holidays there as a boy and knew the place well. Sure enough, when we reached the shore there was a small boat-house. Heinrich forced the door and came out with a rowing boat. He loaded it with the bags and the parcel of clothes. Then he held it steady for me as I climbed in.

It was cold, of course, but not as cold as it can be in February. I mean it wasn't actually freezing. I don't like to think what would have happened if it had been. We cast off and I thought, that's my last contact with German soil, maybe for ever. I wasn't sorry. 'How long will it take?' I asked. I was huddled in the stern. 'What, to row to Switzerland? Not long, an hour, perhaps an hour and a half.' He didn't speak again for a long interval. He was pulling single-mindedly at the oars, concentrating, scowling. Gradually the little lights on the other coast were growing bigger. It was still very dark. Suddenly he stopped. 'This'll do,' he said. Everything was very quiet, all you heard was the lapping of the water. 'What d'you mean?' 'This'll do as a place to get rid of that parcel with my uniform in it. Throw it into the lake, will you?' I took it in my hand – it was heavy with the stones – and I half got up to throw it. As I moved I was aware of him moving too. The boat wobbled and lurched. The next thing I knew I was in the water. He had pushed me, and pushed me hard. Of course I cried out, but not much: the shock of the cold of the lake water almost killed me. And the bastard just pulled away quickly. It was the last I saw of him. He left me to die. He had decided – I don't know whether he'd decided it now or he'd known all along – that I was surplus to his requirements, a piece of excess baggage to be jettisoned like his parcel of uniform. I'd seen him kill a man in cold blood in our street in Dresden. Now he had tried to kill me.

It was my anger that kept me alive, you know. I was furious. I was not going to allow this bastard to get what he wanted, I wasn't going to die. Of course it helped that the night was a little milder than it had been lately. That and the fact that I'm an excellent swimmer. I mean, I won all the prizes at school, no one could touch me. So I kept moving, fighting through the water towards the shore. There were moments when I all but lost consciousness, but I kept seeing those lights, getting larger and larger. I think he'd miscalculated: looking back, I think he threw me out much nearer to the Swiss coast than he'd intended. Suddenly I was there, stumbling out of the water on to a bank of shingle. I couldn't tell you how long I'd been in that lake. I fell to the ground exhausted, suffering from exposure, shaking, but relieved; my God, I was happy just to be alive. And I was in Switzerland, I was in a foreign country. It was the first time I ever left Germany.

The rest is a strange story, but not so relevant to the question of Heinrich Wenglein. So far as I know he caught his plane in Zurich under his new identity, probably reached Lisbon, then took the boat to Argentina. That was where he said he had relations. Yes, Buenos Aires, that's what he said. He was such a lucky bastard, I'm sure he made it. Me, I was found by kind people, Swiss people, who took me in and looked after me. I was ill for two weeks, but they nursed me through it. They didn't ask questions, but they gave me work on their farm. I worked hard for them, I loved them. They were the kindest people I ever met. If I could, I'd still be with them now. But then it all finished: at the beginning of May they told me that the war was over, that Germany was beaten. I was happy, but it was the final defeat which did me in. You see, the Swiss authorities suddenly tightened up, tried to weed out all illegal refugees crossing the border at the end of hostilities. They got me, found I had no papers, and arrested me. I said I was Austrian, I don't know why. I thought it might be better in Austria than in Germany now we had been defeated. So they took me to the Austrian border in a van and bundled me across with nine or ten others. None of us had any papers, so we were not people any more; we had officially lost our identities. I didn't know what was going to happen to me. I ended up in this displaced persons camp.

I just felt numb at the end of it all. There is very little future for me, not that I can see. I wouldn't want to go back to Dresden, not now, even if I could. I don't really care any more, I've got nothing left. But one thing has become clearer and clearer to me over the past months, and I won't give in until I see something done about it: what Heinrich Wenglein did was a crime, and if you claim you come here as liberators, if you claim you stand for justice, then you must pursue this criminal, hunt him down. He killed at least one man, in our street in Dresden, and probably he murdered a lot more. And then he tried to kill me. That is why I am giving you this statement, now, at the first opportunity. It is your duty to find him and to punish him.

Interrogator's note: In my judgment Gerda Helgemann is honest and her story is credible. However, Wenglein's case cannot be classed as a priority. Apart from the testimony of this woman, there is an absence of corroborative evidence against him. On top of that the likelihood of apprehending him is small, now that he has apparently escaped to South America. Hold on file.

Oswald laid the last page of Gerda Helgemann's statement down on the ochre-coloured sofa next to him. He felt sick, sick with apprehension and excitement. Sick because of what he'd read; and sick because of something else, something that he couldn't quite identify, some deep-seated but as yet formless unease which the unfolding of the story had disturbed within him.

Derek said at once: 'What do you think?' His hand was tightly gripping the arm of the sofa where he sat.

'I think that's one of the most extraordinary documents I've ever read.' Oswald could feel his own heart beating now.

'But am I right?' Derek demanded.

'Right about what?'

'Right about the picture they found?'

'Well, I suppose . . .' Oswald began, but he was interrupted by Derek continuing, insistently:

'The moment I read that girl's statement I felt sure she was describing a specific picture. It sounded familiar somehow, familiar in the context of Dresden. Then it came to me: it's something that was lost from the museum in the bombing. Look, I'm absolutely not an art historian, but I know a little bit about Courbet. He's an artist I've always been interested in. This is "The Stonebreakers", isn't it? I'm right, aren't I?'

Of course, he was right. There could be no mistaking what Helgemann and Wenglein had come across on that horrendous morning of 14 February 1945 when they opened the door of her house and stared at the smouldering debris of the street before them, smelled the horrendous desolation of Dresden. The canvas that they had miraculously picked up from the roadway, after it had been thrown clear from the wreck of the furniture van, that canvas could only be one thing. God knew how the picture had come to be lying there then. Oswald had a dim recollection that the lorries containing the cache of museum art treasures had been parked overnight on Bruhl'sche Terrasse. That's where they had last been recorded, anyway. But someone must have moved one of them. A thief? A hero? A madman? Who could tell? But the result was that Major Heinrich Wenglein had taken possession of 'The Stonebreakers'. Then he'd rolled it up carefully. Then he'd put it in his car and fled with it, far, far away. Far from Dresden. Far from Germany. Far from the war itself.

'Yes, I think you're right,' said Oswald. 'It must be "The Stonebreakers" .' He couldn't deny it. His closely guarded secret was out. Someone else knew about 'The Stonebreakers'. Someone else had independently come into the same knowledge. Clever, smug Derek Gilbert.

Derek smiled. He stood up, visibly relaxed. For a moment he looked like a dog whose trick has met with acclaim beyond expectation. 'I'm pleased I haven't wasted your time, then,' he said. 'I was so curious, you see. Having read that statement, the question of what the picture was began to obsess me. I felt pretty sure, but I had to check with someone who would know. So I thought of you.'

'I'm very glad you did.' Oswald paused, choosing his words carefully. 'The strange thing is, I'd already been alerted to the possibility that "The Stonebreakers" had in fact survived the firestorm.'

'Really? How?'

'It seemed it was being discreetly offered on the art market. But it was proving impossible to discover its present whereabouts.'

'So this may help?'

'I'm sure it will. It certainly puts everything in a new perspective.'

'What should be done now?'

'That depends.' The dust still hadn't settled. Oswald still couldn't clearly make out the lie of the new landscape. He added cautiously: 'I suppose one of the crucial questions is what happened to Wenglein after all this? Do we know anything?'

'A little. I'll tell you all I know, anyway. It seems he got to Argentina and built himself a fairly successful business career in Buenos Aires. And he died there earlier this year. There's a widow. But don't ask me for addresses or telephone numbers, please, because I simply don't have them. His file didn't rate a very high priority.'

At that moment a number of realisations hit Oswald. First, that he wouldn't be going to Vienna that afternoon. The trip to Austria would be pointless now. Pointless because Grunwald was not, after all, a link in the chain. Pointless because the picture had evidently never been to Russia, never been plundered by some acquisitive Soviet and spirited home to Moscow. Pointless because the picture was in Argentina. It was part of the estate of a fugitive SS major named Wenglein who had arrived there with it in his luggage in 1945. Somehow it had recently been offered to Bernard Tumbrill. Bernard must have been in South America just before he died. Oswald realised, too, that he had been very, very lucky. If eagle-eyed Derek hadn't spotted the significance of Gerda Helgemann's story, if he hadn't chosen Oswald to check his hunch out with, then Oswald would have been about to depart on the mother and father of all wild-goose chases.

And yet the unease remained.

'Will you leave it all with me now, Derek?' he said. 'I can try to follow up one or two lines of enquiry.'

'Of course. But you must promise to let me know how you get on. I'm only happy that my instinct about the picture's identity has been confirmed by you. No more sleepless nights.'

'And you won't say anything about this to anyone else,

will you? At this stage the fewer people who have an inkling the better.'

Derek looked pained. 'My dear chap, I thought I had explained. I'm hardly likely to talk to anyone else about it. I'm not in the habit of publicising the contents of classified documents. As I say, I only made an exception with you in order to satisfy my own insistent curiosity. If you quote me as your source of information, I shall deny everything. We must agree a mutual pledge of silence.'

Both of them laughed then. It was all so absurd. And all so momentous. And just below the surface there was something else, something niggling, something that gave Oswald unease.

'I think a small toast to Gerda Helgemann is in order,' suggested Derek.

Gerda Helgemann. It was then, as Derek mixed them both one more celebratory drink, that it began to seep through to him, that he began to understand what it was that had disturbed him about Gerda Helgemann's story, that he began dimly to recognise what ghosts her narrative in all its vividness had aroused. He saw Dresden again, Dresden in its agony. He saw a woman in Dresden. The woman was alone, and she was unhappy. Images grew confused. He saw the bombs falling, he smelt the burning, heard people screaming. Was it Gerda, crouched in her basement? Was it Saskia? He shivered.

When Derek, with a little fastidious shuffle, handed him his whisky and water, Oswald took it and said suddenly: 'Why did we bomb Dresden?'

The abruptness of the question made Derek look back at him, eyebrows raised a fraction. Perhaps he was checking whether it was serious. 'There were good strategic reasons at the time, I believe,' he said firmly.

'What strategic reasons?'

'I've no doubt it was important as a gesture of solidarity

with the Russians, being seen to be doing something to help them on the Eastern Front. And it was intended to lower German morale.'

'But it didn't really shorten the war.'

'Who can say? You can't ever compute it.' Derek drummed his fingers thoughtfully on his glass and frowned. 'But I'd have thought it was arguable that the lives lost in Dresden were to a certain extent counterbalanced by the Allied lives saved due to diminished German resistance.'

'Civilian lives lost.'

'Civilian lives lost, that's true.' Derek shrugged.

'We must have known, mustn't we, of the number of civilians packed into Dresden that night, what with all the refugees from the East?'

'Both sides accepted that civilian targets were legitimate in the last war. Look at the Blitz. Sometimes you can only defeat an enemy by fighting him with his own weapons.' It was the old Derek, the undergraduate Derek, relentlessly marshalling points to support his argument. Oswald felt a surge of his old impatience with him, spiced now with a new bitterness. For Derek, Dresden was just an abstract fact of history, to be justified or shrugged away. His arrogance bordered on the callous.

'More civilians died in that one night in Dresden than in the whole war in Britain,' said Oswald.

'So we did it better than them. That's why we won the war.'

Oswald was silent for a time. Soon afterwards he said he must go. On the doorstep Derek asked: 'So what will you do now?'

He replied immediately, as if he'd known it all along: 'I'll have to get down to Buenos Aires as soon as possible.'

The first thing Oswald did when he got back to the gallery

was cancel his ticket to Vienna that afternoon. Then he telephoned Mrs Tumbrill. He imagined her, standing amongst the mayhem of her household, picking up the receiver with the mixture of ineptitude and petulance that had characterised her manner on their first meeting. He felt sorry for her.

'It's coming along slowly. It's a hell of a mess still,' she told him in answer to his polite preliminary enquiry about her clearing-up operation in the flat. 'You don't know anyone who might want to buy Bernie's shell collection, do you?'

'I didn't know he collected shells.'

'Well, he did. Bloody boxfuls of them. They're a bloody nuisance, spilling everywhere. I suppose I could just chuck them out.'

'Perhaps you should show them to an expert first.'

'An expert? Such as?'

He had to admit he knew of no one who could help her. He promised to look into the matter on her behalf. Then he asked:

'I don't suppose you have come across any more information about Bernard's most recent travels? It would be so helpful to me, if you could just think over everything one more time.'

Of course it was a forlorn hope. But he had to check again. Bernard's movements, after all, held the key to everything.

'Hold on,' she said abruptly, 'I've got something here, I think it arrived yesterday.'

He held his breath as he heard the noise of papers being shuffled.

'Yes,' she continued after a moment, 'this might be something. It's his credit card statement. They don't let up, do they, the bastards? God knows where the money's coming from to pay it. Yes, here we are.'

'Are there any hotel bills, for instance? Any from South America, perhaps?'

'They use such bloody small print,' he heard her complaining. 'Hang on, I'll just fetch my glasses.' There was a lengthy pause. 'Yes, you're in luck. On 28 August he was charged 368 dollars by – what's this? – the Hotel Excelsior, Buenos Aires. That's South America, isn't it?'

'It certainly is,' he said. He could have kissed her.

Later that afternoon, Leonard summoned him to a meeting. He'd done a lot of thinking in the meantime, reached a provisional plan. He knew he would have to tread carefully if he was to get what he wanted. But he was prepared.

Magnus and Eugene were also there. They were frowning, looking serious.

Leonard announced: 'There have been some developments. And not all good, as such.'

'Developments,' echoed Magnus, nodding authoritatively.

'But first,' said Leonard, assuming a smile of sickly solicitude, 'Eugene, will you tell us how Lady Lindisfarne is today?'

'Considerably better in spirits, thank you. On the mend, in fact.'

'Did you communicate to her the whole firm's best wishes for a speedy recovery?'

'I did indeed. She was most appreciative.'

Oswald found the whole exchange nauseating. 'Is she any nearer to being prised away from her Corot?' he asked brutally. Leonard and Magnus looked shocked. And guilty. He'd clearly expressed exactly what they were both thinking.

'I really think this is hardly the moment,' sniffed Eugene.

'No, no, of course not. The last thing on our minds at this time,' Leonard assured him.

'The last thing,' agreed Magnus.

'But on to business,' continued Leonard. 'Bad news from Salzman, I'm afraid. He doesn't like the Murillo.'

'Oh dear.' Secretly Oswald was pleased. It meant that Salzman's appetite was still unsatisfied. He would still be in the market for a great Courbet. And Oswald would have the not altogether unpleasurable task of telling the Duke of Santa Ponsa that he was not, after all, the richer by three million dollars.

'And a strange fax in from Osaka. Nikohito and Takomara seem very anxious for us to find them pictures. So far so good. But they also appear convinced that we can negotiate them things from museums. They're even talking about buying from the National Gallery. I can't think where they got that idea from.' He stared around at his three colleagues with annoyance.

Oswald was thinking fast. Christ, 'The Stonebreakers' with its major museum provenance would blow their minds. They would kill for it. He said: 'Well, at least they're keen to buy. And to buy through us. We'll just have to tell them that the particular examples they're asking about aren't available for the time being. But we're on the track of other pictures of similar importance.'

'What? What pictures, Oswald?'

For a moment the image of 'The Stonebreakers' came to him so vividly that he was convinced the others must be seeing it too. He suppressed it. He said quietly: 'I think I'm on to something. Something pretty big.'

Everyone sat up and looked at him. He knew he mustn't give too much away. But equally he had to whet their appetites.

'What have you found?'

'I haven't found it yet. But I'm on the track of it. I've

been tipped off about it, unofficially. By an old museum contact.' He had to improvise here, but give the story plausibility. Tantalise them by making it clear that it was information to which he alone could be privy, by virtue of his previous job. 'There's a particular picture in South America which is just about to become available. It went out there some time ago when the British owners emigrated. It should never have been allowed to go, but export controls were laxer in those days. Now there's been a death in the family. They'd listen to offers.'

'Is it a British picture?'

'No. A French one. Nineteenth-century. Really important. But you'll have to forgive me, I can't say any more at this moment. It was one of the conditions laid down when I got the information. I gave my word to my source to keep the thing utterly discreet.'

'You can't tell us the artist, as such?' Leonard was dismayed. But Oswald could tell he was hooked from the excited way he was drumming his fingers on the desk.

'I'm so sorry, but not yet. Later, of course, if and when we get to the point of making an offer. But if it comes to anything it'll be worth it, I can assure you.'

'So what do we do now?' asked Magnus.

Oswald grasped the nettle. 'I'm going to have to fly out there. To Buenos Aires, as soon as possible. We don't want anyone else cutting in.'

'How long will it take?' Leonard was looking steely again. But he was using the future rather than the conditional tense.

'At least a week. Possibly even two. But I wouldn't propose it unless I thought it was potentially extremely worthwhile.'

'Could you arrange for photographs as soon as you know? So that we'd have something to show our clients?'

'I'd do my best, of course.'

'Will it be fiendishly expensive?' persisted Magnus.

'Not for what it is,' said Oswald firmly. Now for it. Now for the news that would really knock them sideways. 'If we buy it, it's a picture we could ask eight or ten million pounds for. And get it, without any trouble. I don't know what it's going to cost, but I've been told it won't be that expensive. The owners are a little out of touch. What I'll need is readily available cash, to be wired to me in Argentina as and when I need it. Even if it costs three or four million, it's still going to show us a fantastic profit.'

Everyone sat there calculating. Not least Oswald. The plan was designed to benefit him most of all. He'd been looking at Bernard's letter again, the one in which he'd alerted him to the availability of 'The Stonebreakers'. It won't be expensive, he'd said. Whatever the picture on offer, a million pounds would have struck Bernard as expensive. He wouldn't have phrased it like that if the price had been in seven figures. He knew the way Bernard's mind worked. No, the chances were that the picture was going to be buyable at a fraction of its true value. Say five hundred thousand pounds. But Oswald would make sure then that it cost Fortescue's 3.5 million. Sitting in Argentina, he'd have control over the situation. And the three million extra would go straight into Oswald's pocket. After all, he would have earned it. Dead right he would. And Fortescue's would still make a few million selling the thing on, so everyone would be happy. But Oswald would be free. He'd have enough to cut loose.

'Well, of course, we couldn't spend that sort of money without having a very clear idea of what the picture was, and its condition. We've got a line of credit that could be extended to that sort of figure, but it would have to be something utterly exceptional to warrant it, as such.' Leonard spoke carefully. But you could tell he was seduced. Seduced by the difference between four and eight million pounds.

'It is. Utterly exceptional,' Oswald assured him. 'It's something that both Salzman and the Japanese will have to have. I can say that without hesitation.'

'You'd better get on out there, then.' Leonard was finally decisive. 'But try and tie something up as soon as possible. We don't want to keep our buyers waiting a day longer than necessary.'

'Roger Fry,' declared Victor, 'was one of the most single-minded bores of the century. He had this obsessional regard for form over content, really quite staggering. Morgan Forster once told me of the occasion when Fry showed him a love-letter of Virginia Woolf's. Apparently it described an act of congress in the most gripping and obscene detail, but Fry had honestly never read it, although he'd had it in his possession for several months and studied it nearly every day. No, he kept it and showed it to his friends as an example of the most astoundingly beautiful calligraphy he had ever seen.'

Orlando laughed dutifully. He remembered once being described himself as the triumph of form over content. It had niggled him, that description, because it was unfair and malicious. Orlando was not stupid; but like many physically attractive people he was sensitive about his intellectual image.

'Anyway, it's good to have you back,' said Victor fondly, patting Orlando's beautifully bronzed hand as it lay on the table next to him. 'Champagne?'

'Why not?' The restaurant was an excellent one, arguably the best in Cannes. In many ways it was pleasant to rediscover the company of Victor after a week or more of Vera's friends. The waiter arrived and filled their glasses.

'Your very good health,' said Victor.

'Yours too. And to good business.'

'Ah, yes. Business.' Victor nodded reflectively. 'We must talk.'

'That's what I'm here for.'

'It's not the only reason, I hope.' Victor's pleading tone was tiresome, but Orlando said quickly:

'No, darling, of course not. It's good to be back. But tell me your proposition. It's the Klimt, isn't it?'

'No, not actually the Klimt. Another picture. Something potentially even more important.'

'Really? Tell me more.' Orlando sat up straighter and concentrated. As summer approached its end his resources were running dangerously low. The coffers needed replenishing. Any money-making proposition, from whatever source, must be considered carefully. Being languid was an expensive enterprise, and he felt the need to galvanise himself into one of his periodic bouts of dynamism. The sojourn with Vera had proved ultimately unsatisfactory, what with the arrant Hollywood philistinism and Vera's persistent physical demands. A further period with Victor was not necessarily the answer, although the conversation was more intelligent. No, he must make a move shortly, probably back to London where there were one or two deals that he might be able to set in motion in the expectation of some sort of introductory commission. Meanwhile anything that Victor could now put his way would be extremely welcome, and something even more remunerative than the Klimt was certainly worth hearing about.

'An old friend made contact with me at the weekend, a man whose sources of information about such things are excellent. He told me, *inter alia*, that one or two rather good pictures are about to become available. One is an outstandingly good Courbet, although my source could not specify precisely which one. Apparently it's something that has been missing for a number of years.'

'Where's this collection?'

'In Argentina. Buenos Aires. A deceased estate, I believe.'

'Come on, Victor. Are you sure? One thing I do know is that there are an awful lot of fakes in South America, particularly in Argentina. It's a long way to go on a wild-goose chase.'

'My source was very sure. He's generally right.'

'Who is this mysterious source of yours?'

'How can I put it? He's an old Intelligence friend. Past experience indicates that he's reliable.'

'So your idea is that I should head off down to Buenos Aires?'

'That's it.'

'Christ, Buenos Aires!'

'Well, don't if you don't want to. But it seems such a good opportunity. It looks as though this really is a top Courbet, not one of those unspeakably boring rocky landscapes which the salerooms specialise in and which often aren't by the artist anyway. No, this is a great one. Now what's a top Courbet worth? At least a couple of million pounds; probably quite a lot more.'

'And what will it cost?'

'I'm told that it needn't be expensive. The owner's not particularly demanding.'

'Well, I'd need finance.'

'That's what I wanted to talk to you about. If you get the chance to buy it and the thing's worthwhile, I'll put up the cash. It could be our joint venture. You and me.'

'That's sweet of you. So we'd go fifty-fifty on the profit?'

'That's my idea of a joint venture, yes.'

Orlando considered the scheme. Buenos Aires was a long way away, and there was no guarantee that this was going to lead to anything. The Argentinians he had come across in fifteen years' seasoned consorting with international café society had struck him as shifty and unreliable, not the perfect people to do business with. He rather hankered after London again for a few weeks: he had been invited to a couple of parties that might be fun. But if he made the effort and actually got down to South America, the potential rewards were indeed on the face of it substantial. He'd never been to Buenos Aires before, but he had heard that it was possible to enjoy yourself in that city. He knew one or two rich polo players there who would no doubt offer him entertainment. Perhaps he should go. London could wait two or three weeks. Better to delay one's return there if it meant coming back later as the joint owner of a multi-million-pound picture. Missing the odd party would be a small price to pay.

'I don't know,' he said. 'It's tempting, of course. But Vera's expecting me back – I've rather interrupted my stay with her.'

Victor looked pained. 'I think you ought to see your way clear to getting down there at once. Surely this is more important than prolonging your holiday with that woman.'

Was Victor broaching this plan simply to extricate him from Vera's clutches? Jealous old thing. It was a situation Orlando knew how to exploit for the maximum return.

'It's a difficult decision. Vera's pressing me to come back.'

'Of course, I'll meet your expenses,' added Victor. 'Air fare, hotel, that sort of thing. It'll be my speculation. You really can't lose, you know. You could catch the plane to London in the morning, then there's a flight out to Buenos Aires tomorrow evening.'

'You have been doing your homework.'

'I've always been thorough where speculation's involved. That's why I tend to be rather good at it.'

'What do I do when I get there? Who are the owners of this picture?'

'I understand they're Germans, called Wenglein. He's just died. There are heirs – a widow, anyway. You'll find them; with your charm, Orlando, it won't be difficult.'

'I'll have to travel business class, OK?'

'But of course,' said Victor. 'This is a business venture.'

'My God! You!' Daphne was halfway through the front door and stood staring at him, transfixed. It was a quarter past midnight and Oswald had walked into the hall to greet her on hearing a key in the lock.

'I didn't go to Austria after all,' he explained. 'Something came up. Sorry to give you a shock.'

She was flushed, and there was a wild look in her eyes; she seemed not so much angry as knocked off balance by seeing him. 'No, no . . . I just didn't expect you.'

She brushed his cheek with her lips, an unfamiliar act, this, indicating she had momentarily forgotten herself. He smelt a mixture of alcohol and scent, and felt something. What was it? A bitterness, perhaps. An oblique sense of exclusion. This was wine drunk from bottles he had not shared; this was scent worn with no thought of pleasing him.

'Anyway, you had a good time? How were the Alstons?'

'The Alstons were fine.' She was still preoccupied; and there was an unfamiliar air of excitement about her.

'How did you get there? I saw the car was still parked outside when I arrived back, but you'd gone.'

'I took a taxi. Then I got a lift back with a couple of

other guests. Look, I'd better nip out and tell them all is well. We . . . we couldn't understand why the light was on. They're waiting to see that everything's OK.'

'I'll go.'

'No, I'll do it.' There was a sharper edge to her voice.

She moved quickly out of the front door again, her jacket half unbuttoned and a scarf in her hand. Moments later he heard a car drawing away. When she came in again she was no longer discomposed, only irritated.

'You should have telephoned,' she said, removing her coat and flinging it on to a chair. Objectively he could see she was attractive. But why didn't she attract him? All he felt with her was a snarled-up, suffocating sensation in the pit of his stomach, which made him want to flail his arms, bite something, break free.

'Why?'

'You should have telephoned to say you were coming back tonight after all. It was inconsiderate of you.'

'What difference would it have made?'

She paused before answering. 'You could have come to the Alstons' with me.'

'You know I didn't want to.' He decided not to re-open old wounds. 'And I had some work to catch up on. Anyway, I'm glad you had a good time.'

She grunted and walked off into the kitchen. He followed her.

'Actually,' he continued, 'I may be off on a rather longer trip in a day or two. It could be for a couple of weeks or so. So I'll be out of your hair.'

'Where are you going to?'

'South America. Argentina, in fact. But it's secret. I mean, it's the most extraordinary thing: I've tracked down something quite exceptionally important, and I've got to go there to try and buy it. The whole enterprise depends on eliminating all possible competition, so I have to keep this trip quiet. The fewer people who know about it the better.'

Daphne switched the light off in the kitchen and pushed past him upstairs.

'Sounds to me as if you're going through some sort of mid-life crisis,' she said. 'And I'm going to bed.'

7

Victor Meer drove Orlando to Nice airport that morning to catch the lunchtime flight to London. Their farewells were brief, because Victor knew that Orlando did not like public displays of emotion, and, having won the major victory embodied in Orlando's departure, he was prepared to yield to him this smaller concession. Only once, just before passport control and the final separation, did he take hold of Orlando's arm a second or two longer than was necessary and apply pressure that might have been a degree too strong. But the moment passed and the boy was gone, and that after all was what mattered. On the journey back to the villa he felt less uneasy in spirit. He was not yet calm, no. There had been too much emotional upheaval in the past few weeks. Most immediately there had been the quarrel with Orlando, of course. But even more insidious had been all this other dreadful business. He'd had no real peace since the arrival of that letter, that letter which had churned up so many dormant memories and fears, revived so many ghosts. There had been comings and goings, telephone calls, unwanted visits from discreet men in suits. And still it wasn't over. But he was sufficiently relieved when he returned home to call quite merrily to Alphonsina for coffee, and, when he had it, to retreat to his desk in the study without being afflicted by either the deadening depression or the alarming procession of ghosts from the past which solitude had alternately induced in recent days. Now he could give his mind to his writing again, surrender to that absorption which had eluded him as long as he was distracted by anxiety. Perhaps he might even achieve some sort of relief by going to meet the ghosts head on, by beginning today a dispassionate account of them for his memoirs. Dispassionate, remember. And honest. And complete. Nothing less would do.

As an art historian, Victor had evolved a rigorous and exacting methodology, a profoundly analytical approach whose inflexibility might have provoked ridicule from jealous colleagues had there not been a grudging acknowledgment that Victor also possessed an exceedingly good eye for a picture. Victor pulled himself up: what did people mean by a good eye? It was, he supposed, an instinctive discrimination as to quality and authenticity in a work of art; it depended upon a brilliantly retentive visual memory, and it implied a flair for attribution, that conjuring trick which could turn at a stroke an anonymous canvas into the plausible creation of a known artist. An eye enabled you to deal with the obvious, the immediate questions about any picture; first, who painted it, and second, was it well painted? But these, in Victor's view, were only the preliminaries, these were what he called the auction-house concerns, the price determinants. For an art historian they were only part of the story, and perhaps the less interesting part. Mere connoisseurship was not enough: you became dissatisfied with its aesthetic pyrotechnics, its showing off, its dangerously unquantifiable, intuitive element; you questioned its viability as the basis for a serious academic discipline. What you needed was a more solid framework for scholarship; and this was provided by attempting to answer not by whom? or how good? but simply why?

Why? Why had it been painted? How exactly had it come to assume the precise form in which the artist gave it to us? These were the issues which his method aimed to address, and his method involved the intricate and painstaking assembly and analysis of as many factors as possible that might have had a bearing on the picture – its subject and treatment, its date of execution, its size, its every physical feature. These factors were myriad: the models used, and the artist's relationship to them; his literary, and in some cases his musical tastes; his religious background; the artistic influences at play upon him, the precedent pictures from which he might have borrowed, intentionally or unconsciously; his preference for certain colours or surfaces, and the availability to him of such things; his physical health, even his diet; his sexual preferences, his love-life; everything was minutely considered and dissected.

Initially Victor wrote novels as an extension of this curiosity. His aim was still to lay bare springs of action, strip them down and examine their mechanism, but now he was dealing with a more general range of human behaviour rather than the specific activity of painting pictures. Establishing motive was his obsession, and in his early books he did it meticulously; on this score they were both prized and criticised. Some people found his tortuous harping on at the question of why characters took such and such an action excessively fastidious; others were fascinated by it, marvelling at the diligence, the agglomeration of detail deftly handled and perceptively marshalled. No one doubted the considerable intelligence at work behind it; and even Victor's critics could not withhold their appreciation of his unfailingly beautiful prose style.

But gradually he had shed this extreme stringency of approach. His later novels were not marked by quite such a rigorous obsession. A change of emphasis began which crystallised in the writing of his latest, and possibly last, literary venture, these vexatious but coronational memoirs. A suspicion had developed into a certainty: analysis of motive, no matter how thorough, was on its own not enough. In any human action you could not account for everything. There remained something indefinable, something wild, the joker in the pack. You simply could not plumb the full depths of the well underlying such complex phenomena as falling in love, or the creative act. The lunatic, the lover and the poet were of imagination all compact: there was a madness, an irrationality present in man's most significant activities. You could identify sexual hang-ups, childhood traumas, environmental pressures; you could trace unhappy marriages, passionate friendships, sources of resentment. But you could never lay bare everything. There was in human actions an infuriating element of illogicality, a tiny blip of unpredictability, an innate cussedness, that defied analysis. And because it defied analysis it exerted a fascination increasingly evident in his later fiction.

The process of writing his memoirs was confirming this direction. Yes, he had determined to be mercilessly honest, to give no one the benefit of the doubt, least of all himself. Yet the discipline of establishing with complete candour the motives behind the crucial actions in the life of the person he knew best in the world, himself, had defeated him. With autobiography you had by definition all the available data about your subject. And yet he found that he had done certain things for which he could not with complete satisfaction account. Superficially he could justify them, but that was something different. No, he could not explain them. He had done certain things for reasons that would perhaps remain mysterious simply because they were too deep within him to be exhumed. The moment had now come to probe one of these actions from the past, to examine it again to see if he could make any more sense of it. To see if its reappraisal could bring some relief to his present anxieties.

Boris. Boris Venetsianov. Almost twenty years had passed after their separation that night in the Soviet Sector before he saw Boris again. It must have been in 1964 or 1965, because Victor was still living in London, and his second novel had recently come out and had been well received by the critics. On the strength of these kind notices, and encouraged by healthy sales, he had just quit academic life: he was no longer a full-time art historian with a literary hobby, but a full-time novelist occasionally asked to review exhibitions by the Sunday newspapers. It was a step that alternately gave him the intensest pleasure and frightened the life out of him. He relished the novelty of the lionising but he feared its evanescence, could not quite believe that the books which had given him such private personal satisfaction to write could also please a wider circle of other people. But apparently they did. As he sat down to breakfast in his flat one winter's morning, his post brought him invitations to address a literary circle in Poole, Dorset; to be one of the guests of honour at a literary luncheon held by a provincial daily newspaper; and to attend a reception at the Soviet Embassy.

He did not go to Dorset; he travelled north in a draughty railway carriage for the lunch and was mildly depressed by the experience; and out of curiosity he accepted the invitation to the Soviet Embassy. He took a taxi to Palace Gate Gardens, that line of stately mansions on the edge of Kensington Gardens commonly known as Millionaire's Row, a pleasingly inappropriate location for the emissaries of the People's Republics. It was a chilling January evening, and the granite-grey nineteenth-century Classical façade of the Embassy looked far from welcoming. 'Hope you get out again, mate,' said the taxi driver as he deposited him at the gate. Victor shivered, and mounted the steps to the front door.

'Ah, Mr Meer, I am Lenkov,' said a balding, uncomfortably unctuous man in his forties who greeted him in the hallway. 'I am assistant to the Cultural Attaché. It is an honour to receive you here. Let me offer you a drink.' He led the way through to a cavernous reception room, cold and poorly lit, in which straggled various knots of uneasy-looking people sipping particularly disgusting white wine. The most interesting feature of the surroundings was the pictures on the walls, two of which Victor could dimly discern as being Italian seventeenth-century and of surprisingly fine quality. He asked Lenkov about them.

'The pictures?' He looked surprised at Victor's question. 'I have no information.'

'One or two of them are rather good,' Victor persisted. 'Perhaps they were acquired for the London Embassy in pre-Revolution times?'

'That I could not say,' replied Lenkov. Victor noticed that despite the cold the Russian was sweating. It is strange how suddenly a distant chord of memory can be struck. The last person he had seen sweating quite so profusely was a man whose existence he had tried to forget, a pathetic, hopeless, doomed figure glimpsed once all those years ago. A man called Kalb. Victor recalled the way the beads had glistened on the unhealthy pallor of his forehead and his upper lip, globules seemingly congealed like Vaseline. Abruptly he put the image from his mind.

'I wish very much to bring you to meet Malakin, of the Tretyakoff Museum,' continued Lenkov. 'He is visiting London and this reception is held in his honour.'

'I should be honoured to be introduced to him.' Victor was looking at Lenkov's tie. He had seldom seen anything so hideous. 'Is Mr Malakin here for a particular purpose?'

'Ah, yes. He visits for cultural reasons.'

'Cultural reasons,' Victor repeated. 'Good.'

Malakin had the furtive, hunted look that characterised most museum officials from Eastern Europe at that time. When Victor asked him, he was no more informative about why he had come to London than Lenkov had been, but this was partly because in Malakin's case he spoke no English and their conversation, conducted in Russian which had on Victor's part grown rusty, was unenlightening on any front. Victor was not much interested anyway. He was just reflecting that the evening had been pretty much a wasted one, and preparing to take his leave, when he felt Lenkov tugging at his sleeve again.

'Mr Meer, there is someone else here tonight who is anxious to see you,' he said. 'He is an old friend, also visiting London. Colonel Venetsianov.'

'Boris Venetsianov?'

Lenkov nodded. 'He is not present at this reception, but he awaits you upstairs. Will you please follow me?'

He led the way out of the main reception room, up a grand, almost baronial staircase and along a passage, at the end of which he knocked on a door. They were told to enter, and there was Boris. The room in which he was seated was decorated as a small drawing-room, in appreciably more luxury than the gaunt reception area downstairs. He rose from his chair, beaming. Victor sensed immediately that his power to dominate a situation was undiminished. He was a little thicker set, and his blond hair was flecked with grey now; but his beautiful blue eyes were as captivating as ever. He wore a smartly cut dark suit, and it occurred to Victor that he had never before seen him dressed in anything but military uniform.

'Victor, this is wonderful,' Boris said, advancing on him and half embracing him. 'Thank you, Lenkov.'

Lenkov, palpably in awe of Boris, made a nervous withdrawal, closing the door quietly behind him.

'You'll drink vodka with me, won't you?' went on Boris. 'You've probably had enough of that cat's pee they're pouring out downstairs.'

'Thank you, that would be very nostalgic.'

Boris laughed and handed him a glass. 'To Augstein,' he said. 'And to Anglo-Soviet relations.'

Victor drank the toast. Boris was looking at him, still beaming, but something as yet indefinable had changed. Why should it not have after twenty years? They were two different people from the young captains who had made friends in occupied Austria. It was unrealistic to expect the instant reattainment of the same level of intimacy. But nonetheless Victor was uneasy. Something was not quite right.

Victor said, 'I have to call you Colonel now, I understand. You considerably outrank me.'

'No, it is I who should defer to you. I know you have become a successful author. Eminence in that field far outweighs the achievement of a simple soldier. What do you say in English? The pen is mightier than the sword.'

Yes, these were things that the old Boris might have said. But now they did not quite ring true. When Victor first knew him Boris's talk was full of bravado and outrageous spur-of-the-moment fantasy. Now, somewhere in the process, an obscure but perceptible element of calculation had intervened.

Of course they reminisced about Austria, about the inn at Augstein, about their dinners, about Boris's cracked Prokofiev gramophone records. But Victor deliberately skirted Murnzee, changed the subject when Boris's memories appeared to be inclining in that direction. Instead he said, 'Tell me about your picture collection, Boris. Has it grown?'

For a moment the warmth was unaffected. 'Ah! My collection. Yes, I still have it, in my apartment in Moscow.

I have such beautiful things, you know, Victor. Not much grown since the war; I am not interested in the second-rate, you see. One picture – a lovely Derain – I have added to my collection a few years ago, but that is all.'

'And you found that in the Soviet Union?'

He nodded. 'A coastal scene, of 1905. A ravishing piece.'

'What else do you have?'

'No, Victor, still I will not satisfy your curiosity. One day you will come to Moscow and see for yourself. Until then I shall leave you to guess.'

'Why are you so secretive?'

'Perhaps because I like to see you curious. And perhaps because you might not believe me if I told you what I have found. One or two of the pictures that I acquired at the end of the war are quite famous in their way. Only by seeing would you believe.'

'I fear I may go to my grave in incredulous ignorance, then.'

Boris shrugged and grinned. Then he reached across and offered Victor a cigar. He refused it. Boris lit one for himself, leant back in his chair, and said:

'Victor, I need your help.'

The moment he spoke, Victor felt a sick, cold apprehension. He suddenly wanted to be out of that room, out of the building, somewhere safe and secure, in the taxi again, in a restaurant, in a cinema or theatre with lots of other people, in a public place away from this dangerous seclusion.

'What sort of help?' he asked with a dry mouth.

'I want some information. Nothing very much.'

'About what?'

'About the people for whom you still do a little work now and then.'

'Which people are you talking about?' But he knew

only too well: that nagging, insistent suspicion had built into horrible certainty.

'Your friends in British Intelligence.'

It was true. In those days Victor still had a tenuous connection, in a discreetly advisory capacity, with MI5. It was a thread that stretched back to his service in the war. It suddenly occurred to Victor that Boris knew much more about his history over the past two decades than he did about Boris's. The realisation of this long and unsuspected surveillance was disturbing, and struck him as somehow unfair.

He tried to laugh it off. 'But Boris, for heaven's sake, what can I tell you that you don't know already? You would be wasting your time with me. I am a very unimportant cog in the machine.'

'You are too modest, my dear, you underrate yourself.' Boris was still grinning at him as he drained his vodka glass. 'I happen to know you can help me quite substantially.'

Then Victor got angry. How dare Boris presume upon him in this way? 'I think this is outrageous. You have me invited to this quite ghastly reception, you inveigle me upstairs to your ridiculous lair with your vodka and your cigars, then you make this absurd proposition to me. Why should I give this information to you, just like that, at the drop of a hat?'

'Why? I will tell you why.' Boris was very calm and reasonable, pausing to draw on his cigar and wreathing himself in its smoke. 'Let me make an appeal to you as a sentimentalist and suggest that you should do it out of regard for our old friendship.'

'Out of regard for our old friendship?'

'Yes. It is not very much that I ask, just a small piece remaining from our jigsaw, a piece that I cannot get elsewhere. It would count a lot for me personally.'

Victor hated him when he said that; he hated him for his shameless trading on the intimacy that had been so important to Victor, the intimacy that had seemed important to Boris too once but was apparently now no more to him than a convenient aid to Victor's exploitation and persuasion to do what Boris wanted. How could Boris make such a brazen play on their old friendship when in so doing he was utterly devaluing it?

'I am not in the least sentimental,' Victor said, 'so your appeal is pointless.'

'Ah.' Boris looked at him, nodding wisely. 'So you are not sentimental.' He drew on his cigar again, enjoying the way the smoke coiled about him. 'In that case I shall have to address the businessman in you. The realist.'

'So what are you saying?'

'I am saying that I must urge you to give me what I ask because you owe it to me. It is a simple debt.'

'Owe it to you in return for what?'

Boris laughed. 'My dear Victor, in return for a picture by Klimt.'

Why? Victor asked himself. Why, all those years ago in Austria, why had he ever accepted the picture when it had been offered to him? And Boris Venetsianov, his Boris, his first truly intimate friend: why had this man been transformed so grotesquely into his tormentor? And, looking back now over the decades from this vantage-point in the comfort of his villa outside Cannes, he asked himself one further imponderable question. Why, when faced with Boris's outrageous demands, had he reacted in the way that he did?

He did not panic. He felt sick, of course, but at the same time preternaturally clear-sighted, as though the events that were unfolding were happening to someone else.

Another person, but someone over whom, like a character in one of his own novels, he had ultimate control. He made arrangements for future discreet communication with Boris. He left the Embassy unmolested. He went back to his flat and made an omelette. Then he sat in his study and thought for a while, staring up at the picture above the fireplace.

It really was sensationally good, that Klimt. There was an orchard in the foreground, a dazzling design of foliage and blossom. How many times had he lost himself in those leaves and flowers? It was painted in that jewelled blend of forms both natural and contrived that had captivated him from the moment he had first set eyes on it. He had often tried to analyse the intensity of its appeal. It struck the perfect balance between nature and decoration, he supposed. It occurred to Victor once again that the artist's genius for this sort of interplay was most perfectly and purely expressed in landscape, that his better-known figure subjects were often compromised by the anecdotal distraction of the human form. Yes, this was perfection of its type.

And it was Victor's. It was so beautiful that for a moment its possession seemed worth anything. Even this.

The next day he caught a bus to Green Park. He didn't often travel by bus. Normally close proximity to large numbers of other unknown people depressed and annoyed him. But now he derived an obscure and unexpected comfort from it. He wanted to feel the camaraderie of his countrymen, to be one of them. To be average, just like anyone else. Not to be different. He walked up to Berkeley Square, and there, in the web of little streets just off it to the west, he found the unobtrusive little office where he'd been told to come when he'd rung earlier that morning.

The man he met was called Barker. He had never found

out whether Barker was his real name. Never, not in all the years afterwards during which Barker had flitted in and out of his life. Discreetly flitted. A quiet late-night telephone call here; a polite request for a meeting there. But it hadn't really mattered. He'd quite taken to Barker from the beginning, felt at ease with him, rather liked the wistful look in his eyes when he spoke, appreciated his kindly manner. Even his thinning grey hair, immaculately brushed, was reassuring. It hadn't been difficult to tell Barker everything. Or nearly everything. He told him of his original contact with Boris Venetsianov in Austria; he told him of his recent invitation to the Soviet Embassy; he told him of his re-encounter with Boris and the demand Boris had made of him. He also told Barker that he was being blackmailed.

Barker nodded wisely and offered him another cup of coffee. Victor sensed him jumping to precisely the conclusion that he had anticipated. Victor was not indiscreet about his sexual preferences, but equally anyone who cared to make enquiries about his private life would not, by this stage, have found difficulty in identifying them. No doubt Barker had read his file. The strange thing was that Victor preferred him to make the inference that a sexual peccadillo was the cause of the problem. At all costs, Barker and his colleagues must have no inkling about the Klimt. Beyond everything he wanted this information to be kept from them. Why was that? Because its acquisition shamed him to the quick and the other thing did not, he supposed. But equally it was not the picture itself that shamed him. He derived the intensest pleasure from owning it, and he had no wish to rid himself of it. He just wanted to have purged for ever from the memory how it had come into his ownership. How once a terrified man had stood before him with beads of sweat wobbling on his upper lip. How for a brief moment that man had looked up at him with frightened, pleading eyes, but no sound had come. How he had walked on past him. How that man had ended his life with a bullet in his back.

So he did not correct Barker's assumption about the hold exerted over him.

He got the impression that Barker and his colleagues were actually rather pleased with him. He had a series of more gruelling meetings with them over the next week or so, in which they went over a lot of old ground, probed a lot of painful areas of the past. That was an embarrassing experience, undignified, something he would have preferred not to have suffered. But at the end of it all they assured him that he had done the right thing in coming to them, that perhaps the situation could after all be turned to their advantage. Boris was henceforth christened Xenophon, presumably on the basis that he spoke English well. Victor was given the go-ahead to pass the information requested to Xenophon, but to pass it in a form suitably doctored by Barker and his colleagues. At first it sounded convoluted, complicated and dangerous. In fact it was very simple.

When it came to the point, he found he had no fear about the operation. Or if he did it was outweighed by anger and sadness. He was angry and sad at Boris, resentful that he was putting him through all this. That this was what he had reduced their friendship to. So he caught the plane to Budapest soon after on the pretext of some sort of writers' conference, and gave over – to some grey Eastern European academic, in the bar of some depressing Hungarian hotel – the information that had been demanded of him. The information as approved by the men off Berkeley Square. Then he flew home. That was it. There persisted in the back of his mind for some time an unease that the request might be repeated. He was under instructions to report back to Barker the moment any contact was made. But nothing followed. Complete silence. Not a word from Xenophon, not a word from anyone. It went on like that for years.

It was not until 1977, over a decade later, that he received the second and last summons.

He went straight to Barker and told him what he had been asked to provide. Barker had been surprised. He had needed a couple of days to consider the situation, to evaluate the demand. Apparently the surprise was caused by the fact that what he'd been asked for by Xenophon was very low-grade material indeed, stuff it was thought they already had. But it was duly put together and preparations were made to hand it over.

Once again he flew out east, this time to Prague. As usual elaborate and – to Victor – rather foolish arrangements had been put in place for the rendezvous. He was to meet his contact in a café in a small street off Wenceslas Square. He took his seat there a few minutes before three o'clock on a wet autumn afternoon and ordered coffee. The agreed copy of the *International Herald Tribune* lay next to him on the table. He was idly glancing at it when he became aware of a figure sitting down opposite him.

He looked up and saw Boris.

He was changed from when Victor had last seen him. He had aged considerably. It wasn't just that his hair was thinner and greyer and his face more lined, but his manner had lost a lot of its boldness and gusto. It was as if his batteries had run low. One no longer felt the same invigoration, the same energy in his company. Victor greeted him coldly. Boris ordered vodka and offered a glass to Victor which he refused. The fact that Victor showed him no warmth seemed to disturb him.

'It's good to see you again, Victor,' he said. 'How have you been?'

Victor shrugged. 'Let's just get this over with, shall we?'

'I thought we could have a talk.'

'I've got very little to say to you.'

Boris laughed, but without much conviction. 'You know it's a game, Victor, don't you?' His voice was tired. Victor was no longer conscious of any calculation in his words. 'It's all a game.'

'If you say so, Boris.'

'We're all getting older, after all.'

'Maybe.'

'We go back a long time, you and I, huh?'

Victor was angry at the man, sitting there with a drink in his hand, apparently trying to lay the ground for a cosy chat about the old days. This was the man who had once been his closest friend. This was the man who had betrayed him so callously. Very well, then. If he wanted to rake over the past, if he wanted reminiscence, then the bastard could have it. Victor would give it to him. Victor said, 'May I ask you something? Something I've been curious about?'

'Please, my friend.'

'Do you remember what you once told me? A long time ago, in Austria?'

'What was that?'

'You told me that there were only two really important things in life. You said they were music and pictures. You said you would abandon socialism before those things.'

He looked surprised, then perplexed. 'Perhaps that was a young man speaking.'

'And the older man is a different person, is that what you're saying?'

Boris peered out of the window at the rain-swept Prague street. 'No,' he said at last. 'Probably he isn't.'

'So your picture collection is still intact?'

He nodded. 'Yes, that is still there.' He paused, then added: 'I am sorry that maybe you won't get to see it now.

228

I would have liked you to see it, you know. I have some very special things.'

Victor did not reply at once. Instead he pushed over the newspaper enclosing the material Boris had requested. 'Thank you,' he said finally. 'You've clarified things for me at least. Pictures and music are more important than socialism. It's just friendship that isn't.'

'You have the right to make that interpretation of my behaviour. But if you do, you make a mistake.' Boris spoke ruefully, examining his vodka glass. 'At least I can assure you about one thing: this will be the last time it is necessary to ask you for this favour.'

'I am relieved to hear that.'

'I want to explain to you something: you see, it is not the information you have given me which is important. It is the fact that you have given it.'

'If you say so, Boris,' Victor repeated.

'Do not think that I did not know you would go straight to your bosses when I first asked you for your help. For me that did not matter. In fact, I hoped you would go to your people, for your own protection. No, what you have done has met a need, for me personally.'

'What need is that?'

'To be perceived to have sources. Apparently reliable, highly placed sources, answerable only to me.'

'I filled that need?'

'It was a great service you did. For me personally.' He repeated the phrase, as if it needed reinforcing. As if it excused everything.

'And that need has passed?'

'Perhaps. Perhaps there are changes ahead. Big changes, a new era. Anyway, I will not be part of it. My time is nearly done.'

Before he left, he said: 'And the Klimt? You still have it?'

'Yes.'

'I'm glad.'

As Boris walked out, Victor reflected that it was the first time he had seen him melancholy, almost forlorn. He seemed no longer in command of the situation. Yes, Boris had exploited him unforgivably. But perhaps Boris in his own way had also been the victim of something beyond his control. Now, by a strange reversal of fortune, Victor sensed him suddenly to be the more vulnerable of the two. What Victor had witnessed had been a rather pathetic attempt at an apology. Victor still couldn't bring himself to feel sorry for the man. Not under the circumstances. But a little tenderness towards the memory of their friendship in Austria seeped back into his heart. And, as the ageing figure disappeared into the rain, was lost among the bedraggled Sunday-afternoon promenaders, Victor sensed too that he would not see him again.

He didn't see him again. But he had heard from him. Just once. Two months ago. When that bloody letter had arrived.

8

Oswald took off from Heathrow two evenings later, bound for Buenos Aires.

Argentina, for God's sake. It was an unimaginably long way when you looked at the map in the airline magazine. It made you catch your breath when you realised that the aircraft you were in, this strange, cigar-shaped construction of metal and machinery, was going to carry you such a prodigious distance, deposit you suddenly in fourteen hours' time in an utterly alien environment. Another continent, another hemisphere. But those two figures, Gagey and his young mate, they were there, somewhere. They were beckoning him. He was going to find them. He peered out of the window into the fantasy-land of the stratosphere at sunset and thought about the two of them, Courbet's monumental pair of stonebreakers. Theirs had been an extraordinary history. They had hung for half a century as one of the chief adornments of one of the major museums of Europe, the Dresden Gemäldegalerie; they had taken refuge in the vaults of some obscure East German schloss for most of the war; and then they had been harried back across Saxony one grim February day in 1945, in a last-minute flight from the Red Army; that night they had spilled from the burned-out lorry, lain for dead in the ravaged street of that Dresden suburb; and been rescued by two frightened people emerging at first light the next morning. But that hadn't been the end of it. Those stonebreakers had apparently been torn asunder, and the separate pieces of canvas rolled together to make for easier transportation. Then an even more incredible leg of their journey had followed. Through Germany, across the dark waters of Lake Constance. To Zurich. Then what? Perhaps a flight to Portugal; a crossing to South America, to Buenos Aires, where their new owner had presumably had them rejoined, restored, and rehung. Where? In some private apartment in the city? Perhaps. Somewhere, anyway, where they had been photographed. That photograph had been passed to Bernard Tumbrill when he had been in Buenos Aires no more than a few weeks ago, when he had been offered them for sale. They were available again now, now that their original abductor had died. And Bernard had carried that photograph back with him, the one he had sent to Oswald before he himself had died. How to find them? The route must be through Wenglein's widow. She was the first priority.

The night passed as nights on planes do. He dozed off periodically, dreaming fitfully vivid dreams about disconnected subjects, a procession of disturbing images. Once, strangely, he dreamed of Daphne. Daphne, getting into a car and driving away. He called to her in the dream, but she didn't hear him, paid no heed to him. She just drove away, for ever. People commiserated with him. It was an understood thing that she would never come back. He didn't know why he woke up so unsettled, so uneasy. He sat there, wedged uncomfortably in his seat, his eyes wide open in the half-light of the dimmed cabin, hearing only the steady drone of the plane's engines as it set course across the Atlantic. He was keyed up, of course, tense. That was the explanation.

The next morning his eyes stung. But there was deep blue sky. It was another day and another world. He walked through into the airport terminal, and was suddenly reminded of that other arrival, at Tegel, five or six years ago. Then he had been approaching enemy territory, about to cross the Wall that divided the world. He had been nervous, on his guard. Now, as he passed through Customs into the teeming arrivals hall and negotiated a way through the families of screaming children under the sullen eyes of the heavily armed policemen, he felt a similar apprehension.

It was hot; early spring, but the temperature was in the upper seventies. The place smelt hot, too, in the way that the Mediterranean does after England, heightening the sense of unfamiliarity. Oswald queued for a taxi. The vehicle he got into was so decrepit that it made the most beaten-up New York yellow cab seem a luxury limousine by comparison. For most of the journey he had to clutch the passenger door closed, as there was no catch to prevent it from swinging open. They ground out of the airport on to a bumpy concrete-surfaced dual carriageway. The landscape was green but alien, dotted with eucalyptus trees hung with strange draping foliage. Oswald noticed sprayed across a bridge they passed under the defiant but slightly wistful declaration that the Malvinas would always be Argentinian. He looked away, vaguely uneasy. Before long they reached the first suburbs of the city, suburbs that straggled interminably, a hotch-potch of poverty-stricken apartment blocks and ugly concrete constructions, abandoned half built and now colonised by the poor, with corrugated iron strung across at irregular angles to create haphazard dwelling places, joined by countless washing-lines. Here and there the eye picked out the ubiquitous Coca-Cola sign advertising the existence of squalid-looking bars. The sun beat down uncomfortably. When the traffic was stationary, a small army of entrepreneurial youths in grimy tee-shirts darted in and out of the line of cars, trying to sell fruit. There was a sort of menacing exuberance about them. He clutched the door closed and sweltered with the window unopened. What was this place he had come to?

The sheer size of Buenos Aires was baffling. The dual carriageway continued through an apparently endless urban wasteland of cheap concrete architecture and occasional Spanish-looking churches. Then, quite suddenly, the tempo changed: they pulled into a broad and bustling avenue, its carriageways separated by a green and tree-lined central reservation, its flanking buildings tall, grand and heavily hoarded with neon advertisements. It spoke of prosperity, but a prosperity of the past. Oswald imagined it resembled a big North American city of the 1930s or 1940s. They pulled off this main thoroughfare into a web of narrower streets, and the mood changed again. He caught a whiff of Paris, or of Manhattan, as they passed smart shops and well-dressed women; held up in impatient lines of traffic, he inspected the passers-by, and marvelled at the style of the girls, the way they walked, the poise with which they held themselves. And then finally they reached the hotel, reputedly one of the city's best. He registered, and was ushered up to his room on the second floor. He tipped the bellboy, heard the door close behind him, and at last he was alone. He looked about him. The room was large, and oddly unwelcoming. He sat down on the bed and felt that sense of desolation which accompanies arrival in a strange city after a long journey. What was this place he had come to? he asked himself again.

What he had set out to do here was beyond him. This was a far bigger and more alien city than he had suspected. What resources had he available by which to trace these people, the Wengleins? They were one family – just one widow, perhaps – amongst so many. He thought of the millions who lived here, the endless tracts of urbanisation he had just driven through. He was close to despair. How could he have deluded himself into thinking that the enterprise was possible? He walked across his cavernous bedroom to the window, then back to the telephone by the bed. He felt enormously depressed. He lifted the receiver and put through a call to Daphne, but when he finally got a connection there was no reply. Strange that he did that then.

Thank God, he felt better the next morning. The sleep did him good, and his resolve hardened again. You didn't travel halfway round the world in pursuit of something as valuable as 'The Stonebreakers' just to cave in bleakly the moment you got there. He ate breakfast in his room and leafed through the Buenos Aires telephone directory. There was one Wenglein in the book, and he rang the number immediately. The man the other end was helpful, but regretted he didn't know of a Heinrich Wenglein who had died recently. There was no one in his family of that name. That would have been too easy, of course. So Oswald went downstairs and called a taxi to take him to the German Embassy.

'American?' asked his driver.

'English,' he mumbled, thinking of the graffiti on the bridge.

'Welcome to Buenos Aires,' he said delightedly. 'My name is Enrico Brown. My grandfather, he was born in Nottingham.'

It seemed a good omen.

As they drove through the streets of the city, he began to get some sort of impression of the place. Buenos Aires struck him as more and more intriguing. It did not fit into his preconceived scheme of things; he had nothing solidly to relate it to. What he saw struck occasional disparate chords, but there was no coherence. They passed along elegant *avenidas* lined by palm trees, off which were set smart white nineteenth-century mansions with cool court-yards such as you might see in Madrid; later, down by the docks and near the railway station, he glimpsed arcaded warehouses that reminded him obscurely of Covent Garden, hints of an unexpectedly British colonialism. The city hovered schizophrenically between the two extremes of provincialism and sophistication: on the one hand you felt you had flown so far south to get there that you had hit the very edge of the world, reached the furthest frontier of the most distant backwater of civilisation; on the other hand the sheer size of Buenos Aires, its implied metropolitanism, its evident Americanisation, made you think of New York; but not a present-day New York because, as Oswald soon learned, the place had an oddly dated air. Many of the cars looked antiquated, and the inhabitants too gave the impression of having more in common with pre-war Europe than contemporary America. It was fascinating, and at the same time disquieting.

At the German Embassy he spoke to an enormously correct and efficient young man in the consulate department. He happily accepted Oswald's story, that he was trying to locate the heirs of a long-lost relation of his wife's, a recently deceased German called Wenglein. But he politely pointed out that the only German deaths of which they at the Embassy held a record involved tourists or other German passport-holding visitors. It was much more likely that the man Oswald was looking for, if he had lived in Argentina for forty years, would have taken out Argentinian nationality.

Oswald nodded. The man had a point. 'Is there some sort of central records office which collates the births, marriages and deaths of Argentinian citizens?' he asked him.

The German shook his head. 'I regret no. Each town, and each separate district of the city, has, I believe, a civil register, but these are not easy for a foreigner to consult. And it would be difficult to know where to start . . . But I have perhaps a suggestion. Do you know approximately when Herr Wenglein died?'

'Four or five months ago, I think.'

'So why do you not go to the city's newspapers and check the obituary announcements in their back numbers? You could start with the German-language daily, the *Argentinische Algemeine*.'

It was odd how differently people announced death. At inordinate length sometimes, with great shoals of words and dates, followed by interminable lists of names, of relatives, of friends, of business colleagues, all intent on declaring their mourning; or floridly, with verbose expressions of grief, protests of desolation so effusive you knew they must be over-compensating for something; and sometimes baldly, unemotionally, with a minimum of display. Hiding what? A complete absence of feeling? Or sadness too profound for words? He sat at a table in the little office where he had been given space and worked through the editions they brought him, from January onwards. It was hot; a fan turned lazily in the ceiling above him, and a maddened fly buzzed spasmodically at the window-pane. People had been helpful here. He fancied they had found him a bit of a novelty. An Englishman, wanting to check through German obituary notices in Buenos Aires. Amusing, wasn't it? He must be some sort of eccentric. He had fallen in with the role. It was harmless enough. He bumbled about, putting on a convincing act of diffident absert-mindedness Yes, he was looking for a distant relation of his wife's; he was here on business and had a spare afternoon, and had promised to see if he could trace this long-lost family connection for her. More out of curiosity than anything else, you understand.

When he reached it, two hours later, the notice about Heinrich Johann Wenglein was so brief that he almost missed it. It was a bare three lines, tucked in between two much more flamboyant black-edged announcements. But having found it, there was no mistaking it. Wenglein had died on 2 May, aged seventy-nine. There it was. He felt the same feeling of sick excitement that he had felt after reading Gerda Helgemann's statement in Derek's flat less than a week ago. The same sensation of a route miraculously opening up for him – and for him alone – towards the most improbable prize. The same amazement at improbability turning into reality. He stared, fascinated by the three lines of print. Wenglein had come here. Wenglein had died here. That was now proved beyond all doubt. But what had he brought with him when he came? And what was he leaving behind him when he died? A picture collection, perhaps. And in that collection, one particular picture, a simple, monumental, unforgettable image of two men breaking stones by a roadside. Where was that picture now? It wasn't yet within his grasp, but Oswald was a massive step closer to reaching it.

Everything had got serious now. The pressure had risen. He hurried to transcribe the crucial information contained in those three lines. The widow's name was Luisa. There was no indication about where the funeral had been arranged, but flowers were to be sent to an address in San Telmo. Was that where he would find Mrs Wenglein? He wrote it down carefully then checked on the map. It wasn't far. Fifteen minutes in a cab, perhaps.

As he was driven through the centre of the city, past late-afternoon shoppers flocking in and out of stores, past sharp-suited businessmen hurrying down pavements, past elegant women sitting in cafés, he thought, My God, if this is the Wengleins' house I'm going to, if this is where he lived, I could be minutes away from actually seeing this picture. Maybe it's still hanging there. Still hanging there, awaiting disposal. Awaiting offers. Maybe I'm about to touch it. Maybe I'm about to become the first serious scholar to set eyes on it for forty-five years. Maybe I'm about to witness a raising from the dead.

But things are never as simple as that.

The first thing Orlando Verney did after arriving in Buenos Aires and checking into his room at the Plaza was to go to church.

Over the past year or two he had become periodically religious. Perhaps he felt a need for spiritual solace; perhaps he felt it lent him a certain substance. Either way, there had been little doubt about the channel through which his new-found interest should be expressed: the Roman Catholic Church offered advantages and attractions incomparably greater than any of its conceivable competitors. The combination of tradition and beauty in its ritual appealed simultaneously to his innate conservatism and his sense of theatre; its insistence on a clear-cut system of moral values, creating simple equations of sin eradicated by confession and opportunity opened up by prayer, possessed a satisfyingly monolithic charm; the overtones of oppression historically attached to the English Catholic Church endowed converts with a reflected glint of heroism; and the enormous social acceptability of a certain sort of English Catholicism brought with it a cachet on a par with membership of White's. Nor was it merely socially uplifting. Orlando liked the literary connection too, the Catholic tradition of writers like Graham Greene and Evelyn Waugh. He felt comfortable in their company. For Orlando, his religion had both a public and a private face. References to attendance at Mass could be lightly dropped into most conversations to satisfactory effect. It rarely did harm to be perceived as someone with a spiritual dimension, provided that spirituality was understood to be shackled by something as rigorous as the Roman Catholic faith. As to the private side, he found it quite easy to talk to God. But then he found it easy to talk to most older men who had led interesting lives.

'Don't you agree that a novelist needs some sort of belief?' he had asked Victor over dinner earlier in the year.

'Belief in what?' Victor had countered suspiciously.

'Religious belief, I mean.'

'Certainly not. I don't know a single writer who writes better because he believes in God. I know quite a few who write worse.'

'You don't feel the need of anything?'

'Me? Not as a writer.'

'And as a human being?'

'I'm an atheist. I'm much happier that way. Life's complicated enough without cluttering it up with all that unnecessary excess baggage.'

'So you believe in nothing at all.'

'I don't say that. There are some things I value very highly.'

'Such as?'

Victor frowned. 'Such as the preservation of beauty. Such as loyalty to friends. That sort of thing.'

'You sound just like Anthony Blunt.'

'If that's what you think then you're very naive indeed,' Victor had replied with sudden venom.

But Orlando had not been deterred. On the recommendation of a 'grand' friend of his mother he had entered a course of instruction with a middle-aged Irish Jesuit priest attached to a fashionable West End church. Father O'Rourke had been charmed of course by the prospect of Orlando as a convert. But there had been stumbling-blocks along the way, as when on his fourth or fifth visit he had suggested that Orlando should call him Kevin. 'I'd much rather call you Father O'Rourke,' Orlando had replied frostily. Thereafter things had moved forward more slowly, and Orlando had left London in July without having undertaken final reception into the Church. That did not mean, however, that he had abandoned the enterprise. He was fond of wandering into Catholic churches at odd moments, particularly abroad, lighting candles, and praying. His prayers were simple: he imprecated God for things he wanted. He prayed chiefly for money, and in spring, when he had first tried in earnest, the response had been excellent. Within weeks two deals had gone through on which he had earned considerable introductory commissions, enough to set him up for most of the summer. With money in his pocket, attendance at church had seemed less of an imperative. He had not bothered much in the South of France. But now here he was in Buenos Aires in early autumn, buttressed, it was true, by Victor's generous expense allowance, but in need of help in his pursuit of a prize that promised to be substantial. Substantial enough to see him through a period that could be measured in years rather than months.

He set out from the hotel in search of a church and stopped at the first one he came to. He paused at the doorway, glancing back down the sunny boulevard like a swimmer about to dive into icy water, then ducked inside.

It was dark within, the air pervaded by the lingering smell of incense, the scent that had become such a reassuring one to him. He lit a candle, blinked while his eyes became accustomed to the shadows, then knelt before a side altar and prepared to speak to his Maker. It was impossible to do this without envisaging the deity in some sort of addressable human form, and an effort of imagination – now, was this what Father O'Rourke would call Faith? – was necessary here. God for Orlando this afternoon took the guise of a prickly but ultimately amenable elderly gentleman who had to be charmed into granting Orlando his wishes. Indeed, He shared some of the characteristics of Victor in this respect – a potential intransigence and irascibility that must be negotiated with flattery and tact.

'God, look, I know this is presumptuous, but you've been absolutely wonderful in the past, really absurdly generous, and that makes me all the more loath to ask you again now, but could you see your way clear to helping me in an enterprise which I'm undertaking here? It really would be extremely kind of you if you could point me in the right direction for this Courbet and make arrangements for me to buy it at a reasonable price. Smooth the way, I suppose is what I'm asking, nothing too drastic. That would be sweet of you, it really would. You know how grateful I'd be. No, really, I would. And I can assure you that if I do make a decent profit out of this deal, thanks to you, the money will be spent sensibly. Nothing excessive, nothing ostentatious. But of course you know that. And I think I can rely on you, can't I?' Orlando was on the point of telling God that He was a sweet old thing, but restrained himself. He had said enough. He fancied he could detect a twinkle of charmed compliance in the divine eye already. In many ways it was easier dealing with God than with Victor when he remembered all that unnecessary trouble with the Klimt.

He rose and walked quietly out of the church. It had been a job well done. Now he had various people to telephone, people whose numbers he had been given by mutual friends in Europe. People who could be relied upon to welcome him to Argentina with the degree of lavish hospitality to which he had become accustomed wherever he went. People who belonged to a world-wide web of acquaintance, a secret self-serving society that knew no national boundaries, because it joined people with an even more compelling common interest than mere shared nationality: the possession and enjoyment of wealth. And amongst those people – who knows? – there might even be someone with some inkling of the where-abouts of a recently bereaved German family called Wenglein.

The taxi drew up in front of an anonymous doorway. At first sight its only distinctive feature was its number, which coincided with the number on the address Oswald had transcribed from the obituary notice. Oswald paid the driver off and stood for a moment looking up and down the street. It didn't look the sort of place where he imagined the Wengleins living. It had a pungently Latin atmosphere. There was a local bar on the corner, where a few languorous drinkers sat in the shade of an awning, and next to it a greengrocer. You could smell cooking from several different kitchens. Further down, some boys were playing football against a wall. From a nearby open window, tango music wafted out. A man's voice was singing. Oswald recognised it as tango music, but it was unlike anything he had heard before, not the sort of commercially packaged tango you heard in Europe or North America. This was an intensely emotional sound, by turns caressingly gentle and shockingly violent. Under-lying it all you sensed a profound melancholy. He found it rather moving. Also rather unsettling. He shook his head, and turned to the door. There was a bell over a small brass plate, inscribed in flowing italics 'Guttmann. Servicios funerarios'.

So that was it. He was at an undertaker's.

The man who opened the door to him eyed him suspiciously. He looked like an egg. He was oval-shaped, squat, with a domed bald head. He wore large baggy trousers and a tight-fitting shirt which clung clammily to his massive belly. He had large, beetling eyebrows and needed a shave.

'Good afternoon,' said Oswald. 'I wonder if you can help me. I'm trying to trace some people who you arranged a funeral for some months ago. Perhaps I could come in for a moment?'

He stood aside to allow Oswald in, then showed him through to a large bare room where there was a desk and two chairs and nothing on the walls except a crucifix. At first sight it could almost have been a room in a monastery. Almost. Until you looked again at the egg-shaped man, and took in the lurid magazine in his hand and the cigarette packet in the breast pocket of his shirt.

'I regret, it is not possible I answer your questions,' Egg told him. 'Señor Guttmann, he come to you if you wait here. Your name please, again?'

'Ginn. Oswald Ginn, from England.'

Egg paused in the doorway, and before disappearing suddenly gave Oswald a sly, leering grin.

It was perhaps ten minutes before Guttmann came to him. They shook hands solemnly. He was a thin, weasly man with greying hair, and the unnerving habit of suddenly staring straight at you with sharp, almost bird-like eyes. He wore a surprisingly well-cut suit.

'How can we help you?' he asked abruptly.

'I believe that you arrange funerals here?'

Guttmann nodded, then turned a look of penetrating directness on him. 'You want to arrange a funeral?'

'No, no.' Oswald began to laugh, but stopped. 'No, I'm trying to trace someone for whom you did arrange a funeral. Mrs Wenglein? Mrs Heinrich Wenglein? At the beginning of May?'

For a split second Oswald saw the man blink, react with his guard down. He saw surprise. Then he saw anger.

Inexplicable anger. Tight-lipped, Guttmann said: 'Why?'

'Why? I don't quite see . . .'

'Why do you wish to find Mrs Wenglein?'

He was at once wary of him, unwilling to give Guttmann even a hint of the real reason for his search. 'I'm over here from Europe on business, and I had a spare afternoon, so I thought I'd see if I could trace her. It's a private matter.'

'A private matter?'

'Yes. Well, a family matter, if you like.'

'A family matter?' Guttmann laughed almost scornfully.

'That's right.'

'Herr Wenglein was German.'

'Yes, I know that.'

'But you are not German yourself.'

'No, but my wife . . .'

'She is German?'

'She has German connections.' Put like that, it did sound flimsy. He wished he'd worked out a more coherent story in advance. He hadn't expected to be pressed on details. He added again: 'Anyway, it's a private, family matter.'

Guttmann leant forward towards him across the desk, his cuffed hands twisting an ashtray with a suppressed fury. 'I ask myself, why? Why is an Englishman, who says he is a businessman, suddenly so anxious to trace a German family here in Buenos Aires? Me, I am always suspicious of people who come asking questions about things that do not concern them.'

Oswald shook his head. The man's anger was difficult to fathom, but it was real enough. 'I think you misunderstand the situation,' he said.

'Listen to me, Señor Ginn. I do a lot of business with the German community, particularly the older members of it. I look after my clients. They trust me. You know

245

why they trust me? They trust me because I understand that people are at their weakest in bereavement, at their most vulnerable. So I protect them. That is part of my service to them.'

'I assure you I am not a threat to Mrs Wenglein.'

'So what do you want from her?'

'Just to discuss one or two things. It's a private matter.'

'One or two things about the past, am I right? About the past of her husband, perhaps?'

Oswald hesitated for a moment. It was fatal. Before he could speak, Guttmann blazed back at him with a quite unexpected ferocity:

'I knew it! You bastards are the scum of the earth!'

'What do you mean?'

'I know what you are, Señor Ginn. You do not deceive me.'

'I'm here on business.'

'Yes, and I do not like your business, Señor Ginn. You're a journalist, aren't you? I've seen others like you before. Fabricating poisonous stories about men who are too old to defend themselves, about things they are alleged to have done far, far away in the past. What do you call them? Scoops? Exposés? Look, no one here is interested in these things any more, you understand me? That war is ancient history, it was long ago. Forget it, that's my advice to you. Forget Mrs Wenglein. Forget it all. Before you get hurt.'

Oswald did laugh now, in disbelief. It was farcical. And it was disconcerting. This man, with his weasel face and his burning eyes, this man was threatening him. He heard the plangent, sorrowful tango music from down the street. It too suddenly carried a note of menace. He was cut off here. On his own.

'I am not a journalist,' he said. 'I am not trying to dig up anything on anyone.'

'If you're with the Israelis . . .'

'For God's sake. I'm just an English businessman.'

'Then leave Mrs Wenglein alone. You do her a favour that way, OK?' His face was close enough as he leant over the desk for Oswald to smell his breath.

The Egg-man showed him out. On the doorstep, he smiled slyly and asked, 'Which hotel you stay?'

Oswald told him without thinking, then regretted it.

'I call you taxi?'

'No, thank you.' Oswald walked out into the street and the door slammed behind him.

As he wandered through San Telmo, he tried to make some sense of what was happening. He was angry, and a little frightened. He was very, very close to reaching Mrs Wenglein. And therefore, presumably, very close to 'The Stonebreakers'. But this creep Guttmann was blocking his way, preventing him finally making contact. What was Guttmann up to? What was he trying to protect Mrs Wenglein from? Had other people been sniffing around her? If so, why? Perhaps there had indeed been journalists who'd cottoned on to Wenglein's past and scented a story. Guttmann seemed to see himself as some sort of watchdog, scaring off anyone who got too close to that section of the German community in Buenos Aires with Nazi secrets to hide. Or perhaps the real reason why there'd been other people trying to reach Mrs Wenglein was because of something in the late Heinrich Wenglein's estate. Something they badly wanted to get their hands on. A magnificent picture by Courbet, for instance. How much did Guttmann know about that?

But wait a minute; there had been someone else who'd got to her. Or close enough to find out about 'The Stonebreakers', anyway. Bernard Tumbrill. Bernard Tumbrill had been in Buenos Aires barely a month ago. Bernard had brought home a photograph of the picture, together with an assurance that he was in a position to be able to buy the original. How had Bernard dealt with Guttmann? How had he negotiated that barrier? What had been Bernard's reaction to Guttmann's threats? Forget it, Guttmann had told Oswald. Forget it, before you get hurt.

Then he thought of something so appalling that he had to stand still for a moment. Forget it, before you get hurt. That had been the unequivocal message he'd received. Perhaps Bernard had been threatened in the same way. Perhaps Bernard, being Bernard, had paid no attention.

And where was Bernard now? Bernard was dead. Suddenly, unexpectedly, dead.

Come on, now, Oswald told himself, that was liver failure. The doctors in England had been in no doubt about that. You couldn't kill someone and make it look like liver failure. Could you?

The question worried him. It worried him sick. He caught a taxi soon after and it took him back to his hotel. He went straight to his room and poured himself a double whisky from the mini-bar.

Next morning things looked different again. Oswald wasn't going to let that bloody picture escape without a struggle. It was quite possible, after all, that he had been frightening himself unnecessarily. There was absolutely no reason why Bernard's route to Mrs Wenglein should have been the same as his own. Probably Bernard had never even come across Guttmann, never been threatened. There were plenty of other approaches. Bernard could easily have reached her via someone else. But if via someone else, then Oswald had to face the possibility that it was via someone in the local art trade. He had hoped to be able to steer clear of that bunch of crooks, come and go without having contact with them. Now it couldn't be avoided. He must make discreet enquiries. He reached for the telephone book to look up the number of the Galerie Michelangelo.

A minute or two later he had fixed an appointment with the director of the gallery, Dr Oreste Giannini, for 10.30 that morning.

Oswald went on foot. It was another day of flawless blue sky and fresh, invigorating breezes. Despite everything, he found he rather liked Buenos Aires. He picked his way over duckboards in the pavements where holes had been dug and never properly repaired. It was typical of the place: the city was beautiful, the girls were lovely, the restaurants were good; people enjoyed life here, and prospered well enough. But there was a seam of lethargy running through everything. Jobs never quite got finished. Ultimately you sensed pleasure was more important than efficiency. It wasn't an entirely unsympathetic philosophy. But how, he wondered suddenly, had it all struck Major Heinrich Wenglein? How had it struck him, arriving here in spring 1945, fresh from the Germany of the Third Reich?

In order to reach Dr Giannini he had to walk some way along Libertad. You could say Libertad was the Bond Street of Buenos Aires: here, interspersed amongst smart clothes shops, you found many of the city's art and antique dealers. Glancing in at the windows he saw an extraordinary mixture of objects for sale. Most were dross, but occasionally something more interesting caught the eye. There was a little English desk of the early nineteenth century, refreshingly untouched, presumably prised from the local descendants of some emigrant Smith or Brown; there was a sensitive eighteenth-century French drawing from the circle of Boucher; and there was a beautiful piece of Italian majolica. These were mixed in with a variety of more esoteric items: he saw a coloured photograph of the Pope framed in a glass surround decorated with tiny, constantly flashing lights; and in another shop he examined a set of three musical ashtrays which, when the pressure of a cigarette stub was applied to them, played the theme from *The Godfather*. For a moment he thought of Guttmann's ashtray, twisted between his fingers. For a moment he felt a quick shaft of yesterday's apprehension.

He stepped gingerly over the threshold of the Galerie Michelangelo. Above the door a sign boasted that the company had been established in 1972, and offered best prices for pictures by European masters. Oswald was aware that he was taking a risk in coming here, but he could no longer afford to be cautious. A way had to be found of circumventing Guttmann. Dr Giannini had the reputation of being the lynchpin of the Argentinian art trade. It was said that very little went on here without Giannini knowing about it. Oswald had to find out if he had any inkling about the Courbet being available; if so, Oswald had to convey to him that he was a major player with the sort of substantial resources that entitled him to first bite at it; if not, he must avoid arousing Giannini's suspicion or interest. The last thing he wanted was to encourage unnecessary competition for the picture. He didn't want to have Giannini alerted to the enormous potential of the situation if he didn't know already.

The gallery was very white. It was sparsely hung with a carefully calculated selection of European nineteenth- and twentieth-century pictures. There was a large Parisian street scene by Galien-Laloue; there was an English village scene with an improbable sunset by Benjamin Williams Leader; a view of Venice by Federigo del Campo; and an oddly lascivious interior with a cardinal admiring a busty young lady by a Spanish artist called Pablo Salinas.

'Good morning,' said Oswald. 'Dr Giannini? I am Oswald Ginn, from Fortescue's in London. I rang just now from the hotel.'

'Mr Ginn, good morning.' Dr Oreste Giannini came towards him, removing dark glasses to reveal intelligent, bloodshot eyes. He was a good-looking man in his fifties with an easy charm. A bit too easy. 'It is an honour to welcome a visitor from the famous Fortescue's in London.'

'Thank you very much.'

'Can I offer you perhaps a cup of coffee? Won't you come through to my office; we shall be more comfortable there.'

Oswald allowed himself to be led through into a luxurious room that opened through french windows on to a small swimming-pool, built like a Pompeian bath. It looked very welcoming in the sunshine. He sat down and said, 'This is extremely pleasant.'

'It makes working a little less arduous,' smiled Giannini.

A very beautiful girl brought in the tray of coffee. When she had gone again, Giannini stretched and asked casually: 'So, Mr Ginn, what are you doing in Buenos Aires? Is it business or pleasure?'

'A little of both,' replied Oswald carefully.

'Your first visit?'

'Yes.'

'How do you find Argentina?'

'I like it. What I've seen of it so far.'

'You will find the people not easy to deal with, perhaps. The Argentinians, they are a mixed-up nation. I have had a chance to observe them carefully since I first came out here from Milan twenty-five years ago.' Giannini stared out at the pool, apparently thoughtful, but Oswald still had the feeling that he was being surreptitiously studied, evaluated. 'Things are better now, of course. There is more stable government, the economy is stronger, the inflation is a little bit controlled. But it is pitiful to see the mess they have made here in the past. The country had so much in its favour, so much natural resource, a mild climate, space for people to live. Before the war Argentina was one of the richest nations in the world, you know.'

'What went wrong?'

'What went wrong?' Giannini lit a cigarette and thought again for a moment. 'For the answer to that question you should search into the Argentinian character. You see he is feckless, the average Argentine. He possesses the worst characteristics of the Latin temperament, he is the man who puts off until tomorrow what he could be doing today, the man who tells you not the truth but what he thinks you want to hear, the man who cannot do a straight deal but needs always the special angle, the – how can I say? – the illusion of underhand advantage. It is a cliché, but there is some truth in clichés: the Argentine is an Italian who thinks he's Spanish but wants to be British.'

Oswald laughed.

'You think that because I am Latin myself I should not be able to judge these things,' went on Giannini. 'Ah, Mr Ginn, but it is precisely because I am Latin that I can understand them so well. And why I have been able to make good business here.'

'I can see how successful you've been here. And are there still good pictures to find?'

'It depends what you are looking for.' Giannini was suddenly wary. 'There are still many pictures. When they were rich, the Argentinians bought many works of art. Between the wars, in Paris, in New York, even in London. But many fakes, so many fakes . . . no discrimination, tempted always by the special deal, the dubious bargain.'

'And I suppose some good things arrived here after the war, too. With refugees from Europe?'

'Some, it is true.'

'From Germany, for instance?'

'From Germany, yes.' He looked at Oswald probingly. 'You ask for a particular reason? You are looking for German pictures?'

'No, not especially.' He was walking a tightrope now. Giannini was a disconcertingly perceptive man. How much could he ask without arousing suspicion? 'No, if I'm looking for anything, it would be for a really top French nineteenth-century picture. That's what we have clients wanting.' He thought of Salzman. Dapper, greedy Conrad Salzman. He thought of the Japanese.

'A French nineteenth-century picture?'

'Yes. Do you have anything like that? Or know of anything, perhaps? But it must be something truly exceptional.'

Giannini was quieter. He laid down his coffee cup and said, almost softly: 'I think you are lucky, Mr Ginn. You have come to the right place. At the right time. Here we have always the finest European pictures in Buenos Aires. But only last week I have acquired something outstanding. It is the best French picture I have found for many years.'

'I would very much like to see it.' Oswald's mouth was dry.

'I should warn you. It will cost a lot of money.'

'For the right picture, I am prepared to pay a fair price.'

'I think you will not be disappointed. In a way, it is good that you have come. I would show this only to very few people. Only to very serious people.'

They both got up, and Giannini led the way out of the room, up some stairs and into another small gallery, a private viewing-room. Oswald found his heart was beating very fast indeed. God almighty, was this it? Had Giannini got to Mrs Wenglein already? Had he bought 'The Stonebreakers' from her? And if he had bought the Courbet, did he recognise its full significance? What did he mean by a lot of money?

Giannini closed the door behind them. There were curtains drawn across one end of the room, creating the effect of a small stage. The Italian went to the wall and pulled discreetly so that the curtains slowly parted. There it was. Standing alone on an easel. A big picture. A striking picture. A shocking picture.

'So,' he said simply.

It wasn't by Courbet.

It was by William Adolphe Bouguereau. Although Oswald was no expert on the artist, he recognised it immediately. Two putti played in a landscape while a naked woman, presumably meant to represent Venus, slept beyond. It had that distinctive, soapy carnality that had thrilled visitors to the Paris Salon in the second half of the nineteenth century and characterised most of the artist's works. Somehow the preamble of the parting curtains had been entirely apposite for this picture. It was itself a creation of cheap theatricality with voyeuristic overtones. What had Jean-François Millet said about this sort of painting? He'd called it classicism for bankers and stockbrokers. It was the sort of picture that made you want to laugh out loud. Or throw up on the carpet. But Oswald knew it was valuable. He could understand Giannini's excitement about it, as a commercial proposition. In California there were any number of collectors who would happily write out a cheque for three hundred thousand dollars for it.

'What do you think?' encouraged Giannini.

'It's a good example. But not quite what I am looking for.'

'You are a difficult man to please, in that case. It's the most important French picture available in Argentina today.' He spoke as if he knew what he was talking about, as if he was convinced of the truth of what he was saying. 'You will find nothing else of this quality.'

Oswald thought quickly. You had to conclude that Giannini knew nothing of 'The Stonebreakers', that was clear. But then again, why should he? The information that Bernard Tumbrill had acquired about its existence here must have come from another source, a source outside the regular art trade. Who? Perhaps after all Bernard had somehow evaded Guttmann and reached Mrs Wenglein herself. Perhaps Mrs Wenglein had rather liked the idea of dealing direct with a European outsider, preferring to avoid the men on her own doorstep. That was understandable too. But it was all still conjecture. If only Bernard had lasted long enough to fill in these tantalising gaps, to guide him direct to Mrs Wenglein and the picture. If only he could be absolutely sure that Bernard's death was down to natural causes.

Giannini was closing the curtains on the Bouguereau. Oswald sensed a coolness coming from him. His pride had been injured by the rejection of the Venus. Well, no doubt he'd sell it soon enough.

'Perhaps you could give me some advice?' Oswald continued.

'Yes?'

'If I bought a picture from a private collection here in Argentina, would there be any problem in exporting it?'

He was immediately hostile. 'As a foreigner you would not find easily pictures in private collections here.'

'Yes, but say, just for the sake of argument, I bought a picture privately. Could I get it back to Europe?'

'I have to tell you that every picture leaving Argentina needs an export licence. It is government regulation.'

'Is that easy to arrange?'

'An official export licence? Very often impossible. It can take six months. Perhaps twelve months. Perhaps never.'

'So what should I do? Take it with me in my luggage?'

'There are severe penalties for smuggling the Argentinian heritage. Prison, perhaps for several years.'

Oswald tried to imagine Magnus and Leonard bailing him out. He was not reassured. 'But what do you do?' he persisted. 'How do you take pictures out of the country?'

'There are ways, Mr Ginn. But ways known only to the experts, such as myself.'

'What ways?'

'You must be in contact with the right people. The Customs official: perhaps his wife likes a new washing machine. Then he looks the other way when canvases are added to containers of household goods belonging to diplomats returning to the United States. Or the airline steward: he can be persuaded to take small packages with him. The authorities are less – how you say? – vigilant with airline staff. But you must know the right steward. Or stewardess.'

'Is it really as difficult as that?' Oswald queried. 'I mean, a lot of pictures with Argentinian provenance appear on the international art market.'

Giannini shrugged. 'Let us just say that there are many Customs officials here whose wives have washing machines.'

As Oswald was leaving, Giannini subtly changed tack. He told Oswald to come back to him if indeed there was a picture that he wanted to get out of the country. He would help him, give him the benefit of his contacts and experience. In return for a share in it, of course. Oswald thanked him for the offer. He felt that in eliciting it he had won a small victory.

What now? As he walked back to the hotel he tried to repress the feeling that there was no way forward from here. Giannini knew nothing. Guttmann was blocking him. Bernard was dead. Shit.

But when he got to Reception, things changed. He asked for his key and was given the two messages that were waiting for him in his pigeon-hole. The first was from Leonard, a fax which had arrived that morning. It asked him urgently to send details of what he had found. He should get photographs as soon as possible and courier them over. Salzman was due in London next week. It was imperative that they had something fresh to show him. Oswald crumpled the paper and put it in his pocket. He'd reply to it later.

The second was handwritten, in pencil. It was unsigned, brief and to the point.

'If you wish address of German lady you seek, meet me Río Plata embankment opposite Casa Bianca Restaurant 8 o'clock Wednesday. Price is 500 dollars cash.'

Victor strolled towards the verandah. He had just finished lunch. The afternoon was hot again, and the hills higher up once more shimmered in a blue mist. He might as well drink his coffee outside before going back to work in the study. But he paused by the telephone.

The idea had been simmering all morning. Why not, after all? It was 2.30 here in France. It would be 10.30 in the morning, he calculated, in Buenos Aires. Why shouldn't he? Orlando was never an early riser. Now would be just about the right moment to catch him. He would probably be awake, but not yet out of the hotel, perhaps not yet even out of bed. It would be good to speak to him. Just to check on progress. Just to hear his voice.

Miraculously he got through almost at once to the Plaza

Hotel. He was connected to Orlando's room number. He'd guessed right. A sleepy voice said, 'Yes?'

'It's Victor here.'

'Victor. Where are you?'

'I'm in France. I'm ringing to see how you're getting on. I'm not disturbing you, I hope?'

'Not at all. I'm getting on very well. But I'm afraid I haven't found the picture yet.'

'No?' Victor disguised his lack of surprise. 'Any leads at all?'

'I'm still looking for the bloody Wengleins.' There was a rustling noise, audible even on the long-distance line. Victor imagined him, sitting up more comfortably in bed, arranging himself. In those blue pyjamas. 'I've made a hell of a lot of enquiries,' Orlando was continuing. 'I've bored just about everyone I've met here with questions about these wretched krauts. I really could do with a bit more information, you know. Did your source not say anything else at all? A big Courbet, belonging to an old German called Wenglein, who's just died. It's not a lot to go on.'

'I know. I wish I could tell you more, but I simply can't. But keep at it a little longer.' Victor paused. 'Enjoying yourself otherwise?'

'Yes, it's fun here. Actually I'm moving on today; I've been invited to stay with some people called Arnosa.'

'Oh good. So you're having a good time.'

'I am.'

'Worth the trip anyway? Even without the picture?'

'What are you getting at, Victor?'

'Nothing, really. It's just that . . . well, I'd feel rather bad about it if you not only didn't find the picture but also had a rotten time into the bargain. I feel a bit responsible.'

'Don't worry, old thing. I'm fine. But don't write this enterprise off just yet. It's funny, you know, but I've got this very strong feeling, a sort of instinct that I'm going to find this Courbet out here, and going to find it quite soon. Don't ask me why.' Victor wasn't going to. There was a danger the answer would involve some mystical nonsense about God or Divine Providence which would only annoy him. Instead he said:

'Excellent. In that case I look forward to seeing a healthy return on my investment. Keep in touch, won't you; let me know if you need anything. And take care of yourself.'

When he put the receiver down, Victor found he felt uneasy. Talking to Orlando had unsettled him. It was worse now than before; he was no longer inclined to work, he couldn't concentrate. A host of anxieties were stirring within him, some old, some new. Old ghosts, new fears.

In the end he lifted the telephone and dialled another number. Out of curiosity. Out of concern.

'Ah, it's you,' the voice at the other end said when he got through. It was a brisk, efficient male voice with possibly just a hint of preciousness to its intonations. 'Do forgive me, I meant to give you a progress report before now. The situation seems to have been contained, I'm happy to say. And things are finally beginning to happen.'

'What things; can you tell me?'

'I don't want to be too specific on the telephone, I'm sure you can understand that. But everything seems to be satisfactory, as far as we can judge. And I think we're going to get some arrivals fairly shortly. Within a week, anyway.'

'They're actually coming through? Do they include . . . do they include what we expected?'

'I can't say definitely. But there are hopeful signs. Meanwhile I think you ought to hold yourself in readiness to make a trip out here. If you'd care to. In about a week, say? As soon as the shipment arrives?'

Victor swallowed. 'Thank you,' he said quietly. 'I'm grateful for the advance notice. I'll bear it very much in mind.'

Five hundred dollars cash. Not that much, really. No more than you'd pay to take a couple of clients out for a really expensive dinner. But then again, quite a lot to be carrying in your wallet when you were off to an unknown assignation through unfamiliar streets seven thousand miles away from home. He'd cashed the dollar traveller's cheques and wondered. Was it a set-up? Was he on his way to being mugged? He had no guarantee that he was going to get anything out of the proposed transaction. He had no guarantee that he wasn't simply going to be set upon and forcibly relieved of the money in some quiet cul-de-sac. But he couldn't not go, could he? It was the only way forward, the only lead he had on Mrs Wenglein. The alternative was simply to call British Airways and book his flight home.

He'd sat in his hotel room and thought carefully what he should take with him. Not his passport. Not the photograph of 'The Stonebreakers' that he'd kept with him pretty well constantly since he'd arrived. Not his wallet. Just an envelope containing the five hundred dollars. And an extra fifty for taxis and the odd drink. He'd leave behind the pencil-written note, here in his hotel room. It would be found if he failed to return. It would be important evidence in the search for him. He shivered. He couldn't help feeling that by the time anyone had noticed his absence the trail would have gone horribly cold.

As a last-minute precaution he'd sent a fax home to Leonard, in reply to the one he'd received. That would be some sort of insurance. 'Investigations progressing, but slowly,' he'd written. 'Am due at an important meeting this evening, after which I hope to have more positive news. Photographs to follow at the earliest opportunity. Expect another fax from me tomorrow. Keep in touch. Best wishes. O.'

In the taxi on the way out to the Casa Bianca restaurant he thought about Guttmann again. Forget Mrs Wenglein, he'd said. Forget it all. Before you get hurt. What exactly was Guttmann up to? How serious were his threats? And who was the man Oswald was going to meet this evening? Was there a connection? Perhaps this was Guttmann's elaborate and sadistic way of reinforcing his original message. Oswald was going to report for the rendezvous simply to be given a beating. And on top of that he'd have to pay five hundred dollars for the privilege. He suddenly felt very scared indeed. What sort of man had Wenglein been? What sort of a community had he belonged to, that needed to go to these lengths to protect the privacy of its bereaved members?

The route the taxi was following took him out past the domestic airport of Buenos Aires, on to a road that ran along the bank of the River Plate estuary. Soon afterwards they drew to a halt and he was dropped at the entrance to the Casa Bianca. The restaurant terrace fronted straight on to the tree-lined embankment of the river. It was cool and welcoming. Under other circumstances he could imagine this place being rather appealing. He sat down at a table and ordered a beer. He looked out towards the water. It was a strange red-brown colour, stretching out as far as the eye could see. Somewhere beyond the horizon lay the coast of Uruguay. A solitary fisherman stood against the parapet wall, motionless, eternal. There was an almost elegiac quality about the evening light. In spite of everything, Oswald thought again to himself that he rather liked this city.

He finished his beer and looked at his watch: 8.25 now, and the shadows were gathering in. Perhaps after all he was merely going to be stood up. The anticlimax of an aborted rendezvous was the cruellest option of all. He'd have preferred something to have happened. Anything. Anything rather than the depressing journey back to the hotel with nothing achieved. He lit a second cigarette and wandered across to the parapet wall.

He stared into the water. What was he doing here, all these thousands of miles from home? What sort of game was he playing; who was he trying to fool? At heart wasn't he just a jumped-up museum curator who'd deceived himself with a sort of *folie de grandeur* into thinking he was a man of action? Deluded himself with a dream of chasing a war criminal's plunder across two continents, of emerging triumphant with one of the great pictures of the nineteenth century rediscovered intact at the end of it all? And, most ridiculous of all, imagined that he could do it single-handed? He almost laughed out loud.

But he didn't. Because at that split second he heard a voice coming out of the shadows. Speaking to him. Speaking to him quietly but clearly.

'You have brought the money, señor?'

His heart was in his mouth. His first instinct was to run, but he stayed rooted to the spot. He must go through with it now. The voice was strangely familiar. He peered to either side of him. No one. No one except the fisherman. Christ almighty: the fisherman.

It was dark, and it was hard to make out details. But when he looked again, he saw that the outline of the fisherman was shaped curiously like an egg.

He waited till the next morning before ringing Mrs Wenglein. It was entirely possible, of course, that the number and the address in Avenida Alvear he had been given were false. There was every chance too that if Mrs Wenglein were as sensitive to her own privacy as

Guttmann had been on her behalf then she would refuse to see him. But he rang it just the same.

A maid answered. 'Señora Wenglein? A moment, please.'

There was an excruciating pause, then a husky voice said, '*Sí?*' and Oswald launched in.

'Mrs Wenglein? My name's Oswald Ginn.' Stupid, of course, to use his real name, the name Guttmann would have warned her about if he'd been in contact with her at all. He realised it too late, cursed himself, and blundered on. 'Please forgive my ringing you like this right out of the blue, but I'm over from England and I'd very much like to come and see you if you could possibly spare me a few minutes. I am most definitely not a journalist, but I would like to talk to you about your late husband. It's about . . . well, it's difficult to explain on the telephone, but it could be to your financial advantage, let's put it that way. There may be something in his estate that I'd like to buy from you. Is there any time in the next few days when I could call on you?'

'A business proposition?' She was cool and matter-of-fact.

'Yes, a business proposition.'

'Were you an associate of my husband's?'

'I'd had some contact with him.' Oswald paused, sensing he was making headway. Then he took the risk he'd been contemplating. The lie he'd calculated just might tip the balance. 'I was a great admirer of his, Mrs Wenglein. I liked what he stood for. It was a sad loss.'

He could almost hear her mellowing at the other end of the telephone. 'Yes,' she said, 'Heinrich, he was a man of strength.' She sighed wistfully. 'You can come today, Mr Ginn. At three o'clock?'

9

Oswald had been here before.

Not literally. Not to this particular smart apartment block in Avenida Alvear, Buenos Aires. But it was familiar. He'd been to so many others like it in Europe. The art nouveau ironwork of the banisters on the richly carpeted communal stairway; the highly polished panelling in the lift; the greenery of the potted plants; the doorman: it could have been Brussels, or Zurich, or Stockholm. A certain sort of picture-owner lived in these places. There was a uniformity to the experience of visiting them: overheated buildings housing grasping elderly widows or not-so-gay divorcees with works of art to sell. Bitter, suspicious, face-lifted, over-perfumed women anxious to obtain exorbitant prices for paintings that their late husbands had invariably assured them were worth a fortune. These women were an international phenomenon. 'Oh, Mr Ginn, you are of course joking,' he had been informed by Mrs Kaufmann in Munich. 'To offer me so little for this beautiful Teniers, it is an insult to my husband's memory. What do you mean, it is not by the artist? Would my husband leave to me a fake?' He always longed to offer women like Mrs Kaufmann the two most plausible explanations for their husband's oversight: either he had possessed no discrimination at all in the judgment of pictures, or he had left all his decent ones to someone else. Probably to the secretary he had been knocking off on the side for the past fifteen years. But of course you always restrained yourself, didn't you? You muttered soothing words about the difficulty of separating pupils from master with Teniers, and the art market's nit-picking insistence on a standard of condition that this picture – 'owing to a certain amount of over-zealous nineteenth-century restoration quite beyond the control of either your husband or yourself' – now did not quite achieve.

For a moment Oswald stared at the brass plate beside the bell. Wenglein, it said. This was it. He was reaching the end of a road that had begun in a depressing mansion flat in West Kensington, led him up various cul-de-sacs, and now deposited him here, at this doorway. Wenglein. It could be that in this apartment he was about to see a picture of such stupendous importance that it would erase for ever the memory of all the Mrs Kaufmanns in the world, remove the necessity of ever going to visit a single one of them again. He was on the verge of something momentous. Within a few minutes he might be undergoing an experience that would quite definitely change his life. And then there would be Mrs Wenglein herself to deal with. What sort of a woman was she? Could it really be that she was living in this flat, on a wall of which hung Gustave Courbet's 'Stonebreakers', without understanding anything of its significance and value?

When he rang the bell a maid opened the door.

'Señor Ginn, sí, señora Wenglein expects you. Please to wait in the salon, the señora will come to you.'

He walked into the room half expecting to turn the corner and see them there before him. The two of them. Old Gagey and his young assistant at the roadside. He was prepared for the vision of those bleak, monumental figures, the labourers once physically torn asunder in the holocaust of Dresden and now, thanks to some skilful South American restorer, rejoined on the same canvas.

He had braced himself for the shock of it, the shock of recognition, the shock of resurrection.

So when they were not there, not in this room, anyway, it was a disappointment. He stood for a moment, fighting that debilitating sense of anticlimax; and gradually he was aware of a quite separate feeling of disquiet within him. It was the atmosphere of the place. There was something wrong here, some indefinable evil against which he instinctively revolted. He was frightened. He was on dangerous ground. He didn't know how he knew it, but he knew it. He felt with absolute conviction that coming here was disturbing something better left alone. Something buried, something hidden, something over which the dust of time had only recently settled. He looked about him to try to trace the source of this unease. He searched for some physical feature which might have triggered it. What gave this room its threatening atmosphere?

He peered at the pictures that hung there. At first sight the art historian within him was encouraged. No, he didn't covet any of them himself, but they were reasonably serious. They showed discrimination. They were the sort of things that a man like Wenglein might have had. The sort of things that might have been owned by a man who felt strongly enough about pictures to choose to encumber himself in his hectic flight across war-ravaged Europe with an unwieldy roll of canvas from which he could not bear to be separated. There was a mid-nineteenth-century portrait of an aristocratic-looking lady in black, almost good enough to be by Winterhalter; there was a Dutch seventeenth-century landscape, probably the work of van Goyen; there were three Italian Old Master drawings of above-average quality. And then there was another, more disturbing picture, one whose subject-matter simultaneously fascinated and repelled.

It was Italian, painted in the seventeenth century, and

showed an episode of carnage rendered in sickening detail by an artist talented enough and of sufficiently macabre cast of imagination to make its impact both vivid and shocking. The subject was 'The Flaying of Marsyas', one of the most brutal pieces of iconography in the history of art. There hung the victim, suspended from a rail, while his muscular tormentors systematically sliced the flesh from his limbs, exposing ligature, tendons, even the very bone marrow in their bloody and remorseless flurry of cuts and swipes. Despite the appalling violence he had suffered, Marsyas was depicted with his eyes still open, unquestionably conscious and sentient. This was the final twist of sadism that the artist had allowed himself, the look of riven agony he had painted in those eyes. The same look you could imagine being cast even in our own century by other victims in the direction of other torturers. Torturers with whom Major Heinrich Wenglein might even once have been familiar. In Germany. In another life. In a life so long ago that Guttmann had assured him it was no longer interesting.

But what sort of people were they who found this picture a suitable decoration for a drawing-room?

Then his eye was caught by a silver-framed photograph on a nearby commode. He walked over to look at it. Here was part of the answer to his question. It showed a blond, heavily jowelled man of about thirty, in front of a Panzer tank. The first thing you noticed was that he was wearing SS uniform. Oswald had been in houses in Germany where people felt no compunction about displaying their fathers or grandfathers in their Second World War military colours. But always in Wehrmacht uniforms. That was acceptable. What he was looking at here was something different. Something shameless. And something horribly real. A living, breathing human being who had embraced the SS as a matter of choice and served it with enthusiasm. And this was his drawing-room in which Oswald was standing. Heinrich Wenglein suddenly seemed very close. Oswald stared intently at his face. His eyes were narrowed against the sun, and he seemed to be looking out at something beyond the camera, something that pleased him because a hard, arrogant smile was on his lips. One felt that his pleasure was intensified by the fact that what was amusing him was for ever hidden from the spectator. It was his own secret, and would remain so.

After all, he was used to getting his own way. Looking at him, it was not hard to believe. Throughout his life the man had trampled on people ruthlessly in order to get what he wanted. He had lived through a war in which he had become accustomed to giving orders and having them obeyed, in which he had been granted the opportunity freely to plunder the works of art which fascinated him; he had taken his pick of the women he fancied; he had seduced Gerda Helgemann, played her along, and then, when it suited him, jettisoned her, left her to die; he had shot a man in cold blood when that man had threatened to come between him and the Courbet; he had made his escape at the right moment from burning Dresden and defeated Germany; by cunning planning and outrageous good luck he had reached Buenos Aires and ill-deserved freedom. No doubt since then he had pursued a successful and profitable business career. Yes, he had reason to smile. Oswald had thought about him a lot, of course, since becoming aware of his existence that morning in Derek Gilbert's flat in St James's. But up till now he had been an entity in his mind rather than a person. Now, suddenly, he was shockingly real. Seeing this photograph brought it all home. He was looking at Heinrich Wenglein as he had been.

These were the features that had contorted in pleasure at the first possession of Gerda. Where, had it happened, where had her resistance finally crumbled? In some chilly field outside Dresden? In the back of the staff car? These were the features that had twisted in anger when the man had questioned his right to appropriate 'The Stonebreakers' from that street in Dresden as the city burned behind them. He had shot him. Coldly, remorselessly. And Wenglein hadn't changed, not when you looked at what he hung on his wall here in the flat in Avenida Alvear. These again were the features that had furrowed in concentration as he had removed 'The Stonebreakers' from its stretcher, carefully divided the canvas in two and rolled it ready for its long journey to another continent in another hemisphere. And these were the features that had lined and sagged into comfortable old age here in the refuge of Argentina.

Oswald heard the door opening behind him and put the photograph down abruptly. He turned to meet Mrs Wenglein.

He had expected a woman of the same generation as her late husband, perhaps not a geriatric, but certainly an old-age pensioner. He had also envisaged her as in some way Teutonic. But the woman who walked in now was in her late forties, and her looks were unmistakably Latin: sleek dark hair, olive skin, well-defined eyes, a full but petulant mouth whose line indicated a spoiled dissatisfaction with a lot of what she encountered in life. She approached in an aura of scent and cigarette smoke. She was running a little to fat, and yet Oswald's immediate reaction was unexpectedly ambiguous. She was almost attractive. It was a fragile, guilty attraction, the sort that might dissolve at any moment into repulsion. But her plumpness was still voluptuous rather than gross. Just.

She came forward with her hand extended. 'Señor Ginn.'

'How do you do, Mrs Wenglein.'

She looked at him directly, appraisingly, in a way that made him uneasy.

'Would you like a drink? I myself would take a whisky.'

'A whisky? Of course.' He followed the direction in which she was pointing and found the drinks tray. 'How do you like it? With soda?'

'On the rocks.' She spoke abruptly, even impatiently. There was something intimidating about her, as if she too had acquired her husband's attitude of mind and grown accustomed to being obeyed. Although it was only three in the afternoon he felt he also needed a drink. He poured out two glasses and walked over to hand hers to her.

'Thank you,' she said. She sat down and motioned him to do so too. 'So, you found your way here?'

'Yes, thank you. I came by taxi.'

'Señor Ginn, you are wise to travel like this.' She was suddenly animated. 'It is dangerous to walk the streets of Buenos Aires. There are many robberies, many criminals, people are not safe in this city. Once I myself was attacked. It was unbelievable, it was not at night, not in the shadows, but in the middle of the day . . .' She shook her head angrily and reached for a cigarette. 'Fortunately I had one of these. I do not like to smoke in the street, but it is a protection. I used it so . . . in his eyes.' She wielded the cigarette, clenched between fingers and thumb, in a quick, vicious gouging motion. 'He was caught; they could identify him by the burns. But he was not sufficiently punished by the courts; soon he was allowed to go free. The authorities do not seem to realise that these criminals will continue to plague people so long as the judges do not give them the sentences that will deter them.'

'You may be right,' he said warily.

'Violence should be met with violence; it is the only language to be understood by these scum. My attacker, he was most punished by the cigarette, not the court's

271

sentence. The cigarette left a mark. All these criminals should bear a mark.'

Oswald glanced momentarily at 'The Flaying of Marsyas' and said, 'I suppose your husband held strong views about this sort of thing?'

'But of course. What normal man does not? But you knew him, my husband?'

'We only met once,' he lied hastily. But he could have told her truthfully that, after reading Gerda Helgemann's statement, after staring into Wenglein's photograph, after experiencing the atmosphere of this apartment, he felt as though he had met him, even known him well. But he would have shuddered as he said it.

'He was a strong man, Heinrich. Some feeble-minded people even called him a bully. But I believe that men must assert their will, otherwise they lose their manhood. Do you not agree with that, Señor Ginn?'

'I think there are times when one must act rather than talk, yes, certainly.'

She drew on her cigarette. He had the feeling that he had said the right thing. That he'd passed a small test.

'Heinrich was a man of action, yes. And he held on to the old beliefs in many things. Maybe they were no longer fashionable, some of his views, but he would not desert them for the passing whim of liberal fashion. And of course Argentina has its faults, but here at least the mood has been a little more *simpático* for people like him, people who believed in firmness.'

It was true: in some ways Argentina belonged to another world, or perhaps another era, one in which Heinrich Wenglein would undoubtedly have felt more at home than in post-war North America or Europe. To judge from his wife's fierce apology for his life here, he had not felt it necessary to compromise his manner significantly after his flight from Germany.

272

'Of course, you will find people even here who will say bad things about Heinrich. I despise those people. Often they did not properly know him, or they would not have said what they did. For instance, I heard him accused of anti-Semitism. But here he knew many people who were Jews. How could he have been anti-Semitic when he did business with them?'

Oswald nodded. What could you say to a woman like this? She was appalling; but there was a steel beneath the surface which commanded the attention. And there was something else. From where he sat he could smell her scent.

He must handle her carefully, avoid upsetting her. She was his lifeline to the Courbet. He had to do business with her.

'Mrs Wenglein, first of all I must apologise for ringing you out of the blue.' He paused, wondering how to go on, then decided to grasp the nettle. 'I should perhaps tell you that I originally tried to get to you through a man called Guttmann, who I believe arranged your husband's funeral. But he indicated to me that you might not welcome my intruding on you. If that's the case, then I can only thank you for agreeing to see me.'

She looked up, surprised. 'Guttmann. Oh, the man is a fool. But a loyal fool, it is true. He used to worship Heinrich. People did. Some people, anyway.' She gave a little reminiscent laugh. 'You met him, you know what a man of strength he was. Such a willpower, especially when he was younger.'

'I understand that he was also a fine connoisseur of pictures,' Oswald went on. 'In fact that's the reason for my visit. It's about your late husband's picture collection. You see, I'm a specialist in European painting, and I've heard he had one or two particularly good examples.'

'Heinrich, yes, he loved paintings.'

'I can see that he had some fine things in his collection.' He ran his eyes over the van Goyen, the Old Master drawings, and reached 'The Flaying of Marsyas' before turning back to her. 'I believe . . . I believe he brought some of them with him when he came here from Europe after the war?'

She considered the question. 'That may be so,' she said at last. 'But you must understand that these were things that happened before I knew him, so I cannot tell you. I think that when he first arrived in Argentina I was no more than four years old.' She laughed, and shrugged her shoulders.

'No, of course.'

'He was married once before, you know.'

'I didn't know.'

'A terrible woman, she gave him much trouble. They married soon after he came here, but she died twenty years ago. There were no children. It was a great release for Heinrich. He married me in 1979 only.'

'So you know nothing about any of his pictures?'

'I know that some were bought in New York in the fifties and sixties. That, for instance,' she said, gesturing to the Winterhalter, 'and maybe the Dutch landscape. But to be honest, pictures are not so much my forte; I do not have so much interest in them. Now I must sell some of them, so I must take advice.'

'Perhaps I can help. I would be delighted to.'

She barely acknowledged the offer, but continued with annoyance: 'There are many papers to check still and lawyers to consult. You have to be careful, as a woman alone. So many lawyers are not to be trusted, these so-called advisers, they try to exploit you. I must be always on my guard.'

'It's very difficult, I know.'

She stubbed out her cigarette decisively. 'So, Señor

274

Ginn,' she said. 'Perhaps it would be best if you look around the apartment. Perhaps you will find some pictures that interest you. The place is large, you see, and maybe I do not remember everything that is hanging here.'

'Thank you, I'd like to do that.'

She got up, and he rose with her, preparing to follow her. But instead she came towards him and handed him her glass.

'Another drink,' she said.

As he refilled their glasses he asked her, 'Did your husband ever talk to you about the old days in Germany?'

'It was very rare for him to speak of that time.' How much did she know? he wondered. Of Dresden. Of his girlfriends. Of the men he had killed.

As he handed her back her drink, their fingers touched accidentally. There was something about her. She was arrogant. She was petulant. She was difficult. But he sensed that she was ultimately submissive to men. It gave an unexpected frisson to their contact. A frisson of excitement.

She turned away. 'Come,' she said.

It was indeed a large apartment, with a pattern of passages off which opened studies, reception rooms, bedrooms, and servants' quarters. First Mrs Wenglein led the way from the salon in which they had been sitting through to a formal dining-room. Here fourteen heavy gilt chairs stood around a massive table.

'Yes, we have entertained large parties here,' she said, 'but not so much recently. Heinrich was tired in the last years, and the people he wished to see became fewer.'

Oswald had checked immediately for the Courbet. It was not in this room either. There was a series of Brazilian topographical prints, and two large Flemish pictures. One featured a number of dead animals, trophies of the chase.

The other showed dogs fighting over a rabbit, a rabbit whose bloodied body was being wrenched apart between their jaws. He shivered again. It was an odd subject for a dining-room.

'This one interests you?' she asked.

'It's not quite what I am looking for, but it's . . . it's impressive.'

She walked closer to it. 'Heinrich loved this painting. It was particularly this dog here which he admired. He said it reminded him of Gerda.'

'Of Gerda?'

'Gerda was his favourite dog. He bought her when he first came to Argentina; he showed me photographs. She lived to the age of sixteen. I think perhaps that he was more upset when she died than when his first wife did.' There was a hard edge to her laugh.

'It's strange – I wonder why he chose the name Gerda?'

'I do not find it strange. It is a good name for a dog.'

They walked on down the passage and into a study. Once again he was disappointed. The pictures were undistinguished. One wall was dominated by a large glass cabinet containing a collection of firearms, mostly German. There was a Luger there, a hand-pistol. He couldn't take his eyes from it. Suddenly he knew that it was the sort of gun that could have been drawn quickly from a holster on a Dresden street. The sort that could have been used to gun down the miserable interloper who had been unwise enough to argue with an SS major. Gazing at it, a horrifically vivid image of the scene came to him. He could see it happening, hear the stifled scream, smell . . . smell what? Smell a sort of stench of death, perhaps. A whiff of burning flesh.

'Mrs Wenglein, the picture I'm particularly looking for is a large one. It shows two workmen breaking stones by a roadside.'

She thought for a moment, then shook her head. 'I do not recall that one. But let us look in these last rooms.'

It wasn't going to be here, was it? Opening these doors into the maid's cramped chambers was a waste of time. But why wasn't it here, somewhere in this huge apartment, in this opulent refuge Heinrich Wenglein had created for himself? Oswald thought suddenly of another flat, thousands of miles away, where he had called on another recently widowed woman in his quest for 'The Stonebreakers'.

'Does the name Bernard Tumbrill mean anything to you?' he asked.

'I don't think I have had the honour of meeting this gentleman. Should I know him?'

'He was a visitor here in Buenos Aires some weeks ago. I wondered if you had come across him.'

She shrugged. 'No, I did not.'

They were on their way towards one last door. She paused before opening it, turning towards him with a sudden indecision.

'There remains only this room,' she said slowly. 'This was our bedroom.'

It was as if she was contemplating whether or not to go in. Surely she would know if a large picture like 'The Stonebreakers' was hanging here. That couldn't be the uncertainty. There was something else on her mind. Then she appeared to take a decision, turned the handle firmly and pushed the door open. She said: 'Come, Señor Ginn. I show you something now. I show you something which I think you will appreciate.'

He followed her. Almost immediately her manner changed. Once inside there was a perceptible quickening of excitement in her movements, a sense of significance about what she was doing. This room was in some way special to her. He had the impression that in taking him in here she was bestowing some honour on him. She was preparing to reveal to him a secret of some sort. The room they had entered was opulently draped, dominated by a large double bed. The marital bed of the Wengleins. He found he was too embarrassed to look closely at it, and instead he glanced around the walls. He saw no pictures of any distinction. His eye rested momentarily on a semi-pornographic eighteenth-century print. He wondered uneasily if she had brought him in here to show him this.

But no. Now she was opening another door. This led into a vestibule giving off the main room, and she beckoned him in. 'I want that you see this.'

'What is this room?'

'It was my husband's dressing-room. I have preserved it as it was, before he died.'

'Are there pictures here?'

'No, no pictures. But come, you will see.'

Along one wall of the chamber they had entered ran a row of mahogany doors. Slowly, with an air of momen-tousness, she opened two of them. She took a pace back to allow him a clearer view. What he saw was an array of immaculate, slightly dated men's clothes. There were dark suits, light suits, sports jackets, polo clothes, and over-coats, five or six of them, one decorated with an extrava-gant fur collar. They hung there in rows, mute but intimate memorials to one man's life.

Mrs Wenglein sighed, and for a moment they both stood in silence. It was as if they were contemplating a museum. No, it was more than that. A monument. Perhaps even a shrine.

She reached across and touched a heavy tweed jacket. 'He was a man always well turned out.' She spoke in a voice little more than a whisper. 'Feel the excellence of this cloth.'

Suddenly, he didn't want to touch it. He didn't want to

have anything to do with it. The idea was distasteful. But
he felt her willing him to, yearning for it. So he quickly
stretched out his hand and took the material briefly
between his fingers. He shivered. And he felt a quick little
intake of breath from Mrs Wenglein. The tweed was
exceptionally thick. Oppressive on a day like today in
Buenos Aires. He withdrew his hand, letting the jacket's
arm fall back. It had been worn by Heinrich Wenglein.
Worn by Heinrich Wenglein, who had shot at least one
man in cold blood, and tried to drown a woman who loved
him. He recoiled. But there was fascination mixed in with
his horror. He glanced again at Mrs Wenglein. She was
animated, flushed. Looking at her husband's things gave
her an almost physical pleasure. But it was more complicated than that. He sensed that the pleasure was obscurely
heightened by his own presence. She needed him here.
Somehow the ritual demanded it.

Now she reached into the cupboard again. 'And these,'
she breathed, 'how do you call them? Jodhpurs.' She gave
the word a strange, deeply sensual intonation.

The white polo breeches were ancient but beautifully
cut. She pulled them out on their hanger and held them
up.

'Jodhpurs,' she repeated, savouring the word. As her
lips worked breathlessly round the two syllables in lingering appreciation, it sounded suggestive. Almost obscene.
'Jodhpurs.'

The afternoon sun shafted in through the small window
at the end of the room, and it was suddenly uncomfortably
hot, standing here next to this woman in this confined and
disquietingly intimate space. As she leaned forward to
replace the hanger, he caught a hot breath of her scent.
He saw her blouse stretched tight across her breasts. He
saw the buttons open. He glimpsed her cleavage. Her
flesh. A crucifix fell between her breasts on a slim gold

chain. Wenglein. This was Wenglein's woman. Gerda Helgemann had been Wenglein's woman, too. He dominated women, overpowered them. Even strong, arrogant personalities like Luisa Wenglein. The man's sexual forcefulness was communicating itself across the years. She could feel it, through contact with his very clothes. Oswald could feel her feeling it. She was aroused. And her arousal was itself arousing. The two whiskies went dizzily to his head. A balance had been upset. Anything could happen.

'Now, I show you more.' Again she spoke in little more than a whisper, but her voice held enormous tension and excitement. From somewhere she had produced a key. She was unlocking the last two doors in the line. Magnetised, he took three steps to look in.

What he saw made him think immediately and absurdly of a theatrical costumier. Here was a line of heavily braided uniforms, immaculately kept, black adorned with silver. Then he looked again and experienced a shock of recognition. Of horrified recognition. These were not theatrical props: they were genuine SS uniforms. There were tunics, breeches, and further on a jet-black leather coat. These were real. They had been worn by living, breathing Germans. By living, breathing Nazis.

'These . . . these were your husband's?'

'No, not his personal uniforms. But he made a collection. They were not so difficult to find here after the war.'

'Extraordinary.' He swallowed hard. He felt sweat on his forehead.

'In the last years he spent more and more time here with his uniforms.' She reached out wistfully and stroked a lapel. For a moment she was lost in a hazy mist of reminiscence. Then her eye was caught by something in the bottom of the cupboard which she bent to pull out. 'And these,' she said, 'these he spent many hours polishing. Many hours, at the end of his life.'

She held out the black, shining boots. Jackboots. They were proud, splendid things; and they were shocking. She ran a caressing hand over the leather. He saw the brown flesh of her wrist, her ringed fingers, the painted red nails moving against the gleaming black surface. 'See, hold them,' she said. He took them uncertainly, and even as he felt them in his hands he was aware that she was continuing to stroke them. Playing her hands up and down the curves of the calf. Massaging them.

'It is sad,' she murmured. 'Sad to see these boots standing here, these uniforms hanging here no longer used or regarded.' She paused, then added: 'Sometimes I wish they could be worn again, worn by a man. A man of strength.'

Then the suspicion swept giddily over him, sickening and yet subliminally seductive. She was asking him to wear these things, wanted him to dress up in them. Everything. Tunic, breeches, and, God almighty, these boots, these big brutal boots as well. She wanted to see him in them, watch a man's arm swing in the tunic, see the trousers envelop his thigh, hear the click of the heel on the floor.

He saw with heart-stopping clarity how events might unfold: first the dizzy bravado of it all as she eased him out of his jacket and thrust him into the tunic; the enormity of the embarrassment of shedding trousers doused by the clinical efficiency with which she encouraged him into the breeches; then gradually her breath coming quicker as the undercurrent of passion broke the surface, culminating in the battle to get the boots on, she kneeling beside him in a mounting fever of excitement, straining to slide the obdurate leather further up his calf. He envisaged the golden crucifix she wore around her neck jiggling in the cleft of her bosom. He saw her well-groomed hair breaking free, sweeping down across her burning cheek. And then the moment when, with both boots finally in place, he would stand up. Stand up in the full glory of an SS major's uniform, his feet, his legs, his limbs encased in clothes that enmeshed him across the years, brought him into guilty alliance with a proud and horrific past. And she would look up at him, conquered. Flushed, within his power.

He thrust the boots back into her hands.

'No!' he said. 'No, not me . . .'

She held them, motionless. For a moment she stood there, her eyes half closed.

Then the storm was over. With resignation, she put the boots back in the cupboard. Gently, reverentially, she closed the cupboard door, turning the key in the lock.

They retraced their steps back through the bedroom, along the passage and into the salon.

He was still sweating, but in this room it was cooler, less oppressive. He had the sensation that he had been very close to something very dangerous. He had seen something horrible. And worse, for a sickening moment, he'd felt a little part of himself respond to it.

Mrs Wenglein ran a hand through her hair to rearrange a stray lock. She lit another cigarette. She was composed again.

'Of course, there is the camp,' she said thoughtfully.

'The what?'

'The camp. The *estancia*. My husband's ranch – is that what you would call it? I had forgotten about the *estancia*. Now that I think about it, I remember that Heinrich kept some pictures there.'

'My God! Do you remember what they were?'

She drew on her cigarette and looked at him with an icy detachment. It was as if the visit to the dressing-room had never taken place. 'Señor Ginn, I must tell you I have been there only once, soon after we were married. I do not remember the pictures that hung there, but there were some. And yes, one was big, in the dining-room, I think. But I can tell you no more about it. I did not like the place. It was my husband's personal toy, and I had no interest in it. Yes, I like very much to watch the polo, but I have no special wish to see the ponies raised, no curiosity about the cattle. Throughout our marriage I have divided my time between Buenos Aires and Punto del Este in the summer. I am not – how you say? – the countrywoman. And even Heinrich in the last years did not go there very often; he was too tired. But in the past I believe he was very fond of the place.'

So that was where he had taken it. To the seclusion of the country. It had been too precious to be displayed to the world in this apartment in Buenos Aires. He'd taken it to his private lair on the *estancia*. Where he could enjoy it in peace, far from other people's prying. It made sense when you thought about it. Wenglein was no fool. He must have realised the picture's true importance, and judged it wiser to keep it relatively hidden. 'What has happened to the *estancia*?' Oswald asked.

'After Heinrich's death, I instructed the lawyer Dottore Contini to look after the matter. I think that he made a visit there, and I agreed to his advice that the *estancia* should be sold, even though the prices for such properties are absurdly low now; you get nothing for them. Contini told me that there were some items in the house, furniture and I think one or two pictures, which should be sold also. I left it all in his hands, I did not think there was anything important there.'

'But you do not know exactly what is there.'

'No, I do not know exactly.'

'And has Contini disposed of anything from the house yet?'

'No, I do not think so. I have watched him like a hawk, Señor Ginn, because lawyers are mostly crooks. And many are Jewish, of course.' She stubbed out her cigarette, stood up, and smoothed her skirt over her thighs. 'Wait, I have a recent letter from Contini about this matter. I will check.'

He watched her walk to the bureau and open a drawer. He was excited now, but it was a different sort of excitement from the steamy vertigo of the dressing-room. The balance had tipped back again. He saw before him a plump, petulant, disagreeable middle-aged woman. A woman who was getting on a bit. A woman whose ripeness had festered and decayed. Physically she held no more attraction. But in one respect she retained her allure. As a route to 'The Stonebreakers'. Suddenly the picture seemed within his grasp again.

'He says that he will send a *camión* to collect the more valuable items from the *estancia*,' she told him, holding the letter at arm's length in order to read it. 'He has arranged to include them in an auction in Buenos Aires.'

'When is this auction?'

'He does not say. But the *camión* is due at the *estancia* on . . . let me see, on Monday. In four days' time.'

'Mrs Wenglein, where is the *estancia*?'

'The nearest village is called Santa María. It is about a hundred kilometres south-east of Córdoba.'

'If I went out to the *estancia* tomorrow, could I see some of the items before they leave? The pictures, I mean? Would there be someone there?'

'I suppose you would find Juan, Heinrich's manager. He could show you.'

'And could I buy something before it went into the sale?'

Mrs Wenglein shrugged. 'You should negotiate with

284

Dottore Contini in that case. A good price would be necessary.'

'I would make an excellent offer if I can find what I'm looking for.'

She nodded judiciously. 'In dollars, Señor Ginn, payable in Montevideo. Contini will give you the account number.'

He shook hands with her as he left. Physical contact with her again left him unmoved beyond a mild flutter of distaste. She was not a pleasant woman.

'Until the next time, Señor Ginn,' she said.

As he walked thoughtfully down the grand staircase to the street, he hoped that there would not have to be a next time. He could deal through Contini now. She had given him the lawyer's card. He had what he had come for: if not 'The Stonebreakers', then a definite lead on it, a lead that looked more and more conclusive. With the news of the *estancia*, everything fell into place. Of course she had not known Bernard. There was no reason why he should have met her; their paths were unlikely to have crossed. No, Bernard had not met her. He hadn't met Guttmann either. Bernard must have met Contini, and Contini had told him of the Courbet secreted away in the distant *estancia*. Probably Contini had shown him the photograph, without fully appreciating the significance of what he was offering. By a combination of persistence and good luck, Oswald had cracked it. 'The Stonebreakers' was in the *estancia*, the private refuge of Heinrich Wenglein, the place where he kept his most precious things. Of course, Oswald could go direct to Contini now, and get more information from him; but at this stage he preferred to check it out himself, not to alert Contini to something of which he had only imperfectly realised the potential.

As for Mrs Luisa Wenglein, he could forget her, wipe her from the record. He need never visit her again, never re-enter that apartment. Once he'd seen the picture in the *estancia*, he could deal through the lawyer. He need never think of her again. She was part of a sick and fevered dream, with her outdated politics, her sadistic pictures, her vitriolic bitterness, her diseased worship of a war criminal. And her little golden crucifix jiggling tantalisingly between her breasts.

10

Oswald came out of Mrs Wenglein's apartment block on Avenida Alvear. He was elated by his discoveries. He stood for a moment looking up and down the street, as if to get his bearings. Perhaps he was in a state of mild shock. Perhaps he couldn't quite believe that his luck had turned, that things were going his way. Perhaps he was checking to see that no one was following him. Like Guttmann. Like Giannini. Like, craziest of thoughts, Shagger Parks. He laughed a little to himself. Shagger Parks. He should have more confidence. The coast was clear. Of course it was; he'd left the competition far behind this time. He was going to find 'The Stonebreakers'. He was going to find it first, before anybody else. He hailed a taxi and directed it back to his hotel.

In the taxi he lit a cigarette, to calm himself. His mind raced over many things: how he was going to get to the *estancia* near Córdoba, what sort of an offer he should make to Contini once he had seen the picture, where he should turn for help with getting it out of the country. And then selling it. Who should he alert first, Salzman or the Japanese? It was a tantalising prospect. And just below the surface of his consciousness seethed other thoughts, disjointed memories of those monstrous uniforms, the bloodied dog called Gerda, the writhing body of Marsyas. That writhing body, its pleading eyes riven with agony.

As they swung across into Tucman, he looked out of the

window. Idly, as you do in a foreign city. Curiously examining the passers-by.

The shock was almost instantaneous.

'Stop!' he screamed. 'Stop this car now, for Christ's sake!'

The driver stood on the brakes and came to a sudden halt. There was a squeal of tyres behind them, and a hail of angry hooting. Oswald hardly heard it. He tore ten dollars out of his wallet, flung it over into the front seat, and leapt out of the passenger door. He ran into a man with a briefcase, dodged a woman walking her dog, and collided with a barrier. What he'd seen from the taxi he could still see, a hundred yards away down the road. He ran, as he hadn't run for years, crossing a busy street, darting in and out of shoppers. He was closer now. He could see his quarry clearly, halting for a moment, looking in a shop window. God almighty, he was right. She was here, in front of him. In Buenos Aires. Here, in a busy street.

It was Saskia.

It really was Saskia. Since catching the glimpse of her from the taxi, he'd been through it all again. That process of feverish, overheated recognition which had deceived him in the past. That excitement which had caused his pulse to quicken when identifying resemblances in shop-girls or tourists in Bond Street. He saw a woman who moved in that familiar manner, putting one graceful foot in front of the other, swaying slightly as she had done through the tables in the restaurant in Dresden. He saw a woman whose blonde hair was cut short and stylishly. But this time he'd known it was going to be different. There was no sickening moment of revision of the first impression, when the face turned out not to be hers and he died a small death of disappointment. No, there she was, more and more her, with the high cheekbones and the beautiful

288

green Slavic eyes. There was absolutely no doubt about it at all.

'Saskia,' he said.

She was moving on from the shop window. She stopped and turned, surprised at this apparently unknown man calling out her name. Then she saw him. And she smiled. She smiled immediately. He analysed it many times afterwards, that particular smile, and it gave him nothing but pleasure. OK, maybe she didn't instantly recognise him, in the sense of being able at once to recall his name and the circumstances under which she had met him before. But she registered that he was familiar. And the smile meant that their familiarity had been a source of happiness to her, that its renewal was a piece of good fortune. She was not good at dissembling her feelings, she always gave into the instant expression of her emotions. That was part of the joy of her.

'You remember me? Oswald Ginn, from London. We met before, in Dresden.'

'Ah!' She laughed and shook her head as if to dispel disbelief. 'In Dresden, of course. Mr Oswald Ginn. But that was so long ago.'

'A few years now.'

'It seems . . . well, so much has happened since then.'

They stood facing each other on the pavement as other people milled past them. She had changed very little, except that she looked marginally more soignée. She wore trousers, a white tee-shirt, and a well-cut linen jacket. Under her arm she carried an expensive handbag.

'A lot,' he agreed. 'But it's so good to see you again. I can't believe it, meeting you here like this. Are you staying in Buenos Aires?'

'Yes, I just arrived. This morning, from Germany.'

He was suddenly tongue-tied, speechless, incapable of grappling with the outrageousness, the incomprehensibility

289

of their meeting. How could it be that they had spent all these years living relatively close to each other, on the same continent at least, without ever managing to make contact? Why was it only now, after they had both independently travelled thousands of miles to this outlandish place, penetrated to the very edge of the world, that he had found her again?

At last he said, 'Have you got time for a drink, or . . . or something?'

'I am late already for an appointment.' She spoke with genuine regret. Glancing at her watch she shook her head, then turned her wrist to him and added: 'See, I was due there five minutes ago.'

'Could we have a drink this evening perhaps?'

'Of course,' she said decisively. 'I would like that.'

'Seven thirty? At my hotel?'

'Where is that?'

He told her. He felt suddenly at home here, like a long-time resident.

'That is good. It is not far from me, I think. I will look forward to it.' She touched his arm with her hand and hurried on. At the next street she turned, and, seeing him looking after her, she waved gaily back with an enchanting hint of self-parody.

As he made his way back to the hotel on foot, he thought suddenly of Bernard. Of Bernard late one evening in some bar over a final whisky, he could not remember exactly where. Of Bernard holding forth at length with that familiar, slightly slurred intensity, fixing him with burning, bloodshot eyes.

'You know, Oswald,' he had declared, 'once or twice in every bugger's life he hits a purple patch, a time when everything goes right. The strange thing is it's not the failures in life that people are so bloody bad at coping with, it's their successes. You've got to be ready for success when it comes, know what to do with it, how to handle it. When you're on a roller, it's no good just sitting back and admiring it. No, you've got to ride it for all you're worth. Push your luck a bit, make the most of it. Hardly anyone does, though. Most poor sods get nervous, can't believe it'll last; they're almost willing it to end. Not me, not now. Christ, I remember a time when I won three nights on the trot in the casino and got lucky with four different women the same week. It all just kept on coming, it was bloody marvellous. Don't be afraid of things going well, and they'll probably get even better.'

Oswald was on a roller now. On the same unforgettable day, within a matter of an hour or two even, he had brought off the most extraordinary double. He had not only located with reasonable certainty the place where the Courbet was to be found. He had also rediscovered Saskia. Saskia. He had met her again, just wandering the streets of Buenos Aires. She was alive and beautiful and apparently unchanged. It was an inconceivable combination of good fortune. The two biggest ambitions of his life were there for the taking. Suddenly, everything was coming together. This was no ordinary run of luck. It was the roller to end all rollers.

A little under three hours later she joined him in the hotel bar. She stopped a moment in the doorway, looking across the room for him; then she caught sight of him and smiled.

'So,' she said, sinking into the chair he had drawn to the table for her, and crossing her elegant legs. 'Mr Oswald Ginn. At last we have time to talk.'

He had passed the time since their meeting that afternoon in a tumult of activity. He had showered, changed, and booked himself on an afternoon flight to Córdoba the next day. He had also bought a large-scale map and located the Wenglein *estancia* with reasonable certainty. It would be necessary to stay the night in Córdoba, hire a car, and set out the following morning to drive the sixty or so miles into the pampas to reach the end of his quest. He had even managed to speak to Juan Garcías, Wenglein's estate manager, and in broken Spanish warn him of his arrival. The plan was straightforward now. See the picture. Assess its condition. Negotiate with Contini. Do the deal. But he had made all these preparations mechanically, despite their momentousness. In a diminishing number of minutes he would be with her again. Seeing her. Speaking to her. Laughing with her.

'So,' he said. 'Now. What will you have to drink? Schnapps, for old time's sake?'

'No, no, not schnapps.' Then she caught the allusion to that other night in Dresden, and laughed. 'Not so early in the evening anyway. Perhaps a glass of white wine, thank you.'

He ordered. She ran a hand through her short blonde hair, touching it into place with a movement that suddenly seemed wonderfully familiar.

'Where can we start?' he said. 'I have so many questions to ask you. Tell me first what you are doing now.' He set out deliberately to control his tone. To avoid alarming her with the intensity of his excitement at seeing her again.

'What am I doing? It takes quite a lot to explain. Many things have changed in my country, you know. But I suppose I still work for the State.'

'But a different State?'

'Ah yes, a different State, you are right.'

'And is it better?'

'It is a shock for many people, this sudden change. Because it was sudden, you know. Suddenly we were exposed to the West, to a new way of life. Everything crumbled away from one month to the next. Of course, many things are better now, but also some things are gone which are missed. So we are undergoing a process of adjustment which can be a little painful. Perhaps you must ask me the same question again in five years' time.'

'I hope I don't have to wait another five years before seeing you again.'

She reached forward to take a nut from the bowl on the table and smiled up at him. 'It would be a pity,' she said softly.

By comparison with their last meeting she gave the impression of greater self-assurance. She was happier, perhaps, more settled in her life. The last time he had spoken to her had been that sad grey morning in Dresden Museum. That morning came vividly back to him now. His hangover, his frustration, his sense of something magical slipping irrevocably from him. And Saskia then. Saskia, in her scarf and white raincoat. Trying to smile brightly, efficiently, as if the previous evening had never taken place. Saskia, succeeding, just about, until that moment when they had stood in front of that magnificent sunset landscape by Caspar David Friedrich. Then she had gone silent, almost overwhelmed by an unspeakable melancholy. Now, five years later, as they sat in this bar in Buenos Aires, he wanted to ask her about all these things. He was impatient to reattain the intimacy of that moment in the museum, so as to put it right, to comfort her, to justify himself. But not yet. He must not be precipitate. He must tread gently.

She was asking him: 'But you must tell me what you are doing in Buenos Aires. It is so strange to meet you again here.'

What should he tell her? Everything? Nothing? For the moment he said, 'I am here on business.'

'But still for the museum?'

'No. I left the museum. I . . . I took your advice.'

'Oh! My advice. That can be dangerous sometimes. Sometimes I do not even know how to advise myself, let alone other people.'

'But in this case your advice was excellent, you were absolutely right. I should have left the museum sooner; I was getting nowhere there and driving myself mad. I am very grateful to you, for giving me that final little push.'

'You haven't regretted it?' It was that wide-eyed, enchantingly ingenuous concern for his well-being that he remembered from Dresden.

'Never regretted leaving, no. I joined Fortescue's. Perhaps you have heard of them. They are a well-known firm of art dealers in London.'

'So you are buying and selling pictures?' She looked at him with interest.

'That's it. Trying to, anyway.'

'And you have come here for what? Not to sell, I think, not in Argentina. You must be buying something.' It was not so much a question, more a meditative statement of fact.

'Perhaps,' he said. 'But just at this moment it's all . . . it's all rather delicate.'

'I don't want to be an intruder in your secrets,' she said, amused by his uncertainty. 'I shall not ask any more if you cannot tell me about these things. But perhaps you can help me: you have contacts here in the art market? You know people you can introduce me to?'

'One or two.' He thought of Giannini with his intelligent, bloodshot eyes. Giannini, with his little cigar. He didn't trust him. The idea of introducing him to Saskia didn't appeal at all. 'But you have to be careful of dealers here: they are crooks, most of them.' He paused, and then added: 'Why don't you tell me what you need help with?'

She sighed. 'I suppose my situation is a little like yours. My reason for being here is something delicate, something not to be too much spoken about. I have to make some enquiries, but I must make them discreetly.'

He was intrigued. 'I understand. But I'd like to help you. Please tell me about it if you can. We could . . . we could have dinner together if you're free.'

'You know something? When you look at me like that I remember you so clearly in Dresden, in that restaurant. It was a funny evening, wasn't it?'

How had he been looking at her? he wondered. In Dresden with a mixture of anxiety, dissatisfaction, and pleading, no doubt. And now not much had changed, it seemed. Except perhaps for a glimmer of extra optimism, a determination not to let her slip away so easily this time.

'Let's have another evening like that, shall we? For old time's sake?'

'I should like it very much, Oswald.'

'Let's go to the Recoleta. You'll like it there.'

She shrugged, and smiled. 'You seem to know everything about this city.'

They caught a taxi from the hotel.

'What's the Recoleta?' she asked him.

'It's a sort of little park where there are a lot of good restaurants. It's built round a cemetery.'

'A cemetery.' She seemed to shiver for a moment.

'Don't worry. Now it's the place to see the beautiful people of Buenos Aires parading themselves.'

'Dancing on the graves.'

He laughed, then saw she wasn't laughing. Suddenly he realised that there were parts of her that he didn't know at all. Areas of sadness that he could not reach. Not yet.

He chose an Italian restaurant, remembering how once she had told him that she loved Milan. He walked in with her, and as they were shown to their table he felt a joyous illusion of possession of the beautiful woman with him, a pride that other diners might look up and see them together, marvelling perhaps at the combination of such a lovely woman with such a ramshackle man, but registering nonetheless an automatic assumption of their closeness, an impression of intimacy. The clothes she had changed into – a skirt and a silk blouse – were more modishly cut than those she had been wearing in Dresden. In one way assimilation of the West must have come easily to her. She'd been born with a natural grace and stylishness, qualities that the DDR had been unable to extinguish in her. Full access to the elegance of Western fashion had enabled her to fulfil herself. She had flowered. For a moment a shadow of doubt passed over him: how could he ever hope to keep hold of someone so beautiful?

They ate and drank happily enough. Gradually her story emerged. In East Germany she had stayed on in the Ministry of Cultural Affairs. Right up till the end. Why, he asked her, had he been unable to reach her when he rang her the week after his return from Dresden?

'You rang me?' She was surprised. 'From London?'

'I did. They said you weren't there any more.'

'No one told me this.' Her brow furrowed with concern. 'But then frequently the system failed, you know. Stupid people dealt with telephone calls, messages didn't get through. But I remember that I did make an unexpected journey soon after your departure. I was sent almost at once to Bulgaria for two weeks on a project for the Ministry of Foreign Trade.'

'Ah, well. That explains it. I was worried about you.'

'You were worried about me?'

'I imagined you'd fallen into disgrace and been sent to organise postal collections in suburban Leipzig.' They were Bernard's words. He repeated them light-heartedly, but hearing them again from his own lips suddenly made him ashamed. He knew why. He'd told Bernard he'd slept with her. It had been the pathetic, empty boast of a man trying to laugh off deep disappointment. Bernard had believed him. Now Bernard was dead. He wished he could put the dishonesty right. For Bernard's sake. For Saskia's sake. For the sake of his own self-respect.

'I'm sorry, I don't understand.' Saskia looked at him mystified.

'Just a silly joke. Forget it.'

'But why did you wish to speak to me?'

'It was . . . oh, some detail to do with the exhibition. Nothing important.' He had wanted to hear her voice again, of course. Yearned for it with all his heart.

'But the exhibition never took place.' She was suddenly concerned again. 'Surely this was not because you were unable to speak to me?'

'No, no, that wasn't the problem. No, there were other reasons why it didn't happen: lack of sponsors, lack of money. Then I announced my resignation from the museum and I suppose the whole idea was shelved.'

'Ah.' She seemed relieved. 'But you could have spoken to Dr Dresch if it had been necessary.'

'Dr Dresch!' Now he could laugh at the memory of the man. 'What has happened to him, I wonder?'

'Dr Dresch? I do not know. I think that the recent developments would have been more difficult for him to accept.'

'How diplomatically you put things.'

She smiled uncertainly. 'He disappeared. Perhaps he has retired, living quietly somewhere.'

'Perhaps.' Oswald had a vivid vision of him morosely contemplating the tide of encroaching Mercedes sweeping inexorably over East German roads.

After the upheaval of reunification Saskia had been attached to a newly constituted all-German organisation that worked to promote German culture abroad. The job suited her, she said. She loved the travelling, seeing new places, meeting different people. Hadn't she once told him that this curiosity was her weakness? Yes, she was in Buenos Aires now as the first stop on a tour of Latin American countries, investigating how her organisation's activities could be expanded on this continent. She had arrived only at lunchtime on a flight from Frankfurt. They agreed again that it was the most wonderful coincidence to have met all these thousands of miles away from home.

'Do you remember?' she said unexpectedly. 'We once spoke about that?'

'About what?'

'About coincidences. I thought about it often afterwards, your distrust of these things, your fear of chance.'

'You reassured me,' he told her. 'You showed me that chance could be kind.'

'And it has been kind to us again. Here.' She was very definite, as if to stifle any doubt he might be feeling.

Discreetly, little by little, he drew from her more details of her present life. She still lived in Dresden. She still had her same flat. But he recoiled from asking her the ultimate question. He didn't want to know about her husband. Not if he'd come back from Moscow and they'd decided to make a go of it again. The evening was too pleasant for that sort of information. And he didn't want to face her reciprocal enquiries about his own situation. Not yet, anyway. He didn't want to have to lie to her again about Daphne. He didn't want to have to gloss over his continuing unhappy inertia.

'Yes,' she said, 'Dresden is my home always. I am happy that I still live there. That is where my roots remain. It is strange – as I have told you, I love to travel, but always it is special to come home to Dresden.'

'And how is Dresden now? Is it changed?'

'What, since you were there? You would notice a difference, perhaps. There are more tourists. There is much building, much restoration going on. They are working extensively on the Schloss, for instance, and there are many more plans.'

'And the Frauenkirche – will they restore that, too?'

She thought carefully before she spoke. 'Personally I think it is too soon to rebuild it. It is right that people should have this symbol, should continue to remember what happened. The wound went too deep, it would be unnatural if there was no small scar remaining somewhere visible. This is not something which is changed by reunification. It still hurts me to think of my uncle, my mother's brother, and all the others who died. They should not be forgotten.'

After dinner she reached into her bag for cigarettes and lit one unthinkingly, without offering them to him. Her movements were practised and assured. She laid the packet and her lighter neatly beside her on the table. She no longer needed to play with them as she talked.

'Now tell me,' Oswald said. 'How can I help you here in Buenos Aires?'

She drew deeply on her cigarette and inclined her head fractionally closer to him. He remembered how at another table in another restaurant he had reached out and stroked her hair. 'It is a sensitive matter,' she said. 'But, after all, I cannot proceed alone. I will tell you because I trust you and I need your help.'

'I am glad you trust me,' he said. 'You can always trust me.'

She stretched out her hand and touched his in a momentary gesture of gratitude. 'I think you are my friend. From the beginning I hoped it, when I first saw you in Dresden.'

'Did you?' he whispered.

'Yes. It was strange. You were so different from the person I expected. I had not met anyone like you before.

But I was drawn to you at once, I hoped you would have a sympathy for me. It was my intuition, perhaps.'

'Thank God for your intuition.'

The waiter came with coffee and filled their cups. When he had gone, Oswald said again: 'Now tell me what I can do.'

She still seemed unsure how to continue. There was a little bit left in the wine bottle and he used it to refill her wine glass. 'Go on,' he encouraged her.

She drank gratefully, then the uncertain words came out. 'You see, there is another reason why I am here in Argentina, a more secret reason. It is not just for my work for the Institute.'

'Another reason?'

'Yes. This trip was always planned by the Institute to take place later in the year. But then this extraordinary thing happened, something completely unexpected. Because of this thing happening I realised I must bring the visit forward, undertake it now. So I am here today already, several weeks sooner than intended.'

'What was the extraordinary thing that happened?'

'I was given some information. Unofficially, confidentially. I don't even know if it's correct. But to me it was so important that I felt I must come at once, to find out.'

'What was this information?' Suddenly his own heart was beating faster. Suddenly he felt an unaccountable apprehension.

She lowered her voice. 'I heard about a picture, a very important picture from the Dresden Museum, one which had been missing since the end of the war. A friend in the museum told me that they had been alerted, indirectly and unofficially, to the possibility that this picture was not destroyed, as everyone thought, but was stolen and has now become available here in Argentina. The story is incredible, I know, but these strange things sometimes

300

happen. My friend was very concerned and did not know what to do. And the more I thought about it, the more it upset me. If this picture was indeed in Argentina because of some men's evil in the past, it must be recovered. For Dresden. It is our heritage. When so much has been destroyed, it is important to reclaim what can be reclaimed.' She looked at Oswald full in the eyes. She was flushed, almost angry, appealing to him for support.

'So . . . so you came out now?'

'Yes, I came out now. I brought forward my trip as quickly as possible, there could be no delay. And I promised my friend in the museum to find out all I could, even to find the picture, if it existed.'

'And is this . . . this second, more secret mission . . . is it also official?'

'No, not really official. It couldn't be. You see, the information given was not conclusive. I was warned that it is not possible for our government to make representation to the Argentinian authorities so long as we do not know if the picture really exists here. That is what I must find out, before anyone else gets to it and it disappears again.'

'If it really exists,' he heard himself saying.

'Yes, if it really exists. There are many uncertainties. Perhaps it is no more than my intuition speaking to me, but I have this very strong feeling that the picture is here. And I am determined to do what I can. This is a very important thing for me, perhaps you can understand: it is for my home, for Dresden. A reparation that I can ensure is made for the suffering of the past.'

Yes, he did understand. Of course he understood. He knew how profoundly this beautiful woman felt what she was telling him. There were many different emotional seams buried here, immensely powerful ones, some crossing each other and entwining, all running very deep. How could you begin to extricate them all? Wounded pride.

The desire to right the wrongs of history. The grief of the bereaved, the anger of the robbed. And once again, drifting back to him from across the years, he smelled a sickening scent of burning flesh.

He must find his balance now, make the right response. A response that didn't give himself instantly away. He said: 'What is the picture exactly? Do you know?'

She looked up again, angry, imploring, but at the same time almost triumphant, relishing the impact on him of the momentous information she was about to impart: 'It is Courbet's "Stonebreakers".'

'My God!' he exclaimed. There was nothing else to say.

He was vaguely aware of a plate clattering in the distance, of other diners' voices ebbing and flowing about him. She was saying, 'Yes, it's unbelievable, isn't it? You remember, we spoke of it in Dresden?'

He nodded, aghast, but nonetheless registering how lovely her animation made her.

'But I need help,' she went on. 'Now I am here I do not know how to start to look for this picture. Can you give me advice?'

There it was.

Suddenly he was faced with an utterly horrific decision. The challenge was stark and unequivocal. What he said in reply to her question would decide, decide the rest of his life: either he was with her, or against her. There was no halfway house; he couldn't prevaricate. Things had gone too far for that. Either he had to tell her everything. Or he must betray her. Either he made for her the supreme sacrifice, laid at her feet everything that he had discovered about the Courbet, offered it to her as a kind of tribute – and, in so doing, resigned all claim to the personal benefit of it, lost it for ever – or he told her nothing, kept it from her entirely. And betrayed her, betrayed Saskia. There could be no relationship between them after that. He could kiss goodbye to any future intimacy between them, any lasting friendship. The choice lay there before him, with absolute clarity. Either he put what he had found out into the public domain, with the quest almost complete now after his visit this afternoon to Mrs Wenglein and his trip arranged to the *estancia* for the moment of climax; either he gave back its own to Dresden, earning enormous gratitude, but earning nothing else; or he kept it to himself, evaded Saskia's question, flew out to Córdoba, negotiated the purchase of the picture privately, sold it discreetly on to Salzman or the Japanese at a profit of several million pounds, and looked forward to the rest of his life in luxury. Without her.

Either he kept Saskia, and jettisoned the picture. Or he kept 'The Stonebreakers'. And lost her for ever.

Oh, Christ. Bernard again. Bernard, blearily through the mists of time. Another of those late-night drinking sessions round about the time of his resignation from the museum. Bernard, adopting the role he had enjoyed playing with him so much. The role of father confessor cum devil's advocate.

'Have I got it in me?' Oswald had asked, peering into his glass. 'Will I make a dealer?'

'OK, old cock, I'll give you a test. See if you pass it.'

'Go on, then.'

'What do you do in this situation? Some bugger comes to you with a picture. A bloody good picture. He offers it to you at a cheapish price. You know you can sell it on at a sodding great profit to a buyer who won't ask any questions, no comeback guaranteed. But you also know that the picture's stolen. Say not recently, but some way back. What do you do? Tell the fellow to get lost? Call in the police? Or do the deal?'

Oswald had thought before he'd answered. He'd contemplated a procession of images. There'd been the sanctimonious face of his director at the museum. There'd been the nauseating Denzil Burke with his absurd pink spectacles drivelling on about duty to the public. There'd been his own wife, telling him he'd never have it in him to make any money. Any serious money.

'I'd offer him ten per cent less than he was asking,' he'd replied, only half joking.

And now, six years on, the big one really had appeared. 'The Stonebreakers'. The way was open for him to buy it, without strings. Then Salzman's collection beckoned. Salzman wouldn't be inclined to ask too many questions if he had the chance to acquire a picture of this importance. He'd have the money on the table quick enough. Very big money indeed. Or alternatively the Japanese. If they were offered it, they'd have to have it. For them the Western museum provenance was a positive attraction. And once the picture disappeared into Japan, there would be absolutely no recourse for the original owners. Not legally. In Japan possession was ten-tenths of the law. Everything would be water-tight. And Oswald stood to make a very large sum indeed out of the deal. Enough to liberate him for ever from Leonard and Magnus. Perhaps even from Daphne. The Stonebreakers were poised to perform their final act of manual labour: once and for all they would sledgehammer down the walls about him, the walls that had always hemmed him in.

And Dresden? What of Dresden's claim to the picture? It had been a question he'd preferred not to confront. And he hadn't had to. It had been swept away in the slipstream of his own personal sense of mission. Swept away until this moment, that was. He'd felt he could disregard Dresden, he'd come to terms with that. But Saskia. Dear God almighty, that was different. The one person he couldn't disregard was Saskia.

There could be no further evasion. The issue must be decided now.

She sat anxiously opposite him, almost childlike in her enthusiasm and her uncertainty, waiting for him to answer, not suspecting the scale of the sacrifice she was demanding from him. He remembered the words he had spoken not half an hour before. 'You can always trust me,' he had told her, meaning it. If ever he had meant anything he had meant that. And what had she said? That she had hoped, from the very beginning in Dresden, that he would be her friend.

In fact it came out very easily when he finally spoke.

'Saskia,' he said, 'I can help you with this. I can help you more than you think. You have come to the right person.'

She was alert, excited. 'You know something about this?'

'I do. I know a lot about it.' He was conscious that every word he spoke now fastened ties between them. 'Listen, are you free for the next two days?'

'For two days? Of course I could cancel my appointments here if it was important.'

'Then you must come with me tomorrow on the afternoon flight to Córdoba. I think I can take you to "The Stonebreakers". '

'You? You can take me to it? You know where it is? But this is unbelievable.' She was almost tearful with excitement and relief.

'I think I know. This information has only come to me today; it is very fresh. I'm pretty sure that I have discovered exactly where it is now hanging. It is about a hundred kilometres from Córdoba, in an *estancia* on the pampas.'

'But how, Oswald? How did you find it?'

How? It was difficult to answer her question. What

should he tell her of his protracted struggle, the letter from Bernard, his call to Grunwald, the encounter with Derek Gilbert, his mad mission to Argentina, the mercenary intervention of the egg-shaped man, his horrific but ultimately productive afternoon with Mrs Heinrich Wenglein? Could he present all these to her as disinterested actions, recount them without rousing her suspicion of his motives in his relentless pursuit of the picture?

'How I found it is a long story,' he said. 'It's too complicated to tell you everything now, but I suppose you could say I came across it by chance. By a very lucky chance.'

'This is wonderful. I knew my intuition was right, that your friendship would be important to me. You have found "The Stonebreakers". If you take me to it, you will make me . . . oh, happier than I have ever been in my life before.' She paused, as if suddenly suspecting that the whole thing might be some sort of cruel hoax, and added: 'You will really take me to it?'

'I will do it, but on one condition.' He reached across and held her hand, on the table-top between the glasses. He felt he couldn't be denied this small reward.

'What is that?' she asked.

'The condition is that you understand that you are the only person in the world I would do it for.'

She was silent for a moment, apparently absorbing what he was saying. Then she smiled, and squeezed his hand in return. She murmured: 'I think maybe that I do not deserve this.'

He said, 'I am the judge of that.'

In the taxi back to her hotel there was loud tango music playing on the radio. It swept over him, alternately gentle and violent. And desperately sad. He suddenly had an inkling of the essence of Argentina. Proud, melodramatic, melancholy. He still held her hand in his own. He looked out at the lights, the lights of the cafés and bars of Buenos Aires, the city that only came to life at midnight. Whatever happens, he told himself, I will have known this moment. It cannot be taken from me. Obliquely he sensed that perhaps it made up for everything he had just sacrificed.

'Thank you for dinner, it was lovely,' she said when the car stopped at the entrance to her hotel.

He put his arms around her and kissed her on the cheek.

'Tomorrow Córdoba,' she breathed.

'And the next day "The Stonebreakers".'

She turned her face to him and kissed him on the lips. Then she opened her door and slid quickly out.

As the taxi drove on, he was conscious momentarily of the same sense of loss he had felt when they had parted in that other hotel all that time ago. But it was not quite the same. She was bound to him now by bonds that had not existed before. And even as he walked to his room, he still had the scent of her in his nostrils, the feel of her body in his arms, the taste of her lips on his lips as vivid intimations of what might come.

When he lay on his bed he found it impossible to sleep. He thought of the day that had passed, of its momentous discoveries and rediscoveries, of its irrevocable decisions and allegiances. And he thought of the days ahead, of the flight to an unknown city, the journey to Heinrich Wenglein's *estancia*, above all of doing these things in the company of Saskia. How would it be when they actually stood together in some godforsaken war criminal's bolt-hole in the distant expanses of the Argentinian pampas, face to face with the picture of two simple peasant stonebreakers, the picture that in different ways had come to dominate their respective lives?

Then, when he finally drifted into a fitful oblivion, he had a dream. He dreamed that he was running down an endless corridor, running because somewhere off that corridor opened the room where he would find her. And when by a supreme effort of will he reached her door, opened it, and took her in his arms, he looked again and saw he was embracing not Saskia but Mrs Heinrich Wenglein. Luisa Wenglein. And he could not stop himself. He could not stop himself as her flesh spilled from her silk blouse, as he chased the crucifix with his tongue across her breasts, as her skirt rose up round her hips, as her stockinged and suspendered thighs parted to receive him. He could not stop himself as he drove up her, as she sweated and writhed and moaned evil imprecations, as in her final ecstasy she reached down his leg. Reached down to grasp for something he hadn't realised he was wearing. Reached down to clutch convulsively at the leather of his jackboot.

On the whole Orlando found he got on better with women than with men in Argentina. The Arnosas were a typical case. They had both overwhelmed him with their hospitality and their eagerness for his company from the moment he had met them, at a drinks party in the house of a mutual friend the day after his arrival in Buenos Aires. But he'd felt more at ease with Cara than with Enrico.

'Where do you stay?' Enrico Arnosa had demanded. He was in his early thirties, tall, good-looking and rich, with a passion for polo.

'At the Plaza,' Orlando replied.

'That place is a tip. You should come and stay with us. Shouldn't he, Cara?'

'But of course you must,' agreed his wife. 'Our guest suite, it is at your disposal. And do not worry, the apartment is large.' Cara was a beautiful, burnished woman with vivid eyes and lips, a sinuous figure and a gravelly voice.

'That's awfully kind of you.'

So Orlando had packed his bags, vacated his room in the Plaza and moved in with the Arnosas. It was certainly comfortable. But there were wearisome aspects to his host and his constant displays of machismo. He spoke English in a cool Hispano-American accent, shouting a lot, and making jokes about fairies. It was easy enough to play him along, of course, to act out the role that Enrico expected of any male who was to be his friend. His favourite topics of conversation were horses, skiing, women, cars, drink and restaurants, and Orlando in his company simulated a like range of interests, reminiscing about Gstaad, New York, and Maseratis, whilst idly speculating what it would be like to fondle Enrico's bum. Cara's company, on the other hand, he enjoyed, because he could relax with her; he could make her laugh effortlessly.

'Oh, Orlando, you are so funny,' she would exclaim with delight. 'You know something? I never met anyone like you before.'

It was no doubt true. His carefully cultivated, essentially English brand of sophistication was a glorious novelty, and he sensed she was fascinated by him. He himself harboured no pressing carnal desire for her, but he admired her style, the way she wore her clothes, the way she cut her hair, the way she walked.

That night the three of them arrived back in the apartment around 2.30 a.m. It had been an exhausting evening of arduous pleasure-seeking. There had been drinks at someone's house, dinner with ten other people in a restaurant, then on to a night-club.

Enrico strode over to the drinks table.

'Scotch?' he demanded, waving the opened bottle in Orlando's direction.

'I think I've had enough.' Orlando unwound himself on the sofa and stretched languidly. 'You know what I would like, though?' He looked up at Cara who was perched on the arm next to him.

'What?' she enquired tenderly.

'A cup of tea.'

'Tea?' repeated Enrico with disdain.

'*Si!*' exclaimed Cara. 'Of course he must have tea. He is an Englishman, after all.' She shimmered off towards the kitchen, shedding her jacket on the way and shaking her magnificent mane of hair loose over her shoulders.

Enrico rattled the ice in his drink and sat down opposite Orlando. He ran a bronzed hand round the back of his neck and loosened his tie. 'So, we are off tomorrow,' he said.

'Where are you going?'

'To the camp.' He paused. 'Hey, what you say you come with us? You got to see an *estancia* while you're in Argentina.'

'Well, I really don't know. I've got some business to do here in Buenos Aires.'

'Hey, you think about it.' Enrico lit a cigarette.

Cara came back into the room with a tray of tea.

'Thank you, darling,' said Orlando, smiling at her. 'A life-saver; you are an angel.'

'I've been saying to Orlando, he should come with us tomorrow, visit the *estancia*. He should do this once when he's in Argentina.'

'*Si!* Is a wonderful idea!' Cara was ecstatic. 'We can all fly out tomorrow, together. It is Enrico's private plane; it takes only one hour and a half.'

'But will I like it? Who'll be there?'

'There'll only be us. And the horses and the cattle, of course.'

'Gauchos – will there be gauchos?'

'Sure there'll be the gauchos.'

Orlando sipped his tea thoughtfully, and then recited:

'An Argentine gaucho named Bruno
Said, "There is one thing I do know:
A woman is fine
And a boy is divine
But a llama is número uno." '

Enrico looked at him dubiously and swigged his whisky, but Cara laughed loudly. 'Oh, Orlando, you're so funny.'

Orlando giggled with her, and said: 'So you think I ought to come too?'

'Sure. Maybe we find Bruno.' She collapsed into hoarse laughter again.

'The llamas had better watch out.'

For a moment she was serious, galvanised by a sudden memory. 'Hey! And something else. Those people you asked me about today, those Germans: what was their name?'

'Wenglein.'

'*Sí*, that's what I thought. Enrico, who's that German with the *estancia* near Santa María, the one your father never liked, the one that just died?'

'He was called Wenglein. Difficult old bastard.'

'There! I thought so.' She looked at Orlando triumphantly.

'What? Wenglein had a ranch near you?'

'Sure. There were a bunch of Germans had camps to the east of us. Enrico's papa used to call it Krautland. I knew one of them was called Wenglein.'

'But did you know him?'

'Not really.'

'But he was an old man? In his seventies? Who died this year?'

Cara nodded.

'Did you go to his house, at least?'

311

'I, never. Did you, Enrico?'

Enrico shook his head. 'Nope.'

'Christ almighty!' said Orlando. 'Then I'm certainly coming with you tomorrow.'

It was divine intervention, of course. His prayers of the first afternoon were being answered. It was little short of miraculous the way God was so responsive, ordering this sort of disclosure to reach his ears at precisely the right moment with a minimum of inconvenience. This, it seemed, was what Father O'Rourke had called the reward of faith. He felt a glow of spiritual repleteness, coupled with a resurgence of rapacity as he contemplated what might be possible once he actually laid hands on the picture.

'Is wonderful,' exclaimed Cara, leaning over to squeeze his arm. 'I'm so glad you're coming.'

Oswald met her at the reception desk of her hotel at lunchtime the next day. Saskia was wearing jeans and a tee-shirt and carrying a single bag. She looked fresh and lovely. She was a woman who did not need complicated decoration. Seeing her again, he was struck by the fact that while her figure was undeniably flawless, it was to her eyes and cheekbones that one was drawn for the spark of her beauty. He did not kiss her, just put out a hand and touched her arm. For the next forty-eight hours or so he realised that they would be almost exclusively in each other's company. It was a prospect as compelling as finding the picture itself.

'This is exciting, I think,' she said in the taxi to the airport. 'I could hardly sleep last night.'

'Nor could I.'

'Oswald, are we truly going to see this picture?' There was a beguilingly innocent quality to her excitement.

'I think the likelihood is very high,' he said. 'But I can't

312

guarantee it. I mean, everything points to the picture being in this *estancia*. But we can't know until we see for ourselves.'

They bumped along over the pot-holed dual carriageway that led to the domestic airport. He had been on this road the night before last, heading out to his rendezvous at the Casa Bianca. Then he had been apprehensive, uncertain. Prepared for the possibility of being beaten up, of being robbed of five hundred dollars. In fact it had been the best-spent five hundred dollars of his life. It had opened up the road to Mrs Wenglein. And indirectly to Saskia herself. Now he felt her gaze upon him, and he heard her giggling.

'You are very mysterious man, Mr Ginn. You sit there looking very serious, very discreet. I think now is the time you tell me a little more about how you found this painting. I am so curious to know. It would be a kindness to me if you satisfied this curiosity.'

So he gave her a more expanded version of the story. After all, why not? Now she knew the crucial fact of the picture's apparent survival and existence here in Argentina, there was no longer any point in keeping other things from her. He had decided to give everything to her, so there was no need to hold back on these details. He told her about Bernard Tumbrill, how 'The Stonebreakers' had been offered to him and how he had in turn alerted Oswald to it. But alerted him without giving him the crucial information of its whereabouts before his sudden death locked away the secret. He told her about the highly opportune meeting with Derek Gilbert, and how this had led him to the evidence of Gerda Helgemann and the extraordinary account of how 'The Stonebreakers' had miraculously survived the night of destruction in Dresden on 13 February 1945. Saskia listened absorbed, and at the end of his repetition of Gerda's story she asked:

'So this man, this Nazi – what was his name, Wenglein? – he and the girl were in Dresden that terrible night? They lived through it?'

He nodded. 'Her evidence was a very vivid document. It came across as a particularly hellish experience.'

'My God,' she said quietly. She was silent as the car drew up at the departures entrance and they gathered together their luggage. Oswald collected their tickets from the Aerolineas Argentinas desk and they checked in for the flight. It was only when they were sitting waiting to board the plane that she spoke again.

'So they survived,' she said slowly, shaking her head as if trying to dispel the horror of what she was contemplating. 'The Nazi Wenglein survived when so many innocents died.'

'He did survive. Both he and Gerda Helgemann survived. You see, the girl's aunt's house, where she and Wenglein spent that night, seems to have been a little to the south of the centre of the city, not actually in the old town. That was what saved them, of course.'

'My God,' she said again.

He went on to explain how Gerda Helgemann's testimony indicated that Wenglein had escaped to Buenos Aires with the picture; how news had come through of Wenglein's recent death; how it must have been here that Bernard had been offered the picture, as there was evidence that he had travelled to Argentina recently; and how Oswald had followed the path out here and finally tracked down Mrs Wenglein.

She nodded, but she was preoccupied. She had drifted away into that area of private melancholy where he could not follow her. He watched her uneasily.

'Somehow personal stories about the bombing always move me,' she said at last. 'Perhaps I have too much imagination about these things, but I can see so clearly that girl in her aunt's house on that night. It makes me

314

think of my own uncle, the one who died. I suppose he was not so lucky: his house was nearer the centre. You know, I sometimes walk past the place where it stood. Now there is a travel agency there.'

For a moment he saw it all again. What he'd sensed so vividly immediately after reading Gerda Helgemann's statement in Derek's flat. He too saw Dresden again, Dresden in its agony. He saw a woman in Dresden. The woman was alone. The woman was frightened. Images grew confused. He saw the bombs falling, lighting up the night sky with their prodigious explosions. He smelt the burning, heard people screaming. Was it Gerda, crouched in her basement? Was it Saskia?

They boarded, and settled in their seats for the short flight to Córdoba. She was silent again for a while after take-off, then she turned suddenly to Oswald and said:

'So now they have put up a statue to him in London, I think.'

'To who, Saskia?'

'To that man – was his name Harris? The one who organised the destruction of my city. I have read it in a newspaper.'

'Harris.' He laughed awkwardly. 'Yes, I read that too.'

'Why do they do that in your country?'

'As I understand it, it's more to commemorate the British airmen who died in the war, not the destruction of Dresden.'

'That distinction is a difficult one for us to understand, you know.'

'I can imagine it would be.' He was uncomfortable now.

'But why was Dresden bombed?'

He'd been dreading that question. And he was perplexed by it. He was perplexed by the sadness, the bitterness that underlay it. 'Why was Dresden bombed?' he repeated.

'Yes. I have never known an Englishman well enough to ask him that question. I would like to know your answer.'

It was unfair, of course. He had no responsibility for the action. He had not even been born when it took place. Yet now he was being asked to justify it, to Saskia of all people. He would have preferred to have avoided the issue, let it be, but she was looking at him with such an intensity that he felt it would help her if he said something, that he owed her some sort of reasoned reply.

'Well, there were strategic reasons at the time, I believe,' he began. 'I have heard it argued that it was important as a gesture of support for the Russians, being seen to be doing something to help them on the Eastern Front. And it was intended to lower German . . . that's to say Nazi morale.'

'But it didn't really shorten the war.'

'Who can say? You can't ever precisely compute it.' But he found his reasoning didn't carry Derek Gilbert's assurance. He added: 'I've heard it argued that the lives lost in Dresden were to a certain extent counterbalanced by the Allied lives saved due to diminished resistance.' How could he expect her to accept that?

'But the lives lost in Dresden were civilian lives.' She was sad rather than angry. She seemed genuinely to be searching for an explanation. 'The Allies must have known, mustn't they, of the number of civilians packed into Dresden that night, what with all the refugees from the east?'

They broke through a thin layer of cloud and emerged into the vivid blue sky above the weather. But he felt no elation. He said dully: 'Both sides accepted that civilian targets were legitimate in the last war. In London there was the Blitz.'

'More civilians died in that one night in Dresden than

316

were killed in the whole war in Britain.'

He shook his head, defeated. 'I know,' he said. 'In every war I admit there is no monopoly of right on either side. Everyone commits some acts of which they're ashamed. I can tell you, no one's very proud of the Dresden episode. No one with any feeling, anyway.' He paused. 'I'm sorry.'

She turned to look at him again and this time he saw there were tears in her eyes. 'Oh, Oswald, I do not want your apologies. I am sorry too, for inflicting on to you all this. Of course we cannot rewrite history, we cannot take away terrible things that have happened. But just occasionally there is something we can do, and I think now is one of those times. If we could find "The Stonebreakers", it would be as if we had clawed something back, saved a small part, made the destruction a little bit less. That is why I am so grateful to be here with you, why I am full of hope.'

She was subdued for the rest of the journey. They caught a taxi to the hotel in Córdoba, and when they arrived she said she would go to her room to rest for a while.

'Saskia,' he said gently, 'are you all right?'

'I'm fine,' she replied, smiling, 'really OK. Perhaps just a little tired after the long journey yesterday, but that will pass.'

'Are you sure? Can I get you anything?'

'No, honestly. Just a little sleep, and then tonight you are my guest for dinner. We're going to have fun.'

They did have fun that evening. She came down refreshed three hours later, and they drank their way through nearly two bottles of wine. They laughed a lot, reminiscing about Dresch and the hideous waitress in the restaurant in Dresden, the one Oswald had suggested might represent her country at shot-putting. Saskia told him about her childhood and her studies in Leipzig. He talked about his time at Cambridge and in the Courtauld. They ate well, cocooned by each other's company from the utter unfamiliarity of their surroundings. Oswald registered the alienness of the place to which they had come, but in her company found it piquant rather than threatening.

'It's strange here,' he told her. 'In leaving Buenos Aires I had the distinct impression we were falling off the edge of the map.'

'You are right,' she laughed, 'I have that feeling also. We have reached a land where we have lost contact with reality. It brings a sensation of liberation, even irresponsibility.'

'That's the wine.'

'That helps, you are right. But out here we are so far from places and people we know that I feel we have lost them, moved out of their jurisdiction.'

'Are you under anyone's jurisdiction?' he asked.

'I am responsible to people at my work.'

'No, that's not what I meant.' He paused, then jumped into the abyss. 'Did your husband come back from Moscow?'

'Yes,' she said, 'he came back.'

'And?'

She stared at the tablecloth.'And we separated three years ago. Our marriage had been a mistake, we both agreed it. He lives in Berlin now, but I never see him.'

He closed his eyes in grateful relief. For a moment there was silence, then she looked up again and said: 'And you, Oswald, do you ever see your wife, the one you were separated from?'

He found it quite easy to tell her dismissively, 'Almost never.'

Saskia said: 'They are strange, aren't they, those dead relationships? You certainly enter into them expecting them to be immortal; but circumstances change, you change, and suddenly the other person is no longer relevant, no longer giving you what you thought he could, and the love dies.' She halted, and then added: 'You know, I came to have that feeling about the Party too.'

'The Communist Party?'

'Yes. I think I gradually realised that I had no more wish to fight to save the system than I had to fight to save my marriage.'

'Were you sad?'

'No, not sad. I think I was relieved.'

'So you have no regrets? About communism, I mean.'

She shook her head. 'Not when the end came.'

'And everyone lives happily ever after?'

'No, it's not quite as simple as that. I wish it was. You cannot change things overnight. And Western democracy as a political system has its flaws as well. No change is ever totally for the good. Nothing is absolutely black and white.'

'Nor are people,' said Oswald. 'We all have our guilty secrets.'

'Oh, Mr Ginn,' she said, affecting shock, 'you have guilty secrets?'

'I do. One day I'll tell you about them. Not now.'

'You disappoint me.'

He laid his napkin on the table and got up. He thought suddenly, this is the woman for whom I've given up 'The Stonebreakers'. She's cost me three million pounds. But it's worth it. He said, 'I will tell you one thing, though, truthfully. Because I'm a little drunk. You're the most beautiful woman I've ever had dinner with.'

She got up too. As in Dresden, the restaurant was now deserted. It was midnight. She put her arm through his and kissed his cheek. 'Thank you,' she said. 'You pay me a wonderful compliment.'

They walked out together into the foyer of the hotel.

He stood with her at the doors to the lift. He felt euphoric, in that rare state of mind where neither the future nor the past has any power over one. Only what he did now, this moment, had any meaning.

'So, what is it to be?' he said.

She looked at him sidelong, with those hooded, almost Oriental eyes, and murmured: 'Oswald, this has been a lovely evening, but tomorrow is even more important. Now I think I need my sleep.'

But even as she spoke her words carried less and less conviction. When the lift came, she didn't move. She stood there, irresolute. Suddenly he clutched her arm and led her in.

The doors took an eternity to shut after he'd pressed the button. They waited, avoiding each other's eyes. For a moment their proximity was unbearable. Then abruptly they were enclosed by clanking doors. And it was as if a process as irresistible as their ascent had been set in motion. His cheek brushed her ear and he smelt her scent. She gasped as he touched her.

Once inside his bedroom there was intent to their every movement. As he eased the jacket from her shoulders, his tongue was already working against her teeth. Her tee-shirt rode up and he felt her naked skin. Their jaws ground in a feverish mutual mastication. Saliva and sweat. Sweat and saliva. Then there was a purposeful shedding of clothing. He registered odd intimate details, like the zip at the front of her jeans, the button that he lost from his cuff, the darkness of her skin against the white of her underwear.

His hand set out on a magnificently daring journey across limitless expanses of thrillingly unfamiliar flesh, exulting in the possession of unknown territory. He traced an exploratory path from the nape of her neck, just below her tousled blonde hair, over her breasts, under her straining buttocks. His fingers trembled now on the inside of her thighs. Trembled there before reaching the place where he wanted her most. He touched her and she cried out in German words that he did not understand. Then her lips were clamped back on his own.

Soon they were no longer bodies on a bed. They became some mad mobile sculpture manipulated this way and that in the throes of its own creation; two forms in search of positions of perfect linkage. He wondered in a moment of dislocated lucidity: has she been waiting months for this to happen, has this beautiful, supple, passionate woman been somehow saving herself for this encounter? He had the sense that he was releasing something long dammed up inside her.

She was single-minded now, concentrated, oblivious of him, superb in her oblivion, impossible to resist, as her pursuit of pleasure fed his own desire, driving him inexorably towards the abyss until that big beautiful barrier burst and Dr Saskia Benz and he lay exhausted on a bed in the best hotel in Córdoba.

In Córdoba, Argentina. Somewhere a little beyond the edge of the map.

11

He awoke before she did. The sharp sunlight, filtered through the slats of the shuttered window, cast a ribbed pattern across the whitewashed wall. He lay and looked at it for a moment, thinking how pleasing it was. Gradually the events of yesterday ebbed back into his consciousness, redefining his bearings: he was in a hotel, but a different hotel. In a place he had never been to before. And simultaneously he recognised that he had arrived in an unfamiliar emotional territory too: he was happy. He turned and lay watching her in the bed next to him. Saskia slept on her side, her head turned away, the sheet draped across the curve of her thigh, exposing her back to his view but drawn up protectively to her breasts at the front. He marvelled at the soft, bronzed quality of her skin, from the tender angle of her neck beneath the short tousled hair down to the first gathering swell of her buttocks. There were fine, fair hairs at the nape of her neck, repeated at the bottom of her spine, a down he could see only when his face was a few inches away from her body.

The fingers of her left hand clutched her upper shoulder and he ran his eye over them once more. To reassure himself. She wore no wedding ring, no rings of any sort. She was free, under nobody's jurisdiction. And finally his mind engaged the question that had to be faced: what were the chances that this closeness could be prolonged? How could he secure this new emotional territory for good? Where could he envisage a future for them together? No, not in London. He could not see her in London, setting up house with him in an alien country. He could not see her happy or fulfilled in some cramped apartment in Fulham or Hammersmith or Clapham. But equally he couldn't see himself abandoning everything to live in the polluted yellow mists of Dresden. What would he do there, for God's sake? Either way it would put the emigrant at an unfair disadvantage. It would set up an unmanageable imbalance in their relationship from its outset. There remained only the fantasy of complete escape, escape to somewhere that was totally new for both of them. Somewhere they could create a joint *tabula rasa*, both start again from nothing. But not with nothing. That wouldn't work. They would need money, a lot of money, to create a livelihood. Where would that come from?

She stretched contentedly, and as she turned towards him he took her in his arms again. She opened her eyes and smiled.

'Hallo,' he said.

She eased her warm body against his. 'Good morning,' she murmured.

They lay for some minutes without speaking, then he said: 'You know, this should have happened all those years ago in Dresden. Why didn't it?'

'What, that first night?' She pulled away from him gently and rested her head in the crook of her arm, considering him.

'Yes, that night. I felt so close to you then.'

'And I felt close to you.'

'Why didn't you stay with me then?'

'It was better not then. Better for both of us.'

'How can you say that, Saskia? How was it better for both of us to deny ourselves unnecessarily for all those years? And you know something? It might very well have been for ever. The chances of our meeting again were negligible.'

'You do not understand, do you?' He sensed she'd retreated again. Into that mysterious part of herself where he found it difficult to follow.

'No, I don't understand,' he said. 'How is it different now? Was there something about me you didn't like then?'

'You do not understand. The reason I did not stay with you that night in Dresden was not because I didn't like you. It was because I liked you too much.'

'What do you mean?' He was not impatient, only mystified. Now there was silence. Then he realised that this was special. That she was trying to reveal to him one of the hidden parts of herself. She was trying to tell him something that she found very difficult to put into words. She turned her head away and sank her face into the pillow.

'Saskia, my darling. Why are you crying?'

She looked up again and he kissed her tears.

'It is so stupid, I am sorry,' she said. 'Those things were in the past, they are gone now.'

'What things?'

'Horrible things.' She breathed deeply and wiped her eyes with the back of her hand. 'There were some things which were happening in my country at that time which were horrible. They are hard to believe now, looking back, but they were real then. Sometimes there was pressure to do things – for the good of the State, they said – which were unnatural.'

'What did they want you to do?'

'Well, I can say it like this: if we had slept together in Dresden, they would have been pleased.'

'Oh, my God.'

'It was made clear to me beforehand that you belonged to a special category of official foreign visitor, and it might be in the interest of the State to compromise this sort of person, to have some sort of hold over them.'

'But why? I had nothing to offer.'

'Maybe not then; but they figured that there might be some need, or some opportunity, in the future. Probably there was nothing specific. They were crazy, those people. Sometimes I think they engineered these things just for the sake of doing them, as simple practice. They wanted to build up a – how do you say it? – a stockpile of compromised Westerners. It reassured them that there were many potential enemies of the State who might be blackmailed. Well, I hated the idea. It made me sick, and I never did it. But in certain situations I felt the pressure from above. Afterwards, after perhaps I had had dinner with foreign visitors, those above would ask with hope in their voices if it had happened. Always I told them no, and they were disappointed. But I wasn't going to be a whore, not even for the good of the State.'

'Of course you weren't,' he said, stroking her hair. 'What these people were doing was unforgivable.'

'So with you it was difficult,' she went on. 'Part of me wanted to. But I liked you so much, you were funny, you went to my heart. So I realised that it was better for both of us that we should not do anything. They would get to hear of it, and then you would be at risk.'

He kissed her again. 'How could you have tolerated a system that put these pressures on you?'

She looked at him very seriously. 'Not all the things were bad, you know. I still believe the ideals were good. It's just that many of the methods were wrong, particularly this mania for security. There was a neurosis about it, it led people to behave in this unbalanced way, to make these unspeakable demands. It wasn't necessary. In the end it was this mad obsession with security more than anything else which convinced me that the system was no longer worth fighting for.'

'I wish I had known all this at the time.'

'What difference would it have made?' she asked wearily.

'I could have thanked you, at least.'

She said, smiling again: 'You've done that now.'

'How?'

'You have been very lovely to me. You have made me feel so good. But more important than that, you too have made a sacrifice for me.'

'What sacrifice are you talking about?'

'The picture we are going to see: what would you have done with it if you had not met me?'

She still lay with her head in the crook of her arm, looking searchingly at him with her beautiful eyes.

'I suppose I never really thought it through,' he replied slowly. He rolled on to his back and fixed his gaze on the ceiling. He found it easier to answer her like that. 'As I told you, I only came upon the picture by chance. Once I knew about it, my energy was directed totally into finding the thing, that was my only priority. After that, I hadn't thought. Probably it would have ended up back in Dresden.'

'I think you could have made money from this, no? You are a dealer in paintings now, after all, it is your profession.'

'It's hypothetical.'

'No, Oswald, tell me: there are people you could sell this picture to, who would not ask questions?'

This picture. 'The Stonebreakers'. They were going to see it today, he felt it with a gathering certainty. Everything was going right, after all. He was on the roller to end all rollers. What was it Bernard had told him? Don't stand back and admire it, go for it, make it even better. In three, maybe four hours they would drive up to Wenglein's *estancia*. The doors would open. They would be shown into a room. And there it would be hanging. He would finally be meeting them, old Gagey and his assistant. Face to half-obscured face. For a short moment he would greet them, savour their company. And then all too quickly he would have to point their path back to the world. And that would be that. Official representations would be made by the German government to the Argentinians; with much pomp and ceremony the picture would be shipped back to Dresden; Oswald Ginn would have a few brief days' fame as the man who rediscovered 'The Stonebreakers'. Then finish. Bitter anticlimax.

But did it really have to be like that? Was it inevitable? There was another scenario. The original one. Perhaps after all he had jettisoned it too quickly? Things were not the same now. They had made love. That changed the situation dramatically. They had new obligations to each other, new priorities. So, under the altered circumstances, perhaps the old scenario should be reconsidered. That way it would all be very different. There would be no official representations, no Dresden homecoming. Just a series of transactions, discreetly conducted. And at the end a fat bank draft in his pocket, a bank draft easily negotiated anywhere, a bank draft that could be his passport to a new life. But a new life with an extra, unspeakably wonderful dimension: a new life with Saskia. Here was the financial security he was looking for. The financial security that could enable them to start afresh, not in London, not in Germany, but somewhere completely new for both of them. Somewhere they could wake every morning like this in each other's arms, untrammelled by the past.

'Yes,' he said slowly, 'there are people I could sell it to, who would not ask questions.'

'My God!' There was horror in her exclamation. But he

fancied there was also an element of wonder. Of interest, even.

Later she got up and half dressed, retrieving her clothes from the floor where they had been abandoned in the urgency of their love-making last night. He watched her graceful movements as she slid back into her jeans, hooked her shoes over her feet. She kissed him quickly and went back to her room to get ready for their journey. They agreed to leave the hotel in an hour. That way they should reach the *estancia* by twelve, as arranged with Wenglein's man. With Juan Garcías.

After she had left him he lay there for a while, in the debris of the bed they had shared, where the sheet was still warm from her body and her scent still lingered. He thought about Saskia, about how it felt to touch her. To have her limbs entwined about him. To come inside her. And then he thought about how it might have been to make love to Mrs Wenglein. How the two experiences might have mirrored each other in their physical actions, even in the sheerly animal pleasure they gave. But how different their emotional fall-out would have been. And then he thought of Daphne suddenly. He remembered that once their love-making had had something of the same breathless excitement of last night. The same undamming of irresistible forces. Once, long ago.

Orlando also woke up that morning disoriented. He was in the middle of nowhere. The Arnosas' *estancia*, where they had arrived yesterday, wobbling down on to the private landing-strip, was set in a rolling expanse of green pampas stretching out monotonously as far as the eye could see. The estate manager had met them in a jeep and driven them over bumpy tracks to the *estancia* house. A light drizzle was falling, and Orlando's spirits had sunk with every yard they travelled. He was cut off here. He yearned for the city, for any city. For the bright lights and the smart apartments of Buenos Aires. He was not a countryman at the best of times. Wellington boots depressed him. This place brought back grim memories of interminable wet weekends in Scotland, of damp huskies, Hermès scarves, smelly dogs and biting winds. The sooner he did what he'd got to do here and flew back to civilisation the better.

Not that the Arnosa *estancia* was uncomfortable. They lived as well here as they did in Buenos Aires. But it was the bleakness of the surroundings, the desolation, that was insupportable. As he dressed he looked out of the window at the grasslands undulating away into the distance. He shuddered, and wandered off in search of breakfast.

He found Cara in the kitchen.

'Did you sleep well?' she asked him.

'Very well, thank you, darling,' he said, kissing her on both cheeks.

She smiled back at him. 'I'm making coffee. You like?'

'Yes, please, I certainly like. Where's Enrico?'

'Is out, with the horses. He does not return till the afternoon.'

'I thought I would drive over to your neighbour's ranch this morning. Could I borrow a car?'

'You should take the jeep, of course. But what is so special about this Wenglein? Why do you need so much to see his *estancia*?'

'I believe there is a picture there that I want to buy.'

'A painting?'

'Yes, a very good one.' He sipped his coffee. 'French, nineteenth-century. I want to make sure I get to it before anyone else.'

She shrugged. 'Is possible, I suppose. That he had good pictures in the *estancia* house.'

'But you've never been there? Never seen inside?'

'Never. I remember that once I met Wenglein, though. It was two, perhaps three years ago, in Buenos Aires. He was old man, but he stood very straight, very stiff. He said very little. But he had eyes that were hard. Cruel eyes. I did not like him.'

Orlando finished his coffee and asked, 'How long will it take me to get there?'

'One hour, perhaps a little more. The roads are not good. Come, I show you on the map.'

He felt a mounting sense of urgency. He wanted to be off. He wanted to get to that *estancia*, see inside it, check it out. He wanted to find that Courbet, buy it, and go home. He didn't want to arrive and find that someone else had been there already. Suddenly it seemed essential to get moving. He went with her to the study where a map of the local area hung on the wall. The route was straightforward. He must follow the road to Santa María for twenty-five miles or so, then branch off.

'Good luck!' she called to him as he turned the jeep and headed off down the drive. 'Watch out for llamas!' He laughed and waved back. The next time he saw her he hoped to be considerably richer. Or certainly well on the way to it. He glanced at his watch: the time was 10.15. Even on these roads, he should be there by 11.30.

They set out for Santa María in the hired car. Oswald drove and she nursed a map. They negotiated the suburbs of Córdoba, and soon they were in the pampas, flat green grazing lands extending as far as the eye could see. The small streaking ribbon of asphalt along which they travelled was to be their route for the next thirty miles. There was very little other traffic. Occasionally they overtook horse-drawn carts, and once a large petrol lorry belching black smoke. Even in the cramped passenger seat Saskia held herself gracefully, her legs tucked sinuously away beneath her. Out of the corner of his eye he followed her movements, the way she peered at the map, searched for something in her bag, ran her hand through her hair.

'Oswald?' she said.

'Yes?'

'Do you mind if I smoke a cigarette?'

'Please do.'

'It's the excitement, I think. Perhaps it will calm me.'

He laughed, not taking his eyes from the road. He was concentrating. Trying to look ahead. Trying to hammer out the best way of ensuring that they stayed as close as this for as long as possible.

'But you feel it too, the excitement?' she persisted. 'You must feel it. You are so close to the end of your search.'

'Oh God, I'm excited, of course I am. But perhaps I've already reached the end.'

'What do you mean?'

'In a way I feel I reached the end of one sort of search last night. When I found you. Now this journey is not as important as it seemed before.'

She drew on her cigarette and contemplated him before replying. 'You frighten me a little when you say those things.'

'But you make me so happy. I'm sorry, I can't help it.' He reached out and put his hand gently on her knee. She covered his hand with her own and patted it thoughtfully.

'Don't be so quick, Oswald.'

'But don't you feel I can make you happy?'

'Yes, now. Now you make me very happy. But now is different. Look at us: we are in a place that is unreal, we are removed from our responsibilities, we live outside normality. But what is to happen in the future? What is to happen when we return to Europe? So many problems, so

many differences to force us apart. There is so little
ground to join us.'

'We must try.'

'Look, you are English. I am German. Our backgrounds are different. Now it doesn't matter, in this
beautiful interlude here, off the edge of the map, as you
said it. Looked at from this distance, all the way from
Argentina, England and Germany seem very close
together up there in Europe. Hardly any difference. But
in the real world, once we are back in the northern
hemisphere, we will see Europe in perspective again.
Then we will perceive the distance apart once more. Then
it would not work. For how should we be together? Me in
London? You in Dresden? I do not think so.' She sat
staring ahead, drumming her knuckles against her lips.

That picture. That picture by Caspar David Friedrich in
the Dresden Museum. He remembered it suddenly, how
they had both once gazed into it with a similar sense of
despair. He saw it all again: its breathtaking panorama of
distant clouds strung across the yellowing sky, the series of
waterways, the comfortless trees, the lone bobbing sail,
the melancholy of dusk. He remembered the sickening
sense of the gulf between them which had afflicted him
then. Flimsy bridges had been thrown across the chasm
since, it was true: the Wall had come down. Ideologically
they were no longer officially divided. East had edged a
little closer to West in the sense that they were both now
free to travel to each other's countries. But perhaps she
was right. Perhaps one short night's passion in an Argentine hotel room could not diminish the feeling of distance
that persisted. The distance between the Elbe and the
Thames. Between Friedrich and Constable. Between the
bombers and the bombed.

'We must fight this, Saskia,' he said.

He refused to be separated from her. They had made

each other happy, that was all that mattered. He refused to succumb to the melancholy fatalism of that Saxon plain, acquiesce in the beautiful hopelessness of Friedrich's sunset. If their future was not workable in England or Germany, then they owed it to themselves, to each other, to reconsider. To examine other ways of living together.

The forbidden scenario resurfaced seductively. Now they were no more than forty minutes from Wenglein's ranch. At that moment they would have to decide. 'The Stonebreakers' would stand before them ready to be possessed. She must see that there was this other way, this alternative plan whereby the picture might be used to ensure their happiness. She herself had asked him earlier that morning if there really were people he could sell the picture to, people who would not ask questions. Surely she could not have made such an enquiry if the possibility of acting upon it had not fleetingly crossed her mind too? With the profit in their pockets they could give themselves a new start. A fair start. Somewhere perhaps away from Europe, away from the old ties. Where they could begin together undistracted, free to concentrate only on each other.

This was the roller he had to ride for all he was worth, push his luck a bit. He was not going to let her drift away for want of decisiveness now. It wasn't going to be like the foyer of the hotel in Dresden at the time of their first meeting, when he'd seemed to lose her through not grasping his opportunity. You didn't often get a second chance in life. He knew how lucky he'd been. And he knew he wasn't going to let her go this time. The original plan suddenly seemed almost irresistible. OK, she had said certain things about Dresden yesterday. But that was before they had made love. Priorities had changed. Their closeness was what counted now.

'Saskia,' he said. 'About this picture.'

' "The Stonebreakers"?'

' "The Stonebreakers". I've been thinking, my darling.
There is another way.'

'Another way?'

'Another way of handling it.' Outside, a solitary roadside café sped by. A couple of desultory tables beneath a
Coca-Cola sign in an otherwise deserted landscape.

'How do you mean?'

'A way that could be best for us. It could give us a
new start, together. Look, I have to suggest this plan to
you, it's stupid not to consider it. We've got to get our
strategy straight before we arrive there when it may be
too late.'

'Tell me what you are suggesting.'

'I could buy it.'

'You could buy it?'

'I could buy the picture for both of us, yes. Negotiate
with Dr Contini, Mrs Wenglein's lawyer. Apparently it
wouldn't be expensive, not compared to . . . to what it
could be sold for.'

'But if you bought it, then what would happen?'

'Then I would sell it. The profit would run into several
million pounds.'

'Several million pounds?' she repeated incredulously.

'Enough for you and I to start together, a new life.
Completely new, without having to think about the past or
the future.' Suddenly the whole plan felt right. He knew in
his bones it was the way forward. One day in the future
they would both look back on this moment and say to each
other, thank God we did it. 'Look, trust me, my darling.
Leave it to me. It'll be better like this.'

'Better?'

'Much, much better.'

'Don't say any more,' she said.

She was crying, softly. It was understandable: after all,

she was a spontaneous, passionate woman and it had been an emotional time for both of them.

He stood on the accelerator. They would have to speed up if they were going to reach their destination by midday.

Orlando took his eyes from the way ahead momentarily to look at his watch. He had been driving for just over an hour now and he reckoned he must be pretty close. He'd left the road to Santa María at the point Cara had indicated on the map. Since then he'd driven just over fifteen kilometres. Within the next five he calculated he would reach the signpost directing him up the driveway to the Wenglein *estancia*. Yes, he'd be there by 11.30.

Then what? Orlando paused to consider his strategy. Assuming he gained entry to the house, assuming he found the Courbet hanging there, then he must prevail upon whomever was in charge to reserve the picture for him. Secure it. Ideally he would meet the widow in person and be able to negotiate with her direct. Presumably the place had a telephone. He could put a call through to Victor at once, if necessary, to make arrangements for funds to be sent over promptly. With a bit of luck he could sew the whole thing up on the spot. Otherwise, if there was no widow and only a housekeeper of some sort, he would have to tread carefully. In that case he'd have to exert his charm on the housekeeper to secure the picture for the time being, then negotiate later with Mrs Wenglein. Charm. That was what would win the day. He felt suddenly calmer, more confident. If it all depended on charm, then this was a situation he could handle.

And the Courbet. What would it look like? It was large, he knew that. And it was an exceptionally good one; Victor had been very positive on that point. Orlando felt confident enough in his own judgment and eye to rely on being able to recognise it. The indications were that its quality was going to be self-evident; there would be no doubt about it. If it turned out to be doubtful, he'd reject it: by definition it wouldn't be the one he was looking for. He allowed himself a few moments' dreaming about the money he could be on the point of making. What would he do, once he had this picture under his control, once he'd brought it back to Europe? Technically half of it would belong to Victor, of course. It was Victor whose money was going to finance the purchase. But he had the feeling that the reselling of it would be largely up to him. Would he do it privately, or perhaps put it up at auction? Say he made three-quarters of a million out of the transaction, how would he spend it?

Oh, Christ.

Suddenly, on this deserted stretch of track, he was confronted by a massive van travelling towards him at speed. He saw it late, and swung the jeep violently to the right to avoid it. The road surface had been bad all the way and now he seemed to hit an exceptionally large pot-hole. The van swayed past him, but he had to fight to control the jeep and finally brought it to a halt slewed across the grass verge. It had all happened in a matter of seconds, and he sat there for a moment catching his breath, aware of the van receding into the distance behind him. What the hell had a van that size been doing on a back road like this? Its presence here gave him a vague sense of unease. Then he opened the door and gingerly let himself down on to the ground.

'Oh, shit!' he exclaimed. He had a puncture.

There was no way of summoning help. If he was going to get anywhere today he was going to have to change the wheel himself. The delay was infuriating, but there was no alternative. He took off his immaculate jacket and distastefully began to roll up his shirt-sleeves.

★ ★ ★

There was a smell of burning.

They had followed the drive, signposted simply Wenglein, for nearly three miles since leaving the road. Oswald had halted the car in front of the remote, white, low-built *estancia* house. As he helped her out of the car, he noticed her eyes were still red-rimmed. He said quietly: 'Well, this is it.' The double front doors were open. There was no bell, so they walked into the hall.

There was a smell of burning. It hit you immediately you came in, an acrid smell of smoke lingering unpleasantly in the nostrils. At first he thought something had caught fire in the house itself, that someone had carelessly dropped a cigarette. He hurried through to the next room to check. Here he realised that it was smoke wafting in through the open window. He suppressed his alarm. It was a simple life out here, all these miles from the city. Rural, almost primitive. Out in the courtyard they were probably burning the rubbish of the household. It was nothing unusual.

But there was another anxiety, another source of unease. It was confirmed by moving from the hall into this second room. Why was everything so empty, why were the walls bare? It was a desolate shell: no chairs, no table, no carpet. And no pictures. Here were whitewashed walls, grimy with the dust of age. Here were floorboards, worn, uneven, unused to exposure. It was as if the house had been cleared, as if the last removal van had just rolled out of the gates. Someone had made a mistake, a hideous mistake. It would all be explained in a moment, all be put right. Wouldn't it? Why did he suddenly have this sensation that something appalling had just taken place here? Why was he not prepared to confront the possibility of what that horror might be?

She had followed him through now. For the first time since they had come into the house, his eyes met hers. She

looked perplexed, confused, fearful; and, as she saw her
emotions mirrored in his own eyes, betrayed. He sensed
that betrayal and looked away. It wasn't his fault, for
God's sake. He had as much to lose as she did.

'What's happened here?' she asked, giving the second
word a panicky emphasis.

'I don't know.'

'Where is it? Have they taken it?'

'I don't know,' he repeated. 'There must be someone
around who can explain.'

He walked over to the window and saw the bonfire. It
was impossible to make out what exactly had been
burned. You could distinguish fractured spars of wood
collapsing in whitened ash, licked by little flickering
flames. But otherwise there was nothing left. It was nearly
over now. Then he saw the man, short and squat, with the
bowed legs of a horseman, standing motionless, staring
into the embers. As Oswald watched he turned away and
began walking towards the house. He was in his late fifties
or early sixties, and his face, which was weathered and
brown from a lifetime spent outdoors, bore a look of
sadness. No, more than sadness: in that moment when he
thought himself alone, he looked grief-stricken. What
could have stirred such feeling? He turned back a last time
to watch the flames, as if to reassure himself about
something. Then he caught sight of the unfamiliar figure
at the window, and his face was instantly reset into a scowl
of suspicion. He hurried in.

Oswald spoke first. As the man came into the room, he
asked him: 'What's going on?' The question subsumed
everything. The empty rooms, the burning, the sadness on
his face.

The man replied in short, sharp, aspirated bursts of
Spanish that were difficult to understand. He was angry,
uncertain, self-justifying. Oswald, remembering that

Saskia's command of the language was better than his, turned to her in desperation and said: 'Do you understand him?'

'I think I do,' she said slowly.

'What's happened to it? Ask him what's happened to it?'

The man continued to talk agitatedly, moving his arms in sharp, jerky, awkward motions. 'He's just telling us,' she said.

Juan Garcías mumbled on bitterly in his infuriatingly unintelligible patois. He was a gaucho – melancholy, surly, with the gaucho's chronic suspicion of people from the city. You could tell it from his eyes. He paused, and Saskia interpreted:

'It seems that the lorry of the transporters arrived at eight o'clock this morning to take the things – the furniture and pictures – to Buenos Aires. It was two days earlier than expected.'

'Oh, Christ almighty!' exclaimed Oswald.

'They began loading. They loaded everything. There were several small pictures. And then they wanted to take the big picture.'

'The big picture?'

'That's what he calls it: the big picture. It was the only big picture in the house. He says the transporters were wrong. They were not to take that picture. He says that Señor Wenglein before he died forbade it. He had told Juan that it should never leave this *estancia*. Those were his orders. No one ever disobeyed Señor Wenglein's orders.'

'So Juan kept it back?' Oswald hardly dared hope.

'Wait, I'll ask him more.' Saskia spoke to him again, and he continued his narrative. She broke off to tell Oswald:

'Yes, he kept it back. They went away without it.'

'Thank God for that.' He paused, savouring the relief. 'Where is the picture? Can we see it now?'

'Wait.' Juan was talking again, anguished, bitter. She continued: 'He says it was the big picture, hanging here.' She pointed to the wall behind them. It was clear that a canvas had recently been removed, for the space where it had hung was shades lighter than the surrounding white-washed plaster. Two sturdy hooks were still implanted at the upper edge. Oswald knew the original size of 'The Stonebreakers' by heart, without having to check. It was 158 by 260 centimetres. He didn't need a tape measure to recognise that these measurements were tantalisingly similar to those of the rectangle exposed on the wall.

'I've asked him what was the subject of the picture that hung here,' she went on. 'He will only say it showed "*figuras*". He won't tell us any more. He says that nobody was to know about it, it was his last promise to Señor Wenglein. He is breaking his promise even to speak of it. It was the picture which Señor Wenglein valued above all others. He thinks it may have been one he brought with him all the way from Germany.'

'But can we see it, for God's sake?'

'He says no.'

'This is ridiculous. We can offer him money.'

'He still says no.'

'Christ, he's got to show it to us. Where's he put it? It can't be far away.'

But Juan was talking again. As he spoke, something drew Oswald's eyes away from the gaucho and on to Saskia's face. He watched her registering what he said. And suddenly he saw her expression change. Shatteringly. From shock, to disbelief. To profoundest horror.

She exclaimed in German. The words came out uncontrolled, savage. And momentarily familiar. They were the same ones she'd cried out when he touched her last night.

Touched her there, for the first time.

Now she was sobbing.

'What is it, Saskia? What does he say?'

She gasped, as if something was strangling her: 'He says he burned it.'

'He says he did what?'

'He says he burned it. It was the big picture hanging here. He was convinced the transporters would return very soon and try to take it away again.'

They all looked out to the bonfire. The last remnants were smouldering in the sun.

'But why did he have to burn it?' Oswald too felt close to tears. The futility. The waste.

'He says it was the instructions of his master that the picture should never leave the *estancia*. After all, it was only wood and canvas. Those are his own words.' Saskia bit her lip. She could not go on.

They stood there, desolate. The tragedy and its implications were too enormous, not immediately comprehensible. Then a languid voice behind them spoke in English:

'That's not by any chance a picture by Courbet you're talking about, is it?'

Oswald rounded on the stranger. He registered a tall, thin, good-looking man with dark hair, standing at the entrance to the room with a jacket slung elegantly over his shoulders. 'Who the hell are you?' he shouted. But in a way the intrusion was a relief. Anything was better than the numbed silence. God knew how long the intruder had been waiting there in the doorway witnessing this horror. God knew how he was aware of the existence of the Courbet. But shouting at him was some sort of outlet for Oswald's frustration and despair.

'Orlando Verney.' Calmly he held out his hand. Oswald paused, then shook it bleakly. There was no point in screaming at him any more. No point in screaming at anyone.

'Oswald Ginn,' he said. 'And yes. That was a picture by Courbet. That, out there: that smouldering rubble.'

'Jesus!' Orlando peered through the window. 'That's it, is it? That's what I came seven thousand miles to find.'

'It's what we all came for, I believe,' said Oswald quietly.

Almost casually Orlando led the way out of the room into the open air of the courtyard, picking a path in his expensive suede shoes.

'I suppose it has to be this one?' he asked. 'There's no chance the Courbet was another picture? Didn't he say something about a van having come earlier? It couldn't have gone on that, could it?'

'No chance. All the pictures that went on the van were too small. There were only a few of them, anyway. No, this is it. It's got to be; it's the only one approaching the right size.'

'Shit,' said Orlando simply.

Like some grotesque funeral cortège they stood around the ashes. The ashes of what they knew once to have been a milestone in nineteenth-century European art. There were the irregular spars of charred and blackened wood, sad, amputated relics of the picture's stretcher. But of the canvas nothing identifiable remained. Oswald contemplated the ruins of everything he had striven for, lying there before him on the paved yard of the *estancia*. Where the combined might and power of Bomber Command and the United States Air Force had failed in Dresden on the night of 13 February 1945, Juan Garcías had now succeeded. He had single-handedly destroyed Courbet's 'Stonebreakers'. The old man Gagey, bending on his arthritic knee, and his young assistant labouring under his tray of chippings, had both been put to the flames for ever. They had dreamed a dream of immortality, an illusion prolonged in secret here for nearly half a century. Now that was gone. What they had witnessed was the final recrudescence of the Dresden firestorm. Here, thousands of miles away and forty-five years later, it had flared up again and burned. A tiny recrudescence, it was true, by comparison with the original inferno. But a heart-breaking one. And, like the original, it was combustion instigated without any conception of the human damage it would entail.

He looked at Saskia. The tears were coursing down her face, and when he tried to put his arm around her she turned away.

He kicked at the embers in a futile gesture of defiance. There was nothing else to do but go home.

12

They got back into the car. Oswald turned it round in the
estancia courtyard and drove back the way they had come.
Later in the afternoon they caught a plane back to Buenos
Aires. They travelled in long periods of anguished silence.
They were in shock. It was as if they had just witnessed a
horrific car accident. A car accident in which someone
very close to them had been killed. He found he couldn't
get the image of the smouldering pieces of stretcher out of
his mind. He kept seeing that rectangle of wall again. The
place where up till an hour or so before their arrival the
picture had hung intact.

He dimly recognised landmarks they had noticed
along the road that morning: the desolate café with its
Coca-Cola sign, a stunted group of trees at the cross-
roads where they joined the main highway back to
Córdoba. His own misery was compounded by Saskia's
retreat into herself. She'd taken refuge in that place
where he could not reach her. If she spoke, it was in
monosyllables. It was irrational, but he felt a growing
conviction that she was holding him in some way
responsible for what had happened. Dear God, did she
think he had dragged her all this way out into the
pampas simply in order to inflict on her the discovery
that the picture had been destroyed? That he had in
some obscure way engineered it? He wanted to hug her,
he wanted to shake her, he wanted to hit her even. He
wanted to snap her out of her mood of unyielding,

self-regarding gloom. He wanted to make her understand that she held no monopoly of grief over the picture's sickening fate. It was as lacerating to him as it had been to her.

They were back at her hotel in Buenos Aires by eight o'clock that evening.

'I am very tired,' she said when he suggested dinner. 'I am going to bed.'

'But Saskia, my darling . . .'

'Please leave me, Oswald.'

'Shall we meet in the morning?'

'I must go to my Council's office early. There are appointments to catch up on.'

'But we must talk.'

'What have we to talk about?' She spoke dully.

'Us. You and me. Please, when can I see you?'

She looked up at him with eyes that had lost all animation. 'I don't know. I think there is very little left to say. I'll ring you, OK? But now I must sleep.'

She didn't ring next morning. He waited, inert, tense, by his telephone. He waited till midday. Then he rang her hotel. There was no reply from her room. When he checked at Reception they said she had gone out.

He found the number of her Council's office via the German Embassy. They said she was engaged in meetings for the rest of the day and could not be contacted, but they were prepared to give him her hotel number. She might be there that evening. He put the telephone down. He felt that if he could only see her, talk to her, be with her, he could retrieve the situation. But he must get hold of her first.

In the end he installed himself in the bar of her hotel. He sat where he had a clear view of the main door and the reception desk. He ordered brandy and waited. He watched people coming and going. He watched other people waiting for appointments. He watched appointments being kept. He smoked several cigarettes. And occasionally he thought of that large rectangle of whitewashed wall.

What had persuaded Wenglein to take the picture there, to convince the simple-minded gaucho Juan Garcías that it must never leave the confines of the *estancia*? The slavish hero-worship that the man apparently inspired in underlings – Guttmann was another example – had found tragic expression in Juan's literal-minded interpretation of his master's wishes. So the picture had been dragged out into the courtyard. The canvas had been doused in petrol. Juan had struck a match. And that had been that. Finish. The end of Oswald's dream. But it wasn't the loss of the Courbet that was killing him by this slow death. It was the loss of Saskia. He realised now that the sacrifice of the Courbet would have been a small price to pay if it had meant keeping her. But the two disasters had somehow become grotesquely entwined. By some crazy but apparently irresistible process of fate the destruction of one had come to mean the loss of the other. His happiness now depended on disentangling the two.

'Ah, Mr Ginn. I thought it was you.' Oswald looked up and saw a familiar figure standing over him. Dr Giannini. 'I am sorry if I startled you. I had been meeting a client here, and I recognised you from the lobby.'

The Italian sat down next to him and smiled enigmatically. 'So have you had good hunting in Argentina?'

'So-so.'

'Forgive my curiosity, but did you manage to buy that picture from the private collection?'

Oswald gave a little laugh and stubbed out his cigarette. He hadn't the energy to play games with Giannini any more. 'No, I'm afraid I didn't,' he said. He kept his eyes firmly on the glass doors to the street.

'Ah, so you see I was right. It is not so easy for foreigners to buy from private collections in this country.' Giannini was not to be denied his satisfaction. His territory had been preserved. But he seemed to feel the point needed underlining, as a warning for the future. 'Is it too late for me to help you in this matter? My resources are at your disposal.'

'Too late. I'm sorry.'

'Perhaps next time, then. Remember, I am at your service here. Call me if you need me.' He smiled again and rose to go. Then he held out his hand. 'Goodbye, Mr Ginn. It was a pleasure to meet you. Have a safe journey home.'

A safe journey home. He was being politely ushered out. Like a drunk who has made a fool of himself at a party.

Saskia came in at six. He saw her at the door, and ran to catch her by the arm the moment she passed through it. She didn't seem surprised to see him. But her greeting was cold. Depressingly cold.

'Over here,' he said. 'We've got to talk.' Mutely she allowed herself to be led to the bar.

'Drink?'

She shook her head. Her eyes were still red-rimmed.

He said: 'Look, I've been thinking about our future. I can't be without you. I'll come to Dresden if necessary.'

'No. It would not work.'

'Think about it. Why shouldn't it?'

She stared at him. 'I would not want you in Dresden. Not now.'

It was as if she'd thrown a drink in his face. 'Why not now? For God's sake, Saskia, what happened?'

'You cannot see what you did, can you?'

'This is crazy. It's not fair of you to hold me responsible for the way the picture was destroyed. You can't blame me. It hurts me just as much as it hurts you.'

'No, it's not that.' There were tears in her eyes again. 'You still don't realise, do you? That's what makes it impossible, that you still don't realise what you have done.'

'What have I done?'

'You showed you do not really love me.'

'Saskia, this is ridiculous. How can you say that?'

'No. You may think you love me, but it is not the right way for me. You are not the right person. For me it cannot work any more.' She paused, then the words came faster. 'If you had really loved me, really understood me, you would never have suggested what you did. Never even considered such a thing. How could you imagine I would be prepared to sacrifice this picture, betray my city and my people's heritage, just for money? What sort of principles did you think I had? I could never have lived with myself after that; and I certainly could not have lived with you.'

'Oh my God: that.'

'Yes, that. You say it as if it wasn't important. But I tell you it was. More important than anything. It could not work for us after that.'

'But I only suggested it because there was no other way to make us happy together.'

'If that had been the only way to save my own life then I would rather have died.'

'But this is all hypothetical anyway.' He was floundering, desperate. 'The picture's gone now, no one's going to get it. We have to forget it now, put it behind us, concentrate on the rest of our lives. You must see that.'

'I do see that. I am concentrating on the rest of my life.'

'I believe we can still make each other happy.'

She shook her head miserably. 'No. I am sorry, Oswald.'

'You're wrong about this, Saskia.'

'No, you are the one who is wrong.' She looked up at him abruptly, engaging his eyes very firmly with her own. She was animated now, not so much with anger as with a sort of passionate sadness. 'Have you ever thought what it's been like this past year or two? What it's been like since the Wall came down, and suddenly we were changed, we were Westernised at a stroke? I can tell you, it hasn't been easy. They call us Osties and they laugh at us. They reckon we are impossibly naive. Well, maybe we are, but I don't care. Of course the West has a lot to offer us, of course we are grateful to have the old tyranny broken, but that doesn't mean that all the West's values are the right ones.

'You think you can solve anything with money, don't you? You think everything can be bought and sold in the end, it's only a matter of price. Well, I will never accept such a creed. It sickens me. That Courbet represented something more than money, something that it was imperative to save, both for the past and for the future. You saw it differently. But you are a Westerner. When you proposed to me that we should sell that picture and profit from it, I felt . . . I don't know, I felt violated. You think I am naive, perhaps, but I felt it as the violation of the East by the West. I knew it would be impossible for anything to work between us after that. Nothing you can say will change it. Believe me, it is not the loss of the picture that has broken us. That was an intolerable blow to suffer, of course it was, but it was a separate grief. No, we were broken before we reached the *estancia*. The moment you suggested . . . what you suggested. I am sorry, Oswald. You have been kind to me. But now it must end. You should go now.'

'Go? Go where?'

'I think you had better go home.' She paused, then

added, 'Go home now. It will be better for both of us.'

She picked up her bag and the linen jacket which she had been carrying over her arm. Her handkerchief was clutched in her fist. She made as if to say something else, stifled it, and walked towards the lift. He got up to follow her, hesitated, and stayed where he was. The doors shut behind her and she was gone.

The roller had broken. He was very, very tired.

Orlando accosted Oswald at the departure gate in Buenos Aires airport. Oswald had recognised him a moment or two earlier, sitting elegantly on a seat by the duty-free shop reading a magazine. He'd been uncertain about whether to make contact. Not sure whether to interrupt him. Nor indeed whether he actually wanted Orlando's company at all. Then Orlando had seen him, waved, gathered his things together and come over.

'Hallo again,' he said breezily, taking off his dark glasses. 'So you're going home too, are you? It'll be a relief to get out of this godawful country.'

'I suppose so.' He'd lost 'The Stonebreakers' here. He'd lost Saskia here. But he doubted whether he'd feel much relief just by getting out of the place. It didn't seem to matter very much any more where he was.

'Look, where are you sitting on this flight? Why don't you come and join me? We've probably got quite a bit to talk over.'

'I'm already checked in,' said Oswald bleakly. He showed him his economy-class boarding pass.

'Don't worry. I'll arrange it.'

He did. Oswald watched his performance with a distracted fascination. Charm, good looks and strength of will were deployed in an irresistible harmony. It was always instructive to see anything done supremely well. They were actually in the body of the aircraft before he

351

took any action. They paused in the galley area immediately opposite the entrance, the point at which Oswald should have turned right to his cramped economy-class place.

'Wait here,' said Orlando.

He removed his dark glasses again and caught the eye of the stewardess. He advanced on her, smiling brilliantly. You could see her melting even before he spoke.

'I'm so sorry to be a nuisance. Can you tell me, is tourist class full?'

'I believe it is, sir,' she said, going a little pink.

'In that case I'd like you to upgrade my colleague Mr Ginn to sit with me. Would it be an awful bore? I'd so much appreciate it. It would be sweet of you if you could manage it.'

'You've got a bit of a nerve, haven't you,' she said admiringly.

'It's a bit naughty, isn't it? But don't worry, we'll be frightfully discreet.'

She giggled. 'I'll see what I can do. Just hold on for a moment.'

After that you knew there wouldn't be a problem. In fact Orlando even managed to prevail upon the initially recalcitrant purser to open champagne for them before take-off.

'It's an old trick, that upgrading to business class,' he confided. 'If economy class is full, the chances are it's slightly overbooked. That means they've got to upgrade one or two people in order to fit them all in. Why not you?'

Oswald lay back in his chair and took the champagne glass in his hand. Perhaps Orlando interpreted his silence as temporary contentment. The truth was, he felt too miserable to speak.

Later Orlando said: 'There was no doubt, was there?

About the picture that lunatic set fire to being the Courbet? "The Stonebreakers?" '

Oswald shook his head wearily. 'Not really, no. We know Wenglein had it. We know this was the only picture of the right size in his entire collection. We know he prized it more than anything else. I think we can be pretty certain that was it. As certain as anyone can be who hasn't actually stood in front of the thing and checked it with his own eyes when it was still intact. And we got bloody close to that. Forty-five minutes earlier, and who knows?'

'Forty-five minutes,' Orlando mused. 'Shit, if I hadn't had that bloody puncture. It's enough to make you weep.'

Forty-five minutes before their arrival. A horrific thought struck Oswald. That must have been almost exactly the moment he was putting the idea to Saskia in the car. The proposal to buy the picture themselves, to secure their future. The proposal that had had exactly the reverse effect on their relationship. The proposal that had meant he would never see her again. Just as he'd been speaking the words to her, Juan Garcías had been dragging the thing from the wall, heaving it into the courtyard. Looking around for his can of petrol. Coincidence, of course. Bloody coincidence.

'This steak is disgusting. It's so overdone it's inedible.' In the seat next to him Orlando laid down his knife and fork and pushed the tray of food to one side. 'It'll be a relief to get back to civilisation.'

'Do you live in London?' Oswald asked. In the background droned the low, even hum of the jumbo jet's engines, barely perceptible as they set course across the Atlantic.

'I've got a flat in Lennox Gardens. I'm looking forward to a few days' rest there. I've been invited to Los Angeles by Vera Maskell, but I think I'm going to give that a miss. I suppose what I must do is get in touch with Victor to tell him how all this wretched business ended.'

'Victor?'

'Victor Meer.'

Oswald was mildly curious about Orlando. He dropped names liberally. And yet he managed to convey the impression that he did so not in order to impress but rather because he assumed that his listener, like him, moved naturally in the same stratum of society. You were in fact being paid a rather delicate compliment. But why, of all people, had this elegant social butterfly been the only other person in at the death in the quest for 'The Stonebreakers'?

'Was Victor Meer the one who told you about the Courbet?'

'He was, as a matter of fact.'

'Do you know how he knew?'

'Anonymous sources. Victor can be very mysterious at times.'

Anonymous sources. No doubt Saskia couldn't have been any more explicit about where her friend in the Dresden Museum had got his information. He wasn't in the mood to pursue the point. Not if it made him think of her again. 'Oh, well,' he said. 'It's academic now.'

'It was a colossal waste of energy,' said Orlando bitterly. There was silence for several minutes. Then suddenly he added: 'Tell me something. If you don't mind my asking. Do you believe in God?'

The question was unexpected. 'Why do you ask?'

'No particular reason.' Orlando paused, peering out of the window at the darkening skies, then went on: 'It's just that if there is a God, He's behaved in a particularly shitty way over this picture.'

Oswald glanced at him, unsure if he was serious.

'He has,' he agreed at last.

They sat in silence. The stewardess cleared the uneaten

dinners away, and the lights were dimmed for the night.

Orlando reclined his chair and lay back, preparing for sleep. 'By the way,' he said, yawning, 'what happened to the woman you were with at the *estancia*, the German woman? Did she stay on in Argentina?'

Oswald kicked off his shoes and loosened his tie, but he knew he'd be awake for some time.

'Yes, she stayed on,' he said quietly. 'She had other commitments.'

Autumn had arrived in west London. When he had set out it had definitely still been summer. But now he was back it was cold and grey. As he pulled his suitcases from the taxi and paid the driver, a sudden gust of wind sent leaves, sweet-papers and beer-cans rushing down the gutters and across the pavement, and blew open the gate leading to his own front door. It clacked several times with an annoying persistence. He was back. That clacking gate precipitated a surge of familiarity. Here they all were again, the things he was used to. The depressingly routine sights and sounds of the place he had lived in for sixteen years. This was the norm of his life. This was what he had briefly fantasised about escaping. And this was what he had come home to again. He remembered that he had promised Daphne he would mend the catch on that gate several months ago.

He had rung Daphne from the airport, but there had been no reply. He let himself in through the front door and found the house silent. He left his luggage in the hall and opened the door to the drawing-room, hoping to see something new, something different. But it was unchanged: the cold blue carpet, the off-white sofas, the yellow curtains, the magazines, the drinks cupboard; the early nineteenth-century Morland prints; that dull landscape by Daubigny left to Daphne by her uncle. All these things had gone on existing, unmoved throughout his absence, oblivious to his elation, unresponsive to his disappointment. He closed the door then peered into the dining-room. There the table and chairs were also unchanged, impassive. He thought suddenly of two other rooms he had been in since he had last seen this one: the Wengleins' dining-room, with their vulgar gilt chairs, and their hideous bloodied dogs; and the simple whitewashed, bare-boarded room in the *estancia*. The one with the large light mark across the wall where a picture had hung. The last time he had looked into this room, he had known nothing of either of these.

The kitchen was immaculate; only an irregularly dripping tap disturbed its silence. A neatly folded dishcloth lay across the sink, a symbol of the perfection of the cleaning job that had been carried out. The cleaning-lady must have been. He climbed upstairs, pausing to look into the boys' bedrooms, airless and unanimated, uninhabited for the weeks that had elapsed since the beginning of term. It was a dead, deserted house. Finally he turned the door-knob of his own bedroom, the one he shared with Daphne. He paused, suddenly apprehensive about something he couldn't quite define. But when he went in, nothing was out of place. The bed was neatly made. He heard the wind whistling at the window. Looking down, he saw that the gate was clacking again. What had he expected to find? He retraced his steps to the drawing-room and poured himself a drink.

I know it is over, he told himself, I have accepted that. In coming home I have admitted it. But I cannot bear to think of her now, the memory of our brief intimacy causes a physical pain, the thought of her closeness lacerates. I shall never get her back. She is gone as surely as 'The Stonebreakers' is gone. I was driven a little mad, I see it now; my madness convinced me that any means was legitimate provided it secured what I wanted, a future of happiness together. I lost my judgment, and I lost her, destroyed her trust in me. I cannot quite get out of my head the idea that the two destructions are linked, the idea of their literal coincidence. The idea that in putting the fatal proposition to her, that we should appropriate the Courbet for our own benefit, I put the match not only to our relationship but also to the picture itself, set in motion its physical destruction as surely as Juan Garcías himself.

He found himself wishing he had never taken her with him to Córdoba, never discovered the intensity of pleasure she gave him, because if he had avoided that he would not be experiencing the intensity of misery he was feeling now. Suddenly he found himself crying. Because it was all so futile. Because it was all so sad.

He didn't hear Daphne come in. Afterwards he wondered how long she had been standing there in the doorway, unbuttoning her coat, looking at him sitting on the sofa, bent forward with his hands over his eyes. Sensing her, he straightened up and took out his handkerchief.

'How long have you been back?' she asked.

'Half an hour or so. I'm sorry. I tried to ring you from the airport.'

'What's the matter with you?'

'Some sort of allergy,' he said. 'It must be the long flight. It seems to make the eyes water.'

Unexpectedly she came over and kissed the top of his head. 'Why don't you go and lie down? I'll bring you something. You look as though you've really been through it.'

'No, it's all right. Really.' He stood up and faced her, blowing his nose.

She paused there for a moment, looking at him. Then

she turned away. 'Suit yourself,' she said, and went out into the hall to take her coat off.

A minute or two later she called through to him: 'So did you find it?'

'Find what?'

'Whatever it was that you went all the way to South America for.'

'I suppose you could say I found it, yes.'

'And have you managed to bring it back with you?'

'No.'

'Why on earth not?' She was back in the room now. It was one of those rare moments when an activity of his seemed briefly to have engaged her curiosity.

'Daphne, it's a very long story.'

'I'm listening.'

'I really can't go into it now, I'm exhausted.'

'Christ almighty, Oswald, will you never bloody talk to me? Open up, for God's sake. You go away for the best part of two weeks, you travel halfway round the bloody world, and when you get home you can't even be bothered to let me know what you've been up to. Do you think I'm not interested, is that it?'

He sensed the challenge, the spoiling for a fight. She wanted him to say no, you know you're not interested in anything I do. Then they could really get their teeth into each other. 'OK, OK,' he said wearily. 'I'll tell you very briefly what happened out there. I made the sort of discovery that, if you're lucky, happens once in a lifetime. I was very close to getting possession of it. But just as I was about to, it was destroyed. In a sort of accident. I lost it.'

'What was it, this discovery?' she asked, suddenly suspicious.

'It was a picture. A wonderful nineteenth-century picture.'

'Did you actually get to see it?'

'No, I never actually saw it. I saw only the ruins of it, the ashes of it. It was burned, you see. But I knew it was what I was looking for.'

She looked at him doubtfully. 'So this wonderful discovery of yours was destroyed before you could make any use of it. You got there too late, you mean?'

'That's about it.'

'I'm sorry,' she said, her interest dulled. 'It seems to be the story of your life.'

She walked out towards the kitchen and called over her shoulder: 'By the way, it's half-term this weekend. Are you going to collect the boys or shall I?'

The next morning he set off for Fortescue's early. He had woken at five, remembered the way the sunlight had cast vivid patterns over the wall through the slatted shutters in Córdoba, and been unable to sleep again. Now he walked up Bond Street jaded by the same sense of deadening familiarity which he had felt yesterday. He was depressed by the realisation that all this had been going on implacably – shops, cars, deliveries, purchases, deals – while he had been away. Going on oblivious to what had been happening to him. It seemed almost indecent that his recent experience should have left no mark here.

He felt someone touch his arm and looked round to see Shagger Parks. Shagger was wearing a cashmere overcoat with a velvet collar. He looked sleek and prosperous, like a mongrel in ermine.

'Wotcha,' he said. 'Bit nippy today, ain't it?'

'It is cold,' Oswald agreed.

'Had a bit of luck this week,' he continued.

'Really?'

'Bought this Stubbs in a house sale in Wales. Filthy dirty, but it's right, no question. I've got a couple of

American clients flying over on Thursday. I'm going to trouser on this one, mate, I don't mind telling you.'

'That's good.' They walked on together for a while in silence.

'I haven't seen you around for a while. Been away?'

Oswald nodded.

'Anywhere interesting?'

'South America, actually.'

'Find anything?'

He paused. They were approaching the door to Fortescue's. 'I found the most important French mid-nineteenth-century picture to resurface since the war,' he told him.

For a moment Shagger looked disconcerted. Then he laughed. 'Bloody good,' he said. 'And my name's Napoleon Bonaparte.'

As they parted, he went on quickly: 'Listen, I've been thinking. If you boys in Fortescue's have got a client for this Stubbs of mine, let me know. It's a bloody good one. But get your skates on, because it may not be around for long. Be seeing you.'

He walked on in the direction of Sotheby's and Oswald pushed through the gallery door.

Olga was at her desk. The book she was currently reading was laid aside, spine up. Kafka had been abandoned for Gabriel García Marquez.

'Good morning,' he said.

'Ah. You are back.' She paused, then added unexpectedly: 'The wanderer returns.'

She said it almost playfully. The line of bitterness that normally informed her mouth lightened perceptibly as she spoke. Something, somehow, had happened that had pleased her.

'Is all well?' he asked. 'Any excitements in my absence?'

She reached up to tuck an errant wisp of greying hair

back behind her ear. She had that distinctively pale middle-European skin whose faintly unhealthy enamelled quality in certain lights suggests the embalmer's art. But now Oswald was aware of an unusual pink moistness, an animation he didn't see very often. She must be very moved indeed. By something.

'You have not heard?'

'Heard what? Look, I only flew in yesterday from Buenos Aires.'

'Then you would not know.' She drew herself up straighter in her chair. 'The news broke at the weekend. Eugene has prevailed upon Lady Lindisfarne to sell her Corot.' She made the announcement with a triumphant flourish, as if she herself had conducted the negotiations. She was actually proud of what had happened, that was it. Her admiration for Eugene Crabbe was as nauseating as it was inexplicable.

Oswald greeted Gloria, deposited his briefcase in his room, and climbed the second flight of stairs to Leonard's office. There was no point in postponing their confrontation any longer. But it was a moment he had been dreading since his return. He anticipated an inquisition about Argentina. An inquisition that would grow increasingly hostile as his lack of success became apparent. Well, if that was the case, then stuff them all.

There they all were. Leonard, Magnus and Eugene, sitting in Leonard's office together. They all looked up as Oswald came in, Eugene squinting myopically in his direction.

'Oswald! What a pleasant surprise. Come in.' Leonard was beaming. 'No one told me you were coming back today. Take a seat and tell us about your trip.'

'Plenty of tango?' enquired Magnus as he pulled up a chair.

'Never stopped,' Oswald told him.

'I love a good tango,' Magnus continued reminiscently.

'What luck with the picture?' asked Leonard.

'None so far, I'm afraid.' He'd decided on the plane what he was going to tell them. 'The wretched heirs aren't, after all, selling for the time being. They are inclined to hang on. They're not as pressed as it at first seemed. Of course, I made my number with them, and I think Fortescue's will be to the forefront of their thinking when the moment does come to sell, as it undoubtedly will. But not yet.' That was his story and if they didn't like it they could screw themselves.

'Tiresome,' said Magnus.

'But I have made useful contacts,' Oswald added. 'It was not at all a wasted trip . . .' Making contact. He thought suddenly of the undulating line of her back, lying exposed by the sheet rucked across her buttocks, as she slept next to him. He had a vivid and breathtaking image of the fine blonde hairs running down her spine. Of reaching out a hand to stroke her warm flesh. For a moment he felt too sick to go on. He fought to exclude these memories from his consciousness, tightening the grip of his fist around the arm of his chair with such intensity that it hurt.

But Leonard had lost interest. 'Yes, yes,' he was saying impatiently. 'Meanwhile, however, Eugene has made his little coup.' He flashed a rare little gold-toothed smile in Eugene's direction.

'Olga did mention something as I came in.'

'He has persuaded Lady Lindisfarne to sell, as such.'

He had forgotten how annoying he found Leonard's absurd little quirks and mannerisms: the garnet cuff-links in the black shirt, the Cubist-design tie, the way he drummed the end of his pen on the paper in front of him as some sort of attempt to assert his authority, the meaningless 'as suches'.

'How did you do that?' Oswald turned to Eugene.

Eugene shrugged modestly.

'We shall be offering the Corot on Wednesday,' Leonard continued. 'Salzman is due. I am optimistic.'

Corot. Bloody Corot. What was a Corot, even the very best Corot, compared to his 'Stonebreakers'? What was anything any more? Would any picture ever galvanise him again? Was there any canvas left in the world that would enthuse him enough to pursue it, rouse him enough to sell it, now that the Courbet was gone? And the bitterest frustration of all was that no one would ever know how close he had come to acquiring it. How close he had come to landing the biggest prize of all. There was no one he could tell. Who would believe him now? His achievement, unlike Eugene's piddling little victory, would remain an unsung secret.

'That's excellent,' he said. 'I'm delighted things have worked out so well.'

13

'We have now commenced our descent into Vienna airport. Would you therefore please return to your places, and make sure your seat belts are securely fastened, your seats are in an upright position, and your tables stowed safely away.'

The words were delivered mechanically over the air-craft address system, like liturgy at some cathedral even-song, thought Victor, liturgy so well worn by repetition that scarcely anyone registered what it meant any more. This was the airline equivalent of the *Nunc Dimittis*: familiar phrases incanted largely for their reassuring sonority. He himself had not moved from his position by the window at all during the flight. He had sat there, mute and anxious. He sighed. Nearly there now. Nearly at the end of the trail.

Yes, this whole trip was a dreadful upheaval. And yes, of course he was apprehensive. But he felt curious too. If he hadn't felt curious, he wouldn't have agreed to under-take the journey. He would have got his doctor to forbid it on medical grounds. It would have been perfectly justifi-able: after all, he was an old man; they couldn't force him. But on balance he had judged it worthwhile, despite the apprehension. Once and for all, he was going to lay a ghost. A ghost that had haunted him for most of his adult life.

He had spent the first part of the flight running his eye over a copy of the *Financial Times*. But his eye only; his brain dwelt on Orlando. Orlando was back in London now. He had arrived a couple of days ago from Buenos Aires, and they had spoken on the telephone last night. He had sounded well. Surprisingly buoyant when you considered he'd been halfway round the world on a wild-goose chase. He had given Victor a confused and slightly unsatisfactory account of events in Argentina. A very strange story. What was the truth of it? Victor had not been able to fathom it out. Not for the moment, anyway, not with this present journey to Vienna hanging over him. Perhaps afterwards, once he was back in the villa and everything was resolved one way or another, then he'd see the boy and get the full details of what had happened from him. Orlando had said he might come out again soon, just for a weekend. Early October on the Côte d'Azur could still be very beautiful, Victor had assured him. The good news was that la Maskell had pushed off back to America. And as far as Victor had been able to discover, without annoying the boy by prying too closely, Orlando had no apparent plans to follow the bitch out there. With a bit of luck, that whole incomprehensible *engouement* was over. The Argentinian trip had achieved that much, at least.

It was only now, a quarter of an hour from landing, that Victor opened his briefcase and took out the letter to look at it again. That bloody letter. He held it in his hands for a moment, reflecting that it had caused him nothing but turmoil ever since its arrival three months ago. It had come towards the end of June, in one of those first very hot weeks of summer. Alphonsina had brought it to him with his breakfast, which he'd been taking on the veran-dah. Already the heat was shimmering round the hills in a haze of blue. He'd glanced at the envelope and noted its Vienna postmark and its antiquated typescript. At once he had felt a flutter of alarm. Then he'd opened it, discovered it was written from Moscow, and the alarm had turned into a sick sensation of panic. A panic that he thought he'd laid to rest once and for all some years ago. In a café in a small street off Wenceslas Square.

He opened it again now and read it once more:

Dear Victor,

You will be surprised that I am writing to you once again. Perhaps it will not be a very pleasant surprise, but let me reassure you: this will I promise be the last time, the very last time that you hear from me. You see I have been told by the doctors here in the hospital that I have not much longer left. They say it will be days, a week or two at the outside, but no more than that. I do not expect your sympathy, nor do I seek it. I am simply trying to put things in order, arrange all my outstanding business before I die. That is the reason for this letter.

The outstanding business which most concerns me is my picture collection. I am faced with a problem. None of my heirs, such as they are, care much for pictures. I have no wish to leave to unworthy people the four unsurpassed examples which are the jewels of the group. If I lived in another country – your country, perhaps – I might be disposed to leave them to the nation. But in Russia now there is still much confusion and uncertainty, and these are not the right conditions under which to make bequests to the State. So I am making other arrangements. Three of the four I am sending discreetly for sale in the West. The fourth I am also sending in the same shipment, but that one is not for sale. It is my gift to you.

You can accept it as recompense for the demands I had to make of you some years ago. Perhaps you could accept it as a final gesture of friendship. But, Victor, please accept it. Because it is a very wonderful picture, the pride of my collection, and it will mean very much to you once you see it. You will understand why once I had hopes to surprise you with it by showing it to you in Moscow. You will certainly recognise it. I would like to think of you owning it now. Will you do me this honour? And when you look upon it, will you think of me with a little less disfavour?

The details of how the four pictures are coming out of my country need not concern you. I have all that in hand, there are discreet and reliable channels. When they arrive in the West, you must go to the man who is arranging the sale, and he will release to you your picture. He is used to this sort of operation, and he will expect you. You must go to him in Vienna. Yes, Vienna. I think perhaps that to make this journey will not be too onerous for you. I remember how once very long ago you told me that you wanted beyond everything to see Vienna. You were bitter because although you were very near you could not get there. Do you remember that, Victor? No doubt you have visited the city many times since. But here is an excuse to go there one more time.

Make contact discreetly with the agent there. The pictures will take time to arrive because they must pass by an indirect route, but they should be with him in a few weeks. On a separate card enclosed I give you his address and telephone number. His name is Grunwald. Go to him, and he will release the picture I have chosen as my gift to you. But do not leave it too long: no man is to be trusted for ever.

I am very tired now. It is almost the end. You must admit, the situation is a little ironic. When we first met, forty-six years ago, we were on the same side, you and I. Now the wheel has turned full circle, and our countries are once more allies. It is strange, is it not?

If you can find it in your heart, Victor, try to understand me and forgive the pain I have caused you.

Your friend,
Boris Venetsianov

Victor folded the poor-quality Russian writing-paper and put it carefully back into the briefcase. He remembered the horror of reading it that first time. He'd sat there that June morning, staring out into his garden, wondering what the hell to do next. The heat was stifling, oppressive, stultifying to the brain. Why couldn't Boris leave him in peace? Why couldn't the man even die without disrupting his life yet again? Well, he knew where his duty lay. He'd given a binding undertaking to the authorities always to let them know whenever Xenophon made contact. It didn't matter how brief or seemingly insignificant the communication. He had to let them know. That was the deal. It still held. But, God almighty, there'd been a temptation to take that bloody letter there and then and put a match to it. Deny he'd ever received it. Then perhaps the whole thing would go away. Or perhaps it wouldn't. There were bound to be repercussions about this business, and his name would probably be drawn into it. If he destroyed the letter now, he'd always be wondering. Worrying. For the rest of his days.

So later that morning he'd picked up the telephone and dialled the special number in London again. The number he hadn't rung for fifteen years. When it was answered he'd asked to speak to Barker.

He had been told that Barker was no longer there. He had felt let down by the news, almost betrayed. Then he had suddenly felt very old. Still, the codenames he had quoted, including Xenophon's, had ensured that he'd received immediate and concerned attention. Ultimately he was put through to a polite but unfamiliar voice.

'I think I'd better come and see you at once,' the voice had said. 'We must get this all sorted out. I'll fly out tomorrow. Be with you about three, that OK?'

Victor had been inclined to tell the voice that it wasn't OK, that he generally rested after lunch, that five o'clock would be a better time, when it was cooler, and anyway he didn't really want to see him at all. But then he'd thought, why make trouble, why fight it? Let's just get this thing over and done with. So he'd said quietly, 'Right, I'll expect you at three.'

'Good afternoon, Mr Meer,' the man had greeted him next day. He was a dapper, neatly dressed figure in his forties, with a hint of preciousness that Victor always found intriguing. 'It's a great pleasure to meet you. I'm a

369

tremendous admirer of your novels, but I suppose you get quite sick of hearing people say that. My name's Gilbert, by the way, Derek Gilbert.'

Victor had been fully prepared to take exception to him. His visit was an intrusion. If there had been a single annoying element in his behaviour, Victor would have pounced on it. Almost gratefully. But Derek Gilbert had turned out to be polite, well mannered, and palpably intelligent. Victor had rather enjoyed his company. A little bit later, he'd been surprised to find himself opening a bottle of champagne for him.

Derek had asked to see the letter, absorbed it, then nodded. Nodded sympathetically.

'I know this will be a bore for you, Mr Meer, raking over old coals. But I'm afraid, as I suspected, this letter opens up a potentially embarrassing situation, potentially embarrassing in several different quarters. That's why we've got to handle it very carefully, keep the lid on it as far as possible. I hope you won't mind too much if I ask you a few questions about the past, go over some old ground.'

The questions had mostly been about Boris's taste in pictures. Were these things that Xenophon was apparently sending to Vienna for disposal likely to be good? Victor had been forced to admit that they probably were.

'Do you know of anything specific?'

'He did once mention he had a Derain landscape. Of 1905.'

'1905?' Derek paused, then added: 'That's a Fauve one, isn't it? The best period?'

Victor had looked up, impressed. 'Yes. The very best.'

'Any idea about anything else?'

'He once told me he had acquired pictures in Germany with the Red Army at the end of the war. I don't know what exactly, but I'm pretty sure there were one or two exceptional ones. You see, Xenophon knew about pictures, he understood them. He would have recognised things other people might have disregarded.'

'I suppose there were certainly opportunities at that time.'

'Tremendous opportunities. And . . .' Victor hesitated for a moment.

'Go on,' said Derek gently.

'Well, the thing about Xenophon was that – how can I put it? – if he'd set his heart on something he generally wasn't too scrupulous about how he got hold of it.' Victor had added a half-hearted little laugh. To indicate, what could you expect from a Russian?

'Was there anything particular that makes you say that?'

'Anything particular?' Victor was on his guard.

'I'm sorry. It just sounds as though you might have had a specific incident in mind?'

'Oh no,' Victor had said firmly. 'Nothing specific. You just got that feeling about him. He was very strong-willed.'

Derek nodded. 'I can imagine.' Could he imagine? wondered Victor. Could he imagine that pathetic man sweating with terror, rubbing his hands together distractedly to ward off the horror he saw coming? Could he imagine Kalb lying dead with a bullet in his back?

Victor had closed his eyes to blot it all out. 'I'm sorry,' he said, 'it's the heat today. It's hard to concentrate.'

'Of course. I do apologise for putting you through this. I'm sure there are many things you'd rather be doing than answering all these questions.'

Victor had sipped his drink then smiled back politely. 'It's all right now.' The moment of danger had passed, and he could go on. He asked: 'But perhaps you would answer me one question, just out of curiosity: why are

Xenophon's pictures of such interest now?'

'I can't go into it in too much detail at the moment,' Derek had said. 'The whole thing's very sensitive. It's to do with our Russian friends, our new allies. We do what we can to help them these days, and they do us one or two favours in return. Anyway, for various reasons, they'd be very anxious to lay hands on the Xenophon pictures if they knew they were coming through. Our idea is to field them for them, hand them over, and then ask them to do something for us. In return. A bit of co-operation, I suppose you might call it.'

Victor nodded cautiously. 'What do we hope to get as a quid pro quo from them?'

'If we return Xenophon's pictures to them, we think we can get them to destroy the Xenophon file. Cover all tracks, eliminate all possibility of a leak their end that could prove embarrassing to you. And embarrassing to us. We've had quite enough recent revelations about KGB penetration of our own service in the Cold War years. We don't want any more, not if we can help it. That's why we're choosing to handle this business ourselves, for fear of re-exposing what happened in the past between you and him. Obviously this letter draws unwelcome attention to your relationship, so we're keeping it quiet.'

Victor had said hotly: 'But it would be an appalling misinterpretation of the facts to speak of KGB penetration in my case. If you look at the file . . .'

'I do beg your pardon. I expressed myself badly. What we hope to achieve is the removal of any further possibility of misinterpretation of your relationship with Xenophon. And there is that danger, given the sensationalist times in which we live.'

'Yes, I see,' Victor replied quietly. Derek was right, of course. Given the sensationalist times in which we live. 'So what do you want me to do now?'

'Leave it in our hands,' Derek had told him. 'We'll contact Grunwald, as if on your behalf, and we'll check him out. We've got to field these pictures, as and when they come through. Make sure they don't escape the net.'

'And this letter?'

'Keep it. I've made a copy.'

On the way out, Victor had seen Derek's eye rest momentarily on the picture visible through the open door to his study. The picture with the breathtakingly beautiful foliage and blossom. The picture of the jewelled orchard.

'That's rather lovely,' Derek had said.

'It's a nice room, isn't it?' Victor had replied, deliberately misunderstanding. 'It's where I do most of my writing.' He had hurried him on into the hall.

At the front door Derek had said: 'Thank you so much for seeing me and being so helpful. I'll let you know if there are any developments.'

There had been developments over the summer. A lot of them. A sequence of events had been set in motion culminating in this present momentous journey to Vienna.

The aircraft jolted and shuddered. Victor looked up and realised they had landed. Very soon now. Very soon indeed.

Victor always took too much luggage with him, wherever he went. He had never learned the art of travelling light, not even in the Army. He stood at the baggage reclaim area and cursed. There didn't seem to be any porters about. There never were when you needed them. He'd had to commandeer one of those lop-sided pushing contraptions on wheels and wait anxiously for his huge suitcase to appear. He was only staying one night, or at the most two. But his possessions had resolutely refused to be accommodated in anything smaller than the trunk-like container that was now approaching him on the carousel. He laid a hand on it and tugged ineffectually. Finally a young woman moved across and helped him manoeuvre the thing on to the trolley. He thanked her sourly and shuffled off through the green channel.

'Good journey?' asked Derek solicitously on the other side. He was wearing sun-glasses, which he removed the moment he saw Victor, grey flannels and a lightweight jacket. He looked cool and on top of the situation.

'Reasonable.' Victor allowed him to take control of the trolley. In Derek's hands it moved straight ahead, no longer lurching sideways like a mobile crab as it had done infuriatingly when he'd been pushing it. There must be a knack, a knack he was too old to learn now.

'Is it all right with you if we drive straight to the flat?'

'The flat?' Victor felt breathless, suddenly uncertain.

'The flat where the pictures are. The embassy was deemed an inappropriate place to unpack them. There must be no official involvement, I'm sure you'll under-stand that.'

'No, no, of course not. Let's go straight to the flat, by all means.' The sick feeling was there in his stomach again, stronger than ever. Perhaps he shouldn't have come.

'The parcels were picked up from Grunwald yesterday.'

Victor negotiated the double doors out to the open air, then asked with a dry mouth: 'They're not unpacked yet?'

'Not yet, no.' Derek halted for a moment and smiled at him, not unkindly. 'We thought it wouldn't do any harm to wait for you to be present when they were.'

There was a car waiting for them. The driver lugged Victor's heavy case into the boot, then held the door open for the two of them to get into the back. It was hot for early October.

Once the car had glided off, Victor said: 'So Grunwald made no trouble?'

Derek shook his head and gave one of his tight, knowing little laughs. 'I think he's finally been cowed into submission. Not that he isn't a devious little bastard, but I think we finally persuaded him that he had to play along with us on this one. He's been kept under constant surveillance, of course, and I think he got wind of it and realised there was no chance of doing deals with the Xenophon pictures after all. Not with us breathing down his neck, anyway. In fact, although we knew through other channels that the shipment was on its way last week, he actually alerted us too. Trying to chalk up a few brownie points, I suppose.'

'And he's still claiming he doesn't know what the shipment contains?'

'For what it's worth, yes.'

'What did he say when he was quizzed on Ginn's call to him?'

'He claims that call was totally unsolicited, and that he knew nothing about that particular picture.'

'About "The Stonebreakers".'

'About "The Stonebreakers".'

'Do you believe him?'

Derek fingered his cuff-links. Victor had noticed the mannerism before, whenever he was asked for an opinion as opposed to a statement of fact. 'Frankly, no, I don't believe him. As I say, he's a devious little bastard, and I wouldn't trust him an inch. I mean, let's look at the evidence. Ginn was offered the picture by Tumbrill. Ginn had definitely got the idea that the picture was coming out of Russia. Tumbrill had done business with Grunwald before with pictures coming out of Moscow. We tap Grunwald's phone as a precaution once we know from the letter you received that the pictures are coming via Grunwald. We overhear him discussing "The Stonebreakers" with Ginn. It seems to me highly probable that the Courbet is a Xenophon picture and Grunwald was quietly preparing the ground for doing a deal once it arrived. He denies it now. Probably because it's been made clear to him that handling a stolen picture of that importance could have put him in deep trouble with the authorities. And when we open up the Xenophon shipment and find "The Stonebreakers", he'll just claim it's the most extraordinary coincidence.'

Victor swallowed. 'Are any of the packages large enough?'

'To be "The Stonebreakers"? ' Derek gave another of his tight little laughs. 'Look, I don't want to alarm you. But I have to tell you that the only one about the right size is the package that Grunwald now says is earmarked for you. The one that wasn't for sale, the one that Xenophon said was to be handed over to you.'

'God almighty!' For a moment Victor thought he was going to faint.

'Of course, we can't be sure,' Derek continued. 'All the pictures have arrived in cuts of linoleum.'

'Linoleum?'

'Yes. Apparently that's one of Grunwald's methods. He's had a long-standing relationship with a Moscow business that produces the stuff, and he's been importing it for a number of years. The rolls of linoleum contain the carefully wrapped canvases, you see. Your linoleum roll is the only one large enough to contain a canvas the size of . . . of "The Stonebreakers".'

'I see,' said Victor. Boris, you idiot, he thought. You bloody idiot.

They were approaching the outskirts of the city now. They passed a huge oil refinery, a massively ugly construction of pipes, tubes and gantries. These days even the most beautiful cities of Europe were set in suburbs of uniform hideousness. He wished he'd seen Vienna before the war. Just once. It would have been different then. He glanced across at Derek, sitting there neat and discreet. But even Derek was apprehensive. Victor could tell from the way he was drumming his well-manicured fingers on the armrest next to him in febrile little spurts.

Victor said suddenly: 'What happens if it is?'

'I'm sorry?'

'What happens if my parcel is "The Stonebreakers"?'

Derek considered the matter. 'It'll be a relief on balance, don't you think? If it is? The picture will be discreetly handed over to the Russians for them to return to Dresden. And we'll be able to congratulate ourselves on a delicate enterprise successfully completed. All potential damage contained. Everyone will be satisfied.'

'Everyone?'

'Just about everyone. If you remember, I explained the nature of the informal arrangement with our Russian colleagues when we first met.'

'Yes, indeed. And that still stands?'

'Certainly. That's the basis on which we've gone to these exceptional lengths to help them out. Keeping Grunwald's telephone tapped has been quite an investment in time and manpower. But it will be worth it if we end up producing a few looted masterpieces for them. Including "The Stonebreakers". They'll be in our debt then.'

'I've never quite understood,' said Victor, 'why they would be so anxious to get these pictures back.'

'The Russians have become extraordinarily touchy about the public reappearance of art treasures that were plundered from Germany by Soviet personnel at the end of the war. They're making every effort discreetly to retrieve anything that falls into that category, then to be seen to be getting it back to the German authorities. It's part of their current obsession with remaining on good terms with the Germans. They don't want anything to happen that might rock the boat. Of course they're quite right: they're very dependent on German aid and investment for the future. So any help we can give them now will be gratefully received. And repaid.'

'By the elimination of Xenophon's records?'

'That's it.'

'The lid will be kept on,' said Victor softly. No more scope for misinterpretation. Given the sensationalist times in which we live. The fear had always been there, when he'd allowed himself to think about it. The fear of the potential misinterpretation. Look what had happened to Blunt. That was an entirely different case, of course. Blunt had been a traitor. Victor himself had been something quite different, Victor had been a victim. But it was a difficult distinction to get across to stupid people. You could see what might happen, given the unwelcome emergence of more details. Given their likely misinterpretation. Given the sensationalist times in which we live.

After a while Victor added thoughtfully: 'Of course, there will be tremendous publicity if "The Stonebreakers" does resurface. I mean when it's actually handed back to Dresden.'

'There probably will,' agreed Derek. 'But that doesn't matter. For the Russians it'll be the right sort of publicity. It'll show the world how they're cleaning up their act, rejoining the family of nations. Becoming house-trained.'

House-trained. It rang some bell across the years. Colonel Keith, of course. Colonel Keith had known the Russians could never be house-trained. Don't make the mistake of thinking of them as Europeans, he'd warned. If you do you'll come to grief. No, they're Asians, and that's a very different cup of tea. A very different cup of tea indeed. Remember that and you won't go far wrong. Don't get too friendly with them. Colonel Keith couldn't imagine anyone wanting to, anyway. Personally he'd never met a Russian he wasn't perfectly happy to keep a healthy distance from.

The cruellest thing of all was that Colonel Keith had been right. Heartbreakingly right.

They reached Ringstrasse and prepared to cut across it into the maze of little streets leading towards the cathedral. The maze of little streets that, between the shopping precincts garish with their neon hoardings, allowed occasional glimpses of the old Vienna.

'By the way,' asked Derek, 'any news from Argentina?'

'As a matter of fact, yes.' Victor smiled, half embarrassed. 'I must say, that side of things seems to have worked out better than either you or I could ever have dared hope.'

Derek raised his eyebrows. 'Really?'

'I had a brief report from my . . . from the man I as it were "tipped off" about Wenglein. He got back two days ago. The extraordinary thing is that he and Ginn seem to have traipsed halfway across Argentina and tracked down a picture which they've convinced themselves was the Courbet. It was a large picture in the Wenglein estate alleged to have been brought out with Wenglein when he fled from Germany.'

'But didn't they get to see it?' Derek was intrigued.

'That's the extraordinary part of the story. Some lunatic set fire to it just before they could get there. Some servant of Wenglein's with a bee in his bonnet about this picture never being allowed to leave the house. It was burned beyond recognition, so there's no way of checking.'

'How incredible. But convenient, too.'

'Indeed.'

'I wonder what this picture actually was, the one that went up in flames?'

Victor thought for a moment. The question was suddenly a welcome distraction from everything else.

'Probably some frightful piece of Third Reich art,' he speculated. 'Healthy naked Aryans in absurd and mildly erotic poses, you know the sort of thing.'

Derek frowned. 'So does that mean that Ginn's convinced that his quest is over?'

'I understand from my man that he is. They both are.'

'It was a perfect deflection.'

'You could say so.'

'I must admit,' continued Derek, 'I had my doubts about that idea of yours at first, when you originally suggested it. But it came off like a dream.'

'My idea.' Victor nodded reminiscently. 'Yes, it does seem to have worked rather well, doesn't it?'

Victor's idea.

He closed his eyes for a moment, there in the back of the car negotiating the traffic in the narrow Viennese streets. He closed his eyes and remembered his idea. He remembered – with the almost unnatural clarity that age sometimes bestows on distant events – what exactly it was that had inspired it. It was a meeting with someone, an encounter that had also taken place here in Austria. Not actually in Vienna, but about a hundred miles away to the south. In an old monastery, then commandeered as a Brigade HQ for the British Army. An encounter that had taken place one late autumn morning nearly half a century ago.

Colonel Keith. It had started with him. He could see Keith now, sitting opposite him, with those absurdly held shoulders, his pompous manner, his neat little moustache, his careful vowels. Keith was angry. Someone's incompetence had enraged him. That meant he was swearing a lot: it was the way he expressed his authority. Curiously his fury had been incurred by the military police on sentry duty.

380

'What a frigging shambles, I ask you, Meer. They're behaving like a bunch of bloody fairies down there on the gate. They're wet-nursing about over some bloody woman who won't go away. Christ almighty, you'd think they could pull themselves together sufficiently to tell her to frig off. But oh no. Apparently she arrived yesterday afternoon and she's been camped outside in the road all bloody night. She won't push off home until she's seen someone in authority, she says. I'm afraid you're going to have to get down there and find out what all this bloody nonsense is about. Take a quick statement from her if you have to. Then get her to bugger off, will you? Piss off out of it?'

Victor went down to the room where they had installed her. She looked up as he came in. She was young, not more than twenty or so. Her head was wrapped in a scarf tied under her chin, and her eyes were angry. But she was memorable. Even like that she was strikingly good-looking: tall, broad-shouldered, with clear, healthy skin. She had survived her night out in the open remarkably well.

'You are an officer?' she said at once, half rising from her chair. 'In the British Army?'

'I am. My name is Captain Meer.'

'Thank God. At last. I have been trying for many weeks to reach you. I have important information, you must listen to me.'

Victor sat down opposite her and opened his notebook. 'You wish to make some sort of statement, Fraulein . . .?'

'Fräulein Helgemann. Gerda Helgemann. Yes, I must tell you many things. But it may be too late.'

'Fräulein Helgemann, where are you from?'

'Where am I from?' She paused and pulled off her scarf, shaking out a mass of blonde hair. 'Well, at the moment I am living at the camp for displaced persons at Matterhein,

twenty-five kilometres from here. I have been there
nearly two months. Every day I have told them, I must
make a statement. I have important information for
the . . . for the British authorities. They said always next
week, next week, someone will come. But there was never
anyone. I was forgotten, no one paid any attention to me.
Finally I could not wait any longer, I had to speak to
someone about these things. So I set off yesterday morning and reached here in the afternoon. I am determined
not to leave without telling you what I know.' She looked
across at him defiantly.

'You are Austrian, Fräulein Helgemann?'

She laughed, as if the suggestion was a rather stale joke.
'No, I am not Austrian. I said I was Austrian when I was
deported without papers from Switzerland in May. I
thought perhaps it would go better for me if I said I was
Austrian. But no, I am German, from Dresden. Up till
February I had lived in Dresden all my life.'

There was something compelling about her. Victor
leant across and offered her a cigarette. She took one and
he lit it for her. 'What is this urgent matter you have to tell
me about?' he asked.

'I have to give evidence about a criminal. A man who
has committed serious crimes at the end of the war, a man
who must be brought to justice for the crimes he has
committed. If you come here as liberators, as you claim, if
you stand for justice, then you must pursue this man, hunt
him down. He must not be allowed to go free.'

These outbursts were not new to Victor. He had dealt
with many of them already. Resentful, bitter men and
women, burning to settle old scores, do down old
enemies. But there was something about this girl. Something different. Something that commanded attention. He
took up his pen and asked: 'Who is this man and what did
he do?'

'His name is Wenglein, Major Heinrich Wenglein. An officer in the SS. He killed at least one man, a civilian, gunned him down in cold blood. I was there, I saw him do it, in our street in Dresden. Probably he murdered many more. And he tried to kill me. That's why I'm giving you this evidence, now, at the first opportunity you have allowed me. It is your duty to find him and punish him.'

'Fräulein Helgemann,' Victor said, 'I think you had better start at the beginning.'

She was a natural storyteller, that girl. Her narrative had been absorbing in a way that Victor had been quite unprepared for. He wrote it down, all of it, as a record. He felt it was worth writing down, regardless of what happened to Wenglein. Perhaps it was the embryonic novelist within him.

At the end she stood up and said, 'Is that enough for you?'

'Yes. Your account has been very clear and helpful.'

'What will you do now?'

'We'll make some enquiries.'

'What sort of enquiries? In Argentina, will you make enquiries there?'

'Fräulein Helgemann, I can't go into any detail at this stage. Appropriate action will be taken, but you must leave the matter in our hands. There is nothing more for you to do. You must go home now.'

'Home?'

He wished he hadn't used the word. 'Back to the camp.'

A look of despair passed over her face. Such profound despair that Victor felt obliged to summon Dakins and tell him to drive her back to her displaced persons centre. Even then she barely acknowledged the kindness. Perhaps she had known in her heart the note Victor was going to append to the record he'd made of her statement. The note recommending no further action. After all, there

383

were cases with much higher priority than Wenglein's. From a window he watched her climb into the jeep. She pulled herself up slowly, finally acknowledging her exhaustion.

But it had been an unforgettable story. One that he'd not only ordered to be held on official file – whatever good that might do – but also kept in his own private memory bank. It had never deserted him, through the years, as a document of human drama.

And Gerda Helgemann's evidence had come to mind again, very recently. Barely a month ago, in fact, on the occasion of Derek Gilbert's second visit to the villa. This second time there had been a tension about his manner, a suppressed urgency. There had been new developments, worrying developments, calling for immediate action. Derek had come out again to consult.

The previous day the phone tap had exposed Grunwald in negotiation with a London dealer over the sale of what could only be a Xenophon picture. This when Grunwald had been told to keep the existence of the Xenophon shipment to himself, told very forcefully indeed. The bastard was trying to do a deal on the sly. The lid was in danger of being blown off the whole business. And what made it worse was that the picture in question was not just any picture, not something that in the last resort could be quietly forgotten about if it escaped the net. It was something quite staggeringly important.

It was the news that Victor most emphatically had not wanted to hear. He was fraught enough already: Orlando had decamped last week to Vera Maskell's, and Victor was sunk in misery, distracted, unable to work properly. To have this extra anguish visited upon him was intolerable. But despite everything, what Derek told him had engaged his attention. It was a damnable intrusion, this whole business, but part of him was curious. He had leant forward in his wicker chair on the verandah, podgy hands clasping a champagne glass between his bronzed knees. He had asked: 'What is the picture, can you tell me?'

And Derek had replied: 'It's Courbet's "Stonebreakers".'

Courbet's 'Stonebreakers'.

'My God!' He had reckoned back quickly. 'But surely that picture was destroyed in Dresden in 1945?'

'Believed destroyed. Last heard of in Dresden in February 1945. Now Grunwald's apparently offered it to this dealer in London.'

'Shit!' It had all come to him suddenly, with shocking and unexpected clarity.

'What is it?'

'Now I think about it, of course, it all ties in. Boris was in Dresden at the end of the war, he told me.'

'He was, was he?' Derek had frowned uneasily. 'I hadn't checked that part of it yet. Well, it makes the situation all the more sensitive. If it's "The Stonebreakers" that's involved, we've got to take this London dealer right out of it, stop him interfering. That's the first priority.'

'What's the dealer proposing to do about it, do you know?'

'I think there's every likelihood he'll be on his way to Vienna in a few days, to negotiate with Grunwald.'

'Not a good idea,' Victor mused.

'Definitely not. He's got to be stopped.'

'Who is he?'

'He's called Oswald Ginn, of Fortescue's.'

'He's the only one involved up till now?'

'I believe so.'

'If I know anything about picture dealers, he'll try to keep it that way,' said Victor meditatively. 'That's one small mercy. I think you can count on his discretion for the time being.'

'Yes, but he must be deflected. Diverted away from Grunwald, at least until we've had a chance to check the whole thing out, to contain the situation, to get Grunwald under control.'

Perhaps it was then that the idea had bubbled from Victor's subconscious. Perhaps it was then that he had first been aware of its vague possibilities. He must have sensed something, because he'd said with sudden optimism: 'You know, achieving that might not be quite as difficult as it seems. Not if it's properly handled. In my experience art dealers are infinitely suggestible people.'

Derek sat up, his full attention engaged. 'What are you saying?'

'I'm saying that it's a question of implanting the right suggestion.'

'This is exactly what I hoped you might advise me.' Derek paused. 'And there is one advantage to the Ginn situation: I happen to know him personally. Not well, but I was at Cambridge with him. As I see it, what I've got to do is make contact with him again and, without arousing his suspicions, point him firmly in an alternative direction. Well away from Vienna and Grunwald. How do we do it?'

Derek looked at him expectantly. Victor sensed again the urgency underlying his words. There was a compelling necessity for Victor to come up with something, and come up with it quickly. To keep the lid on. To save his own skin. And at the same time the question intrigued him as a problem in the abstract, engaged his novelist's imaginative intelligence.

He said finally: 'At this stage there's no point in trying to deny the picture's existence, because Ginn's had his appetite whetted now, he thinks he's on the scent. No, putting him off would only make him suspicious, increase his curiosity. What you have to do is present him with positive plausible evidence that the picture is to be found elsewhere. A long way away, somewhere he'll have to go to at once to pursue it. And at the same time a little bit of a rumour could be started in one or two other strategic quarters, to back the story up, lend it conviction. The art market is very sensitive to rumour.'

'What would be plausible evidence in this case?'

It was then that it had all come to him. Miraculously. With perfect clarity. The whole interview, the whole harrowing story of Gerda Helgemann's affair with Wenglein. Major Heinrich Wenglein. Perhaps the moment had finally arrived, nearly fifty years on, for the girl's evidence to be put to good effect. To be recycled slightly, to fit the present need.

'Look, I'm thinking out loud,' Victor had said slowly, sitting there listening to the crickets and watching the breeze animate the cypresses at the end of the garden, 'but what about this?' Briefly he described the Wenglein case and how he had come across it. He thought that the records of those immediate post-war interrogations were still on file. Could Derek get access to this one?

'I believe so,' said Derek. 'But forgive me: I don't quite see what use this evidence will be to us now.'

'No use, as it stands. But with a little adaptation it could become a very persuasive document indeed. I can see how it would work.' Victor had leant forward, excited now, expressing himself with rapid little movements of his hands. 'Look, the girl tells how the pair of them emerged the morning after the bombing of Dresden and decided to make a break for it together. Wenglein shot a man who disturbed their preparations for departure. That bit's all there. What isn't there, what needs inserting now, is a small further detail: a brief account of Wenglein's discovery that morning of an oil painting, intact in the ruins. That picture could be described in such a way as clearly to identify it as "The Stonebreakers". The rest of the girl's evidence would indicate that Wenglein escaped with this picture to Argentina. If you put the whole thing across convincingly enough, your man Ginn will be off out there in pursuit at once.'

'What, you mean tamper with the girl's statement?'

'Just a little. Just to add in the Courbet.'

Derek had considered Victor's idea in silence for a moment. Then he had said: 'I think it might work, you know. Particularly as I know Ginn personally; that will help. I could show him the girl's statement as a curiosity and ask him his opinion of it – emphasising that it's classified material, of course. See how he jumps. It might just do the trick. It's worth trying.'

'You'll have to move quickly.'

Derek nodded. 'I'll set things in motion at once. And to add verisimilitude, as you suggested, we could just drop a hint or two elsewhere. Perhaps in Germany, in Dresden itself, to distract attention? There are Intelligence channels that could be used for the purpose. We could start the odd unsubstantiated rumour about the picture's possible reappearance in Argentina. As a temporary smoke-screen.'

Victor had added cautiously: 'I have one channel myself which might discreetly also be brought into play. Someone in the art market I could alert who would probably be tempted away from . . . from what he's doing at the moment by a trip to Buenos Aires.'

'By all means,' said Derek. 'I just hope I can lay hands on this file now.'

He had succeeded. It had all worked out even better than Victor could have imagined. Derek telephoned him from London the next day, the Sunday, to say that he had the record of the interrogation in front of him. Even more conveniently, further checking had revealed that Wenglein himself, by the happiest of chances, had died earlier in the year in Buenos Aires. That would help: his estate would now be on the market. It all fitted in. Derek had got hold of a typewriter of Second World War vintage. The text would be suitably amended, to introduce the reference to the Courbet. And fed to Ginn on Monday morning.

Victor also took action on that Monday morning. With trembling hand he telephoned Vera Maskell's villa and asked to speak to Orlando. To put a proposition to him. A business proposition.

The car turned a corner, slowed, and drew to a halt. They had arrived. The driver opened the door for them and Victor followed Derek out into the bright afternoon sunshine. His legs felt uncertain and he stumbled as he stood up. Derek put out an arm to steady him.

'Feeling all right?'

'I'll be fine.' Victor managed a weak smile.

The narrow street seemed very quiet. He looked down it, saw it for a terrifying moment with the eyes of a man who has lost his memory and recognises nothing, not even his reason for being where he is. There was a bookshop opposite; next to it a confectioner. A girl stood outside, peering in at the window. The scene seemed extracted from time, held in a surreal state of suspended animation.

'Let's go up,' Derek said. He was holding the door open for him, the door that led off the street into a building. Blindly Victor shuffled in and found himself in a cool hallway, at the foot of a sweeping staircase. 'It's on the second floor,' Derek was continuing, 'but there's a lift.'

The panicky moment of disorientation dissolved, and with it the glimpse of dementia. He knew where he was again and clutched gratefully at reality, like a man gasping in fresh air after too long under water.

'Something I forgot to ask,' he heard his own voice

saying. 'It's stupid really. But did Xenophon die? Did anyone actually check?'

Derek looked at him oddly. 'Sorry. I should have told you. Yes, he died the second week in July. It was confirmed from Moscow.'

'Ah. That's all right, then.' Was it? He couldn't quite think any more. He found it difficult to tell whether what he was saying made sense. Boris was finally dead. Was that all right? He summoned every reserve of reason and concentration he could muster and decided that it probably was.

He was ushered into the lift. The driver was with them. It was the driver who pressed the buttons, and when they got to the front door of the flat, it was the driver who produced keys and let them in. It occurred to him that he didn't know what the driver's name was. Not Dakins. No, not Dakins. That was another time. Another time, long, long ago.

The flat had high ceilings and was elegantly furnished. He wondered vaguely who it belonged to. Someone with taste, certainly. They walked through double doors into a salon, and Victor's eye picked out odd details: a lovely piece of Meissen in a cabinet; an unexpectedly good early-nineteenth-century drawing by Peter Fendi.

'Why don't you sit down for a moment?' Derek suggested.

He did, thankfully, on a Beidermeyer sofa. 'Do you think I could have a drink of water?' he said softly.

'Of course.' Derek turned to the driver, who was on the point of leaving the room. 'Would you get Mr Meer a glass of mineral water, Bannon? Then I think we'll have the packages in here.'

'Very good, sir.'

Dakins, Bannon. What was in a name? What had he said to Dakins that time on the road to Augstein? What do you make of them, Dakins, the Soviets? Probably some decent chaps amongst them, wouldn't you say? Wouldn't know, sir, Dakins had replied. Couldn't tell you.

He sipped his water and watched as Bannon pulled in the rolls, one by one. They were wrapped in brown paper and secured with tape. Bannon, who was a big, burly man, stood them in a line like factory chimneys. Three smaller chimneys. And one taller one.

'Quite a moment, isn't it?' said Derek. 'Shall we make a start?'

Victor nodded. The water had revived him and he felt clearer in his head, better prepared for what was to come. But it was still hot here. Derek took off his jacket. He was wearing braces over a light blue shirt, and he was sweating at his armpits. That was unusual for Derek. Even Derek must be feeling the strain. It was there, Victor sensed it again: the tension, the uncertainty, communicating itself amongst them, informing the movements of each of the three men in the room.

Bannon took a pair of scissors and cut the packaging on the first of the smaller rolls. He ripped off the paper with a series of short, jerky actions, then laid the brown linoleum roll on the floor, ready to unwind it.

'Careful now,' said Derek, stepping over to help him. 'Let's do this gently.'

Slowly they unwound the horrifically ugly floor covering. Its cheap, swirling design as it arched out across the floor contrasted absurdly with the delicate Persian carpet next to it. Suddenly an edge of tissue paper emerged. This must be it. This must contain an unstretched canvas.

A moment later they held it up for him. It was a flower picture, a very fine one. Not large, but of exquisite quality. It was by Fantin-Latour. Not bad, thought Victor. And despite himself he added mentally, well done, Boris.

'There's something on the back,' Derek was saying.

They turned it round and peered at the inscription on the reverse. It was handwritten, very finely, in old German script. Collection Brauner, Leipzig, it read. Leipzig. Germany. Not so well done, Boris, thought Victor. But Derek was smiling, relieved, pleased at the development.

'Our Russian friends will be happy with that,' he declared. 'That'll earn them a bit of credit when they hand it back to the German authorities.'

The two remaining smaller rolls were undone. With each there was the same anticipation as the tissue paper emerged and then the unstretched canvas was unravelled and held up. Despite everything, Victor felt a mounting fascination. He left the unpacking to Derek and Bannon, but he sat further forward on his seat. Absorbed, anxious, trembling slightly.

The first to come out was an unusually well-painted head of a woman by Renoir. It erred on the side of sweetness, and Victor wouldn't have chosen it for his own collection. But it was right. Unquestionably right. And it was a good one. What was it worth? he speculated. Between one and two million pounds, at a guess. Funny to think of it rolled up in that quite ghastly cheap linoleum.

Then came the Derain. A coastal scene, a riot of untamed colour, painted in vivid blues, reds and greens, and dated 1905; 1905, the very start of the Fauve movement. It was a gem. Bannon held it up by the edge of the canvas, where the little nail-holes that had once tacked it to its stretcher were visible, and Victor marvelled at it.

'This is good stuff,' breathed Derek.

Victor nodded. 'You see, Boris knew about pictures,' he said again. 'He had a feeling for them.'

For a moment he was almost happy. In a strange way the better the quality of the paintings emerging from the rolls of linoleum, the more he felt his relationship with Boris was being vindicated. Anyone with sensitivity could look at these pictures and understand. Understand what it was that had drawn them together. Understand that for both of them pictures had been more important than politics.

'Nothing on the back of the Renoir or the Derain?' Derek asked. 'No indication of provenance?'

'I don't see anything.'

'Even if they don't come out of Germany the Russians will be pleased to have them back. After all, they have been illegally exported and they're beautiful things. Valuable, too.'

'Certainly valuable,' agreed Victor.

But his attention was now absorbed by the only roll remaining. His eyes were drawn irresistibly to it. This was the biggest roll. His roll, the one containing the painting meant for him. Was it what he thought it was going to be? What Derek thought it was going to be, too? Had Boris somehow saved from the ruins of Dresden one of its museum's most prized adornments, and carried it back to Russia for his own private enjoyment? Were they about to see Courbet's masterpiece after all these years? After the years of incarceration in Boris's Moscow apartment, were the Stonebreakers about to be restored to freedom? What had Boris said in his letter? You will recognise it, Victor, and you will be surprised. And what had Boris told him a quarter of a century ago when they had met one cold night in London at the Soviet Embassy? One or two of my pictures are famous in their way, he had said. Only by seeing them would you believe.

Now he was going to see. Now he was going to believe.

The waiting was suddenly almost unbearable.

Victor watched as Bannon lifted the tallest roll. The only roll left. He took up the scissors again and worked an initial slit in the paper wrapping. Derek moved forward now to hold the roll as Bannon pulled the brown paper clear. But it wouldn't come away immediately; the tape had been stuck round in thicker bands which refused to yield without a struggle.

'Cut it. Cut it with the scissors,' said Derek urgently.

Then it was off, and the large roll was on its side, ready to be spread out. They cleared more room for it, moved chairs and tables aside, because when this piece was unrolled it would occupy a considerable floor space. They both knew that 'The Stonebreakers' was not a small picture.

It was hot in the room. Suddenly Victor had a very clear image. Of Boris. Of Boris as he had been, nearly fifty years ago. Of Boris in the rubble of Dresden, Boris threatening a cowering German, holding him up at gunpoint. Boris, forcing from the grasp of the man a large roll of canvas. The frightened, desperate eyes of the German. And then a shot rang out, and Boris was suddenly Wenglein, and the dying, writhing German was suddenly Kalb. The scene dissolved abruptly, into the confused mists of time. But the horror remained, stark and sickening.

'Here we go,' said Derek breathlessly, kneeling down and beginning to unroll.

At first there was nothing. The absence of a canvas as more and more linoleum was revealed seemed like some macabre practical joke. And then, there it was: the edge of tissue paper, the little package emerging, absurdly small against its massive container.

'It's not it . . .' whispered Derek. 'Not big enough. But what is it . . .?'

They held it up.

'Oh no! Oh, God almighty!' exclaimed Victor. He thought he was going to cry.

It was by Klimt. A mountainous landscape this time, with a breathtaking expanse of lake, the water jewelled with glittering reflections. It was an almost identical size to the orchard: it might have been its pair. If possible it was even more beautiful.

'There's an inscription on the back again,' murmured Derek. 'It doesn't make much sense. Just four letters – look, here, – KALB. Not much help.'

'No,' said Victor, turning away. 'Not much help at all.'

'I'll get them all back into Russian safekeeping as soon as possible,' Derek was saying. 'It's a pity about "The Stonebreakers", but it's still quite a haul. I think they'll be grateful. You'll be kept out of it, of course.'

'Thank you. I . . . I appreciate it.'

'Can I drop you at your hotel?'

'That would be kind.'

'You're probably tired.'

He was. He felt drained. Derek was talking again: 'It's just a bit of a bore that we haven't quite tied up all the loose ends. But I suppose one never does in these cases, does one? I mean, I think it's fair to assume that "The Stonebreakers" wasn't part of the Xenophon consignment after all, and that Grunwald was telling the truth when he said he knew nothing about the Courbet. But if that's so, then who offered it to Tumbrill for him to offer it to Ginn? How do you explain that?'

Victor shrugged, exhausted. Someone had offered Tumbrill 'The Stonebreakers'. Apparently it wasn't Grunwald. Apparently it hadn't come from Boris. Victor had spent a lifetime trying to find explanations for things. Sometimes you just couldn't do it. Sometimes you just had to admit defeat.

14

It was early November. The crowds still surged up Bond Street. Olga still sat reading a book at the reception desk. Jack the porter wheezed malevolently as he stacked frames in the basement.

Six weeks on from his return Oswald still thought of her, of course. But he had found ways of suppressing the grief of her loss. Memories of his intimacy with her were already breaking free of their tenuous connection with reality. Drifting off to some ethereal region of the imagination, taking on some of the characteristics of events in a beautiful dream. Thus the bitterness of their parting could be rendered no more painful than the inevitability of awakening from such a dream. The secret was to keep it like that. To stifle the little-remembered details that pin events back in the real world. To forget the way she turned and waved at him in the crowded street after their first chance meeting in Buenos Aires; the way she tore her cigarette packet to pieces in Dresden; the tears she shed lying in bed that sunny morning in a hotel in Córdoba.

Christ almighty, things weren't that bad. Not by comparison with some people. He wasn't dead like Bernard. He wasn't being burned alive in some Dresden cellar in February 1945. He had a job, a house, children and books to read. Wasn't it better to be an art dealer in late-twentieth-century London than a mid-nineteenth-century stonebreaker in provincial France? Yes. Except that in a way everyone was like Gagey. Everyone was chained by circumstance to their own personal pile of rubble, with their own more or less serviceable pickaxe to hack away at it. The people who were happiest were the people who recognised their lot and accepted it. Came to terms with the routine. Once in your life, if you were lucky, something extraordinary would happen to break that routine. Like Gagey, with the madman jumping down from his carriage and offering him the chance to pose as a model in a picture. Offering him unwitting immortality. Like Oswald himself, when Saskia came into his life. But these were brief holidays from the grind. Everyone went back to being a stone-breaker in the end.

That morning he was sitting at his desk in Fortescue's when he came across something curious.

He was going through his post and there it was. A letter from Mrs Tumbrill. He knew who it was from before he opened it: the flap of the re-used brown envelope was sealed with Elastoplast. In fact she turned out to have incongruously neat handwriting, every letter meticulously formed, the lines straight and unblemished by crossings-out. She explained that she was enclosing something that she was sure he would find interesting, something that Bernard would have wanted him to see. She signed herself Anna Tumbrill. Anna. Funny that he had not known her Christian name up till now. He pulled out the accompanying offprint and found it was of Bernard's article, the one he had glimpsed in typescript when searching through Bernard's desk. It had been published that month in a journal called *European Environmentalist*. There it was, 'The Barbizon School: The First Greens', an analysis of early ecological awareness – real or imagined by the author – in French nineteenth-century painting. Oswald settled down to read it as an act of piety to Bernard's memory.

He skimmed the opening paragraphs, and suddenly his eye was caught by a reference to 'The Stonebreakers'. Now this was a strange coincidence. Here was Bernard writing about the picture that he was on the point of rediscovering so dramatically in South America. Coincidence. Bloody coincidence. For a moment he caught another chilling glimpse of the randomness of things. He shivered and read on: 'The Stonebreakers', according to Bernard, was informed by Courbet's concern with the peasant's fundamental working relationship with the land, and by extension with man's whole relation to nature. For illustration, the writer added in parenthesis, see following page.

Oswald turned over, curious to see the thing illustrated one more time. And then he blinked. There was a mistake, the most ridiculous mistake. They had printed the wrong photograph. The caption said ' "The Stonebreakers" by Gustave Courbet, destroyed in Dresden in 1945'. But the picture showed no Gagey, no picks or shovels, no young assistant with the tray of chippings.

What was reproduced where 'The Stonebreakers' should have been was a repulsive image of a recumbent Venus and two putti playing in a landscape. Repulsive. And familiar.

Christ, it was the picture by Bouguereau. The one Dr Giannini had shown him in Buenos Aires. The one revealed when the velvet curtains had been drawn aside. The one Giannini had assured him was the best French picture available in Argentina. What was it doing here? What the hell was going on? What was the connection between the Courbet and the Bouguereau?

★ ★ ★

It came to him gradually, as he went back over everything that had happened. The connection between the Courbet and the Bouguereau was Bernard, of course. Bernard had sent the wrong illustration to the magazine. He'd meant to send the Courbet, but he'd sent the Bouguereau, and he hadn't lived long enough to correct the error. But how had Bernard been in possession of the Bouguereau photograph? That wasn't too difficult to explain when you thought about it: when Bernard had been in South America he must have been offered the Bouguereau, and he'd brought a photo of it back with him to London. Brought it back with him intending to send it to someone in London as a commercial proposition.

Oh God. He'd intended to send the Bouguereau to Oswald Ginn of Fortescue's. But he'd sent it as the illustration to his article. That meant that what Oswald had received was the correct illustration to the article. The Courbet. Reproductions of 'The Stonebreakers' were simple enough to come by, from old photographs. It was a straightforward transposition. Oswald opened a drawer in his desk and pulled out Bernard's original letter to him, the one that had accompanied the photograph he'd received. He read it again carefully, analysing every phrase. Yes. There was nothing in it that couldn't have applied just as well to the Bouguereau as to 'The Stonebreakers'.

The truth was that Bernard had never been offered 'The Stonebreakers' at all.

For a moment Oswald stared at the papers in front of him. The letter. The photograph of 'The Stonebreakers'. The offprint of the article. Then he shook his head and bundled them all back into the drawer marked 'Private'. He turned the key in the lock. There was no point in dwelling on it.

Whether Bernard had or had not been offered 'The

Stonebreakers' was irrelevant anyway. Irrelevant, since Derek Gilbert had shown Oswald the testimony of Gerda Helgemann. Irrelevant, since he'd personally kicked at the ashes of Juan Garcías' tragic bonfire.

But what a tosser Bernard had been. What an incompetent, disorganised tosser. Right up to the very end.

15

'Beware the month Lenaion, ox-flaying days.'

In the dark apartment, Dr Arnold Weil sank
exhausted into his bed without troubling to undress. It
was a clear night, and as he had stumbled home through
the crowds he had been aware of the icy shafts of a
gathering wind. It was bitterly cold. He murmured the
line once more as he drew the covers about him. Where
was it from? he asked himself again. But it was too late
to look it up now. He had not the strength to lift himself
from his bed and shuffle to his bookshelves. He was
already wrapped in his great-coat and he still had no
confidence in enduring warmth. He must get rest. It had
been a shattering day, but the exhaustion brought with
it an infuriating sleeplessness. He turned over and
clutched himself in frustration. Tomorrow would be
even more draining, what with the early rise, the seven
o'clock departure from the Bruhl'sche Terrasse, the
menacing and obstructive company of Gotz and
Walther, the journey to Schieritz, the depositing of the
pictures and the supervision of their secure stowing
away, then the return to Dresden once more. By this
time tomorrow, he would be more dead than alive. But
at least the job would be done, and that particular
weight, the overpowering one of personal responsibility
for so many irreplaceable paintings, would be removed
from his shoulders. Once more he felt the resentment
surge up within him: it was not fair to make him oversee

this operation alone, to impose such a task on someone so old, with such inadequate and insubordinate assistance. One final time he visualised the two lorries, parked together on the road overlooking the silent Elbe. They were secure, he reassured himself. They were locked up. And early tomorrow morning, they would be on their way again.

He was just beginning to sense intimations of a welcome drowsiness when the air-raid siren sounded. He listened motionless as it wound itself up to its familiar but nonetheless disquieting pitch of insistent whining, echoing across the cold, clear skies and intruding unforgivably into the privacy of his top-floor bedroom. This whole war had been an unforgivable intrusion, of course. But to be assailed by this cacophony tonight of all nights, when rest was imperative, that was intolerable. Experience taught that these alarms were almost invariably false. He recalled the theory he had heard that afternoon, from Gotz of all people: Dresden was safe. It had been agreed, even by his country's enemies. Security from attack was guaranteed here. The more he thought about it, wrapped shivering in his bedroom up under the eaves in the oldest part of the city, the more plausible it seemed. Oh yes, he knew the drill, they'd all been made aware of that. When the warning sounded, everyone in the building – the Corneliuses on the floor below, Frau Wagner with her noisy children on the floor below that, old Frau Schwind on the ground level – they were all meant to gather in the basement till the danger had passed, to herd together in that confined space in uneasy proximity, uncomfortable, ill-tempered, faintly ridiculous. Well, he wasn't going to bother now. It would be a waste of time; and he would lose sleep. Sleep was far more important to him tonight than going through the futile motions of taking refuge from a danger that was itself illusory. He would stay here. He would stay here because he must be ready to face the morning.

Meanwhile, Gotz and his companion were preparing to take a drive. Preparing to drive, despite those bloody sirens.

'They're always false alarms, you don't need to worry,' the woman said. She was breathless, flushed. She wriggled in the passenger seat to adjust her skirt, which had ridden up above her knee. There was a glint in her eye that made Gotz impatient to get away, to free himself from the peasants thronging the road beneath the Bruhl'sche Terrasse. Ignorant pigs.

At last the crowds parted momentarily and the lorry was able to force a way out to the carriageway. An angry fist beat on the outside of the door, but Gotz paid no attention, jerking forward in short violent bursts that scattered the oncoming pedestrians.

Suddenly there was a more serious obstruction. Two helmeted, uniformed figures barred his way. Military police. With guns. He braked hard and swore again. One of the soldiers ran round and tapped on the window.

'There is no unauthorised movement of vehicles after the siren is sounded.'

'Who says I am unauthorised? I have priority.'

'Priority? What priority?'

'I'm on special duty. For Dr Weil of the Museum. I have to get this load of pictures to safety tonight. I have priority.'

The other man wavered. 'Show me your papers, then.'

'God almighty! Weil has the papers.'

'No authority. No movement.' The policeman was

implacable again. 'I saw you. You came out from beside the other lorry, under the Terrasse. Return to that position immediately.' He blew sharply on his whistle.

'Shit!'

For a moment Gotz was tempted to drive on. Run the sods down, make a break for it. What right had they to tell him what to do, dictate to him with their petty regulations, to interfere with his pleasure? God almighty, didn't they realise what lay ahead for him? Later on tomorrow, after he had unloaded the pictures at their destination, he would have to report back to his unit; within seventy-two hours there was every chance he would be back in the front line fighting the desperate and doomed battle to hold back the Russians; by this time next week he might well be dead. And these bastards were trying to stop him getting a few moments' enjoyment with a tart who wanted it just as much as he did. Yes, what had he got to lose by defying them? But it was the woman who restrained him.

'Go back, it's not worth it,' she urged. 'We could go to my room, it's not far.'

'To your room? Why didn't you say you had a room? We could have gone there in the first place.' He spoke angrily as he began to manoeuvre the van round, to return it to its original position. The sirens continued, strangely persistent.

'It's my daughter. She's asleep there. But we can be quiet, can't we?'

'*Ja*,' said Gotz shortly. It wasn't exactly what he'd had in mind, but it would have to do. It was better than nothing. He reversed into position next to the other van, got out, helped the woman down, and locked the door to the cab.

They stepped over the Silesian family who still lay against the wall, apparently too exhausted to respond to the plaintive cry of the sirens. The police and wardens were still urging people to head for shelter, but the two of them set out purposefully in the direction the woman indicated.

'What are those lights?' she asked suddenly. He looked up and saw that the sky to the west of the city was lit by a series of flickering red flares. At first he thought they must be some sort of firework display; after all, it was carnival night.

'God knows,' he said. 'Which way now?'

'Perhaps we should take shelter?'

'No. We go to your room.' Even as he spoke, he was conscious of a mounting uneasiness. Those flares: there was a man in his division who had been in Kassel in 1943 when the enemy had destroyed whole sections of the city with a massive air attack. The details had been suppressed officially, but the man had told him how before a really big raid the first enemy aircraft dropped marker flares, signposting an area, delineating it, so that the big bombers that came after knew exactly where to deposit their cargoes. It permitted a terrible degree of concentration and destruction.

They walked on. Fewer and fewer people were on the streets now. Unconsciously they increased their pace, till they were almost running.

'Here. At last.' She pulled him into a doorway, then fumbled with a key. They were aware of a macabre droning, as of an approaching swarm of bees.

It was twelve minutes past ten when they finally got inside. Sixty seconds later, just as Gotz's hand found the flesh above her stockings, the first volley of four-thousand- and eight-thousand-pound high-explosive bombs hit the inner city, smashing windows and ripping the roofs off the highly combustible old buildings. Many were already on fire when the massive wave of incendiaries followed a minute or two afterwards, engulfing whole streets in one flaming inferno. Engulfing Gotz and the woman. Engulfing Dr Weil. And engulfing two locked furniture vans drawn up forlornly side by side on the Bruhl'sche Terrasse embankment by the Elbe.